DYING BREATH

Books by Wendy Corsi Staub

DEARLY BELOVED

FADE TO BLACK

ALL THE WAY HOME

THE LAST TO KNOW

IN THE BLINK OF AN EYE

SHE LOVES ME NOT

KISS HER GOODBYE

LULLABY AND GOODNIGHT

THE FINAL VICTIM

MOST LIKELY TO DIE

DON'T SCREAM

DYING BREATH

Published by Kensington Publishing Corporation

DYING BREATH

Wendy Corsi Staub

DOUBLEDAY LARGE PRINT HOME LIBRARY EDITION

ZEBRA BOOKS
KENSINGTON PUBLISHING CORP.

This Large Print Edition, prepared especially for Doubleday Large Print Home Library, contains the complete, unabridged text of the original Publisher's Edition.

ZEBRA BOOKS are published by

Kensington Publishing Corp.
850 Third Avenue
New York, NY 10022

ISBN-13: 978-0-7394-9471-4

Printed in the United States of America

For Lisa Corsi Koellner and Rick Corsi,
two of my favorite people in the world
(and the only ones who share my bloodline),
with love from your big sister.

And for Mark, Morgan, and Brody.

ACKNOWLEDGMENTS

With gratitude to my editor, John Scognamiglio, for all the tireless feedback and brilliant inspiration; to all the staff at Kensington Books who made this come together; to my agents, Laura Blake Peterson and Holly Frederick, as well as Tracey Marchini and the rest of the gang at Curtis Brown Ltd; to my publicists, Nancy Berland and Elizabeth Middaugh; to Kim, Carol, and Jennifer at Nancy Berland Public Relations; to Carol Fizgerald, Joe Rivera, and Sunil Kumar at Bookreporter.com; to Rick and Patty Donovan, Phil Pelletier, and staff at my favorite store, The Book Nook, in Dunkirk, N.Y. Finally, thank you, Mark Staub, for the long hours stooped over this manuscript and for seeing things I didn't see.

God grant me the serenity
To accept the things I cannot change,
Courage to change the things I can,
And wisdom to know the difference.

—excerpted from The Serenity Prayer,
Alcoholics Anonymous

Prologue

New York City
January

It always begins with the dizziness.

In her office high above East 46th Street, Camden Hastings is editing yet another inane fashion article, *"Not Your Grandmother's Belts and Brooches,"* when the words begin to swim on the page.

Light-headed, she looks up warily. The desk lamp is glaring, the small room distorted and tilting at an impossible angle.

Oh, no.

She braces herself.

Here it comes.

It's been awhile—a month, maybe more—since the last episode.

Sometimes after that much time has passed, she actually allows herself to relax a little. She'll lower her guard, wanting to believe she's free and clear, that she'll never have to deal with the unsettling visions again.

But they always come back.

Cam's fingers involuntarily release her pencil. It rolls off the desk onto the floor. Ignoring it, she rolls her chair back slightly, just enough to rest her elbows on her lap and lower her face into her hands to stop the spinning sensation.

She can hear her heart beating, hear her own rhythmic respiration . . . then someone else's.

Inhale . . .

Exhale . . .

Inhale . . .

Cam's head is filled with the sound of erratic, shallow breathing, in some kind of bizarre syncopation with her own.

"Please, you have to let me go."

The thin, uneven pitch of the voice is typical of male adolescence, but she can't see the speaker yet. Can't see anything at all; her eyes are tightly closed against her palms and her mental screen remains dark.

"Why are you doing this? Who are you?" she hears the boy ask brokenly.

He's so afraid, she senses, so terribly afraid, it's all he can do to just stay conscious, keep breathing . . .

Inhale . . .

Exhale . . .

Cam's own lungs seem to constrict with the effort.

But that's crazy. You can breathe. You know he's only in your head, like the others.

All of them—all the characters she alone can see and hear—are figments of an exceptionally vivid imagination Cam's English teachers liked to call "a gift," back when she was in school.

Ha. A *gift?*

Hardly.

But then, her teachers didn't know about the strange visions she's endured for as long as she can remember. If they knew, they might have understood that a vivid imagination can be—more than anything else—a curse.

They'd have suggested a shrink for

her, instead of creative writing courses. Because that's what you do when you hallucinate on a regular basis, right? You see a psychiatrist.

That's what her sister Ava did at college.

But no one in Cam's world ever realized that she had stumbled across the truth about beautiful, brunette Ava. About her mental illness. For all she knows, Pop never even knew about Ava's troubles in the first place.

In any case, no one in her life has ever suspected that Cam is aware she might have more in common with her older sister than an uncanny physical resemblance. She might also have the genetic potential to go stark, raving mad, just as Ava so obviously did twenty years ago.

Why else would a person—perched twelve stories in the air—take a headfirst dive to the ground?

You don't kill yourself just because your mother abandoned you when you were a teenager, or because your college course load is overwhelming . . . do you?

Okay, some people might. But Cam

found her sister's diary years ago. She's suspected, ever since, what was going on with her. She's come to believe the voices in Ava's head told her to jump.

The voices in Cam's aren't anything like that.

For one thing, they're invariably laced with fear. Terror, even. They never speak directly to Cam; they're always addressing someone else, some shadowy person who intends to hurt them.

And most of the time, those voices belong to children.

Cam knows that because she can usually conjure their faces if she focuses hard enough.

Funny . . . even though she's the one who dreams up these tortured characters in the first place, she can never quite anticipate what they're going to look like, or whether she'll even get to see them at all.

For instance, this boy today, the frightened boy with the cracking voice, sounds like he's small, and pale.

But when he begins to take shape in Cam's mind's eye, he's older than she expected. Dark-skinned, too—Hispanic, maybe, or Native American. He has a mop of curly dark hair and big brown eyes.

He's huddled in a confined space—she can see carpet, and metal, and a small recessed light, as if . . .

Yes, it's a car trunk. It's open. Broad daylight. Dappled, fluid shade spills in, as if trees are gently stirring overhead.

Then a human shadow looms over the boy; someone is standing there, looking down at him.

Cam's heart races, her throat gags on the boy's panic.

Calm down, she tells herself—and him. Even though he's not real. Even though he exists only in her head.

Is he wearing some sort of uniform? Boy Scouts, maybe? Khaki shirt, badges, and pins. A kerchief is tied around his neck. On his sleeve, a couple of sewn-on numbers, but Cam can't make them out.

Which doesn't make sense because she's the one who made him up—so she should know which numbers he's wearing, shouldn't she? She should know his name, and his age, and, dammit, she should be able to make him stop sounding so helpless.

But no. He's crying now. Crying and cowering in the car trunk, his elbows bent on either side of his face, his hands clutching the back of his head.

Cam can't bear to see him like that, can't bear to listen to the unnatural, keening sound.

Stop, she commands her overimaginative, gifted brain, lifting her head and shaking it back and forth. *Stop doing this to me.*

Mercifully, the boy's voice gradually grows fainter. The image begins to fade.

Cam breathes deeply to calm herself.

There. That's better.

She sits up in her chair.

Sips some tepid tea from the mug on her desk.

Slowly, her breathing returns to normal.

That was a bad one.

They usually are. Bad like a nightmare that grips you when you're having it . . .

And ends when you wake up.

But lately, the hallucinations stay with her. She doesn't forget them the way you would a nightmare. They seem more real than ever before. Why?

Who knows? It's hard enough for Cam to believe she's capable of creating such emotional drama out of thin air—let alone comprehend *how* and *why* she does it.

Lord knows she's got enough to worry about without her mind being cluttered by imaginary people in trouble.

Her promotion from Assistant to Associate Editor is on hold until the next fiscal year begins. Mike's been laid off for almost a month. They're running out of money.

That's *real* stress.

That's what she should be worrying about.

Not daydreaming, or hallucinating, or whatever one would call the unsettling visions that pop up in her head.

Maybe I should go see someone about them, she thinks—same as always, whenever she comes out of one of these episodes.

Then—*no. No way,* she tells herself—same, too, as always.

She can't go see a shrink. They can't

afford it, and anyway, what would Mike do if he realized he was married to a crazy person?

Probably the same thing Pop did, all those years ago:

Make himself scarce.

I can't lose Mike. I need him. I love him.

She can barely remember her parents' married era. Not that Ike and Brenda Neary had ever divorced, though they often spoke the word.

Spoke? Ha. *Screamed* it.

Back then, they still lived in Camden, a New Jersey suburb of Philadelphia and Mom's hometown, for which she named her second daughter. Obsessed with glamorous old Hollywood and lingering girlhood dreams of becoming an actress, Brenda had named her firstborn after her favorite movie star, Ava Gardner.

The irony: the real Ava Gardner lived a long, gilded life. A different brand of irony: once thriving Camden, New Jersey, has steadily deteriorated into poverty, urban blight, and staggering crime rates, notoriously dubbed the "most dangerous city in America."

Cam dimly recalls her mother's face, her voice, her tears. Not much more than that, though. On the rare occasions her father was around, there were arguments and accusations—usually ending with her mother hysterical and Pop slamming the door behind him as he left.

Then came the day that her mother was the one who left—for good. Cam was three years old; Ava a college freshman at NYU. When Ava arrived at their small Camden apartment, summoned in the crisis, she gently told her little sister that they'd never see their mother again.

Pop protested.

But as it turned out, Ava was right.

"Don't worry, baby girl," Pop reassured Cam that night, holding her close as she sobbed. "I'll take care of you. Lean on me. You can trust me."

"But you always have to leave."

"Not anymore. I never will. Never again. I promise. Not unless I take you with me."

And that was what he did.

And she leaned on him. Trusted him.

Yet in all those years the two of them

spent together on the road, or down the shore, or in between gigs—somehow, she never found the nerve to tell Pop about the visions.

Nor can she bring herself to tell her husband.

Or, God forbid, her friends or co-workers.

Cam wonders sometimes if she might have eventually confided in her big sister. But she never had the chance.

Ava's "tragic accident," as everyone chose to call it—her "falling" to her death at NYU's Bobst Library—happened less than a year after Mom left.

As for Cam, she has no choice but to deal, silently and alone, with her hallucinations whenever they strike, reassuring herself that she has no reason to fear something that exists only in her imagination.

November

The day's weighty stack of mail in her hand, Cam sinks her bulky form onto the maroon brocade couch.

Ahhh . . .

That's better.

Much better than the hard plastic seat someone offered her on the downtown number six train a little while ago. Not that it wasn't preferable to standing, as she's been forced to do lately more times than one might expect.

As Cam told her husband just the other day, it's amazing how invisible an eight-months-pregnant woman can be, on board the subway in New York City.

Mike—the sort of guy who gives up his seat not just for pregnant women but for any random passenger who might need it—was predictably outraged.

"You need to start taking a cab home from work," he decided—as if they could possibly afford the rush-hour meter fare between the magazine's offices on East 46th and their apartment on the unfashionable fringes of Chinatown.

"Okay, I'll take a cab, don't worry."

"No, you won't. You're just humoring me. I can tell."

"Well then," she said, "how about if I promise to take a cab on nights when

I'm so wiped out that I really don't feel up to the subway?"

That would be every night—if she meant it.

Of course, she didn't.

Mike has been treating her like an eggshell throughout her pregnancy, but Cam can handle the physical symptoms. Just as she can handle the fact that she and Mike are pretty much broke, same as always, even now that he's working again.

So she'll have to suck it up and brave the subway until the baby comes. An extra mouth to feed will be enough strain on their budget.

The pregnancy wasn't unplanned. It just happened sooner than they expected.

Cam had read—and edited, and, yes, even written—her share of articles on conception. She knew going in that a woman shouldn't count on getting pregnant right away. Figuring it was probably going to take a few months, at least, she told Mike they should start trying the minute he got a job.

So they did.

Just weeks later, there she was: knocked up, due around Christmas.

So much for the best-laid plans: scraping up enough money for skiing in Utah this winter, and taking Mike's parents up on their offer for two plane tickets to visit them at their winter home in Florida over the holidays.

Speaking of Mike's parents . . .

Here's an envelope that bears the familiar loopy blue ballpoint handwriting of Cam's mother-in-law, with a Vero Beach postmark and return address.

Cam is struck by a familiar, and perhaps ridiculous, pang of wistfulness.

It's been years since she went through her mail thinking there just might be something from her own mother.

Mom, wherever she is, intentionally erased herself from the shattered family she left behind. Still, Cam used to fantasize that one day she'd simply show up again, as abruptly as she'd vanished.

Ava's death made the papers in New Jersey and New York. Surely if Mom had seen it, she'd have come back. At the time, Cam felt as though she, and Pop, too, were holding their breaths for that—constantly looking around at the wake, the funeral, for Mom's face in the crowd.

Of course, it wasn't there.

Mom probably never knew, still doesn't know, that she lost one of her children.

She couldn't have known, because if she had, she'd have come back to comfort Cam and Pop. Or so Cam managed to convince herself for awhile, anyway, back when she still clung to faith in her mother.

That faith has long since vanished, though.

Mom is as gone as Ava is; Cam and Pop both learned to accept that years ago. They stoically moved forward together, refusing to become victims of their tragic past.

Cam no longer expects her mother to pop up in her life again, to send, say, a "Thinking of You" card filled with newsy handwriting, the way Mike's mother does when they're away for the winter.

No, but she'll always be wistful—and maybe a little envious—when her mother-in-law pops up in the mailbox.

Her cheerful correspondence will always trigger the familiar aftertaste of loss and futile yearning.

Marjorie Hastings didn't send a card today, and this envelope is addressed just to her son. The only thing in it—Cam can see when she holds it up to the lamplight—is a small rectangle about the size of a check folded in half.

That's what it is, she's certain. A check.

Mike's mom, God bless her, has been sending them a little bit here and there to help out. Probably siphoning it out of her grocery money.

Mike's father doesn't believe in handouts to get grown children on their feet financially, though he can well afford it. Mike's mom never worked; Mike's father doesn't believe in that, either. The woman, according to Mike Hastings Sr., should stay at home with the children while the man supports her.

"Well, what if the woman loves her job?" Cam brazenly asked her father-in-law once, before she knew better than to get him started. *Then what? Does she*

have to give it up when the children come along?

The reply: *"Of course."*

And when she asked why, the answer was equally maddening: *"Because that's the way it's supposed to be."*

She can't stand his attitude—in theory, anyway—but deep down, she can't help but think maybe he's right. Maybe that is the way it's supposed to be. It's definitely the way Cam wishes it had been for her, growing up . . . and the way it's going to be for her own child, if she and Mike can make it happen.

Don't worry, Dad, she silently tells her father-in-law now, flipping the legal envelope forward to rest against her bulging belly as she checks the rest of the mail. *I don't love my job. Lately, I don't even like it all that much*.

With luck, Mike's promising new position in computer technology will pan out while she's on maternity leave. Then she won't have to go back to her job as associate editor at a women's magazine. She can give their child the traditional family life she never had herself, with a father who works a steady nine-to-five job, a mother who's there to dry tears and make meals and keep house . . . Hell, a mother who's just *there,* period, would be a vast improvement over her own childhood.

Maybe, as a stay-at-home mom, she'll even finally be able to get back to her writing.

That's what she always wanted to be in the first place: a writer.

But you can't support yourself in the big city chasing artistic dreams. It's hard enough, she learned early on, to make it on an editorial salary. Most of Cam's coworkers have had their rich fathers' money to fall back on.

Not her. Pop is an aging rocker, living off little more than his fading glory days as a bar band drummer in the Jersey Shore towns.

That's fine with Cam, though. She wouldn't trade him for a blue-blooded businessman with the biggest trust fund in the world.

Nor would she trade Mike for a well-heeled Wall Street wiz with an uptown co-op: her colleagues' perception of essential ingredients in happily ever after.

No, Cam will take Mike Hastings any day—*and* this rented one-bedroom apartment. It's not upscale by any means, but it's cozy, and lived in, and, most important, it's home.

She looks around, drinking in the reassuring sight of the television, the stereo, the cordless phone. There's the official wedding portrait of her and Mike, snapped more than two years ago but finally framed and hung just last month.

Ha. The world's worst procrastinators strike again.

Beneath the portrait is a full bookcase with rows of vertical well-worn bindings and haphazardly, horizontally stacked newer ones as well: *What to Expect When You're Expecting, The Girlfriends' Guide to Pregnancy, The Expectant Father*.

The spine on the last one isn't even cracked. Mike might be thrilled about impending paternity, but unlike Cam, he isn't much of a reader.

In the far corner of the living room, closest to their bedroom doorway: the white-draped wicker bassinet awaiting the arrival next month of its newborn occupant.

Cam feels better just looking at that.

Yes, this eight-hundred-square-foot haven she shares with Mike—and, soon, with their firstborn child—is Cam's whole world.

Too bad that world also consists of so many past-due bills; there are quite a few in today's mail. Con Ed, Verizon, Baby Gap, student loans . . .

Relieved when she reaches the bottom of the stack at last, Cam separates the envelopes from the junk mail. She idly flips through the supermarket circulars, perusing this week's bargains.

She and Pop always got by on fast food, sandwiches, and free pub fare provided to the band and the drummer's daughter, affectionately referred to as a pint-sized roadie. It wasn't until college that Cam learned to like "real food," and she craved it once she left the dorms behind.

So she determinedly taught herself how to cook, thanks to the red-and-white-checked *Betty Crocker Cookbook* someone gave her at her bridal shower.

These days, she finds puttering in the kitchen therapeutic. She even welcomes the challenge of planning ahead, creating menus based on sale items . . .

As she turns a page of this week's D'Agostino's flier, something flutters to her lap.

Scooping it up, she sees that it's one of those small blue and white fliers that arrive with the weekly circulars.

A young boy with dark hair and eyes smiles up at her beneath the headline HAVE YOU SEEN ME?

The answer, to Cam's utter shock, is *yes*.

Oh, my God. Oh, my God.

Yes, she's seen him. Absolutely.

According to the flier, his name is Paul Delgado, and he disappeared on a Boy Scout hike out in the Sierra Nevadas, just six weeks earlier.

Six weeks?

But . . .

This is the same boy who had cowered, bound and gagged, in an abductor's car trunk in one of Cam's visions *almost a year ago*.

He's real.

The comprehension is so stunning, so devastating, that Cam finds herself gasping for air. Panic wells within her, propelling her upward, and she sways to her feet.

She staggers to the kitchen, instinctively seeking to tamp back the frantic barrage of emotions erupting within.

Oh, my God. Oh, my God.

She frantically looks around, for who knows what—and spots . . . something.

A bottle of vodka.

It's stashed on top of the fridge, covered in a layer of dust, leftover from a Halloween party.

Cam finds herself blindly reaching for it on pure whim.

It will numb her—that's all she knows.

With a violently shaking hand, she dumps some into a glass and raises it to her lips, already looking around for her pack of cigarettes.

Where did I put—

Glimpsing a prescription bottle of prenatal vitamins, she suddenly remembers.

The baby.

For God's sake . . .

She lowers the glass in disgust. Or is it dismay?

You're pregnant.

Of course there are no more cigarettes in the apartment; she quit smoking eight months ago.

Liquor is out of the question as well.

Still trembling, Cam dumps the vodka into the sink.

"Help me," she whispers into thin air, clinging to the counter.

What is she supposed to do now? Now that she knows she doesn't have *hallucinations* after all. Nor daydreams.

She has *premonitions*.

Because that boy . . . Paul . . . he's real.

He actually exists somewhere in this world.

And if he does . . .

Then all the others—the anonymous children who have populated the bizarre visions in her head all these years—must exist as well.

PART I: MAY

Chapter One

Fourteen years later

Hearing a door slam somewhere downstairs, Cam is startled from her prenap stupor.

"Mom?" a voice calls up from the foot of the stairs in the foyer. "Are you here?"

She opens her eyes. Tess is home. Can it possibly be three fifteen already?

She turns her head to look at the bedside clock, and sees that it is, indeed, three-fifteen.

"Be right down," she calls to her daughter, and sits up groggily.

So much for catching a much-needed afternoon nap. Somehow, the better part of a Tuesday morning and afternoon seems to have escaped her.

Then again, she accomplished quite a bit today. After getting Tess off to school this morning, Cam belatedly switched over her own drawers and closet from winter to summer. Then she made the usual suburban rounds: pharmacy, bank, dry cleaner, post office, supermarket. Back home, she threw together a pot of homemade chicken soup—an odd craving for an unseasonably hot and humid late-May afternoon. She left it simmering, wearily climbed the stairs, lay down . . . and here she is.

Cam stretches. Sleep will have to wait till bedtime. She swings her legs over the edge of the mattress, half-expecting her feet to encounter a pair of Mike's shoes cluttering the floor beside the bed.

Then she remembers.

Old habits die hard.

The first thing Mike always did every night after work was sit on the bed, take off his shoes, and leave them where they lay. It drove her crazy from the start, but he couldn't seem to remember to pick them up, and she stubbornly refused to be that kind of wife. Instead, she grew accustomed to stepping over and sometimes on his shoes.

Not anymore.

These days, Mike's shoes occupy another bedside about twenty miles away from Upper Montclair, New Jersey. His new place is, ironically, a stone's throw from their old newlywed apartment on Manhattan's Lower East Side, where they spent the happiest time of their lives.

These days, real estate in that neighborhood is booming and the narrow old streets are crawling with hipsters. Who could have foreseen that?

Who could have foreseen any of this?

Not even me, Cam thinks grimly.

How bitterly ironic that Camden Hastings—who once upon a time could foresee the bitter fates of strangers—was ultimately blindsided by her own.

Mike moved out in mid-March.

For all she knows, some other woman is sharing his new bed in his new place in his new life.

If not now, then probably soon.

Mike won't be alone for long. And

when he finds someone new, he'll go for someone who's the opposite of Cam.

That's no premonition. She hasn't had one in years. Just a gut feeling.

Mike will find some woman who is everything Cam isn't, at least not anymore. Some woman who's skinny, financially independent, optimistic, emotionally stable. A woman who is all the things Cam never even was in the first place: blonde, petite and perky, elegant, efficient, self-disciplined . . .

Cam can't bring herself to ask her husband—soon to be ex-husband, that is—if he's started seeing anyone in the two months since they separated.

Nor has she asked their daughter what, if anything, she knows about her dad's new solo lifestyle. It's not fair to expect Tess to spy on him during their scheduled visitations.

Anyway, Cam should probably get used to the fact that after all these years of a shared life, certain aspects of Mike's are no longer any of her business.

Just as aspects of her own life are no longer any of his business.

Right. But one aspect of your life most certainly is *Mike's business, and you need to tell him about it. Soon.*

With the official start of summer a month away, Long Beach Island—a skinny, twenty-one-mile-long barrier island off the coast of central New Jersey—is still relatively uncrowded. The busiest town, Beach Haven, has been a bustling resort for well over a century. On this warm, still Tuesday afternoon, though, all is quiet here.

The sun, dazzling when it rose this morning, is high overhead but its light seems filtered now, more white than golden. Off to the west, above the Victorian rooftops of the historic district, the sky—so blue just an hour ago—is tainted the color of an angry bruise. A pleasant sea breeze has given way to brine-scented air hovering ominously close, as if Mother Nature is holding her breath in anticipation of a coming storm.

The forecast doesn't call for rain.

But that's the glorious thing about the

weather here on the coast. Nobody ever seems able to accurately predict what's going to happen.

So different here than out West, where every day brings more of the same: calm, dry, sunshine. Or the Deep South, where late-afternoon summer thunderstorms are as predictable as the sun going down.

Yes, it's far more interesting to know that on any given day, the weather might remain calm from dawn to dusk—*or* a powerful, exhilarating storm might blow in to wreak havoc on this peaceful little town. This so-called *haven*.

The afternoon may be waning and the weather threatening to turn, but the beach remains dotted with chatting senior citizens in lounge chairs, young mothers chasing after toddlers, and the occasional power walker plugged into an iPod.

Nobody seems to be paying any attention to the solitary figure standing at the edge of the surf, testing the waters, so to speak.

* * *

Cam walks slowly down the stairs, past the framed family pictures that line the angled wall.

There's Tess as a bald, chubby baby, as a tow-headed preschooler, as a gap-toothed first-grader. There's that lone, stiffly posed professionally taken family portrait of the three of them, and a couple of framed snapshots, and, of course, their formal wedding photograph.

Cam averts her eyes as she passes that oversized frame, thinking she probably should just take it down.

Their wedding day was joyful, and every time she sees the picture, she's flooded with memories—now bittersweet.

She remembers exchanging handwritten vows in the little white seaside chapel on the Jersey Shore; the best man's simultaneously funny and moving toast at the reception; her first married dance with Mike to—appropriately—Etta James's "At Last."

Though it took them awhile to hang their large wedding portrait in their first apartment, that was one of the first tasks Mike accomplished when they moved up here to the suburbs. He did so with uncharacteristic efficiency—almost pointedly, Cam remembers thinking at the time. As if he were determined to prove that they were going to create a fresh start here in suburbia—together.

By then, though, the tension between them was already pervasive.

Still, it took almost another decade for either of them to do anything about it.

Now that the marriage is all but over, the picture hangs here still: white lace and broken promises.

I really should take it down, Cam tells herself, not for the first time, as she passes on by. And she will, as soon as she has a chance.

But there are some things she can't keep putting off.

You have to tell him, Cam admonishes herself again, reaching the first floor and heading toward the kitchen where she can hear Tess rummaging through the cupboards for a snack.

Of course I'll tell him. I'll call him and say we have to talk . . .

Just—not yet.

* * *

This early in the season, the Atlantic surf is icy enough to shoot twin darts of pain from ankle to thigh.

But physical pain is nothing compared to what I've been through.

Physical pain, like the tide, eventually ebbs.

Even now, the waterline inches farther from shore with every lapping wave. A flat, soaked, darkened strip at its foaming edge is strewn with glistening relics deposited by the sea: pebbles and shells—mostly shards, with an occasional intact treasure among them.

Gleaming in a relatively empty patch of wave-packed sand is an eye-catching sliver of something wet and black that just washed ashore.

Hmm. Can it be . . . ?

If it is, then it's a sign.

One doesn't come across sharks' teeth very often on these populated northeastern beaches.

Be casual. Don't just snatch it up. Someone will notice.

But this stretch of beach is fairly deserted, and nobody's looking this way, anyway.

Good. Go ahead. Reach down . . .

Ah, promising.

The tiny black object is about the size of a little girl's pinky fingernail, but triangular in shape, tapering down to a sharp, skinny point.

It's clumped with grains of wet sand that need to be carefully brushed away before a positive identification can be made . . .

Yes.

Definitely a shark's tooth.

A sign.

It's time for the hunt to begin again.

Tess Hastings looks nothing like Cam did at her age. Every time she gazes at her daughter, Cam sees Mike.

Tess's coloring is her father's: she's got his light brown hair and green-flecked hazel eyes, as opposed to Cam's chestnut mane and eyes the same dark shade. Tess's shoulder-length layered cut suits her hair's thick, wavy texture and her delicate facial features, while Cam has always worn her own hair long and straight. Cam has an olive complexion that's quick to tan, as opposed to her daughter's fair skin. Tess is short for her age, and slender; Cam lanky and—well, no longer slender.

Not heavy, though, by any means. She's been a fairly stable size 10 throughout most of her marriage. Now, of course, her waist is swelling pretty rapidly, along with everything else, it seems.

She settles at the square kitchen table opposite her daughter, who has dutifully poured chips into a paper towel–lined basket and a small amount of salsa into a little ceramic bowl. At her age, Cam would have eaten the chips straight out of the bag and dunked them into salsa in its low, wide-mouthed jar—double-dipping, of course.

Her father never told her that the saliva would get into the salsa and it would spoil in its jar. She had to figure that out for herself.

Back when she was trying to create the model household, she created all kinds of rules for Tess, to save her from—God forbid—eating spoiled salsa, or something even more undesirable.

Undesirable? Ha. Now that they're dealing with an *undesirable* far more *undesirable* than anything Cam ever imagined, is there any comfort in the fact that the chips are in a basket and the salsa is in a bowl?

"So how was school?" she asks Tess, fighting the urge to grab the damn basket and hurtle the chips across the room in sheer frustration at how it all turned out.

"It was okay."

Cam wistfully remembers Kindergarten Tess, who attended PS 42 in Manhattan wearing cute little dresses and her favorite Lisa Frank plush animal backpack. Every day after school, she reported that her day had been "GRRRRR-EAT!!!"

It's hard to imagine her ever showing that much enthusiasm again. For anything.

"Did you get your grade on your geometry quiz yet, Tess?"

"No. Maybe tomorrow, he said."

"Good. What about English? Did you turn in your paper?"

"Um, it was due today, so *ye-e-ah*." Tess draws it out in the same derisive tone kids used to say *duh* back when Cam was a teenager.

She's been saying that a lot lately. *"Ye-e-ah."*

It's better, Cam supposes, than the sarcastic no's she was prone to before this phase.

As in, *"Did you turn in your paper?"*

"No, I poured gasoline on it and set it on fire."

Well, ask a stupid question . . .

But lately Cam can't seem to think of any that aren't.

She never considered Mike a sparkling conversationalist, but when he was around and they were a family, they somehow always managed to find something to talk about at this table over a decade of family dinners.

Now Cam and Tess are left to sit here across from each other every night, toying with their food and attempting idle conversation, Mike's empty chair between them.

Now that he's officially gone, maybe Cam should remove his chair altogether—get one of those little café tables for two. A black wrought iron one, maybe, to match the sleek appliances.

Or perhaps she and Tess can start eating at stools at the granite-topped breakfast bar across the large kitchen. Even in the living room, in front of the plasma television. Tess used to beg for that when she was younger. She said none of her friends had to eat dinner sitting at the table with their parents.

But Cam insisted on it. She had read somewhere, years ago, that children who eat dinner with their families are statistically far less likely to get involved with drinking, drugs, cigarettes, not to mention sex, truancy, suicidal thoughts . . .

Lord knew she couldn't have her precious only child fall victim to any of those adolescent perils. She would have a normal family, the family Cam never had, the family Mike did have and wanted to duplicate.

They kept up the charade to the bitter end; the three of them sitting down every night to dinner, even when Mike stayed at the office later and later, and those meals eventually consisted of canned SpaghettiO's, buttered Wonder Bread, take-out pizza, cold cereal . . . and, for Cam, a glass—or two—of wine.

Tonight, however, there's not a drop of liquor in the house, and a pot of chicken soup bubbles on the stove.

Last night, they had chili and home-made cornbread.

The night before that, a complete Sunday dinner of roast chicken, stuffing, mashed potatoes, pan gravy . . . for two.

"Daddy would like this," Tess said bleakly, picking at a drumstick. "You should have made it for him sometime."

The message was clear: *If you had acted more like a wife and mother, he wouldn't have left. And I wouldn't hate you so much.*

Of course, Cam doesn't really believe her daughter hates her, despite her having flung the word around lately.

But she does believe, just as Tess does, that it's her own damn fault Mike is gone.

"Do you have a lot of homework tonight?" she asks Tess.

"Not really. Just an essay for English."

"That's good. The teachers used to ease up at this time of year, I remember."

"Not really," Tess says again, sounding deliberately contrary. "It's more like they start trying to cram everything in before finals."

"Oh—that reminds me . . ." *Good thinking. Change the subject.* "I was thinking we'd head right down to Beach Haven the week school gets out instead of waiting till July."

She holds her breath, waiting for Tess's reaction.

Normally, her daughter would be thrilled to get a head start on summer on Long Beach Island. They've been spending the better part of July and part of August, too, at the little gray-shingled house Cam and Mike bought there a few years ago.

This year, everything is different.

Sure enough—"Why do we have to go right away?" Tess protests.

Cam hesitates. "Because you're scheduled to spend the Fourth of July weekend with Daddy, so I thought we could get in some beach time before that."

"Oh."

They're both new to this world of scheduled visitations. With their lives mapped out by lawyers well in advance, everything should be relatively uncomplicated—yet somehow, it all feels anything but.

"What am I doing with Daddy for the Fourth?" Tess asks slowly, not looking at Cam as she busies herself wiping up a ring of condensation her glass left on the table.

"I don't know. Maybe you'll get to see the fireworks in the city. Or," Cam adds, noticing that Tess doesn't seem thrilled by that notion, "maybe he'll take you away someplace."

"Like where?"

"I don't know. It's a long weekend—you've got four days."

"Maybe he can just come down the shore with us like usual."

"I don't think so, Tess."

"You don't want him there."

"It's not that I don't want him there."

It's that he doesn't want to be there.

And that he doesn't belong there anymore.

His choice, not mine.

"Then you should invite him," Tess persists. "I mean, it's not like you're divorced, or anything."

No.

A *trial separation*—that's what they told their daughter—and each other.

But in Cam's mind, it was permanent—if only because she sensed that it was permanent in Mike's.

"Will you invite him, Mom?"

"Maybe," she says, because it's easier than saying no.

Just as *trial separation* is easier to say to a child than *divorce*.

For now, Tess seems satisfied with that *"Maybe."*

And, hell, I will ask Mike, Cam thinks. *Let him be the one to say no . . .*

Or not.

The Fourth of July is more than a month away.

You just never know.

By then, she'll be into her second trimester.

By then, Mike will know she's pregnant.

* * *

The shark has an innate need to hunt, to kill, to feed. It glides stealthily, concealed in the depths, circling the unsuspecting victim.

Great Whites in particular will cleverly blindside a moving target with a ferocious, debilitating strike. The weakened, wounded victim doesn't stand a chance when the mighty beast moves in for a frenzied kill. In its wake, there is nothing but a trail of blood and discarded remains.

A shark's prey is selected opportunistically. Any flesh and blood will do.

Not so in your case. Not so at all.

Sometimes a year, maybe more, can pass before the desire begins to stir.

And sometimes, not more than a couple of weeks go by before it strikes all over again. And again.

It can't be helped, nor the hunger denied.

It's just the way things are, the way they have been since she left.

So. A shark's tooth.

The time has come again to find her.

Claim her.

* * *

Cam doesn't really expect the pregnancy to change anything between her and Mike. Not the big picture, anyway.

He chose to leave; she doesn't want him back by default.

She didn't even think she wanted him back at all, for that matter . . .

Not at first.

But lately, it's as if a haze has begun to lift a little and she's been able to see certain things more clearly. Not just her marriage, but the past in general, and the future as well . . . when she allows herself to think about it at all.

Cam watches her daughter take another tortilla chip and dredge it through the small bowl of salsa. She tries to think of something else to ask. Or say. Or do.

She can't just sit here, hands clasped so they won't feel quite so . . . empty.

Will it be like this from here on in? she wonders, reaching for a chip—not because she's hungry, but because she has to occupy fingers that wouldn't mind being wrapped around a stemmed wineglass right about now.

"I made chicken soup for dinner," she informs her daughter unnecessarily.

Tess makes a face and tilts her head toward the fragrant stockpot on the stove. "I know, I saw. Why?"

"What do you mean, 'why'? And how come you're making that face? You love homemade chicken soup."

"Right, and you haven't made it in years."

"Not *years*." A *year,* though, probably. At least.

Cam, who once considered cooking her favorite hobby, has been shamefully lax in that department.

"So why are you making it now, on the hottest day ever?"

Because I'm pregnant and I'm craving it, that's why.

Of course she doesn't say it.

Tess doesn't know about the baby.

Nobody knows, other than Cam's ob-gyn. When Dr. Advani—a kindhearted, tiny woman she's been seeing for years—confirmed the pregnancy, Cam cried.

It took the doctor a moment to realize the tears weren't exactly joyful.

"If this baby wasn't planned, you should know that you do have options," she began, to Cam's immediate horror.

"No! No, I could never—I. . . . I want the baby. I just . . ."

. . . want my husband, too. I want all of us to be a family. I want to feel the way I did when I was pregnant with Tess and the future was full of promise.

Granted, back then she and Mike were broke. But that was their only real problem, and it was a surmountable one.

This time, Cam is alone, thirty-seven years old and facing what feels like a treacherous mountain whose summit is still obscured by that fog of uncertainty.

But what choice does she have? All she can do is climb, one step at a time, praying she doesn't lose her grip and fall.

"It's good for you," Cam tells Tess. "Chicken soup. That's why I made it."

"I just feel like something lighter."

"That's strange. You don't look like something lighter."

Tess looks up sharply.

Cam wishes she could take back the stupid quip. She said it because it popped into her head; because it's what Mike would have said. A typical Mike line.

"Whatever." Tess glowers.

Cam sighs and crunches another tortilla chip, trying not to long for a Margarita to wash it down.

Margarita?

Ha. Who is she kidding?

Tequila straight up would do the trick, no salt or lime required.

But that, of course, is out of the question.

She hasn't touched a drop of liquor in over two months.

She stopped drinking a few days after Mike moved out—but not necessarily because her husband had decided, out of the blue, that he no longer wanted to live here and she found herself alone with Tess.

Maybe she would have eventually figured out that she couldn't continue to numb herself with booze.

The reality: she stopped because one morning she woke up, threw up, and understood what was wrong with her before the test confirmed it.

Pregnant.

In this life of hers, filled as it's been with stupefying twists and turns, that was one of the most monumental shocks of all.

It was second only to her startling recognition of Paul Delgado's face on that mailbox flier on a dreary afternoon more than fourteen years ago—and the realization that her visions involved real people. That the terrified pleading she heard might very well have been their last words; that the ragged gasps that filled her head might have been their dying breaths.

For a long time after Paul Delgado, she routinely scoured the fliers from the National Center for Missing & Exploited Children, faces on milk cartons, countless websites on the Internet. All too often, she recognized images of strangers who had vanished without a trace.

Her visions came to her before the victims disappeared, in every case. Cam was seeing their future.

Yet she never found a way to identify

any of the victims in advance, or figure out exactly when or where any of her premonitions would come to pass.

Powerless to warn them and prevent the horrific events, all she could do was watch the prophetic dramas unfold.

She made painstaking notes, writing down every detail in a series of Marble notebooks she kept hidden away in her closet.

And, filled with dread, she simply waited . . .

Wondering if perhaps the cruelest fate of all was her own: helpless, hopeless witness to the inevitable.

Chapter Two

Rain started falling an hour ago, pattering into the metal gutters beneath the roof of the brick Colonial. It cools the damp breeze that ruffles the white curtains at the window above the sink and lightly mists Cam's skin as she stands beside it.

Dinner finished, Tess is upstairs doing her homework.

Cam stares out the window as she drinks a glass of milk, Dr. Advani's orders. She never could stomach the stuff, not even in cereal. She'd pour just enough into the bowl to moisten the flakes, then she'd drain it off the spoon before every bite.

Just another of my charming little

quirks, she thinks wryly, trying not to gag as she drains the last few drops.

She drank a glass every day of her first pregnancy, too. Back then, though, it was chocolate milk.

This time around, she seems to have developed an aversion to chocolate, of all things. Usually, she needs a daily fix—preferably of her favorite: Godiva. Now she can't even stand the smell of anything cocoa-related.

Last time, it was coffee she couldn't stomach. And red meat. And garlic. But only for the first three months; then it all passed, along with the morning sickness.

Hopefully that will happen this time as well.

Right now, it's been pure torture getting up and moving in the mornings, and has been ever since St. Patrick's Day, when she discovered her pregnancy. The morning after, Cam did her best to muffle the sound of being sick in the master bathroom. She forced down some crackers before dropping an unsuspecting Tess at school.

Then she drove straight over to the

musty basement of an Elks Club, where she uttered the stunning words for the first time.

My name is Cam, and I'm an alcoholic.

The moment she said it aloud, she felt an enormous flood of relief sweep through her.

Yet with that came a trickle of doubt and disbelief as well.

An alcoholic? How could *she* be an alcoholic?

It wasn't as though she were a barfly with a string of DUIs and cirrhosis of the liver.

She never even drank in public, for God's sake.

And she never once got behind the wheel after a drink.

She never drank herself blind drunk, vomited, blacked out.

Never did any of the uncivilized, abhorrent, illegal things so many people associate with alcoholism.

She was just . . . comfortably numb. That was it. That was all.

Like the old Pink Floyd song her father frequently listened to when she was growing up.

Obviously, the lyrics spoke to him.

It wasn't until Cam was an adult facing demons of her own that the lyrics spoke to her as well.

"I hear you're feeling down.
Well I can ease your pain . . ."

It took her a long time, though, to figure out how it worked.

To realize, as her father had, that booze was a guaranteed escape chute.

When she drank, she could block out not just the painful memories of her past, but the frightening visions that tormented her for all those years.

The premonitions were fewer and farther between. Whenever one did strike, it would be more fragmented than before. A muffled voice, a blurred face, perhaps a snatch of scenery. Wrapped in a liquor-induced security blanket no chilling premonition could possibly penetrate, Cam grew more and more detached from the imperiled strangers in her head.

Finally, the visions subsided altogether.

She hasn't had one since Tess was a toddler.

Now that she's shed the security blanket, though, she's been holding her breath, waiting.

Praying that if—*when*—the premonitions start up again, she'll be strong enough to stay sober.

How many times has she tried to get to this point before, and fallen off the wagon? She'd never made it to an actual AA meeting before March, let alone admitted to anyone, least of all herself, that she has a problem.

No, but she did attempt to cut way back on the booze whenever Mike made her feel self-conscious about it; when he warned her that it was coming between them.

Only now that she's stopped can she see that drinking didn't just protect her from the visions; it insulated her emotions—all her emotions. Fear and sorrow, yes, but pleasure and joy as well. Eventually, she was going through the motions of marriage—and, yes, occasionally even motherhood. But it was the marriage that suffered most, because she mostly drank at night, when Mike was around and her time with Tess had wound down.

She never went cold turkey until now but she did manage, more than once, to limit herself to a single glass of wine with dinner—not the hard stuff, and she'd stop sipping right after they ate. When she got to that point, she'd have hope. And sometimes, hope would last for weeks at a time.

But never more than that.

Something would eventually trigger her to have an extra glass of wine one night, or to chase it with vodka, and the next thing she knew, she was back to her old habits.

She won't let it happen this time, though.

Cold turkey.

That's what it takes.

Cold turkey. Twelve steps. One day at a time, with her sponsor, a woman named Kathy, promising to guide her along.

Now the stakes are higher than ever before.

Now she has to stay sober, for her

baby's sake, and for Tess's, because Cam is on her own. Mike is no longer here to pick up the slack, to pick up the pieces . . . to pick *her* up—quite literally, at times.

That's okay. I don't need him. I'm strong enough now. I can do it, Cam thinks resolutely, setting the empty milk glass in the sink beside the two bowls from their meal. She'll load the dishwasher later. Or tomorrow.

She puts the milk carton back into the fridge, noticing the *World's Best Mom* shopping list pad stuck to the door. Tess gave it to her on Mother's Day, apologetically saying it came from the dollar store—along with a box of drugstore chocolates Cam pretended she couldn't wait to eat when in reality, just the picture on the lid—sickeningly sweet white cream oozing from a half-bitten chocolate—made her want to gag. They could have been Godiva and she'd have felt the same way.

She must not be that great an actress, because Tess said, "Sorry I didn't get you something better. I would have if I could have."

What she meant was, she would have gotten something better if her father had taken her Mother's Day shopping as he had in years past. Last year, Mike and Tess gave Cam a designer handbag; the year before, tickets for the three of them to see *Jersey Boys* on Broadway. There were always flowers, too, delivered from the florist on Saturday: pink tulips, her favorite.

This year, Mike didn't even give her a *"To My Wife on Mother's Day"* card.

Did you really expect that from him?

Too bad Hallmark doesn't make *"To My Estranged Wife on Mother's Day"* cards.

Back at the stove, she ladles the hot chicken soup into a Tupperware container. She's going to need a couple; there's so much left over.

Once upon a time, she—being a model wife and mother, of course—made this whenever Mike or Tess came down with a cold. There's something so comfortingly familiar, so homey about the distinct savory scent of chicken soup.

Maybe that's what I'm craving now,

more than the soup itself, she tells herself. Comfort. Familiarity. Home.

There was a time when she believed this two-story brick Colonial would fit the bill. A time when she, like Mike, believed that by moving to this affluent, desirable suburb, they could somehow reclaim whatever it was that had gone missing. The trust. The security.

Not the love, though. Never the love. That was always there, right from the start. Through everything, there was never a doubt in her mind that she loved Mike, that he loved her.

We still do.

That's what makes all of this so damn hard.

As she inhales the fragrant steam wafting up from the Tupperware container, she begins to feel vaguely lightheaded.

Dizzy.

Oh, God.

Oh, no.

Cam closes her eyes and finds herself abruptly staring at the unfamiliar, tear-streaked face of a child. A girl.

And now, mingling with the milky aftertaste in Cam's mouth is the unmistakable, familiar taste of terror.

Not her own.

It's the girl's—the girl is in danger. She's far from home, Cam senses. Afraid.

And so it has begun again.

Plugged into her iPod, Tess sits at the desk in her room, blatantly violating one of her mother's dozens of rules.

No music while doing homework. And no TV, no phone calls, no Internet unless it's homework-related, and even then, only with explicit permission.

Dozens of rules? Ha! More like hundreds, when you think about it.

Tess is definitely thinking about it, instead of about her English homework on a Shakespearean tragedy.

If she was to write it all down to prove a point—which is tempting—the list of things Tess is forbidden to do would dwarf the list of things that are allowed.

Homework, healthy food, sleep, exercise . . . that's about all that has Mom's stamp of approval lately.

As a result, Tess's life is agonizingly boring.

Especially when she compares it to her friends' lives.

She taps her yellow pencil—which she just overzealously sharpened to a needle point—against the blank lined notebook page before her, where she's supposed to be writing an essay about Shakespeare's theme of fate versus free will in *Julius Caesar*.

No wonder she can't focus. What does she know about free will?

Everyone at school has more freedom than Tess Hastings has; as a result, their lives are much more interesting.

You'd think now that Dad has moved out, Mom would relax the rules to make up for screwing up Tess's life, instead of the opposite.

That's the way it works with other parents. Her friend Morrow Exley said her mother stopped enforcing curfews after the divorce, and Lily Chen, whose parents split when she was a baby and who has had two stepfathers since, has never had a curfew at all.

Neither Morrow nor Lily has to earn

their spending money doing chores around the house like Tess does. Morrow's mother has a live-in maid; Lily's, a live-out housekeeper. Tess's mother has a bimonthly cleaning service and a live-in slave: a fourteen-year-old daughter who picks up all the slack.

Granted, if Mom didn't enforce the rules, Tess would probably keep things orderly by choice. She's always liked to clean and organize. But the house never needed as much of her attention as it has lately.

Not that Mom was ever a neatnik—but lately, she's gotten really lazy. She spends an awful lot of time resting, dozing off in front of the television or even, Tess suspects, taking afternoon naps. Lately, Mom's always upstairs when Tess gets home from school, and Tess has noticed that the bed is usually rumpled.

There could be another reason for that, but she doesn't even want to consider it.

"I guarantee you one of them is having an affair," Morrow said, rolling her dark blue eyes when Tess told her and Lily about the separation that awful day in March. "My dad was having one."

"My mom was, too, when she got divorced the second time," Lily put in. "Like, six months later, she was already married to the other guy. Who she eventually left when he cheated on her. With my cousin, no less."

"My parents aren't cheating on each other." Tess was disgusted at the sordid state of affairs—literally—in her friends' lives.

"Then why are they getting divorced out of the blue?"

"They're not. They're just . . ."

"Let me guess, having a 'trial separation'?"

"Right."

"Yeah. That's the first step," said Lily, who's been through it enough times to know. She tossed her long black hair. "But, hey, join the club. Hardly anyone's parents are together, anyway."

"Plus," Morrow added, "just think: now your mom will be too wrapped up in herself to bug you about stuff all the time."

That was it. No surprise from her friends, no advice, no sympathy.

Tess wanted to cry, but instead she took her cue from Morrow and Lily, pasted a big stupid grin on her face, and acted like her parents' separation was no big deal.

But it is.

Even now, thinking about it, she feels miserable. So miserable that she'd rather think about Julius Caesar's tragedy than about her own.

She looks back at her annotated text again.

Focus. Fate versus free will.

Tess writes:

Because Julius Caesar believed that "Men at some time are masters of their fates"—

Wait—Caesar didn't say that about fate. The quote was from Cassius, talking to Caesar's friend Brutus, right?

She checks the text. Right.

Tess rewrites:

Caesar continuously ignored the omens of his impending death.

Now what?

She should give specific examples of the omens.

Flipping back through the text, she comes up with a bunch: ominous storms, lions in the streets, sacrificial animals that are dissected and turn out not to have hearts . . .

It's pretty creepy stuff, Tess decides, writing it all down.

And what about his wife's foreboding dream about his statue covered in blood? And the soothsayer who warned him to "Beware the Ides of March"?

What are the Ides of March again?

Tess flips through her notes.

Oh—March 15. The day Caesar was assassinated.

Which also happens to be the day Tess's father moved out.

She misses him desperately. The house feels hollow without him. *She* feels hollow.

It's funny, because even when he lived here, he wasn't around all that much. His job—something high-ranking in computer technology, which she doesn't really understand—is demanding, and he was always at the office or traveling. But his stuff was here. When you walk past someone's favorite Yankees cap hanging on a hook in the mudroom, or reach past their leftover midnight pizza in the fridge when you get milk for your morning cereal, it's kind of like they're there.

Now the hook by the back door is bare, and all that's ever in the fridge is healthy crap Mom keeps trying to shove down Tess's throat.

Also missing from the fridge, besides cold pizza: vodka, white wine, beer . . . all the booze that used to come and go, almost on a daily basis.

Mom drank.

Now she doesn't.

Big deal.

The thing is . . .

It's a big deal. Whether Tess wants it to be or not. All of it: Mom drinking, Mom not drinking, Dad moving out, the countless rules that haven't changed since then and the new ones that have been added, the silence, the boredom, the lack of freedom . . .

God, I hate my life.

Tess looks back at her notes again.

Beware the Ides of March.

Yeah. No kidding.

She scowls and jabs the VOLUME button on her iPod, raising it so that the hip hop bass throbs almost painfully in her ears.

She never used to like this kind of music, but lately the angry, rhythmic lyrics appeal to her. Lately a lot of things appeal to her that never did before.

Which kind of scares her—not that she'd admit it to anyone but herself.

The school year's almost over, though.

Yeah. And as soon as it is, Mom's going to haul her down to the beach.

Away from her friends.

Away from Dad.

Away from Heath Pickering.

Standing in her kitchen, eyes squeezed shut, Cam can see the girl pretty clearly: elfin features, upturned nose, straight, wispy, long blond hair. It's hard to make out the color of her eyes, though—they're tear-filled, and she keeps squeezing them closed.

She's about thirteen years old—maybe fourteen, but small for her age.

What else?

She's filthy, caked in dirt, huddled on the ground. She's clutching a purple backpack and wearing what looks like a school uniform. One tail of her once-white blouse hangs below her navy vest, and her legs are scraped and bloodied between her blue knee socks and short pleated plaid skirt. Blue and green plaid—Black Watch? Is that what it's called?

Around her neck, at the open collar of her blouse, is a silver chain with some kind of small, triangular black pendant hanging from it.

Watching the child's narrow little body heave with silent sobs, Cam clenches her hands so hard that what's left of her methodically bitten fingernails dig painfully into her palms.

Her own saliva is tainted by the metallic taste of the little girl's fear; her thoughts by the little girl's frantic introspection:

Oh, please, God, don't let me die. Please.

Hail Mary, full of grace, the Lord is with thee . . .

What if she never gets to go back home?

Home . . .

The girl's eyes squeeze tightly shut.

She's picturing it, Cam realizes. *Picturing her home.*

Yes, show me, sweetie.

Cam does her best to zero in on the image inside the girl's head.

Come on, let me see.

Slowly, it takes shape: a two-story frame house, the architectural style harkening a child's crayoned drawing: a door centered between two shuttered windows on the first floor, three more windows above on the second, and an A-line roof with a brick chimney on one side.

The roof is gray-black shingles. The clapboards are white. The shutters are black.

Towering maple tree sentries guard the front yard.

There are hundreds of thousands of houses like it throughout the Northeast.

That's where it is, Cam is certain—

somewhere here in the Northeast. Not right here in Montclair, though. Maybe not even in New Jersey. New York? Pennsylvania? Delaware?

Where is the girl's house, dammit?

Wait, there's something to the right of the door, beneath the brass, lantern-style light fixture.

It's a house number . . . 42!

But 42 *what? What's the name of the street? Where is it? Show me!*

Helpless, Cam can only watch the image give way to the girl herself again. She's curled in a fetal position in the shadow of a wall, rocking back and forth.

The wall appears to be made of rock, the floor of dirt. She's in some kind of cellar.

Cam zeroes in on the girl's face, memorizing her features, watching her bite her trembling lip, wishing she would open her eyes.

Then, miraculously, she does, as if on cue. Her tear-flooded pupils, Cam sees, are a light hazel shade. Her lashes are sandy, barely visible.

She'll need mascara when she grows up, Cam finds herself thinking idly . . .

Then, *if she gets to grow up.*

A familiar wave of hopeless, helpless panic is beginning to take hold.

Here is Cam's own panic, mingling in her gut with the child's primal fear that even now remains tempered by a wisp of naive hope.

But Cam knows better.

Breathe. Focus, she tells herself. *Focus on that girl. You can't help her if you don't focus.*

Look at the stone wall, the dirt floor . . .

Look! What else is there? Where is she?

Wall, floor—there are no other details; there's nothing more to go on.

She's in a basement of some kind. *Where?*

It, too, feels as though it's located someplace in the Northeast.

Yes. And not far from the house with white clapboards and black shutters.

More. You need more. What else? Don't just look. Smell.

Musty. Damp.

Listen . . .

There's water nearby. Moving water.

Cam can hear it rushing; there's some kind of current. A creek? A stream? A river?

She strains for something more, and gradually, she hears it. But not water.

A faint, rhythmic sound reaches her ears. A sickeningly familiar sound . . .

What is it?

As it grows ominously louder, she sucks in her breath and the smell hits her. The recognizable organic smell of soil. Rich, damp soil, pungent, black, and crumbly.

She begins to comprehend, and new dread sweeps through her.

Oh, Lord.

Lord help that child.

It's a shovel; that's what she's hearing.

Every dull, clanging thud seems to slam painfully into Cam herself.

Somebody's digging, not far from the girl, maybe somewhere above her.

Who are you? Cam demands of the person whose hands clench the wooden handle. *Let me see your face, dammit.*

The shovel merely continues to dig, and all she can see are gloved hands.

They dig, and all the while, the little girl is huddled somewhere nearby, rocking, crying, trying to catch her breath, missing her white house with the black shutters, missing her parents . . .

Mommy . . .

Daddy . . .

Show them to me, Cam calls silently. *I need their names, or at least to see their faces. Something. Some detail. Some clue as to who they are; who you are.*

But the child is too distraught for coherent thought; her mind fraught only with frantic, fragmented images. Every breath she takes sounds increasingly strangled, as if she's struggling for air.

Mom!

Daddy!

I need you!

The terrible sound of her breathing is becoming more labored with every inhalation. Cam senses that she's running out of time.

Who else, sweetie? Who else is there? Mommy, Daddy, Grandma . . . just give me a name. A street. A town . . . Please.

Please keep breathing. Please hang in there.

Dammit. Cam would give anything to actually make herself heard this time . . .

This time?

She's felt this way every time.

But, of course, it's never happened.

In all those years, she could only helplessly observe unsettling scenes like the one now unfolding in her mind's eye. She was no more able to interfere in the action than a viewer of a movie can alter the plot.

Perhaps it's human nature to try anyway. To attempt the impossible and permeate the translucent one-way veil that separates Cam's world from this troubled stranger's.

Give me a name, please, a sister, a brother, a pet . . . anything. Anything more specific than Mommy . . . Daddy . . .

The vision is fading already.

"No," Cam whispers, "please . . . wait . . ."

But the image of the child has already dissolved.

Lingering in Cam's head is an awful, shuddering gasp for air.

Moments pass.

Another gasp.

Then a terrible, deadly silence.

Tess has been in love with Heath Pickering, a senior, from the first time she saw him at the beginning of her freshman year.

She noticed him immediately, passing by her every day in the hall after homeroom. He stood out from the other guys, who always wear what Tess has come to consider the public school "uniform": jeans, sneakers, and a T-shirt—long-sleeved or short-sleeved, depending on the time of year.

Not Heath. He wears jeans, yeah, but he wears them with boots or sandals, depending on the weather, and usually with shirts that have collars and buttons. Not dress shirts, like Dad's, but casual shirts, untucked. A few times, he's had T-shirts on, and once one of them had a familiar L.B.I. logo on the front.

L.B.I.—Long Beach Island.

Tess has a couple of those T-shirts herself. She started wearing them to school more often, hoping Heath might notice, but if he has, he hasn't said anything.

Well, it's not like the two of them are the only kids at school with L.B.I. T-shirts. Plenty of people around here head down there for the summer. Tess can only hope Heath might turn out to be one of them.

She's noticed he's always got some kind of necklace on. Not a gold chain, or anything like that. More like something a surfer would wear.

Someone said Heath moved here not that long ago from California, so Tess finds it easy—and exciting—to picture him expertly riding the waves, tanned and naked from the waist up. She frequently daydreams about it.

Heath's brows and lashes are darker than his hair, which is blond and kind of shaggy. He's got big brown puppy dog eyes—kind eyes, Tess has noticed. Yeah, she can tell he's a really nice guy. The type of guy who would make a great boyfriend.

She imagines that all the time—Heath coming over to her and introducing himself, saying he thinks she's really cute for a freshman—no, just that she's really cute, period, because in her fantasy, he has no clue she's a freshman.

Anyway, he says he's been noticing her. Then he asks her out.

Lately, she's been taking her daydreams a step further: she imagines what it would be like if she marries Heath someday.

"Tess Pickering." Sounds good. She likes to whisper it out loud, when she's alone in her room at night.

Sometimes she even writes it down, practicing her future signature.

She does that now: *Tess Hastings Pickering*. Analyzing it, she decides, as always, that there are just too many *ing*s. But she'd probably get used to that. Or she could drop her maiden name, like Mom did when she married—

Stop it. Don't even go there.

Lately, Tess tries not to ruin rosy thoughts about her imaginary future relationship with Heath by thinking about Mom and Dad.

After all, her parents first met when they were in school. College, not high school . . . but still. Only a few years older than Tess and Heath. Well, Heath, anyway.

Look what happened to Mom and Dad.

But that wouldn't happen to Heath and me.

Nope. When they get together, they'll stay together forever.

Tess Ava Hastings Pickering.

Time is running out, though. The school year is almost over. It's been months since she did some detective work and memorized Heath's schedule so she could detour into his path between classes all day long.

She always tries to lock eyes with him when they pass each other in the hall, but he doesn't seem to notice her. Sometimes she thinks she should just crash into him so he can't help but notice her . . . only then he might think she's just some stupid freshman klutz, and not his future wife.

Tess Hastings-Pickering.

Yeah. Maybe she'll hyphenate.

Her friends aren't even going to take their husbands' names when they get married. Lily, whose mother has had four different last names in her life, thinks it's a stupid, demeaning custom. Morrow said she and her husband will just make up a new name for themselves, so that it's fair to both of them.

Tess thinks that if you're married to someone, you should have their name.

What if you get divorced? Is Mom going to go back to being Camden Neary again?

Tess hopes not. But if her parents get divorced, what her mother chooses to call herself will probably be the least of her problems.

Don't think about divorce. Think about Heath, or homework, even.

Julius Caesar.

Heath.

He plays on the school baseball team. Tess almost died the first time she saw him a few weeks ago in his uniform, those snug white pants and a cap pulled low and sexy over his eyes.

She decided right then that she had to do something soon.

Otherwise school will be out, and she'll go away for the summer, and he'll find a new girlfriend. He used to have one, in the city, but they reportedly broke up last fall, right before Tess discovered him. His single status can't last, though. Tess has to make her move soon—or get one of her friends to make it for her.

Tess Ava Picker—

Oops. The tip of her overly sharpened pencil just snapped.

She shudders. To her, the scraping of the splintered wooden hollow of broken lead across paper is like fingernails on a chalkboard.

She trades the pencil for a fresh one with a slightly duller point, flips to a clean page, and decides she'd really better get busy on her homework.

Fate versus free will.

She flips pages, rereads the passages about Caesar's death.

"*Et tu,* Brute?" he uttered on his dying breath, realizing that his trusted friend was among the conspirators.

Deciding Caesar was a fool for not paying more attention to the signs all along, Tess goes back to her essay.

* * *

It's dark, and it's late, and it's raining.

The drive from Long Beach Island took hours longer than it should have, thanks to a train derailment near Camden. A toxic one, as it turned out, which led to the road being closed and a detour through the suburbs. A wrong turn from there led to the streets of this so-called family neighborhood in East Greenbranch.

A wrong turn?

Or fate?

She's here somewhere, nearby.

I can feel it. I just have to figure out where she's been hiding from me . . . and why.

For now, it's enough just to cruise along these residential streets beneath a canopy of maple trees, passing rows of older houses, wondering which one is hers.

I'll come back tomorrow, when it's light. When all the pretty young girls aren't safely tucked into bed, having sweet, naive dreams.

The shark's tooth—the *sign*—is safely wrapped in several layers of Kleenex and stashed in the glove compartment.

The rain beats down on the car roof, the radio plays soft jazz, and the windshield wipers swish rhythmically, seeming to echo the silent, soothing mantra.

Find . . . her . . . find . . . her . . .

PART II: JUNE

Chapter Three

Cam throws another pair of shorts into the open suitcase on the bed she once shared with Mike.

Then she wonders why she even bothered.

It's not as if they're likely to fit for more than another week, maybe two at the most. She desperately needs to go shopping for some summer maternity clothes.

Shorts with elastic bands at the belly, sleeveless tops to reveal her fleshy upper arms, maternity bathing suits . . .

Yeah, that'll be fun.

But it was, last time around, she remembers wistfully as the warm night breeze stirs the sheers at the open window.

It shouldn't have been fun, shopping on a strict budget in pricey Manhattan maternity boutiques, battling nausea the whole time. But whenever she stepped out of a dressing room wearing some ill-fitting, overpriced garment over a strapped-on foam belly provided by the store, Mike would flash an emotional smile and tell her she looked great.

She didn't look great, and she didn't feel great, and they couldn't afford any of it—the clothes, the medical care, the baby—but that didn't matter. Mike being there with her every step of the way made it all okay.

This time around, she'll have to go it alone. Maternity-clothes shopping, blood work and tests with potentially scary results, labor, diapers, the whole thing.

Unless . . .

Nope. No way.

They're already into June now, and he hasn't come home. Not to stay, anyway.

He comes and goes in the driveway, thanks to his regular visitations with Tess. But he never ventures into the house. If she happens to be at the door, he'll wave and call out a greeting, but that's about it.

They talk on the phone a few times a week to discuss the details of his visitation schedule, household bills or repairs, that sort of thing.

She hasn't even had an opportunity to mention the pregnancy to him—if she was ready . . . which she's not.

When she is ready, though, it's not something she should mention in passing.

Tess has to be home early tomorrow night because of finals, I scheduled the annual cleaning for the hot water heater, and, oh, by the way, I'm pregnant.

No, she'll have to summon him over, sit him down, drop the bombshell, then . . .

What?

Wait for his reaction.

Wait for him to get over his shock, to ask why she didn't tell him sooner, to say that he wants to be a part of this baby's life—all of which is inevitable.

But where do we go from there?

Do they continue on in this state of marital limbo?

Trial separation.

She's *tried* it. She doesn't like it. She doesn't want it.

But Mike, apparently, does. Otherwise he would be reaching out to her, talking about coming home.

All he'd have to do is ask, and she'd take him back.

When he finds out about the pregnancy, he might decide to do just that. But she doesn't want him back that way. She wants him back because he still loves her.

Because I still love him.

She shoves another pair of too-snug shorts into the suitcase.

Mike will be dropping off Tess soon. It's a Tuesday night; he took her to a nice seafood restaurant for dinner to celebrate her terrific final report card. Cam stayed home, planning on eating cold cereal—to take in her nightly milk serving—in front of the TV. Then she decided that seemed pitiful.

So she threw together a stir-fry and ate it on the good china, sitting alone at the kitchen table reading a literary novel and trying not to wish that the raspberry-flavored seltzer in her glass was Pinot Grigio.

Talk about pitiful.

But still better than cold cereal and TV.

All right, what now? Should I catch Mike in the driveway and tell him we need to sit down and talk before Tess and I leave for the shore Friday morning?

Yes. She should.

In the split second after she makes that decision, as if to reinforce it, she hears a car pulling into the driveway below.

Sitting in with the band, Ike Neary spots her in the middle of the first set, during the opening riff of "Brown Eyed Girl."

The shock is nearly enough to make him lose his grip on the drumsticks, but somehow he manages to hang on.

Brenda?

Oh my God, Brenda!

After all these years . . .

"*Hey where did we go . . .*" sings the lead vocalist, a kid named Jimmy.

Ike's drumming.

And miraculously, Brenda's familiar face is here among the throng that's gathered to drink and dance to live music at the Sandbucket Grill on this warm Tuesday night in June.

Oh my God.

What should Ike do? What will he say to her?

What does one say, after thirty-odd years, to a wife who walked away and never looked back? A wife who left you to single-handedly raise one daughter and bury the other . . .

Swept by a familiar surge of fury-tainted grief, Ike blinks away the tears pooling in his eyes.

What is she doing here? How did she know where to find me?

He wasn't even officially supposed to play tonight.

He never does, these days.

But Jerry, the owner, spotted him and asked him if he'd sit in for a set.

"Ladies and gentlemen," he said, "we have a very special guest here tonight to help us inaugurate the Sandbucket's new stage . . ."

Over the winter, Jerry built a fancy new outdoor stage out back. Now he has to pay for it—and compete with the big acts in nearby Atlantic City—so he's stepping up his exposure in the shore papers. This week he took out ads with color photos of all the new bands playing the Sandbucket's new stage, alongside black and white photos of the legendary musicians who played there in the past.

Brenda must have spotted Ike's picture among them. Maybe it triggered her memory . . .

Right. Because she got hit on the head all those years ago, came down with amnesia, and wandered away.

Of all the scenarios he conjured after his wife disappeared, that's the best.

It sure as hell beats the one where she gets abducted from their apartment in the crime-ridden neighborhood, murdered, and her body dumped in a landfill somewhere.

And the one where she just walks away to start a new life somewhere without him and the girls.

"Do you remember when we used to sing . . ."

Forcing his eyes open, Ike chimes in on the familiar chorus.

"Sha la la la la la la . . ."

His eyes scan the swaying, singing crowd below the stage, seeking Brenda.

". . . la la la la te da . . ."

She's gone.

Again.

"So what do you think, Messy Tessy?"

Seated beside her father in the front seat of his silver-blue Saab as he pulls into the driveway, she can't help but smile at the affectionate nickname. It doesn't fit her—it never really did—but she's always liked it anyway.

"What do I think about what?"

"About the Fourth."

Oh. Right. He was just telling her about all the things they could do for the Independence Day holiday in a few weeks.

And she was thinking about other things. Nice things, for a change—like Heath Pickering.

And not-so-nice things, like whether she should feel as guilty as she has been about letting Morrow cheat off of her in the English final the other day.

The thing is, who does it really hurt? No one. Tess is great at English. Morrow, who says she really thinks she might be dyslexic, is not. Tess has been trying to help her with the Shakespeare stuff for the past month, but there's so much Morrow just isn't getting.

When Morrow finally asked Tess if she could copy her answers since they sit right next to each other alphabetically, Tess had to say yes.

Well, she didn't *have* to.

But she feels sorry for Morrow because of her disability, and anyway, if Tess hadn't agreed, Morrow probably wouldn't be doing her this huge favor in return: having her new boyfriend, Chad, a junior and a friend of Heath's, talk to him about Tess.

Bold move, but Tess had little choice. It was either that, or leave town in a few days for the entire summer without Heath knowing she's alive.

She heard he got a lifeguard job for the

summer, at an ocean beach. She wonders where. Remembering his L.B.I. T-shirt, she wonders if it's somewhere down near Long Beach Island. That would totally be fate. Maybe he'll turn up right in Beach Haven itself. Wouldn't that be a dream come true? Spending a summer at the shore with Heath?

That can't exactly happen unless she meets him, which is why she told Morrow to tell Chad to tell Heath about her.

At Lily's pool party tomorrow, she's supposed to find out what he said. Heath might even show up there, according to Morrow, who invited, like, everyone in the school. It's not even her party, but Lily doesn't care. Her mother won't even be home.

"What are my choices again?" she asks her father, reaching out to turn down the radio, which is broadcasting tonight's Yankees game.

He could have been there. Someone he knows through work got last-minute box seats.

Dad loves the Yankees.

"But I love you more," is what he told Tess.

She believes it, most days.

"We can go to Cape Cod to visit the Nortons at their beach house"—he begins ticking off on his fingers—"or we can have a barbecue at Grandma and Grandpa's, or we can watch the fireworks over the East River from my roof in the city . . ."

"What about Long Beach Island?"

"What about it?"

"We always watch the fireworks there."

They always have, even back before they got the beach house on Dolphin Avenue. As a kid, Mom always spent her summers on the shore—mostly Long Beach Island—with Granddad, and she's nostalgic about it. She wants Tess to have that same tradition.

Dad hesitates, either straining to hear the radio announcer, who's shouting about some Yankee who just got a hit and loaded the bases, or trying to figure out what to say.

Tess stares out the window at the red-brick, white-shuttered Colonial that hasn't really felt much like home since Dad left.

Yellow light spills from the black wrought iron fixtures beside the door and along the curved path bordered by long flowerbeds. Normally by June there are pastel-colored annuals planted there.

Not this year—the beds have only dirt and mulch, waiting for blossoms Tess suspects will never be planted.

Mom usually goes to the garden center around Mother's Day to fill the Volvo station wagon with plastic cell packs of blooming geraniums and impatiens. Dad would tell her they can get the landscape service to do it, but Mom never wants that. She says she loves kneeling in the sunshine, working the earth with her trowel, making things grow.

But this year, she doesn't seem to care. About a lot of things—not just the flowers. And Tess, who never paid much attention, is surprised at just how much it bothers her to see plain old dirt in the beds every time she steps into the yard.

"Would you rather just spend the Fourth at the shore with your mother?" Dad finally asks, interrupting her bleak thoughts.

Your mother.

She hates how he's taken to saying it that way. Before the separation, he used to just refer to her as *Mom*.

Your mother—ugh. It's so distant. As if that's his only connection to Mom—that she's Tess's mother, and not his wife.

"Do *you* want to spend it at the shore?" Tess asks her father in return.

"I'm not talking about me. I'm talking about you."

Ignoring that, she repeats, "Well, *do* you?"

"Do I what?"

"Want to spend the Fourth at the shore?"

Dad frowns. "With your mother?"

Your mother.

"You know what? Never mind," Tess snaps, and opens the car door.

"But—"

"I don't know what I want to do yet. I'll figure it out later. It's still weeks away. Thanks for dinner. Night."

"Tess—"

About to slam the car door, she opts to close it instead. Firmly. Then she jogs toward the front door with a backward wave.

Dad just sits there for a few seconds, like he's either trying to hear what's happening with the baseball game or trying to decide if he should come after her.

She wishes he would. She wishes he'd come into the house with her, close the door, and stay.

But he won't, because the bases are loaded and Mom—*her mother*—is here. And he doesn't love her mother more than he does the Yankees. He doesn't love her mother at all.

For awhile there, Tess didn't blame him.

But lately, Mom has seemed kind of . . .

Lost. Sad. Vulnerable.

Okay, so she obviously screwed up their marriage—but maybe she deserves a second chance.

Doesn't everyone?

Yeah. Including Dad.

Tess turns toward the car again, wondering if she should run back and tell him never mind about the Fourth. That she'd love to spend it with him, wherever.

But he's already backing out of the driveway.

* * *

Slipping back onto a stool at the long bar, Ike tilts the icy brown bottle to his lips and swigs a fresh beer.

All the doors and windows are open to let in the salty night air and the live music out back. A new band has taken the stage—a couple of kids who just graduated from college and decided to launch careers as musicians.

Yeah, good luck with that, Ike thinks, setting the beer on a cardboard coaster. In this day and age, it's not easy.

Was it ever?

Probably not.

But for Ike it sure seemed that way. He dropped out of high school to become a busboy at a supper club in Fort Lee, back when the swing orchestra and crooner scene was going strong. Pearl Bailey, Dean Martin, a kid named Frank Sinatra who hailed from right down the Palisades, in Hoboken. There were countless lesser—if not completely *un*—known acts, too.

It was a lesser-known who taught Ike

to play the drums after-hours, and told him he had talent.

By the time he was twenty, he believed it, a cocky son of a bitch. Hitched a ride down to the beach one summer night that changed his life.

That was the early fifties; doo-wop music was taking hold in Philly, spreading to the Jersey Shore. Ike was great with harmony. Classic case of right place, right time. Someone asked him to sit in on the drums, sing a little backup. He did, and a star was born.

Ha. That's what he thought.

Yeah, but he wasn't the only one.

He had quite a following, right from the start.

Easy-breezy.

Then he met Bren in Beach Haven.

She was just a kid then, genuine jailbait. But Ike wasn't old enough—or maybe just not smart enough, or strong enough—to know better. He took one look at Brenda Ann Johnson on the beach in that not-so-virginal white bikini and he fell hard. Got her name tattooed on his right forearm a few days later, rimmed by a heart. Knocked her up in no time, and felt obligated to settle down and support a family.

Sure as hell not easy to do on a rented drum set and a dream.

God knows he tried, though. For her, for his precious baby Ava, and later, for Camden, who Bren always called their "midlife crisis surprise."

But Cam turned out to be Ike's salvation. If he didn't have Cam after he lost everything else, he'd have had nothing to live for.

Then again, if he didn't have Cam, maybe he'd still have his Brenda.

Cut it out!

Ike guiltily steers his brain away from that particular thought process, though not as effectively as he used to.

When Cam was a little girl, it was much easier for him to focus on her many needs and not on his own devastation—or what might have been. For a long time, Ike was able to ignore the truth: it was the second pregnancy that did Brenda in.

She went off her medication, afraid of what it might do to the baby. And she never went back on it—not that he knew, anyway.

So if Cam had never been born, he'd still have Brenda. Sometimes, in his aging, irrationally resentful mind, it's that simple.

"Yo, Ike, what d'ya think of the new digs out back? Nice, huh?" Billy, one of the bartenders, asks as he materializes at this end of the bar to load a blender with ice.

"Nice," Ike agrees, forcing himself back to the present, away from the futile *what if*'s.

"You guys sounded good tonight."

"We always sound good."

"Better on the new stage, though, right?" Billy's bare, muscular, tattooed arms reach for some kind of blue liqueur, some berries, pineapple. He tosses it all into the plastic pitcher with the ice, then flips the switch.

"What the hell kind of drink are you making?" Ike asks above the blender, the chatter, the wailing guitars out back.

"This here? It's for them." Billy indicates a couple of clean-cut guys down the bar.

They're wearing pastel polo shirts, shorts, no socks—cologne, too, Ike's willing to bet. He knows their kind; he's been seeing more and more of them around here lately, and fewer rockers, bikers, working-class types.

Billy pours the fruity slush into a pair of glasses—real ones, not plastic—then plunks in a pair of straws and paper umbrellas, garnishing the whole thing with a wedge of pineapple on the rim.

"Cripes, Billy, a fancy stage, girl drinks . . . next thing I know you'll be wearing a tux."

"That ain't gonna happen."

"Don't be so sure. I think Jerry's trying to change the image of the place, attract a different kind of crowd, like what they tried to do up in Asbury Park."

Billy smirks and heads off down the bar with his girl drinks, leaving Ike to drink his beer and reminisce about the glory days here on the South Jersey Shore.

He keeps an eye on the crowd, though—still looking for Brenda.

In case he really did see what he thought he saw earlier, from the stage.

* * *

Too late.

Mike's car is disappearing down the street when Cam opens the front door. That was fast. Usually he lingers a few minutes, as though he can't bear to say good night to his daughter just yet.

On the doorstep, Tess looks up, startled.

Cam, glimpsing fleeting distress in her face, asks, "What's wrong?"

"Nothing," Tess shoots back. "What's wrong with you?"

Cam scowls. "Watch your tone, Tess."

With a scowl, Tess amends, "All I meant is, what are you doing out here?"

"I figured I'd open the door for you when I saw Daddy pulling up."

Tess's expression instantly softens. "Oh. Well, thanks."

Looking as though she wants to add something, she comes into the house. Cam knows better than to press her daughter.

"He was in a hurry to leave tonight, huh?" Cam asks casually as she closes the door.

"Yeah, I guess." Tess heads immediately for the stairs.

Cam slides the dead bolt and sets the alarm that had once seemed so necessary for a house this size "in the middle of nowhere," as Cam once saw it.

Back when Mike moved into senior management and they first considered moving out of Manhattan, her only suburban experience was her childhood apartment in Camden. There were bars on the windows, junkies on the streets, and sirens screamed all night.

Yeah, and it took her all of five minutes to figure out that this upscale, well-insulated neighborhood couldn't be farther from her roots—or closer to Mike's, even though Connecticut is two states away and not on the list of places she was willing to live.

High on a ridge west of Manhattan, Montclair won them over with spectacular skyline views, historic architecture, and a manageable commute. Though historically the town boomed early last century when Manhattan's affluent built their mansions—and though it remains partially populated by celebrity types, the cultural elite, Wall Street and media royalty—there is, nonetheless, a small-town feel. It is, as the first realtor told Cam and Mike way back when, a great place to raise a family.

So Montclair it was. With a built-in security system. Because you can't be too careful . . . anywhere.

Not when you're a mother tormented by visions of real kids in real trouble.

Cam looks up at her daughter heading up the steps. "Tess? You should pack, tonight or tomorrow morning. Okay?"

"Yeah."

Not very convincing.

"Don't leave it for the last minute," Cam calls, but her daughter is already down the hall, closing the door to her room.

She sighs, remembering Tess's little-girl days, when she was always delightful, always delighted.

When was the last time she heard Tess laugh?

Really laugh, not the staccato, sarcastic sound she frequently emits these days to express just how ridiculous she finds something—or someone, usually Cam.

Well, can you blame her? She started a new school, turned fourteen, and her parents split up, all in a matter of months.

Not exactly a glee-inducing combo.

Only thing that can top that for Tess will be finding out her soon-to-be single mom is pregnant.

Cam shakes her head and starts for the kitchen, thinking she needs a glass of—

Milk. That's all you get tonight.

Or ever.

Cam sighs, longing for wine, for her little girl, for Mike.

For the life she used to have—or perhaps, for the life she never had at all.

Okay, so it isn't the first time over the years that Ike's caught a glimpse of Brenda—only to have her either vanish into thin air or prove to be a figment of his imagination all along.

He's pretty sure he didn't take a hit of acid earlier when Frankie offered—though, yeah, he remembers taking a hit or two off Jimmy's joint before they went on. But it's not like he's stoned out of his mind, blind drunk, or—despite his age—going senile.

Maybe it was just wishful thinking.

Brooding, he twirls the cold, wet beer bottle back and forth between his palms.

For all he knows, Brenda has been dead all these years, just like Ava.

Somewhere in the back of Ike's mind, beneath the weighted shroud of grief and loss, something stirs.

No.

More wishful thinking, and you know it.

Or does he?

Years ago, there was no DNA testing. Ava's body—with all recognizable features obliterated in the fall—was identified based on the contents of the wallet in her pocket.

No one ever questioned it, or the fact that there wasn't a suicide note. Not even Ike. Not back then, anyway.

But as the years passed, he began to wonder . . .

Would his firstborn child, his beloved, beautiful Daddy's girl, really have done that to him after all he had been through? Would Ava—after promising to be a stand-in mom to her little sister—have abandoned Cam as well? Was she that distraught over Brenda's disappearance, or her grades, or a breakup, or any of the things the police said might have caused her to kill herself?

Anything's possible.

And when Ike's stone sober, he's usually fairly convinced that it was her. When he's messed up, though . . . he believes anything's possible.

Like some other girl diving to her death that day with Ava's wallet in her pocket, and Ava still being alive somewhere.

Like Brenda showing up in some bar looking for him . . .

Or on the street in Philly, or in an Atlantic City dive casino, or at his granddaughter's eighth-grade graduation, or any of the other places Ike's glimpsed her—or so he thought—over the years.

Brenda.

As hard as it ever was to believe his wife had really chosen to walk away, it's even harder to fully accept, even now, that she's never coming back.

Maybe that's why he keeps looking for her, for both of them, Bren and Ava, more and more lately.

Or maybe he's seeing Brenda because she's really there.

Maybe she couldn't stay away. Maybe she's been watching him, and Cam, and even Tess, keeping tabs on them. Just waiting for the right moment to come back into their lives.

Any time now, Bren, Ike silently tells her, wherever she is. *Any time.*

"Need another beer, Ike?" Billy asks, and he shakes his head.

The night is young. It's time to move on.

Ike drains his beer and leaves the empty on the bar, then shuffles off toward the door and the neon-lit world beyond.

". . . Bases loaded, two outs, bottom of the ninth on a beautiful night here in the Bronx . . ." the radio sportscaster is saying as, driving past the stately mansions of Montclair, Mike fights the urge to make a U-turn and go back and . . .

What?

Knock on the door and demand that Tess make a decision about where she wants to spend the Fourth of July?

What would that accomplish?

She's not in a reasonable mood. She hasn't been in a reasonable mood since she turned fourteen and he moved out.

Nice timing, you selfish jerk.

Cam didn't say that, but she wanted to. He could tell. He's said it to himself enough times since he made what now feels like a stupid, spontaneous decision to jump off what he'd decided was a sinking ship.

"*. . . The pitcher winds, kicks, and deals . . . outside, ball one.*"

Poor Tess.

Never in a million years did Mike ever believe his own daughter would become the product of a broken home. Divorce happens to other people. Not him and Cam.

Or so he thought, until he woke up one day and asked himself whether he'd be happier with her . . . or without her.

The answer seemed so damn clear at the time. As far as he was concerned, they'd hit an all-time low when she refused to accompany him on the February ski trip with his side of the family, an annual Christmas gift from his parents.

She claimed it was because she didn't want to take Tess out of school for a week.

"We've always done that, and it's no big deal."

"Now that she's in high school, she can't just miss all those days, Mike."

"She can take the work with her."

"They won't do that. They're trying to discourage parents from pulling their kids out for illegal absences."

"That's ridiculous. She's our kid; we can take her out of school if we want to."

"And have her fall behind, and maybe jeopardize her grades? Uh-uh. Let's just ask your parents to wait until March this year for a change, since that's when her break is."

"Can't. I've got to be in Prague that week," he said.

The truth was, Mike hadn't yet scheduled that particular business trip; he just knew it was coming up.

But Mike knew how the suggestion

that they postpone the ski trip till Tess's March break would go over with his father. Mike Sr. wasn't thrilled with Cam's decision to enroll their daughter in a public high school. He's a big believer in private school.

Back when they were living on a shoestring budget in Manhattan, he was aghast that his grandchild was attending PS 42. He even offered to pay for private tuition, but you can't just walk into a private school in Manhattan, where kids are wait-listed from the time they're born.

When they moved to the suburbs, though, they got Tess right into prestigious Cortland Academy, a private day school two towns over, and Mike's salary easily covered tuition.

Cam never liked the private school crowd, though. Especially as Tess got older. She wanted her daughter to hang around with "normal kids," as she put it, as opposed to worldly rich kids. Anyway, the local public high school has a terrific reputation—even wealthy families send their kids there.

It doesn't matter how many times Mike

has defended to his parents the decision—a joint one between him and Cam—to switch Tess from private school to public freshman year. Dad still doesn't get it, and he still blames Cam.

For a lot of things.

". . . Here's the pitch . . ."

Looking back, Mike wonders if things might be different now if he'd decided to forego the annual skiing trip over President's Day. Instead, for Valentine's Day, he gave Cam the biggest box of Godiva chocolate he could find, and Tess a camera that cost a small fortune. Then he broke the news that he was going away without them.

Tess cried.

Cam retreated emotionally—surprise, surprise.

He tried not to care, flying solo out to Utah to meet his parents and his older brothers—Dave, who lives in Chicago, and Jeff, in Los Angeles.

They all seemed so content with their lives—Dad, newly retired, and Mom, a doting wife and grandmother, and Dave and Jeff, with their wholesome wives, large families, big plans, bright futures.

It made Mike's life back home in Jersey seem all the more isolating.

". . . cut on and missed."

A few weeks after he got back, he told Cam he was leaving.

One look at her face when he broke the news, and he wanted to take it back. But he forced himself to hold his ground, forced himself to remember the advice his father had given him one day on the slopes.

"Ask yourself where you'll be in ten years, son, if you two stay together. Do you expect things to get better—or worse?"

Looking into the future on that blustery day, Mike envisioned himself and Cam, middle-aged and living in a household without Tess, who by then would be out of college.

What would they even have to talk about? They could barely keep a conversation going now, even with Tess between them to share the burden.

Mike pictured himself and Cam coasting into their retirement years sitting at the dinner table alone together, night after night, forks clinking against china the only sound in the room.

That, and the ice cubes dropping into Cam's glass as she refilled it yet again.

". . . and the count is one and one. He's two-for-four tonight, with a double and an RBI . . ."

Mike hasn't been able to shake the image of Cam, ten years older, ten years lonelier, angrier, with the drawn, angular face and bloodshot eyes of a longtime drinker. Like her father.

He didn't—doesn't—want himself and Cam to become those people. Workaholic, alcoholic.

Maybe apart, they'll have a chance to escape that fate. Together, it seems inevitable.

At least, that's what he managed to convince himself after talking to his father back in February.

Tess told him that, within days of his leaving Cam threw away every bottle of liquor in the house. She's supposedly gone cold turkey on the booze, which may prove that Mike was right to leave and that his father really does—as he always claims—know best.

". . . Here's the pitch, fastball, in there for strike two."

Yet Dad never was crazy about Cam. Conservative and old-fashioned, he had judged her before he even met her. He took issue with her past, even with her parents' lives. He hated that Cam's father is a musician, that her mother has long been out of the picture.

"What kind of woman just up and leaves her husband and children?" he'd demanded of Mike, back when he first found out about Brenda Neary.

The kind of woman whose daughter might grow up to do the same thing. That's what Dad was thinking, even if he didn't say it out loud.

Maybe somewhere deep inside, Mike was always afraid of that, too.

Hell—maybe it had actually happened.

Only Cam didn't check out physically, as her mother had. She checked out emotionally, putting up walls he couldn't get past.

Why would she do that if she still loves him, as she claims?

All these years, Mike wondered, and worried. But he long ago gave up asking his wife if everything is okay. He's known for quite some time that it isn't.

". . . Two out, the count one and two in the bottom of the ninth here at Yankee Stadium. The bases loaded with Yankees who still trail by two runs . . ."

Mike gave up, too, on believing that the girl he fell in love with still exists somewhere behind the mask of a burdened, bitter housewife.

Still . . . you never know.

"God, I miss you," he says aloud.

". . . It is high . . . It is far . . . It is GONE! A game-winning, walk-off grand slam and the Yankees win! The-e-e-e Yankees win!"

Wait a minute . . .

The Yankees won?

Somehow, Mike missed it . . . And he was right here all along.

Yeah. That's kind of how he feels about his marriage.

Shaking his head, he drives on toward the Holland Tunnel, and the small rented apartment that doesn't feel like home.

Then again—neither does the big brick Colonial in Montclair.

Jesus, Cam, what happened to us?

No, that's not exactly it. More like . . .

What have I done to us? Can I undo it before it's too late? Do I even want to?

Eddie Casalino grew up in Atlantic City; he knows the beach, the boardwalk, and most of the casinos inside and out.

Not that he gambles. What a waste of hard-earned cash.

At twenty-two, he's got better plans for his money: big plans. For a year now, he's been saving every spare dollar from his day job at Packages Plus and his night job as a desk clerk at Bally's. A few more months, and he'll have enough for a bike. Not just any bike—a Harley. Used, but in great condition.

Then he'll be able to move to a better apartment, someplace off the public transportation route.

Yeah, by fall, he'll be riding his bike back and forth to work, living someplace with decent plumbing, maybe even a yard or a balcony. Who knows? Maybe a view of the ocean.

Dream big . . . that's what his mother always told him.

Last week, he went to Kaminski, his boss at Packages Plus, to ask for a raise.

"You need to step it up a little, Eddie. Talk to the customers. Don't just hand them their mail, weigh their packages, take their money. Be friendly. If I see more initiative from you, I'll think about a raise."

He's been remembering to do what Kaminski said. He's stepped it up at Bally's, too, making small talk with guests as they check in and out. He's never been much of a chatterbox, so it doesn't come naturally to ask people where they're from, if they've ever been to Atlantic City before, whatever. He tries to act interested in their answers, but he really doesn't give a shit.

"Night, Eddie," calls Angela, one of the blackjack dealers, as she passes him on his way to Pacific Avenue.

"Morning, Angela," he returns, as usual, and they smile before continuing on in opposite directions. She's about to clock in; he's about to take the jitney to his rented room and catch a few hours' sleep before he has to be back behind the counter at Packages Plus.

Sometimes, he imagines asking Angela—who, he's heard through the grapevine, is divorced with a couple of kids—if she wants to go out with him. But a hot older woman like her wouldn't want to ride the bus to T.G.I. Fridays and the multiplex.

It'll have to wait until fall.

As he walks along the deserted street toward the bus stop, Eddie smiles at the thought of Angela on the back of his new bike, her arms and legs wrapped around him.

Dream big. Yup.

All he needs is—

"Dude!" he blurts involuntarily as a figure abruptly steps out of the shadows in front of him.

Startled, Eddie stops short—he has no choice, the person is standing squarely on the sidewalk, facing him, blocking his way.

"What—"

Then he sees the gun.

In the split second before it goes off,

he looks up. In shocked recognition of the shooter's face, his voice clogged with dread, he begins to ask, "Why—"

Then a flash of blinding pain, and everything shatters: his bewilderment, his big dreams, his skull.

Lying on the sidewalk with his brains spattered around him, Eddie Casalino dies.

The lone witness is his black-clad killer, who whispers, "Sorry, dude," before tucking away the gun and disappearing into the night.

Chapter Four

Wednesday afternoon, Cam lugs yet another packed duffel bag to the heap she's been accumulating beside the back door, ready for Friday's departure.

Tess is upstairs in her room filling a few more. They're going to have a heavy load this year, even without Mike's stuff.

Cam is still undecided about whether to bring the bag she filled with the Marble notebooks—all the notes she'd taken over the years about missing children. She'd been thinking she might have time to go through them down at the beach, when Tess leaves to spend time with Mike.

Go through them . . . why?

For old times' sake?

To dwell on just how helpless you really were . . . and still are?

Maybe she'll return them to the attic. The car is going to be jammed full, anyway.

The phone rings as Cam returns to the kitchen, and she waits for Tess to grab it on the first ring, as usual.

When she doesn't, Cam goes over to check the caller ID window. The number is unavailable.

Maybe it's a telemarketer. She could just let it ring.

Then again, maybe it's her father.

Pop still keeps an apartment over in Hoboken, but he frequently crashes elsewhere—occasionally even here with them, if he feels like it.

"Can't he at least call and let us know when he's coming?" Mike used to ask, early in their marriage.

Cam passed that request along to her father, who tried to honor it . . . for awhile.

Eventually, Ike got back to his old ways, popping up on a whim every now and then.

Tess is always thrilled to see him, and

it doesn't bother Cam. In fact, she's always secretly relieved to see that her father is alive and well.

She always scolds him to call more often to check in. It's not as if she can get ahold of him whenever she feels like it, even now that she got him a cell phone. Half the time he forgets to charge it or doesn't carry it with him, and he rarely bothers to check his voice mail.

But that's Pop.

A free spirit, and God bless him for that. They could all—Cam, and Tess, and Mike—use a little more of her father's easygoing attitude in their lives.

Anyway, this could be Pop, calling from some bar down the shore. It wouldn't be the first time, and those calls sometimes come up on the ID as UNAVAILABLE.

Cam picks up the phone, hoping to hear her father's voice. Almost expecting it, really—she has a feeling she's going to hear from him.

"Cam? It's Kathy."

Her AA sponsor.

So much for psychic ability that doesn't

involve missing children, she thinks darkly.

"Kathy!" she says aloud. "What's up?"

"I haven't heard from you in a couple of days and you didn't make the meeting last night or the night before, so I wanted to check in."

"I'm doing great." White lie. Or maybe not so white.

Then again, for Kathy's purposes, she *is* doing great. Meaning, she's almost three months sober.

"Ninety-in-ninety, Cam . . . that's the goal."

"I know." Ninety AA meetings in ninety days—the AA mantra. One of many, actually.

Cam hates that she has to be accountable to a stranger whose last name she doesn't even know. Even if Kathy is responsible for getting her into recovery in the first place—her own personal AA recruiter, really.

I owe her, Cam thinks to herself.

Aloud, she explains, "I was planning to come yesterday but I had a doctor's appointment I couldn't miss."

"Anything serious?"

"No, just a regular checkup." *With my obstetrician. Because I'm pregnant.*

It's probably time she mentioned that to Kathy. After all, the pregnancy was the initial motivating factor in her newfound sobriety—and remains the ongoing reason Cam won't be slipping, with or without ninety-in-ninety.

But it doesn't seem right to confide in someone else before she tells Mike.

Granted, Kathy knows far more details of Cam's life these days than Mike does.

But the pregnancy involves him directly. He should know before anyone else. And soon.

And you would have made arrangements last night if he hadn't blown out of here so fast when he dropped off Tess, she reminds herself, heading into the kitchen.

Kathy makes weather small talk in her ear as Cam pours oil and vinegar into a cruet for the big salad she's planning to make later, to use up the rest of the stuff in the crisper.

Maybe she should just put aside her reservations and call Mike. She can probably reach him at the office right now. Or . . . She could always call his apartment and leave a message on the voice mail there, so she won't have to talk to him directly. But how would she phrase the message, exactly? And what if he doesn't call her back until it's too late and she's already left for Long Beach Island?

Oh, please, how old are you? Fourteen? Analyzing every possible scenario before calling a boy?

"So can we still have lunch tomorrow?" Kathy is asking, and Cam belatedly remembers that tentative plan for Thursday. It was Kathy's idea. She wanted to talk about maintaining sobriety on vacation, attending AA meetings down in Beach Haven.

Ninety meetings in ninety days—that's the goal.

Which you've already blown, and by the time you get to the shore, it'll have been more than ninety days since you joined AA.

Still, you're sober. Isn't that what counts? You're sober, and you haven't come close to slipping up.

AA was built on a spiritual cornerstone: the concept of opening one's mind to embrace a power greater than oneself.

You've done that. You understand why you were doing what you did for all those years.

Maybe she wasn't even an alcoholic—an addict—in the first place.

She just wanted to make it stop—all the drama in her head. She wasn't equipped to deal with it.

Is she now?

Time will tell.

"I don't know, Kathy," she hedges, "I've got a lot going on before I get out of here . . . and anyway, I'll be coming back and forth once a week to bring my daughter for her visits with my husband, so maybe we can get together then."

"We should still really touch base before you go."

Yes. They really should.

"Okay. I can do lunch if it's a quick one," she says reluctantly.

Kathy names an Asian bistro not far from the library, and Cam agrees to meet her there at twelve thirty, after she drops off Tess at a pool party. Maybe after lunch she can stop at the library and pick up some books to take on the trip.

Reading—once, along with writing, one of her favorite pastimes—fell by the wayside over the years, since it's difficult to focus on a meaty novel when you're comfortably numb. God knows she could use a nontoxic distraction these days, so she's been working her way through all the neglected titles on her own bookshelf, and is thirsty for more.

Not as thirsty as she once was for other things.

One day at a time. That's all it takes.

You can do it.

You have no choice.

She rests a hand against her belly, wishing the baby would kick or something.

God knows she can use every possible nudge in the right direction.

The dude's name, it turns out, was Edward Casalino Jr.

His twenty-two years on earth merited just five lines—six if you count the headline, LOCAL MAN SLAIN ON PACIFIC AVENUE. The short paragraph is buried inside the afternoon edition of the newspaper.

Edward died of a single gunshot to the head, execution-style.

No witnesses.

No suspects.

Police are investigating a possible connection to organized crime . . .

Organized crime?

Why? Because a guy's last name ends in a vowel?

Whatever.

They'll never figure out that Edward Casalino Jr.'s only crime was opening his big fat mouth.

"Here's your package . . . all the way from Texas," he'd commented, setting it heavily on the counter. "Thing weighs a ton." He pointed at the return address. "LONESTAR CATTLE BRANDS, huh? Gonna brand a herd of cows here in Atlantic City, or what?"

He laughed at his stupid nonjoke, oblivious to a tight-lipped reaction from his customer, indicating his fate had just been sealed.

The newspaper lands in a garbage can; no need to read anything else in it.

Why'd you have to say that, Edward? Why'd you have to look at the return address at all? Hundreds of packages come and go, and you have to comment on mine?

It's a shame.

Because really, Edward might well have forgotten all about the package two seconds after handing it over, collecting the fee, and going back to sorting letters into rented mailboxes.

Still . . . You can't be too careful.

The phone rings again as Cam finishes loading the dinner plates into the dishwasher, and she decides to let Tess pick it up this time.

Once again, though, it continues to ring, and Cam is forced to go over to see who it is.

Recognizing her father's cell phone number in the caller ID window, she snatches up the receiver.

"Pop!"

"Cam?" He sounds surprised.

"Yeah. Hi, Pop." Silence. "You called me."

"I know! Of course I know I called you."

No, he doesn't. Either he dialed her by accident, or he dialed her, then forgot, in the seconds it took for the phone to ring and her to answer, who it was that he had called.

It wouldn't be the first time.

Sounding vaguely confused, Ike asks, "Well . . . How are you?"

"I'm good, Pop. How are you?" she asks, though she knows the answer.

Wasted.

The question is whether Ike Neary is just mildly trashed tonight or on something other than beer.

She'll know the answer if he starts telling her he's seeing spacemen or angels or Mom.

"I'm good," he says. "What about my girl? How's Tess?" He slurs the *s*'s.

"She's great."

"Can I talk to her?"

"Sorry, Pop, she's not here," Cam tells him, and wonders when she's going to stop trying to protect her daughter from her father's various weaknesses.

Tess isn't stupid, and it's obvious Ike Neary—with his black T-shirts, gray ponytail and tattoos—isn't exactly a traditional grandfather.

Then again, Tess has never seen him distraught and delusional.

Cam has, enough times to know she never wants to put her daughter through that.

"Where is she?" Pop is asking.

"I'm not sure . . . out with friends."

"You're not sure?" Ike echoes. "What do you mean, you're not sure? You can't just let her go running around in the night."

Cam's stomach turns over. "It's okay, Pop," she says soothingly.

But it isn't. In their world—her father's and hers—things happen to people. They die. They disappear.

In our world?

In *the* world, the big, bad world, where hundreds, thousands of children never come home and Cam gets to witness the excruciating details: sometimes all of them, from that first moment of terror to the dying breath.

Yeah. Things happen.

And then you spend years trying to get over all of it, in your own way. Trying to numb yourself, in your own way.

"Pop, I want to see you," Cam says quietly. "We're going down to Beach Haven in a few days. We'll be there most of the summer. Why don't you come stay for awhile?"

"Maybe."

"Say yes."

"Yes," he says, and laughs.

"Really?"

"I don't know . . . I'll try, honey."

Maybe he's not as wasted as she thought.

"Pop, you have my cell phone number, right? Because there's no phone at the beach house."

"I thought there was."

"There is a line, but I don't bother to hook it up anymore. Tess and I both have cells, and—"

"And Mike, too, right?"

She hesitates. He doesn't know. "Right."

"Okay. I'll call you."

"My cell. Don't forget."

"I won't forget. Give Tess a big hug from me. Mike, too."

She swallows hard. She should tell him.

"Pop—"

"I've got to go, Cam. I'll talk to you soon. I love you. Bye."

And just like that, he's gone.

With a sigh, Cam hangs up the phone.

For a minute or two, she just stands there, missing her father, missing Mike, missing the mother she barely knew, missing the sister she lost.

Jesus, my whole life feels like a tragedy right about now.

She shakes her head, needing to snap herself out of it.

It isn't all tragic.

She has Tess. And soon, she'll have the baby, too.

She's about to turn off the kitchen light when she remembers that she hasn't had her nightly glass of milk.

Oh, ick.

She defiantly reaches for the freezer instead of the fridge. Ben & Jerry's Cherry Garcia contains calcium, right?

Right, but you know it's not as healthy.

She takes out the ice cream anyway and closes the freezer door hard.

The new magnetic shopping list pad drops off the front. It does that frequently—the pad is too heavy for the size of the magnet—but she doesn't dare move the pad around to the side of the fridge. She doesn't want Tess to think she doesn't like it.

Wearily, she bends to retrieve it and sticks it back on the door, glancing at the grocery list jotted on the top page. She's been adding items for the past few days as they occur to her: supplies for the cottage, sunscreen and aloe, bug spray—the usual vacation stuff.

True, she can buy it all on the island, but there's something tremendously gratifying about pulling up to the cottage with everything they'll need for the first couple of days.

With a pang, she realizes that this year, she won't be buying the Pringles potato chips Mike loves to munch on the beach—neither she nor Tess likes them—or Dr Pepper, his favorite soda, or a new kite for him and Tess to fly in the sea breeze . . .

Well, maybe I can start a new mother-daughter tradition instead, like spa massages, or Saturday-night sushi, or . . .

Something. Something she and Tess can do together, just the girls, and not be so acutely aware of Mike's absence.

After all, in summers past, he would sometimes leave the two of them at the shore for a few days while he returned to the city for work or went away on business.

But that was different.

This time, he won't be around to do the driving down the Garden State Parkway, or open and air out the house—last year, there was a bat lurking inside. It swooped out of the closet when Cam was unpacking. She and Tess screamed and cowered in the bathroom while Mike chased it out with a tennis racket.

Who will chase bats this year?

Who will fly the kites and grill the steaks and set up the beach umbrella so that it doesn't get picked up by the wind and go cartwheeling down the sand?

I will, Cam tells herself resolutely. *I'll just have to learn how to do everything by myself . . . since that's how it's going to be from now on.*

Ike looks down at the cell phone in his hand.

Who was he going to call?

Or did he just call someone?

Hmm. He's not quite sure.

You're losing it, Ike, baby.

That's Brenda's voice, in his head.

Or is she here?

He looks around.

No sign of Brenda.

No sign of anything—or anyone—familiar, for that matter.

With a sigh, Ike shoves the phone into the back pocket of his jeans, no longer interested in who he might have called, or been about to call.

What's more important, for the time being, is figuring out where he is and how he got here.

Carrying the carton of ice cream and a spoon, Cam goes into the adjacent sunken sunroom.

This is her favorite place in the house, with its high ceiling, slate floor, and brick walls lined with tall arched windows and French doors.

When they first moved in, Cam filled the space with plants, comfortable chintz-covered furniture, books, lamps, throw rugs. She and Mike used to sit here cozily after dinner, catching up on each other's days while Tess played with the toys that used to fill the antique wooden chest in the corner.

She would take things out one at a time. After playing with a toy, she'd return it to the chest before getting a new one. Model child.

Now the toys are long gone, and the chest is filled with old blankets.

Standing in the dark, Cam looks out over the deep, landscaped lot, lit by strategically placed timer floodlights among the trees. Where she once envisioned the built-in swimming pool she and Mike had always wanted, there's only grass, shrubs, trees.

In the far corner alongside the small shed is an elaborate weathered wooden playset. It has swings, a slide, monkey bars, a climbing wall, a rope swing, a little two-story house . . .

Everything but a hot tub, as Mike used to say.

Last summer, he was talking about having it dismantled and replacing it with a much bigger shed, but Tess wouldn't hear of it.

"So you plan on swinging and sliding your way through high school?" he teased her.

"Dad! No! I just don't want you to get rid of it yet."

"Why not?"

"Because I used to love it, and . . . I don't know. It would be sad."

So they kept the playset.

And Mike got rid of Cam, whom he himself used to love, instead.

Okay, maybe that's not fair. She turns away from the window and flicks on a lamp. *Then again . . . maybe it is.*

Cam sits heavily on the couch and swings her legs onto the glass coffee table. After removing the round cardboard carton top from the ice cream, she moodily jabs in her spoon and swallows a heaping mouthful.

Owwww . . . head freeze.

She winces and wedges the spoon into the carton and sets it on the table. Off balance thanks to the vertical spoon, it promptly tips over.

Ignoring it, her head spinning painfully, she massages her temples with her fingertips.

But it isn't just a head freeze. It's . . .

Another vision. Oh, no.

Ice cream.

That's the first thing she sees.

Not cherry, though. It's chocolate, studded with fudgy chunks, in an oversized waffle cone instead of a carton.

Cam is nauseated. Because of the chocolate? Because she's afraid of what else she's going to see?

A girl.

A girl is holding the ice cream, and it's melting faster than she can lick it. The sun is blazing overhead, and Cam would know it was hot and humid even if it wasn't for the dripping ice cream, because the girl's face is flushed and shiny and her bangs are damp.

She's about Tess's age: cute, petite, a carrot-top with a pair of braids that hang just past her chin. Her freckled cheeks are sunburnt. She's wearing a green cotton top that has spaghetti straps tied in little bows over her shoulders—also freckled and sunburnt. Her feet are in white sandals, her toenails polished hot pink, and—

Oh, God. Oh, God . . .

Around her neck is a silver chain with some kind of small triangular black pendant hanging from it.

Cam saw a similar pendant in her last vision. The one she had of the small blonde in the plaid school uniform.

What does it mean?

Okay, don't get distracted by it. Focus. What else do you see here?

Behind the girl is a brick wall that's been painted bright blue. On it, off to the far left and painted in red bubble lettering, are the letters *L* and *F*.

The girl is laughing, looking at someone Cam can't see.

Then, all of a sudden, her face twists into a grotesque mask of terror, and she lets out a bloodcurdling scream.

The vision fades before Cam can get anything else from it.

Something's going to happen to that girl.

Does it have something to do with the unusual necklace she's wearing?

One thing is certain: wherever she is—or will be—Cam has been there before.

The bright blue backdrop is strikingly familiar.

What else?

Let's see . . .

The red letters . . .

On autopilot, she reaches into an end table drawer, rooting around for something to write with, and on.

Nothing; just the television remote, an old pair of Mike's reading glasses, a tangle of cables from some forgotten electronic device.

Keep going over everything, she tells herself as she hurries toward the kitchen, the ice cream forgotten in the sunroom. *Remember the details.*

The girl . . . about thirteen but tiny, a freckled redhead with short braids, sunburn, green top.

Hot, sunny, melting chocolate ice cream.

Blue painted brick, red letters. *L-F*—those letters mean nothing to Cam.

L-F.

L-F.

What could that be? *Left Field?* Part of a word? Can *L.F.* be the girl's initials?

In the kitchen, Cam grabs the magnetic grocery list pad stuck to the front of the fridge. She finds a pen, flips over the shopping list, and begins scribbling on the back.

She painstakingly writes down all the details of her vision, just as she used to do in the old days . . . back when she thought she could do something about them.

Now that they've returned . . . who knows?

She's a grown woman now, a mother, able to relate with that visceral there-but-for-the-grace-of-God horror only a parent can truly understand. Maybe that will make a difference in what she can perceive . . . and what she can do about it.

Or maybe not.

But it could be worse, she reminds herself with a shudder.

It could be my own child in danger.

She pushes that horrific thought from her mind, along with her father's words: *What if something happens to her? What if she disappears?*

Fighting paranoia, Cam flips back to the shopping list side and sticks the pad back on the fridge. Later, she'll copy the notes over onto a clean sheet of paper. For now, it's enough that she got it all down.

Then she heads upstairs to check on Tess. She hasn't heard from her in a few hours—not unusual. She didn't pick up the phone, either, though, when it rang.

And between what just happened and her conversation with her father, Cam's maternal nerves are on edge.

She tells herself she just wants to make sure Tess is dutifully packing for the trip, when in reality, she just wants to make sure . . .

What?

That she's there, in her room, safe and sound?

The door is closed.

Cam knocks.

No reply.

Heart pounding, she knocks again, calls, "Tess?"

Still nothing.

She reaches for the knob.

What if she opens the door and finds an empty room?

That won't happen. Don't be ridiculous. Of course she's here.

Please let her be here.

Slowly, Cam turns the knob, unable to escape the icy grip of every mother's worst nightmare.

At least it hasn't rained in a few days, though it's forecast for tomorrow.

When it rains, there's mud, and mud is heavy.

Dirt is heavy, too, but not as bad.

Heap after heap of it lands off to the side, near a pile of branches and leaves that were lying on top of everything for added camouflage. Mud or no mud, this is back-breaking work.

Good thing I'm strong. I can handle it. All I need is a heating pad later, and a good night's sleep on a hard mattress. Tomorrow I'll be good as new.

At last, the shovel makes a dull scraping sound as the metal tip encounters hard wood.

"That's it. See? I told you it wouldn't take long."

"Wh-what is it?" the girl asks fearfully, not nearly as friendly as she was earlier, at the bus stop.

Your mother told you how many times never to talk to strangers, and what do you do? You go off with the first stranger who wins you over with the oldest trick in the book: a nice present and a promise to make you a star.

It really is shocking that she didn't know better. It would be maddening, too . . . if the entire plan didn't hinge on that very naive gullibility.

She should have known better. She should have listened to her mother.

Little girls should always listen to their mothers. Mothers know best.

Then again, there's always a chance that she recognized you despite your disguise, and didn't let on. A wig, dark glasses, some padding . . . Maybe she saw right through it. Maybe she knew it was you, and she was relieved that you found her at last, and she's just playing along with the charade.

In which case you can save yourself a lot of back-breaking trouble and come clean right now.

But what if she doesn't really know? What if the minute she finds out, she tries to bolt?

"What is it?" she asks again. "What's down there?"

"A buried treasure chest, remember? Like I told you. An old sea captain hid it here two hundred years ago. Gold doubloons, jewels . . ." *What else would be in a treasure chest?* "Goblets. And . . . priceless heirlooms. More prehistoric sharks' teeth, like the one I sent you . . ."

Is she still wearing it? Stop digging, quick glance—*Yes. Good*.

But a look at her face reveals that the kid doesn't know who she's dealing with, and she isn't buying any of this treasure crap anymore.

"I want to go home."

"Don't you want the grand prize?"

"No."

"I thought you wanted to be on my show."

Reality TV . . . such a great ruse. Amazing how easy it is to convince any reasonably gullible modern kid—one who doesn't heed her mother's cautions, anyway—that she's been selected as a contestant for a new reality TV game show.

All it took in this case was a letter written on fake production-company letterhead. The subject line was marked TOP SECRET, and details about the show followed. The accompanying package contained the necklace, of course, made from the shark's tooth. The girl was instructed to wear it on the designated day and meet the producer at the designated school bus stop at the designated time. All very official.

"I don't want to be on your show anymore," she's almost wailing now. "I just want to go home."

"You will. With a treasure that will make your whole family rich." Just a little more dirt to push aside with the shovel now . . .

Hopefully she won't decide to make a run for it. But then, these days, who doesn't want their fifteen minutes of fame? She's still thinking there's a chance.

"Why aren't you filming this part?" she asks, a little reproachfully.

"I had to dig up the treasure."

Ah, there it is: the iron ring attached to the trapdoor. All it takes is a mighty tug to pull it open, and then—

"What are you doing?" the girl screams, finding herself being yanked toward the gaping hole in the ground. "Stop it!"

One shove, and she tumbles into the black depths with a terrified scream.

Below, there's a dull thud. A moan.

Good. The fall didn't kill her.

"Anything broken?"

No reply.

"Hello down there? Any broken bones?"

"Please . . . Why are you doing this?"

"Because I know who you are—and you know who I am now, right? Admit it. Game over."

"What?"

"Don't play dumb. You thought you could hide from me, but you can't."

"Please . . . I don't know what you're

talking about. Please, I want my dad and—"

"Look out below." A flashlight goes sailing down into the hole. Next, the purple nylon backpack, now missing the metal zipper pull with her name on it, the one she bought with her allowance at a cheap souvenir stand in Seaside Heights a few summers back. She was so thrilled when the spinner rack held one with her name on it—spelled the "right way," no less.

"Heads-up . . . Here comes your breakfast." Down go a plastic bottle filled with water and a white paper bag containing a roll. "Lunch and dinner, too, so make it last. And listen, it's not so bad. Your Christmas presents are waiting for you when this is all over."

From below, hysterical sobbing as the trapdoor comes down with a satisfying thud.

Time to start digging again.

Shovelful by shovelful, the dirt is moved again to cover the door. On top of that: the pile of branches that look like a pile of brush leftover from spring cleanup.

There. All that remains is the barely audible sound of pitiful cries coming from far below, courtesy of the air vents.

That's okay.

There's no one around to hear it.

And if she keeps it up, she'll eventually cry herself hoarse.

Just like the old days.

"Tess!" Cam turns the knob, jerks the door to her daughter's bedroom open in a panic, certain she's going to find it empty, an open window, a ransom note . . .

"Mom! What are you doing!" Tess is standing in front of her open closet with clothes on hangers draped over her arm. She angrily jerks tiny white earphones out of her ears and fumbles with the device clipped to the waistband of her jeans.

Oh.

"I'm sorry, I thought—"

You had been abducted by some psychotic stranger.

Go ahead, Cam, say it.

Say it, and watch her do that eye-roll thing.

"I'm sorry," Cam says again, and decides to leave it at that. She presses a hand against her racing heart, resisting the urge to rest the other one protectively against her womb.

To her shock, Tess's expression softens. "It's just that you scared me, barging in like that."

"I knocked."

"Well, I couldn't hear you."

Obviously not. Cam can hear the music blasting from the minuscule speakers even from across the room.

"What are you listening to?"

"Fifty Cent."

"Yeah?" She makes an effort not to show her disapproval. "Did you ever listen to that Springsteen song Grandpa wanted you to hear?"

"Yeah. It was good," Tess says briefly.

"You didn't listen to it."

"Yes, I did. I liked it. Did Grandpa really play with Bruce at the Stone Pony when he was young?"

"Young*er*." Even in the seventies, Pop

wasn't exactly young. "And, yeah. He did."

Pop has told Tess all about his Asbury Park days. He really was a legend back then—and not just in his own mind, as far as Cam recalls.

"Are we going to see Grandpa when we go to the shore?"

"You mean, see him play with his band? Or just see him?"

"Both."

Cam hesitates.

"I'm sure we will," she tells Tess. "He's always around somewhere down there."

Tess smiles, probably thinking, *Yeah, that's my grandfather, the harmless, eccentric musician.*

"Mom?"

"Yeah?"

Her daughter hesitates. "I was wondering . . ."

"Yeah?"

"Dad really seems like he wants to come down for the Fourth of July. He kept saying he didn't want to take me away from you because he felt bad for you, staying all alone at the cottage."

"He said that?"

Tess hedges for the briefest moment before saying, "Yup."

But he didn't say it. She can tell. Tess is trying to get them back together.

Cam tries to think of a way to tell her daughter that it's futile.

Instead, when she opens her mouth, she hears herself say, "I'll ask him."

Tess lights up. "You will?"

"Sure. But don't get your hopes up, Tess."

And I won't, either.

Home at last after a miserably long day at work, Mike settles in in front of the television.

It's a wall-mounted plasma one, just like in the living room back in Montclair. He bought it last week, thinking it would make him more comfortable here.

Somehow, it's had the opposite effect. The TV seems ridiculously oversized in this urban living room; the couch—leather, also like home, yet not—positioned much too close to the screen. He had no choice, though; the square footage of the entire apartment is smaller than the master suite he shared with Cam.

Which, ironically, seemed to be closing in on them during those last few weeks he lived there. It's not easy to share a room—a bed—with your wife, once you've decided she isn't going to remain your wife.

At the time, he kept thinking it might have been easier, or it might not have to happen at all, if he could just take a step back to think things through. But there wasn't time or space or opportunity; feeling hemmed in, he made a snap decision and fled.

What's done is done.

He's made a fresh start; he should stay focused on the future.

The thing is, there isn't much to look forward to. Work, sleep, take-out, watching Yankees games on TV—maybe a few from the stands, if he gets lucky again. Possibly some golf if he can get out to a course on the weekend. Even the looming summer weather isn't exactly a plus when you're stuck in the city. He's got a two-week business trip to Japan in July, but aside from the sushi, nothing great about that.

There's Tess, always the bright spot in his world, but last evening ended on a sour note that left him wary of their upcoming visits. Especially the Fourth of July holiday, when he'll have to figure out a way to keep her entertained in the city or take her away somewhere, just the two of them.

It's hard enough trying to make conversation with a fourteen-year-old for hours on end over dinner and weekend visits. How is he going to fill four days?

Mom and Dad would help, if I take her to their house for the weekends.

They live in the Connecticut suburbs: Darien. They have a spacious guest suite, a picturesque patio right on the Sound, and a sailboat Tess loves.

The only thing is that Mike's father can be counted upon to touch upon the subject of his soon-to-be-*ex*-daughter-in-law. He won't exactly be singing her praises.

Mike doesn't want to subject Tess to that.

Hell, he doesn't like to listen to it himself, which is why he hasn't returned his mother's calls in a few days. He knows that if he gets on the phone with her, she'll put Dad on eventually. He's always around now that he's retired.

Oh, well.

All Mike has to worry about right now is the Yankees postgame report, so he can catch the highlights he missed.

He's doing just that—feet propped on the coffee table and cold can of Dr Pepper in hand—when the phone rings. In the caller ID box is a New Jersey area code; his home number—old home number, that is.

Tess. Good.

He mutes the television and answers the phone.

"Hi, sweetie."

Silence.

Then . . . "It's me."

Cam?

Mike sits up straight, swings his feet around to the floor. "Oh . . . I thought you were—"

"Tess. I know." She laughs awkwardly.

He quickly considers making a joke about what he might be calling her,

Cam, these days instead of sweetheart. No—bad idea. In fact, he can't think of a worse idea, much less a better one, so he lets her do all the talking.

"Listen, Mike . . . We're getting ready to leave for the shore and I just wanted to talk to you about maybe coming down—"

"You mean, instead of your bringing Tess up for her weekly visits?" he asks, immediately defensive. "Because the separation agreement is supposed to be—"

"No, that's not what I meant at all!"

"Then what?"

A pause.

"I'll bring her up to Montclair for her visits with you, don't worry." Cam's tone is brittle. "I just thought . . . but you know what? It was a bad idea."

Wait, no . . . don't backpedal. Say what you were going to say.

"What was a bad idea?" he asks. Earlier, Tess had the same disappointed, disillusioned tone; the same blurting, then halting, conversational style. Is Cam filling her head with bitterness about him?

"Your coming down to the cottage while we're there is a bad idea," Cam's saying, "because I don't want Tess to get the wrong idea about us. She might think . . ."

"Yeah, she might."

Still—she was actually going to invite him down to the shore? If she had, how could he have turned her down?

Come on, how could you not? You can't let Tess get the wrong idea: that her parents are getting back together . . .

Unless we did actually end up getting back together.

In which case his going to the shore would be the right move *and* a great idea.

"Listen, I should go," Cam says.

"So should I." He wishes he had said it first, hates that he's feeling so childish, wishes she would say something more.

Something other than . . .

"Good-bye, Mike."

Chapter Five

"It really looks like rain. Are you sure Lily's still having the pool party?" Cam asks Tess as she steers the Volvo down a leafy suburban street lined with mansions in various architectural styles: Greek Revival, Federal, Tudor, contemporary.

Whenever she ventures into this particular neighborhood, she realizes that her own two-story brick home—which once seemed so extravagant—isn't the least bit impressive by Montclair standards.

"Lily's got an indoor pool, so it can rain all it wants," Tess informs her.

"Oh. Right. I forgot." Sheesh, an indoor pool. The Hastings don't even have an outdoor pool.

We should have put one in, Cam thinks wistfully, remembering all the times she and Mike had discussed it.

If they had, maybe Tess would be hosting a pool party right now, and there would be annuals in all the flowerbeds, and Mike would be there barbecuing and she'd be picking out paint colors for the nursery and—

And we'd be one happy family, and none of this ever would have happened, is that it?

Yeah. That's it.

Makes a hell of a lot of sense, doesn't it?

You find yourself living a life you never expected, so you overexamine everything that led up to it; you retrace every turn you ever took or didn't take, every possible omen you blithely ignored, trying to figure out where the path veered off in the wrong direction.

Part of the problem is that she was driving under the influence, as it were. If there really was a turning point on her marital journey, she was probably too—

"Stop!"

Cam reflexively slams on the brakes as

Tess cries out, her right arm flying over to shield her daughter.

"You just passed it, Mom."

"What?"

"Lily's! You drove right past her house."

"Oh . . . sorry." She takes a second to regroup, then shifts into REVERSE and backs up along the curb.

Tess bounces a little in the passenger's seat. She seems antsy about this party. Or maybe just eager to get there. Back home, she kept prodding Cam, worried she was going to be late.

"I'll pick you up at three."

"Three thirty? Please?"

"Three, if you want to have time to stop and get Daddy a Father's Day gift."

That was Cam's idea. She'd decided to be the bigger person and actually take Tess shopping for something nice for Mike, same as she always has. Only this year, the gift won't be from both of them—and it can't have anything to do with grilling, or lawn care, or the house, since Mike now lives in a city apartment.

That kind of narrows the field to golf, or something to wear.

Oddly, Tess suggested a necklace.

"Daddy doesn't really wear jewelry," Cam had pointed out, and had to keep from saying, *other than a wedding ring*.

She assumes he no longer wears his, but hasn't had the nerve to ask Tess. Maybe she doesn't really want to know.

"Not a fancy necklace," Tess had said. "Something more like . . . you know, like Granddad wears."

Pop, the aging beach bum rocker?

Somehow, Cam finds it hard to picture Mike wearing puka shells or braided leather around his neck, but if Tess wants to get something like that, it's fine with her.

"How about three fifteen?" Tess persists.

"No! Geez, Tess, stop pushing!" Cam snaps. "We have a lot of stuff to do today, and—oh no."

"What's wrong?"

She sighs. "I forgot my shopping list back home."

"Why don't you go back for it?"

She shakes her head wearily. "I'll just have to try and remember what's on it. Listen, three o'clock, okay?"

This time, Tess doesn't protest.

That's a good sign. Watching her daughter swing her orange beach bag over her shoulder and head through the pillared gate of Lily's house, Cam decides the time alone together at the beach will do them both a world of good.

Plus, once she knows about the baby, Tess is bound to be excited. She always used to say she wanted a little sister or brother.

Who knows? Maybe if Mike and I had—

Oh, for Pete's sake, cut it out! You can't second-guess every move you ever made. It's over. Move on!

Disgusted with herself, Cam drives toward the business district to meet Kathy for lunch.

A few drops splat onto the sidewalk as Kathy walks the short half block to the restaurant from her car.

She looks up at the overcast sky. It's threatening to open up any second now, and she doesn't have a jacket or umbrella.

Normally, she welcomes a good, cleansing rain.

It wouldn't be a problem today if she wasn't wearing this new pale yellow silk blouse. Yes, she bought it for next to nothing at a sale, but that doesn't mean she can afford to have it ruined with water splotches.

Oh, well. She'll just have to wait it out at the restaurant until the storm has passed.

Maybe Camden won't be in such a rush to leave after all. She claimed she had a lot to do, but maybe she was just giving herself an out.

Not that I blame her. I pretty much pushed her into having lunch with me today.

But she's a big girl. She could have said no if she really wanted to, right?

Maybe not. I can be very persuasive, Kathy thinks, smiling to herself.

Cam is waiting in front of the hostess stand when Kathy arrives. She's wearing crisp white pants and a lacy beige top. Gold hoop earrings hang below her dark ponytail; she has on a light floral perfume and makeup, too.

She's much more pulled together than she usually is for the AA meetings, where she tends to wear jeans and T-shirts, as if trying to fade into the background.

Kathy knows the feeling.

"I'm so glad to see you. You look good," Kathy says, even as she privately decides Cam looks a little wan.

"Thanks. I wish I felt good," Cam replies, and her *oops* expression makes it obvious she didn't mean for that to slip out.

Kathy remembers that she said something yesterday about going to the doctor. "Are you sick?"

"No, just tired. Should we be seated?"

It takes a few minutes for that to happen despite a reservation; it's the height of lunch hour. Fairly new and instantly trendy, the narrow bistro has all the requisite elements: high ceilings dotted with dim recessed lighting, exposed brick, blond wood, and attractive staff with an attitude.

They study leather-bound menus while they wait.

"Have you ever been here before?" Cam asks.

"Yes . . . it's good," Kathy lies.

She glances around as the hostess leads them through the crowded dining room, hoping she won't see anyone she knows. This place is deliberately off her beaten path, but you never know. If she runs into anyone, she'll have to make introductions and explanations, and she isn't in the mood to play that game.

One charade at a time, Kathy tells herself, and wishes she could order a vodka tonic.

Of course she asks for sparkling water when the kimono-clad waitress arrives, as does Cam. They both decide on the Pad Thai with Prawns without consulting each other.

"Great minds think alike," Cam says with a smile.

Glad Cam can't read hers, Kathy asks if she's looking forward to getting away tomorrow.

"I will be once we're there. I love Long Beach Island. Have you ever been there?"

"No," Kathy lies. "Obviously you have, though."

"Every summer of my life. And we have a house there now."

Kathy raises her eyebrows as if this is news to her. "How nice. So it's familiar territory."

"Yeah. Although nothing feels like familiar territory lately, so . . ."

"I know the feeling. It's all uncharted when you're trying to get through every day without your crutch."

"Right."

"That's why you need to get yourself to meetings while you're gone, daily if you can."

"I'll try. But my daughter will be with me, so . . ."

"There are a million excuses. Don't fall into that trap."

Cam looks like she wants to defend herself. Then she merely shrugs and flashes a tight smile. "I'll get to meetings."

"And we can check in with each other every day. Should I call your cell phone, or is there a number there I can reach?"

"My cell is best."

Kathy pulls out her own phone and pretends to make sure she has Cam's cell programmed in.

As if it hasn't been there for years.

Sitting in the hot tub up to her bare shoulders, Tess stares through a wall of glass at the sweeping view of the Manhattan skyline twelve miles away. Emilee Pfister is in the midst of an endless description of the dress she's wearing to her godmother's wedding, and Tess wishes she could go dive into the pool and cool off.

She's been in here for at least a half hour and she's feeling like a boiled potato.

Looks like one, too. She's so white. If only she'd thought to get a fake tan like pretty much every other girl here. They all go to this place where you get sprayed and contoured and wind up looking like you just got back from a week in Saint-Tropez, or wherever it is that fancy people spend their beach vacations.

Tess is positive it's not the Jersey Shore.

She's feeling out of her element . . . again.

And that surprises you? It shouldn't. You knew this would happen. It always does.

Yeah, but she promised herself, before she got to Lily's party, that she wasn't going to let it bother her that a lot of the kids are richer than she is and all of them seem way more sophisticated—even the few who aren't upperclassmen.

Spotting Lily sitting on a chaise nearby—barefoot, wearing a sarong and a bikini top, her silky black hair hanging loose down her back—Tess climbs out of the hot tub at last.

She quickly wraps herself in a beach towel, self-conscious about her pale, scrawny body. Then she shoves her feet into the new hot-pink flip-flops Mom just bought her to match her new bathing suit. They're not the thin rubber drugstore kind with the hard plastic strap: these have polka-dot fabric strips tied into bows and a contoured sole.

They had cost a lot for flip-flops, but

she was able to talk Mom into them. Plus a new pair of sunglasses. Her mother's trial separation guilt might ultimately help fill out Tess's wardrobe, even if she still has more rules than a kindergartner.

"Hey, have you heard from Morrow?" Tess asks, going over to Lily. "How come she's not here yet?"

"Oh . . . She's coming."

Is it her imagination or does Lily look uncomfortable?

"Are you sure? Because I tried calling her like three times this morning and she didn't pick up."

"You know how she is. She probably forgot to charge her cell. Did you check out the string bikini Brooke Billings has on? I would kill to look that good in that."

Oh, please. "You *would* look that good in it," Tess assures her friend. "I'm the one who'd look like someone's cross-dressing kid brother."

Lily laughs, but says, "Come on, you know you look great."

"No, I don't." Tess shakes her head and glances down at the two-piece hot-pink bathing suit she ordered because the catalogue said it was supposed to enhance her figure. The twin fabric triangles that make up the top are padded, but she still can't fill it out.

She won't blame Heath if he told Chad he's not interested in her, provided he even knows who she is.

Why couldn't she have long legs and curves, like the other girls here—and everywhere else, for that matter? Even her own mother looks pretty good in a bathing suit . . .

Then again, maybe not this summer. Mom seems to have crossed the fine line from curvy to chubby. Tess noticed in the car this morning that she's getting a bit of a gut, and her face is getting full. She felt like reminding her that she'll never get Dad back if she lets herself go, but she didn't. It seemed too mean.

And anyway, she was kind of relieved to realize that Mom probably wouldn't be letting herself go if she was seeing someone else, like Morrow and Lily claimed. So, all things considered, the weight gain is a good sign.

"So are you having a good time?" Lily

asks her, looking a little restless, like she'd rather go off and mingle.

"Yeah, great party."

And so different from the gatherings she used to go to when she went to private school.

Back then, everyone usually had slumber parties, and just invited girls from their own class. Those parties were stressful in their own way: someone usually brought cigarettes, or wanted to sneak out, or sneak boys in.

Plus, Tess would try to stay awake all night because bad things happened to whoever fell asleep first. The other girls would put ridiculous props around the unfortunate victim and take pictures, or stick her hand in warm water so she'd pee her pants.

Thank God those days are over.

Then again, parties this year have been stressful in a different way.

At the beginning of the year, she went to a few that were given by her old private school friends. But their social circle had branched out since Tess had left and there were always so many new people around. Tess wanted to reminisce with her old friends in front of them, just to remind everyone that they had a history, but no one was really into looking back.

Gradually, the invitations from her old crowd stopped coming, and she was secretly relieved. By then, she had Lily and Morrow and a whole new crowd that invited her to their parties. And she fit in, for the most part. For awhile.

She's been feeling insecure lately, though.

Even more so watching Jordyn Runyan—who is a sophomore and would be even more beautiful if she wasn't always wearing such a mean, pinched expression—emerge from the pool looking like a glistening goddess.

"How's the hot tub?" Lily asks Tess.

"Hot."

"That's kind of the point."

"Yeah, but after awhile . . ."

"Why don't you go in the pool, then?" Lily sounds like a busy mother trying to find something for her bored toddler to do.

"No way. I'll get soaked."

"That's kind of the point," Lily says again, and this time she doesn't smile.

"I'll go in later." Tess had spent a lot of time on her hair and makeup, which is waterproof, but still. This is her big day; her last chance to make Heath fall in love with her, maybe. She doesn't want to look like a drowned rat when he shows up.

"Have you seen what's going on over there?" she asks Lily, and gestures at the pool.

A bunch of girls are floating around on air mattresses, and the guys keep swimming up beneath them and dumping them into the water. The girls shriek and pretend they're furious, then make a big show of shaking out their hair and settling their perfect bodies on their floats again.

Pretty ridiculous.

"Yeah," Lily says, "it looks fun."

Fun?

Tess sighs. "I just wish Morrow and Chad would get here."

"What you mean is, you wish Heath would get here. Admit it."

"Are you sure he's coming?"

"That's what he said, but I didn't actually talk to him. Yesterday Morrow said Chad told her."

"And you're sure she didn't mention anything to you about what Heath said when Chad told him about me?"

"I'm positive." Lily looks bored. They've already had this conversation today. Twice.

Tess tries to think of something else to say, but everything that pops into her head involves Heath.

"I think I'm going to go see if anyone wants another Margarita." Lily swings her feet over to the slate floor. "Do you want one?"

"No, thanks."

Lily's been spiking the blender drinks with tequila from her mother's liquor cabinet. Tess has no interest in ever becoming *Tess Hastings Pickering* with a fridge full of booze.

No way.

Her life will turn out much differently from her mother's, because she's not going to make the same stupid mistakes.

* * *

Cam's car isn't in the driveway when Mike pulls up to the house in the rain. Either it's in the garage or she's out.

He'd figured on a fifty-fifty chance of that, since Tess said something last night about having to go to a party this afternoon.

He had even considered calling ahead but decided not to. The last thing he needs is another awkward telephone conversation with Cam.

Parking the Saab in the empty driveway before the three-car garage, he can't help but think of the rented stall where he's forced to keep it back in Lower Manhattan. A car can be a liability in the city. Too bad he can't just leave his here in Jersey. But that would force him to take the train back and forth whenever he comes to see Tess. No way.

Not that he didn't take it daily as a commuter all those years he lived here.

Still, there's something empowering about coming and going in a car—as opposed to public transportation and a cab from the station or, worse yet, asking Cam to pick him up and drop him off.

Mike climbs out of the Saab, heedless of the downpour, struck by a memory of how she used to drive him to and from the train station years ago, when they first moved here. They had only one car then, and assumed that would work. Cam assured him she didn't mind shuttling him back and forth—often in her slippers and pajamas—with little Tess in back and a great CD on the car stereo.

That lasted a year, tops. Then Mike got promoted and started working later and later, and Tess wasn't thrilled to spend so much time strapped in her car seat, and Cam had begun the slow retreat behind the wall.

So they bought a second car and he took over the round-trip to the station—good thing, because by the time he got home most nights, there was booze on his wife's breath.

Then again, maybe she never would have had an evening drink in the first place if she thought she had to drive.

Maybe it was the second car that did them in.

Maybe everything would be fine between them if she was still driving him to the train in her pajamas, stone sober and singing along to Southside Johnny.

Christ. Why do I do this to myself?

Mike slams the car door and walks across the rain-slicked pavement to the garage, noticing that the empty garden beds have turned to mud puddles. Maybe he should call Ron, the landscaper, and have him come by to put in some flowers.

Then again, what does he care? He's not the one who has to look at the barren beds every day.

But he cares, because Tess has to look at them, and because he still owns the house, and . . .

And it bugs him that Cam hasn't planted the flowers, dammit. Just because.

He peers through the garage-door window to see if the Volvo is there, hoping . . .

Not sure what he's hoping.

That she's in? That she's out?

It changes from one moment to the next.

She's out.

Okay . . . good. That's what he was hoping. At one point, anyway.

He hesitates for only a moment before heading for the front door. After pressing the alarm code, he steps into the house and is struck by the familiar scent. No one specific aroma, just a blend that combines into the unique smell of home.

It hits him hard, and gives him pause.

His own place smells like a recent paint job and his neighbors' cats.

Here, there's something savory lingering from the kitchen, a hint of wood, fabric softener, maybe flowers . . . No, that's perfume.

He recognizes it: it's the designer scent he once bought Cam for their anniversary. She loves it but wears it only when she gets dressed up.

So she's out someplace, wearing perfume.

He tries to ignore a stab of jealousy; tries not to wonder—or care—who she might be with.

Her life is her business these days.

Yeah, right. That's why you're here.

Oh, hell.

Why are *you here?*

Why did he blow out of the office claiming to be going to a client lunch, only to hop the subway downtown to his car?

Because I need my golf clubs.

That's what he told himself.

The weather this weekend is going to be gorgeous, perfect for hitting the links. Never mind that he has no one to golf with in Manhattan; the usual suspects are here in Jersey, along with his regular course. There's always Chelsea Piers, though.

Okay, you're here, she's not, and you need your clubs. So get them, and go.

They're in the storage room off the kitchen. He moves through the first floor, noticing that she's made few changes since he left—that he can see, anyway. She hadn't moved furniture around or taken down every picture that has him in it.

There's a typical amount of household

clutter; she's a packrat. But then, so is he.

Not Tess—whom he started calling Messy Tessy to tease her, because she couldn't be more opposite.

Organized, a little uptight, not a procrastinator . . . When she was little, he and Cam used to marvel that the two of them had managed to create such a fussy little creature, so different from the two of them.

That, of course, was when he thought he and Cam were two of a kind.

How could he have been so wrong?

How could this have happened to us?

In the kitchen, he opens the fridge, remembering what Tess told him. Sure enough, there isn't a drop of liquor in sight. Just condiments, fruits and vegetables, some kind of leftover rice, and milk. A lot of it, considering that neither Cam nor Tess is crazy about it.

Feeling as though he's snooping, he hurriedly closes the door.

Something drops off the front and lands at his feet. He looks down to see a shopping pad—*World's Best Mom*.

Shaking his head at his daughter's

lack of originality, he bends to retrieve it. The gummy strip holding the top page to the pad was severed in the fall, and it comes free in his hand as he picks it up.

He hastily sticks the pad back on the refrigerator, then glances at the loose page he's holding, wondering what to do with it.

Cam's familiar, hurried scrawl jumps out at him. Yesterday's date is followed by a series of phrases that mean nothing to him.

Girl, 13-14, freckled, redhead, short braids, sunburn, green spaghetti-strap top, white sandals, hot-pink toenail polish.

Silver necklace with black pendant.

Hot, sunny—melting chocolate ice cream.

Blue-painted brick, red letters.

L-F.

Girl terrified, screaming.

Mike frowns. What is this?

None of it makes sense. He gives the other side a cursory glance—nothing more than a regular shopping list there—

before folding it in half and impulsively putting it into his pocket.

Thinking twice about that, he takes it out and sticks it on the fridge with a separate magnet.

Then he reconsiders.

Isn't she going to wonder how it got there?

You shouldn't be here.

Yes, technically he owns the house, and holds claim to just about everything in it—with the notable absence of *World's Best Mom* herself. He doesn't belong in this house anymore, though, prying into Cam's new life.

He grabs the shopping list and shoves it into his wallet behind Tess's latest school picture.

Nice move. Get rid of the evidence . . . and steal her stuff while you're at it.

It's only a piece of paper. She'll never miss it.

Maybe she will.

Whatever—grab your clubs and get moving!

His mental tug-of-war leads him toward the closet.

Beside the door leading into the

garage, a heap of packed luggage waits for the trip to the shore. Conspicuously absent: his own set of sturdy brown canvas and leather Filson bags.

With a pang, he remembers snippets of last year's summer vacation. Much of it is a blur: sitting in an hours-long traffic jam on the southbound parkway, finding a bat in the house, arguing with Cam. A lot. Nothing major, just stupid little disagreements.

Enough of them so that he was torn whenever he had to travel back and forth to the city to work for a few days at a time. He wanted to *want* to stay at the beach house . . . but most of the time, he was relieved to get away.

Why?

Because my wife felt like a stranger. Because it was easier to pretend to be the perfect family at home, going about our daily business, than at the shore where all we were supposed to be doing was having fun together.

Yet, they used to have fun together. Long before they could afford a beach house, or had the time to use it.

So what happened?

His demanding career.

Her emotional withdrawal.

Did one fuel the other?

It doesn't matter now.

I should go.

As he reaches for the closet doorknob, he glances into the adjacent sunroom to see if it's still pouring out.

Yup.

Rain is still falling beyond the tall windows. The front yard might be looking bare, but at the back of the property the tall Mountain Laurel shrubs are in glorious pink and white bloom, and the rest of yard looks incredibly lush and green . . . much more so than ever before. Or maybe it just seems infinitely more inviting now that he's perpetually surrounded by concrete.

He notices something else, then, too: a carton of ice cream lying on its side on the coffee table in a pool of milky pink liquid.

It's not as if that's the only thing out of place in the whole house.

Mike can't help but feel uneasy, though, about the blatant—or even merely neglected—mess. It seems out of character to just leave it there, even for Cam.

He starts toward it, thinking he'd better clean it up.

Then he realizes that it's obviously been there for awhile, and anyway, he can't clean it up; he's not even supposed to be here.

Right. So go.

This time he does.

As she steers her green Ford Taurus onto Maple Street, Lucinda Sloan takes a big bite of her Snickers bar and idly wonders whether every suburban community has a Maple Street. It sure seems that way to her.

Here in the Philadelphia sprawl, Maple Streets always seem to be in the older part of town, lined with sidewalks, two-story frame houses set close to each other and to the street, and big old namesake trees.

East Greenbranch's Maple Street, where she's been summoned today, is no exception.

Swallowing the last satisfying chocolate-caramel-nut mouthful, she crumples the wrapper and tosses it over her shoulder into the backseat.

The downpour that followed her off the exit from Interstate 76 has let up significantly, and there are people on the street now. A nearby school must have just let out because suddenly there are helmeted kids on bikes, teenagers with backpacks and basketballs.

It's a public school, though. These kids aren't wearing uniforms like the girl was; there's not a pleated Black Watch plaid skirt or navy vest in sight.

Braking at a STOP sign, she sees a young mother pushing a stroller toward the intersection, holding the hand of a puddle-seeking toddler wearing yellow rubber boots and followed by two older schoolchildren in rain slickers.

"Go ahead," Lucinda mouths at the mom, waving her across.

The woman clutches the toddler to keep him out of the street and says something over her shoulder to the other kids, who stop. Lucinda waves again, but the Mom holds her ground on the curb, shaking her head.

Geez, does she think I'm going to wait until they get into the crosswalk, then run them down? With a shrug, Lucinda drives on. The mom—obviously skittish, overly cautious—must already have heard what happened. After all, it was only a couple of blocks from here, and news, especially tragic news, travels fast.

Deciding she should double-check the address, Lucinda keeps one eye on the road while searching for it on the passenger's seat. It's never been used to transport anything other than stuff she can't fit in her shoulder bag. This month, it's littered with a couple of empty Pepsi cans, fast-food napkins and straws, half a bag of Fritos, and CD cases.

Ah, there it is. She finds the address on the back of the envelope from the insurance bill she was opening when Detective Neal Bullard called a little while ago.

She and Neal go back a long way. She adores him—but she's never happy to hear from him.

"Missing kid," he said tersely today in response to her greeting, and her heart sank.

It's rarely good news when Neal calls. The best she can hope for is closure on one of the cases she helped with in the past: a suspect apprehended, or a body located.

On a handful of occasions, a missing person Lucinda sought will actually be found alive—usually a teenaged runaway, but once an Alzheimer's patient who wandered away from a nursing care facility.

But usually, when Neal calls, someone new has gone missing in the greater metropolitan area. And kids are the worst.

"How long has this one been gone?" she asked Neal.

"Less than twenty-four."

"Parents?"

"Ruled out. I told them about you. They want you there. Can you come?"

"Don't I always?" She was already hunting for her car keys.

"Yeah," Neal said gruffly. "Always. So get your butt over here. And be discreet."

He always reminds her of that . . . as if it's necessary, after all these years.

As if he expects her to stick a screaming light dome on top of her car, and a sign on the door that reads LUCINDA SLOAN, PSYCHIC INVESTIGATOR.

Wouldn't she love to do just that, someday, and park it in the driveway of the Sloan mansion? Yeah. That would go over big with the Main Line crowd.

Finding the envelope on the seat, she checks the address he gave her against the house numbers she's passing. They're descending; yeah, she's going in the right direction.

Another intersection, then one more . . .

She's getting closer. This is the block. She'd know even if it wasn't for the addresses. Not because she's psychic, or because there are news satellite trucks swarming—yet.

She has no doubt that they'll be here.

For the moment, though, there are only telltale clusters of somber-faced neighbors on porches and lawns. They look up warily as the unfamiliar car passes; Lucinda can feel their eyes on her, and wonders if they're dutifully noting her license plate. Just in case a skinny auburn-haired female stranger turns out to be the suspect behind all this.

Lucinda slows the car, crawling along so that she can check the numbers on her right . . .

60 . . . 54 . . . 48 . . .

There. That should be it. An unremarkable house, white with black shutters, just like Neal said. There's a squad car in the driveway and another at the curb. An unfamiliar uniformed officer is behind the wheel of that one, and he turns to watch Lucinda park behind him.

Neal is somewhere in the house. She can see his sedan parked up the block.

She takes her time getting out of her car, taking in every possible detail.

There are two windows on either side of the front door; three more windows on the second floor. Gray-shingled A-line roof, brick chimney, concrete steps, wrought iron railings, low boxwood hedges, an American flag.

Someone's working-class dream home . . . now the scene of every parent's worst nightmare.

To the right of the front door, beneath the brass lantern-style fixture, is the house number: 42.

It's about time.

Cam has finally made it to the head of the world's longest supermarket line ever, and none too soon. She's read enough of the *National Enquirer* to know that, supposedly, Nicole is secretly pregnant, Jennifer is plotting a breakup, and everyone's favorite married action hero has a secret boyfriend.

Hah—they think they've got troubles.

"Do you have any coupons?" The cashier, wearing a name tag that reads KAREN—TRAINEE, which explains a lot, scans Cam's first item.

"No, no coupons." She did clip a few but they're at home with her grocery list. Without that, she went through the store filling her cart with everything they could possibly need.

And a few things we almost certainly won't, she thinks, watching KAREN—TRAINEE ring up a can of Pringles.

Cam bought that on a whim. Just in case. Along with a six-pack of Dr Pepper.

And a Marble notebook.

She spotted that in the office-supplies aisle, which she usually doesn't bother to peruse unless Tess needs poster board for a school project or something.

Today, Cam found herself wheeling her cart up the aisle, stopping in front of the notebooks, putting one into her cart.

Does that mean you're starting the whole thing all over again? The painstaking notes on your visions, the constant searching for would-be victims, the endless sense of powerlessness?

What choice does she have?

If the visions are going to come again, she's going to log them.

And maybe now that she's older, and wiser, with keen maternal empathy—she'll be able to actually do something about what she sees.

The conveyor belt inches agonizingly forward and Cam unloads a few more items from the cart onto the end, thinking that if KAREN—TRAINEE doesn't pick up the pace a little, she won't have time to visit the library for beach books, plus she still has to stop at the—

Her ringing cell phone interrupts her thoughts. Flipping it open, she adds something else to the mental To Do list: she'd better charge her phone as soon as she gets home. According to the screen, she's down to one bar of battery power.

She doesn't recognize the number on the caller ID. It's local, though, and she picks it up.

"Mom?"

"Hi, Tess, what's—"

"Can you come get me?"

"Now?" She checks her watch, wondering if she lost track of time, but it's only two thirty. "Is the party over already?"

"No . . ." Tess sounds miserable, like she's been crying.

Her heart sinks. "What happened?"

"I just need you to come. Please."

"You're scaring me. Are you all right?"

"Not really."

Please, dear God . . . "Are you hurt?"

A pause.

"Tess! Are you hurt!" Cam's heart and thoughts race wildly and she prepares to abandon her groceries and run.

"No . . . I just have to get out of here."

Okay . . . so it's not an emergency, as far as she can tell. Not a life-and-death one, anyway.

"What's going on there? Are the kids doing something you don't feel comfortable with?" In a flash, Cam remembers her own high school party days. Sex, drugs, rock and roll.

Terrific.

"I just want to leave. Right now. I'm going to start walking up Highland."

"In the rain?"

"It's not raining that hard."

"Tess, it's that bad that you can't stay there and wait for me?" Cam asks helplessly, watching the cashier take her sweet old time putting an orange PAID sticker on a twelve-pack of paper towels.

"It's that bad," Tess confirms, sniffling.

"Listen, I'm about ten minutes away," Cam tells her. "Just wait there, and—"

"I'll be walking. Bye, Mom."

"Tess—"

She's already hung up.

Chapter Six

"This is it." Ken Roby holds the door open for Lucinda, who crosses the threshold to the plush lavender carpet of a young girl's bedroom.

A police officer stands sentry in the doorway.

Lucinda's heart aches for Leah's blond, bespectacled father, whose hand is visibly shaking as he reaches for the roller shade to raise it. He's clean-cut, young—maybe a little older than Lucinda is, probably in his mid to late thirties.

The shade goes up and gray light falls through the window, framed in white eyelet curtains that match the bed skirt.

"Do you want me to turn on the light?" Ken asks. The room is dim even with the shade raised all the way.

Her instinct is to say yes. She's never liked the dark, not since she was a little girl, afraid of the boogeyman and convinced bad things happen only under cover of darkness.

Yeah, she knows better now, but the first thing she does when entering any room, even in the daytime, is flip a light switch.

Unless she's doing an investigation.

"No, thanks," Lucinda tells Ken Roby.

She doesn't necessarily need to see every last detail of his daughter's bedroom. It's just as important, if not more so, that she use her other senses . . . especially the so-called sixth.

She walks slowly into the center of the room where thirteen-year-old Leah woke up yesterday morning. Shortly after, she left for Saint Hedwig's school on the other side of town . . . and never came home.

No one in her family has seen Leah Roby since.

Stopping beside the twin bed, Lucinda gazes at the rainbow quilt with matching throw pillows, the lovingly propped stuffed unicorn.

"She has a thing for rainbows and unicorns, huh?" Lucinda comments, gesturing at the bed, the framed prints on the walls, the figurines that line a bookshelf.

"It's all Lisa Frank stuff. Leah loves it. Most of her friends have outgrown it, but she still spends all her allowance on it."

Lucinda nods. How many girls' rooms has she visited, decorated in their current obsession: Barbie, Polly Pocket, Strawberry Shortcake . . .

And how many heart-wrenching funerals has she attended where a doll or a favorite stuffed animal is tucked into the open casket?

She expertly shuts out the disturbing reality of her work and focuses on the business at hand, turning back to the bed.

A pair of violet-sprigged pajamas are draped over the headboard's post.

"She wore these Wednesday night?" she asks Ken Roby, who nods bleakly and turns away to brush away tears.

His wife, Rebecca, couldn't even bring herself to come upstairs. Red-eyed and depleted, she's huddled on the couch, holding an untouched glass of water some well-meaning relative or neighbor put into her hand.

Lucinda has seen it all before, too many times: the shattered mother, voice raw from screaming; the devastated father trying to stay strong. The support system of family and friends there to answer the phone, bring in food nobody eats, and keep the other kids in the family occupied. Police officers with squawking radios keeping a watchful eye on the bystanders and press who invariably show up outside; detectives, Neal included, asking questions and taking notes.

And then there's Lucinda Sloan, who has walked onto scenes like this one too many times to count—but not too many times to be profoundly affected by the familiar unfolding drama.

She's a pro, though, after spending the better part of a decade on this work. And though she left her blue blood roots behind years ago, that impeccable Main Line breeding rendered her an expert at keeping up the façade, masking sloppy emotions.

So she doesn't fall apart—ever—in front of the missing child's loved ones. Or anyone else, for that matter. Not even when she realizes that the child is never coming home again.

Sometimes, that knowledge is instantaneous . . . Occasionally, the terrible truth strikes her even before she arrives on the scene.

That didn't happen with Leah Roby. She still doesn't know whether the girl is alive or dead.

But she probably isn't a runaway. No, Lucinda's gut instinct is that sometime yesterday afternoon, Leah crossed paths with someone who stole her from her family . . . and has no intention of letting her go.

They never do.

Driving toward Highland Avenue with her car full of groceries, Cam curses the rain, the other drivers in her way, and especially the inept cashier who made a mistake that required a thorough perusal of the register tape, followed by the manager's time-consuming attention.

Yes, and instead of hollering "MANAGER!" she simply flipped a switch so that her lane number flashed overhead, then she waited. And waited. Finally, Cam yelled "MANAGER!" Which didn't go over very well with KAREN—TRAINEE or with TRISHANDA—MANAGER.

Too bad.

Cam has to get to her daughter. Tess is in trouble.

She keeps telling herself that it's probably just a typical teenaged crisis—a falling out with her friends, or maybe she unexpectedly got her period, which she has yet to start.

Still, Cam's sense of urgency has grown stronger by the minute. By the time she actually reaches the Highland intersection, she's all but frantic. And of course, the light is yellow.

She speeds toward it, but it's already turning red.

"Damn, damn, damn!" She slams on the brakes and exhales shakily.

Okay, calm down . . . This stress isn't

good for the baby. You're making a big deal out of noth—

Whoa.

A familiar dizziness spins in and she clutches the wheel; the image of a gory wound flashing through her mind.

Just a fleeting glimpse: Bright red blood. Torn, fair flesh.

Cam winces and shakes her head to rid it of the image.

Then another replaces it, again, just a blink, and then gone.

Tess's face, contorted in pain.

Tess hurt. Bleeding.

Cam's daughter is in danger. She knows it, beyond a shadow of a doubt. She can feel it more profoundly than she's ever felt another person's pain in her premonitions. Because this time, the child is her own.

And I have to get to her, before it happens.

Because it will.

The things she sees always, always come to pass.

Clenching her jaw, Cam lifts her foot from the brake, checks for oncoming traffic, and goes through the red light, tires squealing as she rounds the corner.

"Do you mind if . . ." Lucinda asks Leah's father as she reaches for the girl's pajamas, her latex-gloved hand poised for permission.

He turns. "Oh . . . no, go ahead. Touch whatever you have to."

Lucinda picks up the pajamas. Holds them, wraps the soft fabric around her forearms, closing her eyes.

Come on, Leah . . . Where are you?

The detectives on the case are pretty sure she got off the school bus yesterday afternoon at a different stop, about a half mile before her own. A few kids and the driver thought they remembered seeing her get off there, though no one thought anything of it. Kids take the bus to different stops all the time, for playdates with friends.

But it turns out that shy Leah doesn't have many friends—and none who live off Loon Road.

So why did she get off the bus there?

No one knows. She sat alone as usual

and didn't talk to anyone. At the Loon Road stop, the other kids quickly scattered; it was a nice day and they were eager to get home.

Leah Roby never did.

Lucinda opens her eyes and wanders over to Leah's desk as her father stands at the window, staring out.

"We were always so careful with her." He sounds as if he's talking to himself, but Lucinda listens closely. "When she learned to walk, I can't tell you how much duct tape I went through."

Duct tape.

In her mind's eye, Lucinda sees a silver-gray roll of duct tape in gloved hands.

The ominous vision is there, then gone, leaving her with a familiar sick feeling in her gut.

"I used to wrap folded towels around the edges of all the tables in the house and tape them," Leah's father says, "kind of like bumpers, so she wouldn't fall against a hard corner."

Lucinda nods, but Ken isn't even looking at her.

"And when we found out she was allergic to peanuts," he goes on, "my wife got her out of school every single day for lunch so that she wouldn't accidentally come into contact with some other kid's PB&J sandwich. We never took a chance with her, ever. And now . . ."

He trails off, swallows hard, and continues to gaze at the dreary world beyond his daughter's bedroom window.

Lucinda turns back to the desk.

On it is an assortment of adolescent-girl possessions: books, a ballerina music box, a bin filled with colorful, sparkly art supplies and rainbow and unicorn stickers.

There are a couple of framed photos—Leah with her parents and younger brothers; with a friend; by herself, dressed up and holding a flute. Lifting that one, Lucinda stares long and hard at Leah, memorizing her features.

Blond wispy hair, light hazel eyes, blond lashes. She looks like her dad.

All at once, an image barges into Lucinda's mind: the sea. She takes a deep breath, expecting to smell salt air and sunscreen; sometimes that happens.

Not today.

Today, she can only *see* the water; can't smell it, or hear crashing waves.

Then something rises from the green-black depths in the distance, out beyond the breakers: a fin.

A shark?

"What is it?" Ken Roby's voice distracts her, and she opens her eyes to see him watching her worriedly. "Are you having some kind of . . . vision?"

Lucinda hesitates. "I saw the ocean. Does that mean anything to you?"

He shakes his head slowly, fearfully. "Do you think she's . . . in the water?"

"I'm not sure. That's not what I saw, though."

She won't tell him about the fin. Fins are inherently ominous, and anyway, she's not sure whether to take it literally or symbolically. She's learned after years of interpreting what she sees that it works both ways. All she can do is try to work with what she gets.

She closes her eyes again and concentrates, hoping the vision will return.

A few minutes pass.

Nothing.

"Is there anything here that Leah wore

a lot?" she asks Ken, glancing around the room. "Or something she used every day, maybe?"

He thinks for a moment, then shrugs. "How about her school uniform? She wears one every day—a skirt and vest. She has a few. You can see them if you want to." He walks toward the closet. "The only other thing I can think of that would fit the bill is her backpack, but she had that with her yesterday. It was her favorite color, purple."

Lucinda follows him, then notices something on the dresser top as they pass.

A white jewelry-sized cardboard gift box.

Seeing it, she feels inexplicably uneasy.

"Do you know what that's from?" she asks Ken, walking over to it.

"I have no idea."

The box is open, sitting inside its top, where nothing more than a rectangle of white cotton is visible. "Did she get a present recently?" Lucinda asks, turning to Ken. "For a birthday, or . . . ?"

"Her birthday's not until August. She'll be fourteen."

She can read his mind—anyone would be able to do that, though. The ravaged look on his face makes it plain that Leah's father is asking God to please let his daughter turn fourteen in August. Please let her survive, wherever she is.

Lucinda picks up the box. She can tell that it's empty even before she lifts the cotton pad to see if anything slipped beneath.

Nothing.

Nothing, that is, Lucinda realizes, her heart beating faster, but a few grains of what looks like sand.

At last, the rain has passed; the new copper firepit is finally blazing in the nearby clearing.

These days, everyone has one. Families gather cozily around them at night, toasting marshmallows in their own backyards.

It isn't night. And there's no family here . . . not officially.

Still, if anyone in the vicinity was to

randomly happen into the far reaches of the property—and they won't, but even if they did—the firepit wouldn't necessarily give anything away.

No, because I've thought of everything.

What looks like a simple poker is propped with the handle end against the copper rim, the other end buried in burning embers.

A bag of marshmallows sits at the ready on a makeshift log bench beside the pit.

The ladder is propped against a cherry tree nearby in the wooded section, once an orchard. The fruit isn't in season yet, but for all anyone knows, the ladder's been there since last summer.

Today's earlier rain now equals mud: ugly, filthy, weighs a ton.

It's taken fifteen minutes to dig through it to the trapdoor, and it's going to take more than just a heating pad and a good night's sleep to ease the resulting back pain.

Maybe I should have waited a day or two for this part.

After all, it's not like she's going anyplace, or likely to be dying of starvation down there. It's been less than twenty-four hours, and she has bread and water . . .

Ha. Just like prison.

Which is fitting, because that's pretty much where she is, and where she'll stay from now on.

And it's your own fault, little girl.

If she were an obedient child and could be trusted not to run away, she could sleep indoors, in a nice clean bed, the way she used to.

Almost there. One more shovelful should give access to the door . . .

Or break my back. One or the other. That would be her fault, too, just like these blisters on my hands from all that digging yesterday. These gloves are going to be bloody inside by the time I get finished today.

Her fault. All her fault, and I won't let her ever forget it. She'll pay for everything she's done to make my life a living hell.

"You made this happen, you know. You're responsible for your own actions.

So don't you *dare* start crying to me when I open this door."

No response.

Yeah, well, she probably can't hear a thing from down there.

Just as well. That means no one can hear her if she screams.

These nice thick gloves are coming in handy today in every way; the old iron ring handle is cold and caked in mud.

I don't feel like getting my poor blistered hands filthy on top of everything else. What if I got an infection and had to see a doctor? That wouldn't be good.

No, but it wouldn't necessarily be a giveaway. It's not as if the doctor would take one look at a bunch of blisters and connect them to the supposedly kidnapped child miles away in a Philly suburb.

Kidnapped? That's rich.

I'm just claiming what's rightfully mine. Mine.

Soaked hair and smeared makeup are the last thing on Tess's mind as she walks up Highland Avenue in the rain.

Like Julius Caesar, she was betrayed.

Et tu, *Morrow?*

How could she have done this to me?

Morrow is one of her best friends. Tess trusted her. Helped her pass the English final.

Yeah, and if I had just let her fail, this never would have happened.

Tess will never live this down.

The only saving grace is that school is over and she's leaving town tomorrow.

Thank God it'll be a few months before she has to face any of them—Morrow, Chad, Lily . . . most of all, Heath.

Heath, who not only now knows that Tess is alive, but has seen the black and white evidence of her private daydreams about him.

Tess Hastings Pickering . . . Tess Ava Hastings Pickering . . . Tess Pickering . . .

You idiot!

How could she have forgotten that she had written all that in her notebook before she lent it to Morrow?

How could Morrow have not only shown it to Chad, but let Chad show it to Heath?

"You told me to tell Chad you liked

Heath," Morrow protested to Tess, all innocent. "I mean, I thought it was just so cute that you were practicing writing your married name. So did Chad."

Just so cute?

It was just so ridiculous, that's what it was.

If only Morrow and Chad hadn't shown up at the party after all.

Tess shudders, remembering how she ran right over to them the moment they arrived.

Chad promptly announced, "Hey, look—it's Mrs. Heath Pickering."

Morrow immediately swatted his arm and hissed, "You promised not to do that."

Of course, Jordyn Runyan and her friends just happened to be in earshot. And, of course, Chad had to tell them all about the page Morrow had found in Tess's English notebook.

They were all laughing when she bolted into the house. At least Morrow had the decency to come running after her, trailed by Lily—who had also heard about it but was less amused than the others.

"That was a shitty thing to do," Lily told Morrow in the mirrored first floor changing room as Tess collapsed into a chair and buried her face in her hands.

"She wanted me to find out if Heath likes her!"

"That's not what she meant, and you knew it," Lily told her.

"Please don't tell me Chad told Heath," Tess begged, not daring to look at Morrow's face.

"Heath was flattered," was the reply. "Who wouldn't be?"

Lily moaned.

Tess cried.

Spotting herself in the mirror, she saw that the waterproof mascara isn't waterproof at all; ribbons of black were streaming down her cheeks.

She realized this was going to go around school faster than a stomach bug. Around school? Around the world, thanks to MySpace and FaceBook.

"Listen, when Heath shows up—he was supposed to be here already, so I have no idea where he is—I promise I'll introduce—" Morrow began, but Tess cut her off.

"No. No way."

"But—"

"Forget it," Tess said. "I don't ever want to see him again. You, either."

Morrow protested, spewing apologies, and Lily tried to play peacemaker, but Tess kicked them both out of the room. She called her mother, and snuck out of the house without saying good-bye.

She's walked three long blocks already—barefoot, her beautiful, expensive new flip-flops left out by the pool.

How is she going to get them back?

You aren't.

She's not going back to Lily's, ever. In fact, she's never going back to school, either. In the fall, she'll transfer to a private—

"Ow!" A sharp pain jabs into the sole of her foot.

Balancing on her left leg, Tess twists the other to see a shard of green glass sticking out of her right arch.

Wincing, she pulls it out and examines the wound, where a bright red trickle of blood runs from the gash.

* * *

For a split second, waking up in the dark, Leah thinks she's in her own bed, in her beautiful purple rainbow and unicorn bedroom.

But that dark is different. Cozy. Safe. Familiar.

This dark is clammy, filthy, terrifying. The air stinks terribly and the ground is alive with invisible creatures that scurry and slither over Leah's bare hands and feet.

She isn't in her own bed. She isn't home. She knows, in her heart, that she'll never be home again.

Reality hits, hard. So hard that Leah begs God to take her to heaven right now. Her teacher, Sister Mary Luke, said no one should ever be afraid to die, because heaven is paradise, safe and filled with lost loved ones.

Even so, Leah has always secretly been afraid. Afraid to leave her parents and her friends and her house and her life.

That's already happened to you.

Yes, and the thought of what might happen next—in this life—is far scarier than heaven as described by the elderly nun.

Please, God . . . Please help me. Please don't let this crazy person hurt me. Please don't—

Overhead, a dull thud.

Leah knows what that means. She won't be alone for long.

Please, God . . .

Why didn't she show someone the letter when it came? Mom or Dad, or even Sister Mary Luke, someone—why didn't she show someone?

But the letter said it had to be a secret or she would be disqualified.

Leah figured that was how those reality shows worked. They probably didn't want word getting out, because then everyone would want to be a contestant.

Leah kept thinking of how nice it would be to surprise her parents by turning on the television one night and saying, "Hey, look who's on TV! It's me!" And it would have been even better to surprise them with her winnings from the show. They were always worried about money. Their faces would light up if Leah won a treasure. Yes, and the girls at school, the ones who weren't very nice to Leah, would be jealous if she was on television—that was what she kept thinking.

Maybe that's why this is happening to her. Because she had sinful thoughts, and she was greedy—she wanted the treasure, and stardom, and the cool shark's tooth necklace, too.

Above, the heavy door creaks open and lands with a soft thud on the spongy ground beside the hole.

Dear God, please. Please take me now. I don't want to see that awful face again. I don't want to hear that horrible voice calling me by the wrong name, talking about Christmas presents, telling me I've been a bad girl.

All her life, Leah has been a good girl. Surely she's going straight to heaven when she dies.

And someday, Mommy and Daddy will meet her there. That's what Sister Mary Luke said.

Please let it be quick when it happens, God. Please don't let me suffer. Please . . .

* * *

"Tess!" Cam calls through the open car window, rain washing over her along with relief.

Up ahead on the sidewalk, her daughter turns. Her light brown hair is drenched, hanging in sopping strands that are plastered to her jaw and neck. Even from this distance, Cam can see the smudged black makeup running over her cheekbones—and the look of anguish in her eyes.

"Oh my God . . . what happened, sweetheart?" she pulls up alongside Tess, who limps over, barefoot, as Cam throws her door open.

The scenarios running through her head in the few seconds it takes Tess to answer are horrific: Did someone spike her drink with drugs? Attack her? Rape her?

"Morrow—she destroyed me. I swear, Mom, I will never be friends with her again, ever."

"She hurt you?" Holding her daughter close, Cam tries to imagine Morrow—whom she personally considers a little snotty, but certainly not physically threatening—beating up Tess. She can't do it. Still . . . "That's why you're limping? What did she do to you?"

The story that pours out of Tess is so reassuringly benign—compared to what she feared, anyway—that it's all Cam can do to summon a sympathetic expression.

"I'm so sorry, sweetheart," she says gently, helping Tess into the front seat.

Yes, when you're fourteen, being humiliated in front of your peers—and, worse yet, your current crush—is devastating. And, yes, teenaged Internet networking exacerbates the situation, according to a melodramatic declaration from Tess, who is convinced she's about to become a global laughingstock.

But thank God it's nothing worse. Adolescent broken hearts heal, and so do minor flesh wounds. Embarrassment subsides; teen tormentors move on to a new scapegoat.

It could have been so much worse. No one knows that better than Cam.

* * *

Hmm. Not a hint of artificial light from below.

"What's wrong? Flashlight burn out?"

"Yes," comes the hollow, hoarse reply.

"That's a shame. It was new, too. And I'm fresh out of D batteries. I'll tell you what. Behave and I'll leave you this other flashlight I have."

A flick of the switch illuminates the small figure huddled down there in the corner. It takes a few tries to prop the light at just the right angle to light the hole.

"Please let me out of here." The girl's voice is a barely audible croak. "I want to go home."

"You *are* home. And it's about time. Do you know how many months I've wasted looking for you? Wait there. I'll be right back."

First, the ladder. It's a lightweight one that takes mere moments to drag over from the cherry tree and lower into the hole.

"Touch that, and I'll kill you."

The command is met by a pathetic whimper.

"I mean it. Don't you dare try to climb out of there. I'm right here, even though you can't see me."

A quick trip to the firepit, where the proper tool is waiting, and then back to the trapdoor with it.

Good. She listened.

She's murmuring something, chanting, maybe.

Illuminated in the glow of the overhead flashlight beam, she's nowhere near the ladder; still cowering in the corner. She's a meek little thing these days . . . nowhere near the defiant little brat she once was. It's almost a disappointment to see that the fight has gone out of her . . .

Or has it?

It might just be an act. She can't be trusted.

I learned that the hard way.

"Now stay put just like that. Do you understand me? You move a muscle while I'm on this ladder and you die."

No reply, just fervent murmuring that sounds like she's reciting poetry, or . . . Is she praying?

She can't be. She doesn't know how . . .

Unless someone taught her.

The thought is both infuriating and amusing. She's going to need all the help she can get, and it certainly isn't going to come from any earthly source at this point.

"Shut up, do you hear me? Right now. Shut up if you know what's good for you . . . not that you ever did."

She does now. She falls silent.

The ladder shakes on the descent, just as it did on all the practice runs. It wouldn't take much to knock it off balance. A kid—even a skinny little thing like her—could easily accomplish it, if she chose to.

But, wisely, she doesn't. She stays put like a good girl.

Maybe she's changed . . .

Or maybe she's just trying to fool me.

The ladder wobbles crazily to one side.

Whoa . . . close call.

Below, there's a sudden gasp, a high-pitched cry. "What are you holding?"

So she spotted it. There goes the element of surprise. Oh well.

"This is just something that will make sure you don't forget where you belong. Just in case you were tempted to run away again. Now that I've found you, you're staying here with me."

The girl is sobbing again. "Please . . . please don't hurt me."

"Oh, come on . . . It won't be so bad." How much farther to go?

Ah, one more rung, and then another, and, at last, contact with the solid cellar floor.

The darkness is pungent: the musty smell of damp earth mingling with the stench of human excrement and vomit. It's impossible not to gag. Thank God this won't take long.

"This place reeks. How can you stand it?"

The question is met with another question, posed in a quavering, barely audible voice. "Wh . . . what are you doing with that?"

"We can do this in a nice, civilized fashion and it'll be over before you know it. Come here and stand up."

"No! Get away from me!" She tries to crawl away, but there's nowhere for her to go.

"Have it your way. But if you squirm all over the place and make me hold you down, this could get messy. And much more painful than it needs to be."

"No! St—" The girl's protest is curtailed as she's slammed down onto her back. Eyes wide in terror, she watches helplessly as the red-hot brand descends.

A bloodcurdling scream escapes her as the blazing iron encounters tender young skin.

"Shut up!"

The girl ignores the command, screeching as though she's in a torture chamber.

"Don't be ridiculous. It's already over. Stay still, let me see. Stay *still!*"

Ah, there. Perfect.

The brand left an indelible mark in the center of her forehead. Just one word.

The only one that matters, there for all the world to see.

MINE.

* * *

Pulling into the driveway at home with her daughter safe and sound, though miserable, beside her, Cam can't help but think about last night's false alarm.

First she burst into Tess's room, fearing for her safety for no reason other than a gut instinct that she was in danger. Now this.

It's getting ridiculous. She really has to stop jumping to conclusions.

Can pregnancy hormones be responsible for exacerbating her paranoia?

Sure they can, she reminds herself as she drives toward home. Bleeding gums, crying over stupid TV commercials, panicky food cravings . . .

Dr. Advani blames a lot of crazy symptoms on pregnancy hormones.

Cam leaves the car out in the driveway. She'll have to go back out later to finish the last few errands.

"Can you go ahead and open the door for me?" she asks Tess, opening the back gate to start unloading groceries.

Still sniffling, her daughter dutifully hobbles to the front door.

Cam grabs a couple of bags and the six-pack of Dr Pepper and follows, wishing she hadn't bought this stuff for Mike. Tess is going to notice, and assume that—

"Mom? I thought you set the alarm."

"I did. Why?"

"You didn't. You must have forgotten." Tess holds the door open for her.

"Oh . . . I guess I must have." Cam frowns as she steps over the threshold.

She could swear she remembers setting the alarm.

Especially since she was still so jittery about her latest vision last night.

Then again, Tess was rushing her out the door.

And . . . pregnancy hormones. They can cause forgetfulness, too.

You left your grocery list and coupons at home. What makes you think you didn't forget about the alarm, too?

Still, the nagging question lingers in Cam's mind.

What if there's more to the disarmed alarm—and her certainty that Tess was in danger—than pregnancy hormones?

Did someone break into the house while they were gone?

She has the distinct feeling that someone was here, yet nothing seems out of place as she and Tess walk through the quiet rooms to the kitchen.

"What should I put on my foot?" Tess sinks into a kitchen chair and examines her cut, adding almost accusingly, "Since Dad's not here to do it."

First aid was Mike's department. Somehow, he always happened to be around to tend to their daughter's bruises and bloodshed.

"I'll do it. We need to clean it. I'll get peroxide," Cam murmurs, and goes toward the half bath to search the medicine cabinet.

Tess stops her. "The stuff's in the utility closet. In a plastic shoebox. Second shelf from the top."

"Oh. Right."

Tess sniffles miserably.

Come on, Cam, forget about the alarm. Forget about everything but Tess, at least for now.

You're her mom. You can do this just as well as Mike—better, even.

Peroxide and cotton balls in hand, along with antibiotic ointment, bandages, and an empty blue rubber ice pack, she stops at the fridge on the way back.

"What are you doing?" Tess wants to know.

"Getting ice." She opens the freezer.

"Do cuts need ice?"

"Sure they do." *Don't they?*

Who knows? Feeling helpless, hopeless—and as irritated with Mike for making himself resident caregiver as she is with herself for letting him—Cam scoops cubes into the open neck of the ice pack. She slams the door, and of course the magnetic shopping pad drops off the front of the fridge.

Well, Tess does think you're the World's Best Mom, she reminds herself, seeing the slogan across the top page as she bends to pick up the pad.

Then . . .

Wait a minute.

The page is blank.

Where's her shopping list?

Earlier, she checked her pockets, her

purse, and the car before realizing she didn't have it with her.

Meaning, it should be here where she left it . . . right?

Right. So where is it? And why isn't the alarm set?

And what is wrong with me? Am I losing my mind?

"Mom? This really hurts."

"Oh . . . I'm sorry, I'm coming."

Cam kneels beside her daughter. "Here . . . Let me see."

"Ow . . . be careful."

"I'm being careful. When was your last tetanus shot?"

"You're asking *me?*"

"No, I'm asking me, and I can't remember. I should call the doctor. This might sting," she warns, soaking a cotton ball with peroxide as her mind reels.

What if her vision about Tess, bloody and in trouble, was about more than a friend's betrayal and stepping on a piece of glass? The whole nightmare situation with Morrow and the notebook and the bloody foot could have been a mere coincidence—

As the peroxide penetrates the wound, Tess cries out in pain.

Cam's blood runs cold at the sound.

"It'll be okay, sweetie," she says soothingly, struggling to push aside irrational fear as she strokes the ointment over her daughter's wound. "It's just a cut. It'll heal fast."

But what if—*please, God, no*—the real drama involving Tess still lies ahead?

"Here . . . I brought you something."

Lying on the dirt floor, the child doesn't move a muscle. Even a swift kick doesn't rouse her; she might as well be a pile of rags.

Why did I even bother?

The answer is humbling: *Because I don't want it to be like this—captor and captive. This isn't how it was supposed to be.*

It wouldn't have come to this, though, if she hadn't left in the first place. And again, when I found her . . . and again the next time . . .

Over and over again.

She always leaves.

This is the only way.

Clearly, this is the only way it can be. Captor and captive—branded like an animal for all to see so there can be no mistake.

"You know, I could have just left you here to wallow in misery, but I didn't. No, I went all the way up to the house to get you an ice pack for your forehead, and candy, too. Don't you want some?"

Candy: it always was the magic word.

The girl turns her head at last.

Ah, the earlier handiwork is most effective. Beneath the etched raw—but clearly legible—mark on her forehead, her eyes are wary.

"Here . . . see? It's your favorite."

The girl's gaze settles on the proffered peace offering: Reese's Peanut Butter Cups. But she doesn't light up and seize the candy the way she used to.

Well, she's still shaken up, poor thing.

Poor thing? She'll get over it. Don't go feeling guilty. Don't forget for one second she brought this on herself.

"You know what? First, we'll do your hair. Then you can have your treat. Deal?"

No response.

"Look at these tangles! I'm afraid this isn't going to be easy." The brush gets snagged a quarter of the way down the first strands.

That gets a response. "Ouch!"

"Sit still. You haven't been brushing a hundred strokes a night like I taught you, have you?"

The brush is stuck again. This time it takes a few hard tugs to get it loose.

"Oww!"

"Sorry."

Her hair seems silkier, more easily tangled. Maybe the blonde dye has changed the texture.

"There. How's that? One nice braid down your back. And now you can have your treat."

The girl turns away. "I don't want it."

"Go ahead, take it." The gentle tone is fraying fast.

"I can't."

"What do you mean, you can't? I got it just for you! Now take it!"

Her lip trembles. "Stop yelling at me."

"I suppose you want those gingerbread cookies I promised you, don't you?"

"What are you talking about?"

"You'll get them later. It was going to be a surprise. I baked them just for you."

No surprise. No gratitude. No reaction other than apparent bewilderment.

"Look, just take the damn candy. I don't have all day."

"I can't. I'm allergic."

"What?"

"Peanut butter. I can't eat it. I'm allergic."

"Don't be ridiculous. You're not allergic to anything."

"I break out in hives."

"You've never broken out in hives in your life. Stop lying. Here . . ." A quick crinkling of the wrapper, and the candy is open, thrust toward the girl's mouth. "Eat it."

"I can't."

"Eat it!"

The child's jaws are forced open, the candy jammed into her mouth. She writhes, gagging, choking, drooling saliva streaked with chocolate. As she raises her hand toward her mouth, desperate to get the candy out, the overhead flashlight beam catches something metallic at her wrist.

A bracelet.

A bracelet with a flat ID tag on it.

"Let me see that."

"Owwww . . . You're twisting my arm!"

A fierce tug, and the bracelet snaps off.

There. The light is dim down here but if it's tilted at just the right angle, the engraved letters become visible.

LEAH ROBY.

The name means nothing; of course it wouldn't. She's always used fake names; she's dyed, cut, and grown her hair; has even worn colored contacts.

As if she can fool me. As if I wouldn't know her anywhere, even with a disguise.

Beneath the fake name is a fake birthdate and fake contact information, along with a medical alert that Leah Roby has a severe nut allergy.

Yeah, right.

Still . . . She's putting on a good act, going limp, gasping as though she's having a hard time breathing.

"In my backpack," the child moans. "An EpiPen. Please."

"Stop the melodrama."

"Please . . ."

The thing is . . .

There's something on the girl's face that wasn't there a few minutes ago. Some kind of rash that looks like a couple of harsh red bumps . . .

Hives.

"Please," the girl—the wrong girl—begs as her throat swells closed. "Please help me."

The truth hits like a killing frost.

In its wake, hope—foolish, naive hope—withers and dies.

The wrong girl. An imposter.

"Please . . . help . . . Epi . . ."

"You know, I'm really sorry about this . . . Leah? Is that your name? I thought you were someone else. My bad."

This means she's still out there somewhere.

But where?

It's like looking for a needle in a haystack.

Or a shark's tooth on a beach.

The beach.

The one where it all began.
And it's time to go back.

Amazing. It's really happening, just like Leah prayed.

Oddly, it hasn't really even hurt much, other than the hairbrush.

It was scary at first, though. Dying.

Really scary.

Not anymore.

Lying on the floor, no longer struggling to breathe, no longer fighting to survive, Leah thinks of her parents as she waits for the angels and the white light. Sister Mary Luke said that's how it would be—angels and white light.

Mom and Dad are going to be so sad. That's the worst part. They're going to be crying a lot when they find out. More, even, than they did at Grandma's funeral.

Funeral.

What will hers be like? Will they put her in the beautiful pink dress Mom got her for Easter? She only got to wear it once.

Maybe she'll be able to watch her

funeral from wherever she is. In heaven, with Grandma, and God.

God, who heard Leah's prayer and rescued her from the Devil itself, a devil with an angry, accusing voice and eyes that flicker with madness, seeing someone else when they look right at Leah.

Some other girl, a girl who likes chocolate peanut butter cups and gingerbread.

Wherever she is, I hope the Devil never finds her, is Leah Roby's last thought.

Tess's cell phone buzzes late that night.

Someone is sending her a text message.

She reaches for it in the dark, certain it's going to be Morrow with an apology.

The sender's number is unfamiliar.

Hi Tess. This is Heath.

Her stomach lurches.

Chad. It has to be. Thinking it would be a hilarious prank to text her posing as Heath. For all she knows, a bunch of his friends—yeah, and Morrow and Lily and God knows who else—are all there with him.

Shaking, Tess types in a response.

Leave me alone!

She looks at it for a minute.

Then she scrolls back to edit her message.

Leave me the hell alone!

There. Better.

She hits SEND.

Then she holds down the END button until the power shuts down, and tosses the phone across the room.

It hits the wall, hard, and drops to the floor in at least two pieces.

Who cares?

Who needs a phone, Tess thinks, hot tears soaking her pillow, *when you have no friends?*

* * *

Downstairs at the kitchen table, Cam turns to the third page in the Marble notebook, then hesitates, pen in hand.

The first two pages are lined with her handwriting.

One is dated May, followed by as much information as she can recall about the vision she had that night in her kitchen, about the little blond girl in the cellar.

It's surprising how many details she remembered. Maybe it's because it was the first vision after so many years and caught her off guard, or maybe because her brain is no longer affected by alcohol whose very purpose was to cloud the visions. Whatever the case, she wrote down everything from what the girl was wearing to the purple backpack to the house with the number 42.

Most striking of all was the silver necklace with the triangular black pendant. She underlined it several times, circled it, knowing it has some kind of meaning . . .

Because she saw it twice, on two different girls.

The second page, with yesterday's

date, covers the vision of the sunburnt redheaded girl in front of the blue wall that looks so familiar. She already scribbled her notes on that vision, but she's looked everywhere and has no idea what she did with the shopping list. That's been eating away at her all night—along with the alarm she thought she'd set and hadn't—but she has other things to worry about.

On page two, Cam wrote down every image she glimpsed last night, from the red bubble letters *L-F* to the pink toenail polish, to, again, the black pendant on a silver chain.

Again, underlined several times.

What the hell does it mean?

Reluctantly, she puts today's date at the top of the third page.

Then, pen wavering above the paper, she shakes her head.

Go on. What did you see today in the car?

Tess. Tess's skin, Tess's blood.

Okay, she didn't actually *see* her. And it wasn't a full-blown vision.

Just an overwhelming sense that her

daughter was going to be in trouble, and injured . . .

And she was.

Her friends betrayed her, she sliced open her foot. Had to go to the doctor and get a painful tetanus shot, which made Tess squeeze Cam's hand so hard it still feels bruised.

So . . .

The brief premonition has already come to pass. Why bother writing it down?

Because what if that wasn't—

No, Cam tells herself sharply. *It was. It's over. That was it. That was all.*

She tears out the empty dated page, snaps the cap back on the pen, and closes the notebook. After crumpling and tossing the paper, she turns off the kitchen lights and goes over to the pile of luggage by the back door. There, she hesitates again.

Are you sure you need this? Any of it?

No. She's not sure of anything.

She unzips the tote bag, slips the notebook in on top of the others, zips the bag closed again.

Then she climbs the stairs in the dark, silent house.

At Tess's door she pauses.

Then she cracks it open, peeks inside, sees the huddled form in the bed.

Good. She's asleep. Poor kid.

Cam closes the door and goes down the hall to her own empty bed.

PART III: JULY

Chapter Seven

"Does it get any better than this?" Debbie Marriman sighs contentedly. "I mean . . . look around!"

Sitting beside Debbie in a low canvas chair, bare toes buried in warm sand, Cam glances up from the open book on her lap.

Following her friend's gaze, she looks out over the crowded strand.

The island's summer residents, weekenders, day-trippers, and locals are out en force: some well oiled and sprawled in the glaring sun, others well screened and chilling beneath bright-colored umbrellas. Frisbees soar, elaborate sand castles rise, lifeguards keep a watchful eye on waders, swimmers, and boogie boarders in the bracing surf. Out beyond the ridge of foaming white breakers, buzzing Jet Skis cut across the darker blue water of the Atlantic, shimmering in the golden midday sun.

"Nope," Cam agrees, trying not to sound forced, "it definitely doesn't get any better than this."

She's known Debbie for about a week. That's plenty long enough to realize that she's the last person who wants to hear that Mike's conspicuous absence from Cam's life makes everything—even this glorious seaside day—decidedly imperfect.

The first time Cam mentioned that she misses her husband, Debbie's expression soured instantly. "You're better off on your own. Trust me. You're capable of taking care of yourself *and* your daughter. You don't need him."

Maybe she does . . . but she wouldn't admit it to Debbie, who is recently and bitterly divorced. So bitterly, for that matter, that not only does Debbie never have a kind word for her ex-husband, but she's pretty much peeved at men in general. All men. Including total strangers. Like Mike.

"There is one thing I can think of that would be better than this," Debbie says.

"Yeah? What's that?" Cam is positive she's not going to mention Gregg, her ex back in Phoenix.

Debbie doesn't miss him. Far from it. She's moved her kids—Beth, fourteen, and ten-year-old Jonathan—across the country to get away from him. A flight attendant, she transferred her base back East to Newark Airport and moved back to her hometown in Monmouth County, where her parents still live.

Cam senses there's more to Debbie's story than she's heard so far . . . and that the sordid details will come out before the summer's over. She's not in any hurry to hear them, or to share her own in return.

"If we were on a lush Caribbean island being waited on hand and foot by attentive cabana boys. Right?"

Cam grins. "That does sound pretty good."

"Doesn't it? I can get you a flight dirt cheap, maybe even free—how about a girls'-only weekend down there in the fall?"

By fall, Cam herself will be the size of a small Caribbean island.

"That's hurricane season," she reminds Debbie.

"So? What are the odds of getting hit? Hey, do you see the girls?" Debbie cups a hand over her brows and scans the beach for Beth and Tess.

"Down by the lifeguard stand." Cam promptly points in that direction, where her daughter—looking particularly angular and childlike beside Debbie's daughter, who even from here looks like a Brazilian Miss Universe contestant—

"And in case you were wondering," she adds, sensing Debbie's searching gaze, "Jonathan's still over there"—Cam arcs her arm over toward the lapping waterline—"helping those little kids with their sand castle."

"Oh, right. I see him. Wow, Cam, you're *good*."

She *is* good. Unable to shake those visions she was having back home about Tess, she hasn't let her daughter out of her sight for more than a few minutes since they arrived in Beach Haven.

It wasn't all that challenging to keep an

eye on Tess in the beginning. The sky opened up the moment they crossed the causeway onto the island at Ship Bottom the first day here, and it was no fluke. The remainder of June was unseasonably cool and rainy, forcing Cam and Tess to spend the first two weeks here as an inseparable twosome. Cooped up in the cottage, they played endless board games, read stacks of books and magazines, even watched rented movies—something Mike never allowed at the beach, to Tess's perpetual dismay.

Cam had intended to stick with Mike's no-TV-on-vacation rule, but after a few days of rain, she relented. After all, who's in charge here? The gray-shingled cottage on Dolphin Avenue—like the big Colonial in Montclair—is her department now.

There's something to be said for chick flicks and microwave popcorn. Especially when the weather is lousy and the little cottage seems as oddly deserted as the town itself.

Last week, though, the pervasive cold front finally pushed on past the coast, taking with it endless drizzle and gloomy skies. The local action picked up drastically as hordes of summer people arrived, and it started to feel more like summer at last. Even at the cottage. Even without Mike.

Summer without Mike. Unbelievable. It's Cam's first in almost twenty years, and it most likely won't be her last. Will she ever get used to the idea? Will she ever stop rolling over in bed every morning expecting to see his head on the pillow beside hers?

"You know what I want?" Debbie interrupts her thoughts again.

"Ice cream?" Cam asks hopefully. That's what she wants—pretty much any time of the day or night, actually.

"No. I feel like a Frozen Piña Colada."

That's strange. You don't look like a Frozen Piña Colada.

Yeah, that's what Mike would say. One of his favorite corny jokes.

It always made Cam smile.

"What do you think?" Debbie asks.

"Isn't it kind of early for happy hour?"

She waves Cam off with an, "Eh, it's five o'clock somewhere, right?"

Debbie stretches her toned body lazily and flexes her tanned toes—with their glossy coral pedicure and a gold ring on one pinky—over the sand. Slender, dark, and on the short side, with delicate features, she's effortlessly beautiful.

Sitting next to Debbie, when one feels more and more like a beached whale, is no picnic. It's a good thing Debbie—quick, friendly, confident, sharp-witted—is immensely likeable.

Cam is glad Debbie is spending the summer on the island—well, her kids are here full time, anyway. Debbie's on vacation through the weekend; she returns to work on Monday and a hired woman will be staying here with the kids on the days and nights she's traveling.

That's how she phrased it—"a hired woman." Debbie said she met her by chance, that she cleans houses in the neighborhood and mentioned she was looking for more work.

Cam can't imagine leaving Tess with a virtual stranger, but figures Debbie must have no choice. Maybe her parents are too old or frail to help her.

"I've got a can of Bacardi mix in the freezer, and a gazillion of those little airline bottles of rum," she tells Cam. "Should I shoot back up to the house and make a pitcher of drinks? Doesn't a Frozen Piña Colada sound good?

"It sounds a little too fattening for me."

Good one. No one looking at Cam—and not knowing she's pregnant, which Debbie does not—would argue that she doesn't need to watch her weight. Her stomach is growing more and more difficult to camouflage beneath the oversized hardcover on her lap and the oversized white terry beach cover-up that's become her uniform lately.

"Oh, who cares about the calories?" Debbie asks. "Live a little."

Should I just tell her I'm pregnant? Cam wonders fleetingly.

No. Not before she tells Mike.

Okay, then, should I tell her I'm newly sober?

No. Like the pregnancy—and the fact that she's sometimes haunted by disturbing visions—that's too personal to share.

Cam settles on a flippant, "If I drink rum this early in the day, I'll fall asleep."

"Good point. Me, too. And who doesn't love an afternoon nap?" Debbie decisively shoves her pretty feet into flip-flops and grabs her beach bag. "Can you keep an eye on my kids while I go whip up those drinks?"

She doesn't bother to wait for a reply.

Cam watches her amble off down the sand toward her rented first-floor duplex, just a few doors down from the Hastings's cottage.

What do I do when she comes back with those drinks?

Just say no?

Get up and leave?

Tell her the truth?

What would Kathy advise her to do?

Work the program.

That's all Kathy ever tells her. She goes around spewing AA mantras as if they, alone, hold the key to righting what's wrong in Cam's world.

That's why Cam has guiltily ignored her sponsor's phone calls these last few days. Not only that, but she hasn't gone to an AA meeting—down here, or back home—in more than ten days.

Why should I? It's not like I'm going to fall off the wagon this time, she thinks stubbornly, glancing down at her belly.

No way would she risk harming the child inside her.

It's that simple.

Is it?

That's Kathy's voice inside her head—not her own.

Yes, it is, she retorts.

She believes in herself, even if Kathy doesn't.

Lately, Cam's found a strength she didn't know she had.

It's not as if she doesn't long for an escape every day . . . it's just that she'd rather crawl into Mike's arms than into a bottle.

Why hasn't time dulled the ache of her marital separation the way it's dulled the thirst for liquor? If anything, she misses Mike more painfully with every long, lonely, sober day that passes.

She misses him here at the beach; she misses him on the long drives back to Montclair with Tess for her weekly visitations; she misses him whenever she walks into the still, empty house they shared. Most of all, she misses him when she sees him—always from afar, in his car in the driveway. He waves; she waves. They don't talk.

But we have to.

And tomorrow's the day.

"So it really is you. I can't believe it. To what do I owe the pleasure?"

Lucinda looks up to see Randy standing in the doorway of the small, deserted waiting room.

Detective Randall Barakat of Long Beach Township Police Department, to be more specific . . . But to her, he'll always be just Randy. Nothing more.

She learned long ago, the hard way, that more—any kind of *more,* where Randy is involved—is out of the question.

"You owe the pleasure to the usual," she tells him lightly, standing and meeting him halfway for a tight, quick hug. An old friend's hug.

Nothing more.

"You mean the 'I'm on a case' kind of usual? Or the 'I decided to come to Long Beach Island for some sun and sand' kind of usual?"

"Have I ever been the beach-bunny type?"

"Hell, no." Randy steps back and flashes his dimples at her.

Black-haired men with dimples and blue eyes are her weakness.

That's how the whole damn thing started in the first place.

With her weakness.

And, to be fair, with Randy's.

It ended because of his strength . . . if transferring to an out-of-state job shows strength.

She initially thought it was weak and cowardly. Running away.

It's been three years now. Long enough for Lucinda to realize Randy's decision to leave really was best for both of them.

Not having to see each other meant not living with temptation on a daily basis.

Three years—and a string of relationships and breakups with other men—

later, Lucinda has a feeling she could pick up right where she left off in the temptation department, where Randy is concerned.

"Tell me about the case," he says.

"Missing child."

"Aren't they all?"

"Not all. But most."

He nods. "Neal got you involved?"

"He always does."

"I wasn't sure if you two were still working together, or . . ." Randy shrugs, having been out of touch for a few years now. "So how is he?"

"Fine. Erma retired last month, but Neal's nowhere near ready. And they have five grandchildren now, and a sixth on the way."

"That's great."

"Yeah."

"So you see Neal a lot, still?"

She nods, eager to dispense with the small talk, afraid of where it might lead. She doesn't want to discuss her personal life with him, and she sure as hell doesn't want to hear about his.

"So there's a connection to Long

Beach Island with this case?" he asks. "That's why you're here?"

"There might be."

"So can I help you? Is that what you want?"

Is that what she wants?

Lucinda isn't a woman prone to wishy-washy statement or sentiment. She always knows what she wants, and finds a way to get it.

Randy lifts his left wrist to check his watch. His gold wedding band glints on his fourth finger.

Still there . . . in case she was wondering.

Hell, yeah, she was.

So now you know all you need to know about his personal life.

"You might be able to help me," she says. "I'm not sure."

Wishy-washy. Ugh.

Not her style.

"Are you hungry?" Randy asks.

"Always."

He laughs. "Right. I remember that about you. The tiny little thing with a trucker's appetite. Where do you put it all?"

She sees his eyes flick up and down her body—not inappropriately in the least, and only for a split second. Still, she feels her face grow heated, remembering . . .

"Come on," Randy says. "I'll take you to lunch. Nothing beats Long Beach Island chowder."

"You used to say nothing beats a Philly Cheese Steak."

"Yeah, well . . ." *I used to say a lot of things.*

She knows him well enough to read the thought.

Yes, and he knows Lucinda well enough to keep it to himself.

Open that door, even after all these years, and she'll step right through it. She never was one to back down from a challenge.

But that's not why she's here.

She's here to bring Leah Roby home . . . or maybe just to bring some kind of closure to her family.

It has nothing to do with her own unfinished business with Randy.

The fact that the Roby trail led here to

Long Beach Island is nothing more than a colossal coincidence.

If one believes in such things.

Lucinda used to.

But the more she works in this business, the more she realizes there are never any true coincidences at all.

Interesting.

Viewed with the naked eye from this perch amid the dunes, the Atlantic appears deceptively calm today, a crisp, even shade of greenish blue.

But of course nothing, seen from a distance, is ever what it seems.

Only when one looks through the newly purchased pair of binoculars is there evidence of the mighty rip currents that churn beneath the surface. Only via a magnified lens can one glimpse the true palate of splotches that make up the shimmering veneer: not just green and blue, but also purple and gray and a murky charcoal shade in one spot, the shadow of a cloud, perhaps, or a school of fish, or a prowling marine predator.

Ah, closer to shore, hearty swimmers

seeking relief from the heat splash about or stand chatting casually in waist-deep waves, seemingly heedless of the cold water—not to mention other hazards of the sea.

How brazen, when one considers it, this breed of ocean beachgoers really are. Don't they realize that the moment you let your guard down, an errant tide can sweep you perilously far from shore? Aren't they aware that lethal creatures lurk and hunt in the water's chilly depths, creatures that crave the scent of blood and feed on human flesh?

The binoculars tremble in sheer anticipation of a triangular fin abruptly breaking the surface to slice into shallow water toward the swimmers.

That could happen anytime, without warning. Wouldn't it be a sight to behold?

This, after all, is the very beach where, almost a century ago, a great white shark slaughtered an unsuspecting swimmer before moving on up the coast to do it again, and again, and again—even inland, in a creek in Mattawan.

That was an anomaly. A man-eater couldn't possibly dwell in those benign waters . . . or so the naive residents of that small, sheltered town believed.

Until the creek waters ran red with the blood of a ruthlessly slaughtered child.

Standing on line at a crowded Lexington Avenue deli around the corner from his office, Mike feels his Blackberry vibrate in his suit pocket.

He pulls it out, checks the screen. A new e-mail from Kate.

The Subject line reads TONIGHT.

In no hurry to read the message, much less respond, he shoves the device back into his pocket. She said she was working from home today. He'll call her there later.

Or not.

He glances back at the sandwich board above the counter.

As a regular here, he pretty much knows the menu by heart. The sandwiches are all cleverly named after local sports stars. *Heroes-heroes,* get it? Got it. Long over it.

But the hand-holding Midwestern honeymooners in front of him are captivated. They take their sweet time dissecting their options, exclaiming over the prices, and inanely discussing the weather, too, oblivious to the lunchtime crush, the counterman's impatient glare, Mike's growing frustration.

His Blackberry vibrates again.

This time, a call. Kate. Again.

He ignores her. Again.

Maybe he should just cancel their dinner. He needs to get on the road by four thirty tomorrow morning to beat the morning traffic.

Traffic . . .

Once upon a time, he and Cam joked about how they had become a typical suburban New Jersey cliché: traffic seemed to define their lives from the moment they moved across the Hudson. There were certain things you just didn't do if you could help it, like go near the Meadowlands on Sundays in the fall, drive east through the Lincoln Tunnel on a Monday morning, or west on a Friday evening . . .

Usually, they could avoid all of it.

Change the schedule or the route, take a train, stay home . . .

Not anymore. Not Mike, anyway. And he and Cam haven't joked about it in ages.

Mike's visitation schedule with Tess means he spends almost as much time sitting in the legendary Jersey traffic as he does with his daughter.

Tomorrow promises to be a vehicular nightmare.

Hordes of people head down the shore every year to kick off the holiday weekend. The earlier he picks up Tess, the better, since they've got a few additional hours' drive from Long Beach Island down to DC.

After much deliberation, he'd decided that would be a fitting place to spend the most patriotic national holiday. Years ago, when Tess was little girl, he and Cam talked about visiting Washington.

Now he and Tess are going without her. They're planning to watch the parade along Constitution Avenue, attend the concert on the lawn of the Capitol, and cap things off with the fireworks above the Washington Monument.

"You must be so excited about the trip," Kate commented when he mentioned it to her over brunch last Sunday.

He isn't so excited, but he pretended to be.

He pretended, too, not to notice Kate's wistfulness about her own lackluster plans for the Fourth. He also ignored the blatant hints she was dropping by the time brunch drew to a close.

She mentioned that she'd spent a lot of time on the Jersey Shore in the past and was thinking it would have been nice to head down sometime this summer. She all but invited herself to catch a ride with him tomorrow morning. He knew that if he offered, she'd manage to wedge her way into his DC plans as well.

Ridiculous.

Did she actually expect him to ask her—a woman he's dated a handful of times—to spend a long weekend with him and his daughter?

Apparently she did.

He's recently discovered that single

city women of a certain age can be a little desperate. Even beautiful, successful, independent women like Kate.

Thirty-nine and never married, she's a corporate brand manager with a corner office, a designer wardrobe, and a two-bedroom co-op in an Upper East Side high-rise.

Kate is the polar opposite of Cam in every way . . .

Which is pretty much why he asked her out in the first place.

It's also why he's going to stop seeing her after tonight.

She's not Cam; she's nothing like Cam . . .

And I miss Cam.

At least he can freely admit it now—to himself, anyway—after trying to deny it for months.

There's nothing wrong with missing the woman who's been a part of your life for almost two decades. The woman who shared your bed and your bank account, lean or fat; the woman who gave you life's greatest gift.

His daughter.

Tess hates this—the separation—and

all that goes with it: the one-on-one precision scheduling, the stilted conversation over dinner for two, the constant shuttling back and forth from Montclair to Manhattan and lately, from the shore to Montclair to Manhattan and back.

"Now what does a 'B-LT' have to do with sports and why is that hyphen in there?" wonders the clueless newlywed wife in front of Mike, gazing at the menu.

"The hyphen is a typo," replies her equally clueless husband, who's clearly never heard of the Giants' Lawrence "LT" Taylor.

Mike and Cam saw LT play years ago at the Meadowlands, on a crisp October night not long before they were married. Monday Night Football. Someone gave them the coveted tickets; he no longer recalls who it was, or which team the Giants faced, or whether they won. What he does remember: Cam's rosy cheeks; sharing a cozy plaid wool stadium blanket and a thermos of hot chocolate; how she screamed herself hoarse by the fourth quarter.

"I want to know what a Grilled Thurman

Muenster is," the newlywed wife declares.

Mike checks his watch. If he doesn't get back to the office, he'll never get *out* of the office.

"Grilled muenster cheese," her husband replies, kissing the tip of her nose. "You're so cute."

Maybe Mike should just tell Kate he has to work late. It's the night before a long weekend. She's a businesswoman. She should understand.

Yeah, she should . . . but will she?

Kate can be persistent.

She's the one who came after him in the first place. It was raining, and he came out of his office building to hail a downtown cab as he always did when he worked late.

She was already standing at the curb, trying to hail a cab herself.

"I'll make you a deal," she called from beneath her umbrella, a straight-shooting stranger with great legs. "If I get a cab first, I'll share it with you. If you get one, you share it."

Either way, they'd ride together. There was no escaping her.

Yeah, and admit it. You were flattered by the attention.

Okay, he was.

Who wouldn't be?

You're such a cliché, you know that? The newly separated man whose head spins at the slightest glance from a beautiful woman who isn't your wife.

But the novelty is wearing off fast.

Another cliché.

"Shouldn't it be Herman Muenster?" Mike hears the wife ask her husband.

"For God's sake, Herman Munster was a sitcom character!"

The newlywed tourists turn to look at Mike.

"Thurman Munson was the greatest Yankees catcher ever," he adds, as if he's just trying to be a helpful local. As if he's not beyond annoyed with their cluelessness and their youth and their blissful cooing and canoodling.

They exchange a glance with each other, then look back at him.

He realizes they see him for what he is: an impatient, Type A, divorce-bound New Yorker. And an asshole to boot.

The ultimate cliché.

Wordlessly, Mike turns and pushes his way back out of the deli.

Outside on the street, the midday sun glares. Grumpy office workers skirt around meandering tourists. Snarled traffic inches and honks. Sirens wail in the distance. From a nearby construction site, a jackhammer rattles incessantly. The whole nine New York City yards.

And Mike's damn Blackberry buzzes again.

He leaves it in his pocket and makes his way back to the office, missing Cam and wondering what the hell he was thinking when he left.

Wondering, too, what might happen if he told her he wanted to come back.

"Mom!"

Cam looks up to see her daughter waving at her from across the sand.

"We're going to get ice cream! Be right back!"

She nods and watches as Tess and Debbie's daughter, Beth—both wearing bathing suits and shorts, but in very different ways—walk toward the dunes. Sea grass sways there, in the incessant breeze. A weathered board fence, missing pickets and crazily tilted this way and that, marks the sandy path off the beach.

Tess disappears and Cam pushes back an irrational stab of fear.

She still can't shake the vague worry about her daughter, though she hasn't had any specific premonitions about her.

She wants to believe that the frightening episode in the car that day back in Montclair was related to Tess's emotional pain, and nothing more than that. Yes, she's almost positive that the vision was purely symbolic—or maybe related to the cut on Tess's foot. Nothing more.

But she does keep seeing that redheaded girl with the braids and silver necklace, standing against the blue wall with the red letters *LF*. The vision washes over her when she least expects it, bringing with it a growing urgency and a frustrating aura of familiarity.

Why? Is it that Cam has seen the girl

somewhere before? Or does she know the place in the background?

The snippet of a scene never lasts long enough for her to figure it out. Trying to grasp it is as futile as building a sand castle in the path of an incoming tide.

So she tries not to dwell on it.

Lord knows she's got plenty more to worry about.

Tomorrow, Mike arrives at the cottage to pick up Tess for their Fourth of July trip. Before they hit the road, she plans to pull Mike aside and tell him she's pregnant.

Not the ideal scenario, but what choice does she have?

The news has to be delivered in person, and time is running out. Her stomach is literally getting bigger by the day. By the time Mike gets back next week with Tess, it will be too obvious. Then he'll accuse her of hiding the pregnancy from him, and God knows what else, and things will get ugly.

Better to get it right out in the open tomorrow, then let him absorb the situation while he's away. Maybe they can tell Tess together when he gets back.

And she'll react . . . how?

It's hard to say. The child Cam once knew so well has become a mercurial stranger at times. She doesn't share much. Not with her mother, anyway.

Beth probably knew more about what's going on with Tess five minutes after meeting her than Cam has been privy to in a year. Cut off from her so-called friends back home, Tess bonded with Beth—who's in the same boat—in a way only fourteen-year-old girls can.

It usually takes a little longer for grown women to let each other in—at least, back home in the upscale northern Jersey suburbs. There, only Kathy ever really reached out to Cam—but not necessarily because she wanted to be friends. More likely because she sensed a kindred spirit, someone in trouble, and wanted to help.

There's not a whole lot of benevolence about Debbie, with her bouncy brown ponytail and quick smile. But that's okay. She was friendly to Cam from day one, and Cam welcomed the companionship.

Debbie quickly introduced Cam to a number of her friends, almost all of them divorced single moms. At first, Cam assumed Debbie had known them all much longer than she has Cam, but that turned out not to be the case. In the two weeks since Debbie's arrived on the island, she's developed a brand-new social circle and treats everyone in it like an old friend, Cam included.

Already she's joined Debbie and her friend Petra for a pedicure one day this week, and the following morning had breakfast in town with Debbie and her friend Gina. Hanging around with a bunch of single mothers has made her own situation seem a little more bearable . . . and almost universal.

Funny, she never realized just how isolated she was in her suburban life. The alcohol had dulled the loneliness, just as it had numbed everything else. Now that she's been sober for more than three months, she realizes just how much she'd been missing.

Maybe when she gets back home,

she'll look up some of her old friends—the moms she used to know from the playground and PTO at Tess's old school. Amy, Lisa, Janice—no, Janine. Wait, was it Janice? Janine. Right.

Come on, Cam. You barely know their names. Are you really going to look them up?

Maybe. Anyway, sometimes she's not great with names, but that doesn't mean anything.

After meeting Kathy, for instance, Cam kept wanting to call her something else. What, exactly, she wasn't sure. It was just that Kathy didn't seem to fit right.

Still—it's kind of surprising Cam had such a hard time with it, since Kathy is one of the most common names in that particular generation. Must have been the booze doing a number on her memory, since there were no pregnancy hormones to blame then.

Soon enough, though, the hormones will be history. The next thing Cam knows, she'll be back on the playground with a new toddler in tow. There will be new moms to meet . . .

Right, and they'll probably all be, quite

literally, new moms. In their late twenties or early thirties, first-timer visitors to the insular world that revolves around Noggin, Go-Gurt, and Crayola mess-free finger paint.

I've already been there, done that.

But it might be fun to go back. To do things differently this time around. Stress less, linger more, make new friends . . .

You're going to need them, since you won't have a husband this time around.

But she will have Tess. She'll be a big help.

Or will she? She's never been around small children. And she's still pretty needy, herself.

Cam looks toward the beach-access path, hoping to catch a reassuring glance of Tess, safely back with her ice cream.

No sign of her yet.

Cam shifts uneasily in her chair, as a sense of apprehension slips in to make her shiver in the hot sun.

The binoculars will do nicely; the purchase was a success. After dark, the night vision feature can be tested, but it's sure to prove effective.

Back into the shopping bag they go, along with the receipt, the amount paid in cash, of course. There will be no credit card to trace the buyer to the sporting goods superstore out on the highway.

Nor—in the unlikely event that suspicions arise—will anyone ever be able to link a paper trail to the Texas mail order company. No records at the Trenton electronics store where an impressive-looking video camera just happened to be on sale last month, and not at the adjacent Home Depot, where there were a number of supplies to replenish: rope, duct tape, a flashlight. All bought at different times, from a different checkout cashier.

Everything is safely tucked away; no need to bring any of it out here to the beach. The binoculars, though, are a different story. They needed to be tested, to see whether they were worth the exorbitant price.

Yes. Well worth it. They really are as powerful as the salesman claimed.

Perfect.

Now all there is to do is wait for the right time.

The shopping bag slips easily into the bottom of the beach bag, beneath a towel, a book, sunscreen, a hat . . . everything an ordinary beachgoer might need for an innocent day at the shore.

Well, of course. When it comes to charades, I'm as skilled as . . . well, as she is.

But in the end, every game has a winner and a loser.

And I never lose.

Chapter Eight

Tess and Beth are still nowhere to be seen.

Debbie is back at last, though, with a full plastic pitcher in her hand and a stack of plastic cups sticking out of her beach bag. Three of them.

Why three? Cam wonders distractedly, her nerves on edge with Tess out of view.

"Sorry it took forever, but how's this for chair-side service?" Debbie asks. "Who needs cabana boys?"

Oh—Cam realizes why Debbie brought a third cup. She isn't alone. Trailing behind her is a tall blonde in sunglasses, shorts, and a T-shirt. She's carrying a straw beach bag.

"This is Gwen. Gwen, Cam."

"Nice to meet you." Gwen politely extends a hand.

"You, too," Shaking Gwen's right hand, Cam automatically checks the ring finger on her left.

She's been doing that lately—looking to see who's wearing a ring and who isn't. Around Debbie, ring fingers tend to be bare, as Gwen's is.

Is she single? Gay? Divorced? Married, perhaps, but for whatever reason not wearing a wedding band?

My God, why do you care? Cam asks herself, annoyed.

Again, she glances at the dunes. Where's Tess?

Having settled into her own sand chair again, Debbie points to the empty seats that were quickly vacated by the kids. "Sit, Gwen."

Gwen sits.

Debbie begins filling the plastic cups with white slush from the pitcher. Cam wants to stop her before she gets to the third, but she doesn't.

I'll just take it, she decides, *and hold it, and dump it out gradually whenever no one's looking*. That's the easiest way to handle it—especially with a newcomer in their midst, and her growing sense of uneasiness.

She shouldn't have let Tess go get ice cream. She should have just said no.

Yeah, that would go over about as well as insisting Tess wear floaties if she goes into the water.

Cam tells herself Tess is probably fine, and wishes she could push aside the unsettled feeling.

To distract herself she looks at Gwen again, sizing her up beyond the ring finger. For all Cam knows her face might very well be gorgeous beyond the glasses, but her hair has slightly dark roots, she's got cellulite on her thighs and a faint network of varicose veins on her legs. Physical imperfection—a welcome sight, given Debbie's striking beauty and Cam's pregnancy weight gain.

"What, no pineapple garnish and paper umbrella?" Gwen fake-chides Debbie, who cheerfully gives her the finger.

"So you guys just met?" Cam asks, a little taken aback by the easy rapport between them.

"Oh, no—we knew each other back home, years ago," Debbie replies. "What, you think I'd invite a perfect stranger to sit with us?"

Sure I do, Cam thinks, amused. Perfect strangers are exactly Debbie's style. For hanging out, for watching kids.

Aloud, she says, "Wow . . . that's some coincidence."

"What's a coincidence?" Debbie asks.

"That you two ran into each other here." She tries not to look down at the cup in her hand. The sun is hot, and she's thirsty.

"Not really. We're staying in the same house." Careful not to spill her own drink, Gwen adjusts her chair back and kicks her flip-flops into the sand.

"Really?" Cam raises her eyebrows. "That's an even bigger coincidence."

"Didn't anyone ever tell you there are no real coincidences?" Gwen asks with a grin. "We're both renting it from a mutual old friend back home. Harry Myers."

"He's owned the house on Dolphin forever," Debbie adds. "I used to come here with my parents, and then later, with what's-his-name."

"Who?" Gwen asks.

"My ex." Debbie sips her drink, then adds, "I don't like to say his name, because it makes him sound human, and he's not. But it's Gregg."

"Yeah, I know how that goes. I've got a Gregg of my own."

"Gwen's divorced, too," Debbie informs Cam.

Too?

Does she mean, Gwen's divorced like me? *Or Gwen's divorced like* us?

Cam wants to point out that she herself is merely separated, but she doesn't.

Again, she looks at the drink in her hand, wishing she could gulp it down. But only, she tells herself, because it looks refreshing and she's thirsty. Not because there's rum in it and she's growing more tense by the second.

She lowers the cup to the side of her chair away from the others and tilts it, allowing some of the white foam to run out into the sand.

"So when did you say your daughter is coming out here?" Debbie asks Gwen, who is sipping her own drink.

"Not until August. She's a junior counselor this year, at a sleepaway camp in Maine."

"What are you going to do with yourself alone out here for a month?"

"I'll keep busy, I'm sure," Gwen replies.

Cam said the same thing to Tess yesterday when she asked, yet again, what Cam is going to do all weekend without her.

Debbie nods and doesn't press Gwen, unlike Tess, who wanted to know exactly what Cam would do to keep busy while she was with her dad.

"I'll read, and go for walks. Maybe I'll go see Granddad play somewhere with his band, too." If she can track him down. Her father has been making himself pretty scarce lately. "Or I'll just relax here. I'll be fine."

Tess didn't seem to believe that. Cam didn't believe it, either. Still doesn't, now that her lonely long weekend is looming.

She just hopes it doesn't rain.

Or maybe she should hope that it does. That way, she can hole up in the cottage and pretend it's just another stormy day at the beach instead of a family holiday.

"I swear, I'm so used to 'keeping busy,'" Gwen comments, "that I don't think I'd know how to mope anymore if I wanted to."

"There's the spirit." Debbie lifts her glass in a toast. "Life's too short for moping. Maybe I'm lucky I have to work."

"Well, I have to say, I wouldn't mind getting on a plane and flying away some days," Gwen says with a laugh.

Cam checks, again, to see if Tess is on her way back yet. Nope.

"How old is your daughter?" she asks Gwen.

"Casey's fifteen."

"So she's spending the summer at camp?"

"Yeah, she says beaches are boring and she wants to make money." Gwen shakes her head. "How old is your daughter?"

"Tess is fourteen, like Beth." Debbie, Cam has noticed, likes to answer questions for people. That might get annoying after awhile. Right now, though, Cam would just as soon have her own personal spokesperson so she can focus on emptying her glass little by little, and worrying about Tess.

How long can it possibly take to get ice cream?

"I guess Casey will have someone other than me to hang around with when she comes down in August," Gwen says.

"You mean your daughter doesn't want to hang out with you 24/7?" Debbie asks dryly. "Imagine that."

"Yeah, imagine."

"Beth used to want to be with me all the time. Then she pretty much turned into my worst enemy."

"You mean since your divorce?" Gwen asks.

"I mean since she hit puberty. She can be a little beast."

"Can't they all," Gwen agrees.

Cam merely nods and keeps an eye on the beach-access path, wishing Tess would reappear.

"Wow, close call, huh?" Beth asks as they hurry back to the beach.

"Definitely. Your mother would have killed us if she saw."

"Nah," Beth said. "She wouldn't have been thrilled, but she wouldn't have killed us."

"Well, she would have told my mother, and my mother would definitely kill me if she knew."

"Good thing she doesn't know then, right? And she's not going to find out. So no big deal. Right?" Beth flashes her a white, perfect smile.

"Right." Tess tries to smile back.

They made their way along the road, flip-flops slapping. Tess's are constructed of cheap rubber and plastic, bought at a drugstore in town. Mom felt so bad about what happened at Lily's party that she offered to replace the expensive pair Tess left behind there, but Tess didn't want her to. Every time she wore them, she'd only be reminded of that awful, humiliating day.

It's not as if she doesn't still think about it—a lot—but sometimes, she feels like it happened to someone else.

"It's so freaking hot," Beth comments.

"Yeah. We should go in the water."

"You can. I'm not."

"I bet it's not that cold."

"Who cares about cold? There are sharks in there."

"They're way out, though."

"Uh-uh. My mother said a bunch of people got eaten by a Great White really close to shore on this beach."

"A bunch of people?" Tess asks, shuddering. Maybe she won't go in after all.

"Maybe it was just two, but it was horrible."

"When did it happen?"

"Like, almost a hundred years ago or something."

"*A hundred years ago?* So you're not going to go in the water because there was a shark in it a hundred years ago?"

"Nope." Beth lifts her glossy black hair away from her neck. "No way. Sharks live a really long time. Are you going in?"

"Maybe. I mean, it's really hot." Tess wipes a trickle of sweat from her forehead.

"You're not afraid of sharks?"

"Not really. I guess I never thought about it."

"Well, you should. You could die."

"What are the odds of that?"

Beth shrugs and they walk on in silence for a moment.

Up here, away from the water, the briny air smells of hot asphalt, fried seafood, and last night's beer. Tess decides it's kind of sickening in this heat.

"Oh, wait—" Beth stops walking and grabs her arm. "We need to get ice cream before we go back down. That way, they won't get suspicious."

"They might if we show up with, like, full ice-cream cones. They'll know we just got them, because otherwise they'd be melted, and they'll wonder what we were doing for the past twenty minutes till now."

"Good point. You should be a detective, Tess."

She can't help but feel flattered by Beth's approving nod.

Unlike Lily and Morrow, Beth makes her feel good about herself. Like she fits in. Which she doesn't back home.

Tess doesn't care if she never goes back to Montclair again, but that's not going to happen. Summer's going to end and school's going to start and she's going to be stuck seeing Lily and Morrow and Chad every day, knowing they're all laughing about her.

Mom says by then they'll have forgotten all about it, but Tess knows better.

They won't forget.

Her worst nightmare, which was once her most fervent dream, would be to run into Heath Pickering here on Long Beach Island. So far it hasn't happened, but she keeps an eye out for him everywhere she goes. Especially on the white wooden lifeguard stands that tower above the beach.

"Okay, so we'll say we got ice cream and stayed up here and ate it," Beth decides. "Right?"

"Right."

"Cool." Beth sighs. "I wish you weren't going away tomorrow. That sucks."

"Yeah."

"Can't you just tell your dad you don't want to go?"

"He'd feel bad," says Tess, who'd already considered, and ruled out, that idea.

"So what? He's done plenty of stuff that makes you feel bad, right?"

"Not really."

"Oh, come on. How about leaving you?"

"He didn't leave me. He left my mother."

"He left both of you. And don't pretend it didn't make you feel bad, because I've been there."

"I thought you wanted your dad to move out. I thought you hated him."

Beth hesitates.

"Yeah, I did," she says. "I mean, I do. And so does my mom. He's a worthless piece of crap."

Tess had heard Beth's mother say exactly the same thing about Beth's dad. In exactly the same harsh tone.

No matter what her own father did—or does—Tess can't imagine talking about him that way. Either Beth's father is really, really horrible or Beth's mother is really, really bitter. Maybe both.

At least Mom never says anything bad about Dad. Thank God.

Tess gets the feeling she isn't even mad at him for leaving. And Dad doesn't seem mad at Mom, either.

Divorces are supposed to be angry

and bitter, right? That's how it's been for all her friends' parents.

But Mom and Dad are just sad. And wistful.

Maybe that means there's hope.

Maybe, when Dad shows up tomorrow to pick up Tess, he and Mom will realize they're still in love and everything will get back to normal and . . .

And then what?

We all live happily ever after?

Oh, please. Tess is disgusted by her naive wishful thinking. She's not a little girl any more, believing in fairy tales.

The real world basically sucks. The older she gets, the more she realizes that.

The sooner she stops holding out hope for her parents' marriage, the better it will be for everyone.

Look at Beth. She's not sitting around pining for the good old days—though, in Beth's case, the old days weren't very good, to say the least.

But that doesn't matter. What matters is that Beth has put the past behind her and moved on.

I need to move on, too. I need to grow up.

Yeah, and the way things have gone so far, Tess has a feeling that being here this summer, with Beth, is going to accomplish that task pretty quickly.

Sitting across a weathered picnic table from Randy, Lucinda swats at a persistent fly that apparently didn't get its fill on her burger and is now buzzing around her funnel cake. More flies buzz around a nearby garbage can.

The air is still and steamy. A stereo in a nearby house is blasting ancient Bon Jovi through the screens; and around the corner, by the condiments, some little kid is screaming because he dropped his hot dog in the dirt.

Maybe Lucinda should have accepted Randy's invitation to an air-conditioned marina restaurant on the bay in Ship Bottom as opposed to this beachside grill in Beach Haven. But once she glimpsed the blue Atlantic beyond the dunes at the end of the side street, she decided she wanted to eat outside, by the water.

"What better way to soak up the local atmosphere?" she asked him.

"You've been to Long Beach Island before, though, right?"

"Right," she said. *But never with you.*

And she isn't with him now, other than to eat lunch and fill him in on the case.

So here they are, polishing off dessert—a mango water ice for Randy, and this golden, powdered sugar–dusted nest of deep-fried calories for Lucinda. She knows it's crap. She's pretty sure the day is going to come when she'll have to watch what she eats. But at thirty-one, she can still put away anything she wants and still wear size 6 jeans.

The Sloans have always been blessed with good metabolism.

Some back in Philly would say the Main Line Sloans have always been blessed, period.

Lucinda knows better.

"So that's pretty much it," she says at last, having finished a running update on just about everyone she and Randy ever worked with back in the old days, before he fled.

"That's it? You mean there's no more?"

he asks wryly. "No news on the desk sergeant's nephew's cleaning lady's gall bladder surgery?"

She swats at Randy's brown arm instead of the fly. "Hey! I thought you asked how everyone was."

"I did. I didn't expect you to tell me how *everyone* was."

"You didn't seem bored."

"You could never bore me."

Is he flirting with her?

Hard to tell. They're both wearing sunglasses. She can't see his striking blue eyes. That's probably a good thing. Those eyes always did get to her. The eyes, the dimples, the dark coloring—an exotic combination, courtesy of his Arabian father and Irish mother.

Suddenly there's a rush of squawking birds, flapping wings and swooping low. Lucinda turns to see some tourists a few tables away, throwing crumbs from a big pretzel.

"Idiots," she mutters, shaking her head and taking a big bite of her funnel cake.

"Trying to finish that before they start

using it for target practice? And I'm not talking with arrows."

Lucinda looks up in surprise to see Randy grinning at her. "Now who's the psychic?" she asks, returning the grin.

"Nah, not a psychic. I just know you well."

"After all these years? That's pretty amazing."

"What? That I knew you didn't want some bird crapping on your food? Or, worse yet, your head?"

"Now, see, that wouldn't be so bad," she tells him, and pops the last morsel of funnel cake into her mouth. Around a mouthful, she adds, "I heard somewhere that it's good luck if a bird poops on you, and I could use some of that right about now."

"Luck? Planning on heading down to Atlantic City from here?"

She shakes her head. "Unfortunately, no."

"So tell me about the case."

She brushes the powdered sugar off her hands and lap, then folds the grease-stained white paper plate in half.

"It's not exactly dinner table conversation, if you know what I mean."

Randy, more than most people, does know what she means.

With a nod, he says, "Let's go for a walk on the beach and you can tell me about it."

A walk on the beach. She considers making a joke about how romantic that sounds, then decides it would be inappropriate.

Inappropriate?

That's pretty much her mother's all-time favorite word.

"White shoes and handbags before Memorial Day and after Labor Day are inappropriate, Lucinda." So said the formidable Bitsy Sloan. Often.

That and, *"Asking for a rum floater on a cocktail is inappropriate, Lucinda."*

And, *"Laughing at a bawdy joke is inappropriate, Lucinda."*

How about, *"Kidding around about romance with married men is inappropriate, Lucinda."*

Ha.

She isn't in the mood to kid around, anyway. As they make their way down to the beach, she gives Randy the background on the Roby case.

"So if you've had no leads in almost a month," Randy asks as they cross the dunes onto the wide golden strand, "what brings you here?"

"That." She sweeps her hand out toward the sea.

"The ocean?"

She nods, kicks off her black leather flats, and bends to pick them up, scooping a handful of sand in the process. "And this." She lets the fine grains run through her fingers, blowing away on the warm, coconut lotion–scented wind.

"Sand?"

She nods. "The forensics team ran some tests on the little white box I told you about."

"You said it was empty."

"Pretty much. But there were grains of sand in it. They came from here."

"Long Beach Island?" He looks dubious. "You know that for an absolute fact?"

"Let's put it this way: I *know* for an absolute fact that they came from a stretch of shoreline in this general region . . .

and I *feel* they came from Long Beach Island."

Randy's mouth quirks in recognition and he nods. "Gotcha."

"I knew you would."

He always did believe in her gift—or, at least, gave her the benefit of the doubt. He was one of the few on the force who didn't question or ridicule her. That—well, after the dimples and blue eyes—was the first thing that captured her interest.

They walk down the beach, sticking close to packed wet sand at the waterline because the hot, dry sand farther up scorches the soles of Lucinda's feet and she insists on walking barefoot. She wishes she had on a bathing suit instead of black pants and a white short-sleeved blouse. At least she left her blazer in the car.

Not Detective Randall Barakat. He's wearing a jacket, dress shirt, slacks, loafers.

"So you think that little girl is somewhere on the island?" Randy asks.

"I'm not sure. I feel like she was."

"Was?"

Lucinda nods slowly.

"So you're here to find her remains?"

"I'm here to blanket this island with missing child posters that have Leah Roby's picture on them, and hope that somebody saw something and will recognize her. I'm here to find whoever took her before they strike again."

"And you think—I mean, you feel—like he's somewhere on the island?"

Lucinda nods again. There isn't a doubt in her mind.

"How long are you staying?"

The question gives her pause. Truthfully, she has no idea. She figured just for the afternoon, but now that she's here . . .

"As long as it takes," she hears herself say.

The late-afternoon sun has slid low on the horizon, and a steady stream of beachgoers head toward the dunes. Bedraggled, sun-toasted, wrapped in damp towels, people lug chairs, umbrellas, coolers, and boogie boards over the sand. Air-conditioning, aloe, herbal shampoo, dry clothes, deck grills, cold drinks await.

Straw tote over her shoulder and folded sand chair in hand, Cam walks toward the access path with Debbie and Gwen. Trailing behind with a shovel and a sloshing bucket full of shells and sea life is Jonathan; leading the way are Tess and Beth, colorful towels tied low, sarong-style around their waists, their heads close together as they chat intensely about whatever it is teenaged girls chat intensely about.

Boys, if memory serves Cam. Clothes. Music. Some things, she suspects, never change.

Cam is glad Tess has found a summer friend—even if she does look about seventeen and is a whole head taller than Tess, who from here could be a scrawny little girl beside Beth.

Cam wonders if Tess is reluctant to leave tomorrow with Mike. Or maybe she's looking forward to a change of scenery. Cam would welcome one, right about now.

She could always head back to Montclair for the weekend herself.

But what would I do there?

At least here, there's the beach, and Debbie. And Gwen, for that matter, whom Cam found herself inviting to get together over the weekend for a movie or a walk.

"We can keep each other company," she said casually.

"What about me?" Debbie asked.

"You've got your kids," Gwen piped up. "That would cramp our style."

Cam couldn't see her eyes behind her sunglasses, but her mouth was grinning slyly.

"Listen, Jonathan has his heart set on minigolf and I've been putting him off. You two have to come with us."

"Why don't you just make Beth take him?" Cam asked, and added—but only to herself—*or find a hired woman to do it?*

"Are you kidding? Beth is much too cool for minigolf."

"So am I," Cam said with a grin.

But the truth is, she's on her own this weekend at the shore for the first time. By this time tomorrow, minigolf might actually sound appealing.

Or maybe she'll go through all those notebooks, which she stashed on the top shelf of the bedroom closet, where Mike used to keep his golf shoes.

"Don't forget, you're both coming to my barbecue this weekend," Debbie informs them now. "Day after tomorrow."

"Is that an order?" Gwen asks.

"Absolutely. So mark your calendars."

"That'll be the only thing on mine," Cam says wryly.

"Mine, too, pretty much," Gwen agrees. "What time is your ex-husband picking up your daughter tomorrow morning?"

Cam doesn't correct her on the *ex. It's just semantics,* she tells herself, even though it bothers her. "About seven thirty, he said."

"At that ungodly hour," Debbie says, "you should shove her out the door, roll over, and go back to sleep."

Cam nods, wishing it could be that simple.

Maybe that's why she's been on edge all day—even after Tess safely returned from her ice cream mission.

Tomorrow, she'll come face-to-face with Mike.

Tomorrow will either be the beginning of a new chapter in their marriage . . .

Or the end of the final one.

"Let's get cleaned up and go out to dinner," Debbie suggests. "I'm dying for a steak."

"That sounds good," Gwen agrees. "I'm in."

"Cam?"

"With the kids?"

"Are you kidding? G-N-O."

"Don't you mean N-O?" Gwen asks. "Or is the G silent?"

"You goof. I mean G-N-O . . . Girls Night Out. We'll get the kids some pizza and a movie and leave them at my house."

"It's my last night with Tess."

"Ever?" Debbie asks flippantly, and Cam wants to tell her that isn't funny.

Not at all.

But she forces a smile anyway, telling herself she's overreacting. Tess is fine. Safe and sound. Nothing bad is going to happen to her.

"Tess!" Debbie calls. "Hey, Tess, come here."

Tess turns, then trots agreeably toward them.

"Would you rather go out to dinner with me and your mom and Gwen or have pizza and a movie at my place with Beth and Jonathan and maybe Tyler and Ryan if they're not staying with their dad tonight?" Tyler and Ryan are her friend Petra's kids. Tyler is thirteen, tall for his age. Cam heard Beth call him a "hottie."

"Are you kidding?" Tess lights up. "Pizza and a movie."

And the hottie. Cam sighs inwardly.

Debbie directs a slightly smug expression at her. "Great. We're all set. I'll call Petra when I get home."

"You know, I really thought you were going to stand me up tonight," Kate comments, setting her nearly empty wineglass back on the white tablecloth.

Mike forces himself to look her in the eye. "Really? Why did you think that?"

"Because you didn't return my call or my e-mail until the end of the day." Kate leans back in her chair and folds her arms across her black designer bodice.

Her left wrist, encircled by a watch that costs about the same as a year of Tess's school tuition, is positioned on top—probably deliberately. As if that would impress him.

"Either you were completely unreachable, or you wanted to leave me hanging." Kate tilts her head. "Which was it?"

"Which do you think?"

"In your business, you can't afford to be unreachable. That's what I think."

Mike wonders what to say to that, then realizes he doesn't *have* to say anything at all.

He doesn't owe anything to this woman, this stranger, with her bony bare shoulders and pale city skin, black eyeliner, and fancy perfume that smells nothing like the one he bought for Cam on their anniversary.

He asked Kate out the first time, a few weeks ago, because it seemed like a good idea to start dating.

"You might as well," is how his friend Tony—on his second marriage—put it.

For some reason, Mike listened to him.

You might as well?

Is that ever a good reason to do anything?

He slept with her for the same reason. Just once. Because she was willing, and it had been awhile. Yes, he knew it was wrong from the first kiss, but he wasn't thinking with his brain at that point.

Afterward, he couldn't get out of there fast enough. He found his discarded clothes beside her bed, threw them on in the dark, and left.

He might never have even seen her again if he hadn't stupidly forgotten to check and make sure his wallet hadn't dropped out of his pants pocket onto the floor.

He had to meet her the next day to get it back. She made him feel so guilty for running away in the night that he wound up asking her out again.

You're an ass, Mike tells himself, buttering another hot roll from the basket on the table.

Then, realizing what he's doing, he sets it on his plate.

Mike doesn't want a roll. He's had his fill.

"Our appetizers should be here by now. Where's the waiter?" Kate asks, looking around impatiently.

Mike doesn't want to date her. He's had his fill.

If they hadn't already ordered their meals, he'd be tempted to cut this short right now. But that would be complicated, and anyway, after the way he ran out on her the one night they slept together, he's determined to be a gentleman now.

Okay. So he'll share this last dinner with Kate, then see her to her building's lobby with the taxi meter running.

Then what?

Go home to his empty apartment downtown. He can't think of anything more depressing.

"Waiter? Excuse me?" Kate waves her hand, fancy watch gleaming.

Well, there is one thing more depressing than going home alone.

Finding himself in Kate's bed.

He pushes the thought from his mind. Never again.

At this hour of the night, with traffic

thinning, he could make it down to Beach Haven in a couple of hours. Be there before midnight. It's tempting . . .

But not a good idea.

Better to start fresh, in the morning, as planned.

He'll get up early, drive to the shore, and see his daughter . . . and his wife.

Don't you mean soon-to-be-ex-wife?

Maybe not.

What if he told Cam it was all a big mistake? That he was wrong? That he'd give anything for a second chance?

What would she say?

There's only one way to find out.

No one argued with Cam when she volunteered to be the designated driver tonight—a brilliant move. She can sip Pellegrino in peace as Debbie, Gwen, and Petra drink red wine and trash their ex-husbands.

Well, Debbie has done most of the talking, alluding to Gregg's other women, a gambling problem, and a string of lost jobs. No wonder she has to work.

Now, as dinner winds down, she announces, "Dolores will be around this weekend, so you guys will have to let me know what you think of her."

"Who's Dolores?" asks Petra, a heavyset brunette with bleached-blond hair and a smoker's deep voice.

"She's the one who's taking care of my kids while I'm gone. They all need to get used to each other before I go flying away after the weekend."

"Where'd you find her?"

"I actually met her walking down the street. We started talking and she said she was looking for work."

Gwen is incredulous. "You just happened to meet a nanny walking down the street?"

"Not a *nanny*. She's just a hired woman."

Cam sighs inwardly, wishing she were home with Tess, grateful when the check arrives.

"Someone figure out how much we each owe," Debbie commands as they all reach for their purses. "I stink at math."

"I'll do it." Gwen opens her large wallet, revealing a slim calculator tucked into a pocket.

"You're totally equipped," Debbie marvels.

"That's because I stink at math, too. Not to mention, I can't see very well in my old age." Gwen removes a clear plastic rectangle, places it over the bottom of the bill, and presses a little button that lights it up.

"Whoa! What's that, a fancy magnifying glass?" Petra peers over Gwen's shoulder. "What else have you got in that wallet of yours?"

Gwen laughs. "Just the usual. Driver's license. Credit cards. Pictures of my daughter."

"Ooh, let's see."

Gwen passes around a school photo of a girl with dark braids and glasses. "That's Casey."

"Cute," Petra says approvingly. "Want to see Tyler and Ryan?"

"Sure."

Petra fishes in her own wallet for pictures of her boys as Cam sneaks a peak at her watch. She was hoping to spend some time with Tess, but by the time they get home it'll be time for bed, since Mike will be there early tomorrow.

And I need to figure out what I'm going to say to him and how I'm going to say it.

Of course, Debbie has to show off several pictures of Beth and Jonathan, and they all want to see one of Tess.

"You know, she really looks nothing like you," Gwen comments.

"I know," Cam says, longing to just get moving. "People say that all the time. She looks just like my husband."

"Ex-husband," Debbie corrects.

"Not really. We're just separated."

Cam hates the knowing look the other three share.

At last, the photos are back where they belong, the check is paid, and Cam digs for her car keys as they head for the door.

The moment they're out in the steamy night air, Petra lights up a cigarette.

"Sorry," she says, fanning the smoke away from the others. "Been at it since I was twelve and I can't quit. I've tried. Do you guys mind waiting a few minutes before we get into the car?"

"No, that's fine."

"Why don't we just take a walk before we go home?" Debbie suggests. "I need to work off that twice-baked potato. What do you say?"

Gwen says yes.

Not wanting to be the lone party pooper, Cam reluctantly agrees. She keeps a distance from the cigarette fumes as they walk.

The sidewalks are crowded tonight with tourists, strolling retirees, roving groups of teenagers. Debbie buys a box of saltwater taffy as they pass one of the ubiquitous stands, and offers it around.

"Are you kidding? That will pull out every filling I have." Gwen shakes her head.

"Plus, how do you eat so much and stay so thin?" Petra throws her cigarette down on the sidewalk and grinds it with the toe of her sandal.

"Fast metabolism." Debbie blithely unwraps another piece of taffy.

"Casey's like that."

"My boys are like that, too," Petra tells Gwen. "They fill themselves up with all kinds of crap—fast food, candy, soda, chips—and they never gain a pound. Half the time I live on broccoli and salad, and look at me."

"Same here," Gwen says, as Cam sneaks another peak at her watch and Debbie stops walking to peer into a shop window. "And Casey's a tiny little thing, too. Like our friend, here."

"Who, me?" Debbie crumples a taffy wrapper. "Let's go check out this store. I like that beach bag."

"Don't you have one just like it?" Cam asks.

"Not exactly." Debbie tosses the wrapper toward a garbage can. Misses. Doesn't bother to pick it up. "Come on."

Cam reluctantly follows the three of them into the store. It's a beach boutique just like countless other beach boutiques up and down the main drag: brightly lit, crowded, filled with T-shirts, sunscreen, jewelry, souvenirs.

Debbie decides to try on a couple of bathing suits and disappears into the dressing room. Gwen hunts through bracelets, wanting to buy one for her daughter as a gift.

"I'm going to go out for another smoke," Petra decides. "Want to come?"

"No," Cam says quickly, "I want to browse a little."

What she really wants is to go home. They checked in on the kids less than ten minutes ago. They were playing Scene It? and having a blast. Still, Cam doesn't like leaving Tess at night after all that's happened.

Like what? she asks herself, gazing into a jewelry case at a collection of earrings. *Nothing's happened.*

You're just feeling like something might.

"Which do you like better?" Gwen asks, nearby.

Cam turns and sees her holding out two shiny charms. One is a starfish, the other a lighthouse. Both have dangling silver flags etched *New Jersey*.

"They're both nice."

"Yeah? Maybe I'll get her both, then," Gwen says, and drifts away.

Cam looks back at the jewelry case, wondering if there's anything in it Tess might like.

"Can I help you, ma'am?" a dreadlocked, college-aged salesgirl asks.

"No, thank you, I was just—"

She breaks off as something catches her eye.

Her pulse picks up as she leans in to get a better look.

"Would you like to see some earrings, ma'am?"

"Please. The ones right here."

"These?"

"No, those. The black ones with the gold posts."

Cam shifts her weight uneasily as the girl lifts them out and hands them across the glass counter.

The moment they're in her hand, a wave of dizziness sweeps over Cam. But this time, it's not a vision coming on. Just a pervasive sense of foreboding.

"Pretty, aren't they?"

She nods, her trembling forefinger stroking the glossy triangular pendants. "What kind of stones are these?"

"Oh, they're not stones. They're sharks' teeth. Real ones. Found right here on the island."

* * *

What could be more providential than a summer house without air-conditioning on a stifling July night?

Most people could probably think of a number of things.

Not me. For me, this is the jackpot.

The windows are wide open at the two-story bay-front house in Loveladies, a largely residential community on the island's northern end. There are no blinds or shades to hinder what little sea breeze there is. It's a Peeping Tom's dream come true . . .

Not that I'm a Peeping Tom. I'm not out here with night vision binoculars, getting eaten alive by mosquitoes, for kicks.

These people aren't big on conserving energy. Even now, well past midnight, many of the rooms are brightly lit including two on the first floor. It's an island house, so that's where the smaller bedrooms are, with the main living area—and probably the master suite—on the floor above, with the better view of the water.

In a first-floor corner room, the view

is, quite conveniently, a clump of tall shrubs—the ideal hiding place.

Inside, the girl is clearly visible. She's on her bed, painting her toenails a bright, bold pink. It clashes with her sunburnt face and fair, freckled red-headedness, which, if one didn't know better, would appear God-given.

I know better.

I know what she used to look like, who she used to be.

She's wearing a cotton tank top and boxer shorts. Skimpy attire for someone who's sitting in front of a window that anyone might come along and look into, for God's sake.

There's something around her neck . . . Can it be . . . ?

It's impossible to tell at this angle, even through the binoculars.

I need to get a little closer so that I can—

A twig snaps with the forward movement; the telltale sound seems to boom through the night.

Did she hear?

How could she not?

But the girl—whatever she's calling

herself these days—hasn't so much as glanced up from her toes.

Ah—there's the reason: in her long orange-red hair, crimped from its usual daytime braids, thin white earphone cords are plainly visible. She's plugged into something, deaf to a stray footfall outside her window.

Does anyone her age ever listen anymore? Do they really need that constant noise to fill their heads?

It's not noise—it's music!

That's what they probably say to their elders, who just don't get it.

It's what I used to say myself. But that really was music, back then.

What kids listen to today—with its throbbing beat and angry words that are shouted, not sung and thus barely qualify as lyrics—isn't music.

The girl screws the polish brush back into the bottle, leans back on her elbows, and extends her freckled legs into the air, waving her painted toes back and forth as if to dry them.

At this angle, with her head thrown back, her neck is plainly visible.

And, yes, hanging from a silver chain there is a black shark's tooth.

So she got the little gift from a so-called secret admirer.

Does she have any idea who it's from?

Ha. If she did, she wouldn't be wearing it.

There she sits, clueless, unaware that her shameless masquerade is about to come to a close. There she sits, pretending to be somebody else . . .

But I know exactly who she is.

Anger is beginning to seep in, along with a surge of adrenaline that makes it almost impossible to just stand here in the shadows and watch.

But it isn't time yet. Not tonight.

Tomorrow will come soon enough.

And then she'll be mine.

Mine.

Chapter Nine

"Did you pack that extra sunscreen I left on your bed last night?" Cam stands over Tess, kneeling on her bedroom floor, zipping and unzipping the pockets on her bulging duffel bag as if she's looking for something.

"Yeah. Got it. But it's not like we'll be on the beach. I mean, there's no beach in DC, right?"

"There's sun in DC. Make sure you protect your skin. You're so fair, you'll burn in a second." *And I won't be there to remind you.*

A memory flashes into Cam's head: chasing Tess on the beach a good twelve years ago, her little girl wearing nothing but a diaper and a broad-brimmed floppy hat. All that tender baby skin exposed, and Tess screaming when Cam caught her, wriggling maniacally as she smeared sunscreen over chubby legs and arms and wrangled her into a ruffly pink swimsuit.

"Mom, I've got everything you put on the list, and a lot of extra stuff, too. You don't need to stand over me and catalogue things."

But Cam does need to.

"What about the charger for your cell phone?" she asks her daughter. "I don't think I remembered to write it on the list."

"You did."

"So did you pack it?"

"I'm pretty sure." Tess peers into a side pouch.

"Is it there?"

"I'm not looking for it."

"What *are* you looking for?"

"Nothing. Just making sure I've got everything, okay?"

I'm bugging her. But I can't help it.

"Well, if you forgot anything important, let Dad know."

Tess nods and unzips another compartment.

Cam checks the digital clock on the night table, then sneaks a peek at her own reflection in the mirror above the bureau.

She's looking pretty damn good for seven twenty-five in the morning, thank you very much. She's looking pretty good for any hour of any recent day, actually. She's made sure of it.

She set the alarm for five forty-five but was awake a half hour before it rang, nervous about what lies ahead.

She got up and got busy, using a special conditioning pack on her hair in the shower, then blowing it dry, something she rarely bothers to do. She put on makeup that accents her bronze coloring, courtesy of these past few days on the beach.

It took her a good twenty minutes trying to find the perfect outfit—something that would flatter her, hide her bump, and be comfortable. Tall order.

The heat and humidity didn't break overnight so she's forced to show more skin than she'd like. Her upper arms, while fleshier than usual, are nicely tanned, bared in a loose-fitting off-white linen tank. With it she's wearing a crinkly floral print skirt and the beaded hemp anklet she bought last night.

When Debbie and Gwen had come out of the dressing room, Cam feigned interest in the jewelry she was still standing beside. Debbie talked her into the ankle bracelet, saying hemp would look hip.

Still feeling rattled, Cam mindlessly obliged, but it turns out Debbie was right. With her tanned bare feet, coral-pedicured toenails, and cute leather thong sandals, the hemp wrapped around her ankle does look hip. Sexy, even. As hip and sexy as a pregnant middle-aged mom can be, anyway. Even Tess approved.

So, yeah—Cam looks good today. Which makes her *feel* good. It's nice to be out of the terry cover-up and looking presentable for a change.

Her stomach is definitely protruding beneath the layered top and skirt, though. If she hadn't been planning to spill her news to Mike when he gets here, she'd have to carry around a bag of groceries or something.

"Uh-oh, is that Dad?" Tess asks, as the sound of tires crunching on gravel floats in through the screened window.

"Probably . . . it's time. Why 'uh-oh'?"

"Because I'm not ready yet."

Outside, the engine cuts off, a door slams, footsteps on the path.

"Can you tell him I need another few minutes?"

She's stalling, Cam realizes. Her bag is packed, she's dressed and ready. *Why prolong it?*

Then again, who cares why? Cam needs time alone with Mike.

"No problem." *Take five minutes. Take ten.*

She closes Tess's bedroom door behind her and heads down the short hall to the living room, which she straightened before going to bed last night. The simple chintz and wicker cottage furniture, rag rugs, and board floors look charming with the sunlight streaming in the windows. On the weathered pine coffee table: a vase of violet-colored flowers she picked from the yard last night and a stack of magazines arranged in a perfect fan. Too perfect.

She pauses to scatter them a little—*there, that's better*—then picks up a magazine and holds it casually against her stomach, as if she were just reading. It doesn't camouflage the bump entirely, but it helps.

She takes a deep breath and opens the door.

Ah. Mike, up close and in person.

A Fourth of July sky lights up inside her and if she's not mistaken, he's pretty happy to see her, too.

Or maybe he's just glad to be out of the city, glad to have the long weekend, glad about leaving with Tess.

Whatever.

He looks good. Familiar. Clean-shaven, his light brown hair cut short and a little stubbly on top. He's wearing a polo shirt, khaki shorts, deck shoes.

"Hi," he says, and holds out a gold cardboard box. "These are for you."

Chocolates.

Not drugstore chocolates, but Godiva.

Her stomach quivers at the sight of them, and not necessarily out of queasiness.

"Thank you." She tries not to smile too big; tries not to seem surprised.

Mike brought her chocolates. What does this mean?

"You're welcome."

He's smiling at her. What does that mean?

"Tess isn't ready just yet. Come on in."

"Oh . . . thanks." He steps over the threshold he's crossed hundreds, maybe thousands, of times before, into a house that is, technically, still his.

Cam catches a familiar whiff of his aftershave, and scenes from countless mornings of sharing a bathroom sink flash through her brain.

"How's Tess?" Mike asks. "She said she made a new friend . . . What's her name again?"

"Beth."

"Right. Do you like her?"

Cam hesitates just long enough for Mike to say, "Uh-oh."

"No, I like her. She just seems . . . I don't know . . . older than Tess. More mature. Like the rest of the girls their age, I guess. I feel like Tess is still a little girl. I guess that's because she still looks like one."

"Thank God. Is she still hung up on what happened back home?"

"Not really." Cam is surprised Mike even asked about that.

Back in June when she told him what had happened, he didn't seem the least bit concerned.

What he'd said was, "Oh, thank God. She had a fight with her friends? I thought you were going to say something really awful happened, the way you sounded."

Cam, having just spent the rest of the day in a doctor's waiting room for a tetanus shot, then the better part of the night trying to console her sobbing, wounded, limping daughter, knew Mike just didn't get it.

Not because he's a man, because he's always been a loving, tender, sensitive guy.

No, he didn't get how bad it was because he wasn't *there*. Period.

You can leave and say you're going to be a hands-on parent and see your child on every occasion you're officially supposed to—and then some—but when you don't live under the same roof, you just don't get it.

And Cam told him so.

He wasn't exactly thrilled to hear it.

But she doesn't want to remember that argument now. Time to move on.

"Want coffee?" She brewed some, with him in mind.

"If you're having it."

She's not. "Come on into the kitchen," she says, and leads the way.

The beach house kitchen is nothing like the sleek stainless and granite one in the Montclair house. Outdated appliances, worn laminate, stock cabinetry. They always said they'd remodel it someday.

She pours him a cup of coffee, adds milk and a packet of Splenda without asking, and hands it to him.

"Thanks. You're not having any?"

"No, I'm good. Why don't you sit down?"

She expects him to protest, or at the very least, check his watch. To her surprise, he pulls out a chair for her, then one for himself, and sits. The table is in a sunny nook off one end of the kitchen; the morning light casts a warm glow over everything.

How to begin?

Last night and this morning, she rehearsed what she was going to say. But suddenly, the script has been erased from her brain.

What matters more, though, than *how* to begin is *when* to begin—and the answer is *now*. They're on the opposite end of the house from Tess's room; she won't overhear if she stays put. But she won't for long, and Cam has to talk fast.

"Listen . . . I need to tell you something."

The words come from Mike's mouth, but he could have stolen them from her own.

That's it. That's exactly what she was going to say. Every version of her rehearsed speech began with those words.

I need to tell you something.

So now *he* needs to tell *her* something? What can it be?

Judging by the solemn look on Mike's face, it's serious.

But . . . He brought chocolates!

So? He gave her Godiva on Valentine's Day, too—just weeks before moving out. And he gave Tess that expensive camera.

Maybe today's gift was just to appease the pain of whatever's coming.

Is he going to tell her he wants to file divorce papers? Or that he's met someone else? Or wants to put the Montclair house, or this cottage, on the market?

Whatever it is, he'll have to keep it to himself until she's shared her own news, because her news might make him change his mind. About filing papers, officially moving on without her.

"Mike, wait, you need to know . . ."

She chickens out.

Say it. Just say it!

"What?" he asks expectantly.

The words are lodged in her throat.

"Before you say anything, Cam, I have to tell you—"

That's it. That does it. Mike has just unwittingly performed a verbal Heimlich, and a frantic-sounding "I'm pregnant," comes flying out of her.

He goes utterly still.

"I'm pregnant," she repeats decisively, with a firm nod in case there's any doubt in his mind.

There. It's out. At last, he knows.

In Cam's mental rehearsals of this scene—and there were many—Mike's initial reaction to her news was just as it is now: dumbfounded, jaw-dropping silence.

Ah, she knows him well.

But maybe not as well as she thought, because his greenish-hazel eyes turn to stone and he recovers his voice more quickly than she'd expected.

"Whose is it?"

It's Cam's turn to be dumbfounded—but only for a split second.

"It's yours!" Damn him. "How can you even ask me such a—"

"It's mine? Yet you didn't tell me?"

"I'm telling you now. And please keep your voice down," she adds crisply. "Tess doesn't know."

He swallows audibly, shakes his head. And she almost feels sorry for him. Almost.

"Whose is it?"

How dare he?

She glares at him.

He doesn't seem to notice. "What . . ." he begins, then clears his throat. Swallows again. "I mean . . . When are you due?"

"Sometime between Halloween and Thanksgiving."

"You don't *know?*"

"The doctor said it's hard to tell, because I was irregular and . . ." She trails off, feeling like the details are too intimate to share with him. Which is ridiculous, since they've already had a baby together, and lived a life together, and if anyone knows every intimate detail about her it's Mike.

It *was* Mike, anyway.

The sunlight that had seemed so cheerful just a short time ago now feels harsh. In its glare, Mike's eyes are rimmed by dark circles and a fine network of wrinkles. He's tired, and he's getting older; they both are.

Half a lifetime together, and still there's so much he doesn't know about her.

What if she tells him the rest, right here and now?

About the visions that caused her to

start drinking in the first place. And how they've come back to haunt her now . . . fewer and farther between, less graphic, but somehow more foreboding than ever before. About her growing worry—perhaps irrational, please God, irrational—over Tess's well-being.

It would be such a relief to unburden herself on the one person who deserves the whole truth.

But that might be the nail in the coffin.

If she couldn't bring herself to tell Mike back in the old days when things were good between them, how can she possibly tell him now, when their life together is on the brink of destruction?

Maybe, if she keeps all that to herself, they still have a chance.

He sighs. "What are we going to do?"

"I don't know."

We. He said *we.* That's a good sign.

Well, of course he said "we." He's a grown man, she reminds herself, *a husband and father, not some fifteen-year-old kid with a knocked-up girlfriend.*

And he isn't talking about terminating the pregnancy when he asks what they're going to do. He's talking about bringing a baby into the current state of their marriage.

With a pang, she remembers being in labor with Tess. Remembers how at the hospital Mike never left her side for a moment, though the nurse explained that the bedside chair turned into a cot and encouraged the father-to-be to get some rest.

"Your wife is going to need you later," the nurse said.

"My wife needs me now," Mike replied.

"What about later?"

"I'll be there. I'm fine."

Day turned into night and night into the wee hours of the morning.

"Just try to get some sleep," Cam urged Mike, and the nurse turned the chair to a bed, brought sheets, a blanket, a pillow.

Mike spent all of two minutes lying on the chair-turned-cot, as Cam labored in stoic silence in the hospital bed.

Then the chair was a chair again, and Mike was sitting in it, holding her hand, watching her anxiously.

"I thought I told you to get some sleep," the nurse barked when she came back.

"Have you ever tried to sleep on that thing?" Mike retorted. "It's like a torture device."

He never moved until it was time for Tess, a wet, sticky newborn, to slide into his hands.

Cam will never forget the look on his face in that moment.

Just as she'll never forget the look on his face in this.

If she thought her news was going to heal whatever had gone wrong between them, she was wrong.

Dead wrong.

"Did you sleep well, dear?" asks the guesthouse owner, who introduced herself yesterday afternoon as Martha, or Margaret. She's watering a potted fern at the foot of the stairs as Lucinda comes down.

"I slept very well, thanks," she lies. The mattress was a sagging, spring-studded spine-killer, especially after all those exhausting hours spent papering the island with Leah Roby fliers.

"Most people do sleep well here.

There's nothing like fresh salt air. It's good for the soul."

Window air-conditioning, Lucinda can't help but think, would be even better for the soul. Or at least, for the body.

She was initially so relieved to have found a place to stay on short notice that she found herself charmed by the attic bedroom, with its white-washed sloping walls and gabled windows. Sure it was hot up there, but she optimistically decided that that was just the afternoon sun beaming in.

Evenings are supposed to cool down nicely at the shore, right?

Wrong.

After a night of tossing on the miserable mattress and sweating profusely, she has a good idea why she was actually able to find a vacancy at a beachside island inn on the night before a holiday weekend.

She'd love to check out of the Briar Beach House and return to the climate-controlled, pillow-topped comfort of her apartment back in Philadelphia. But something tells her to stick around.

And it has nothing to do with Randy being a stone's throw away.

Or with his parting words yesterday: "Give me a call tomorrow and we'll talk some more."

He wants to help her with the case, she's sure.

The case—the main reason she's here.

The only reason you're here. Keep that in mind.

"Why don't you go on into the dining porch for breakfast?" the owner suggests.

Lucinda hesitates.

"It's included in the room," the woman mentions, as if that will convince her.

She has no idea she's talking to a real-live heiress. An heiress in shorts and sneakers, whose family would have disinherited her if they could have kept it out of the papers.

Publicity is the Sloans's worst enemy.

"Thank you," Lucinda says politely. "Martha, is it?"

The woman nods her white head, pleased.

Lucinda crosses through a wallpapered parlor cluttered with far too many cheap knickknacks, following the sound of clinking silverware and mute conversation to the small screened dining porch. Frank Sinatra is playing jauntily in the background. Overhead paddle fans do little to stir the air, which smells of toast, coffee, and mildew.

There isn't an empty table among the four, where the handful of other guests are sipping coffee and eating breakfast.

Hmm. Lucinda can either choose to join the most harmless-looking of the bunch, or forego coffee and forced small talk and walk right back out again.

That seems rude, so she heads toward the only table that has just one person sitting there.

Its occupant, a middle-aged woman, looks up abruptly from her *New York Times*.

"Do you mind if I join you?"

"No, it's fine," she says a little stiffly, and Lucinda knows that it's not fine at all.

Frankly, she doesn't blame the woman. She herself is never thrilled when forced to share a table, or even a train seat, with a total stranger.

It isn't that Lucinda is shy—far from it—or a snob, or unfriendly.

For her, the problem is that, in close quarters, she tends to get impressions about people. Especially strangers. Sometimes she knows things their closest confidantes might not even know.

For example, not only does this woman, in gold earrings and a trim navy top, not want to be bothered, but she's hiding something.

That's what flashes through Lucinda's head in the moment after she sits down, and she wishes she hadn't.

"Coffee?" asks a teenaged girl in an apron, appearing with a carafe.

"Thank you."

The girl pours, then asks the woman if she'd like a warm-up.

She merely shakes her head.

She seriously wants to be left alone. The unwelcoming vibe is so palpable the girl with the coffeepot can surely feel it, too.

What's up with her? Does she have a deep, dark secret? Did she come here to the island without telling anyone where she was going? She's keeping something hidden, if not herself—that's what Lucinda's intuition tells her.

Intrigued, she wants to know more. She can't help it.

You're just nosy, she tells herself, but she can't help wondering if it's something more than that. If the woman's presence is more sinister than standoffish. Hard to tell.

She stirs sugar and plenty of half-and-half into her coffee, then takes a sip. It's awful. Watery and lukewarm. *Quelle surprise.*

This place really is a bad roadside motel masquerading as a seaside inn.

She sets her cup back into the saucer, then announces to her tablemate, "I'm Lucinda."

"Nice to meet you," the woman murmurs, eyes on the *Times*.

"I didn't catch your name."

Cornered, the woman says, with a look of resignation and a crisp snap of her newspaper as she turns the page, "It's Kathy."

* * *

There are so many questions flitting through Mike's brain, he couldn't get answers to them if he had all day.

And you don't.

Any second now, Tess is going to appear and this conversation will screech to an immediate halt, which is probably best for now.

He needs to get away from Cam; needs to process this news and figure out what to do about it.

He glances at the door; no Tess.

"Say something, Mike."

Cam looks shaken.

That pisses him off and he snaps, "How long have you known?"

"That I'm pregnant?" At his curt nod, she admits, "Since March."

March. Over three months. Staggering.

"You knew before I left, and you let me go anyway?"

"I knew right *after* you left. On St. Patrick's Day. You were already gone."

Yes. He was. He remembers St. Patrick's Day well. Watching the parade. Drinking green beer afterward at an Irish pub somewhere in the East Fifties with a bunch of guys he barely knew. No need to keep an eye on his watch and the commuter train schedule in his head. All he had to do was grab a cab for downtown whenever he felt like calling it a night.

If he'd only known—if Cam had called him the day, dammit, the *second* she found out—he'd have come right back.

Would you really?

He'd felt so damn claustrophobic then, news like this might have pushed him further away.

The most bitter irony of all: he walked into this house today planning to tell Cam he still loves her, that he wants to come home.

Now what?

Now . . . He isn't so sure.

How could she let weeks, months, go by without telling him she was pregnant? Didn't she think he had a right to know sooner?

He looks at her. Just five minutes ago, he was sitting here thinking how glad he was that it's this morning and not last night—how glad he was that it isn't Kate sitting across the table from him.

It might as well be, though. Cam feels like a stranger.

How could you keep something like this from me?

Because that's what she does, a voice answers in his head, sounding suspiciously like his father's—but it's his own. He's older, wiser, wearier. Just like his father.

She builds walls, and hides behind them. She's been doing it for years.

How can anyone have an honest relationship that way?

Frustrated, Mike reaches for the coffee he didn't really want, just for something to do.

It's too milky and not hot enough, and lands in an acrid pool in his stomach.

He'd already drunk too much of it in the car on the way down, in an effort to combat a mostly sleepless night after telling Kate he was going back to his wife.

She didn't react well. Accused him of using her, asked why he hadn't just told her before, instead of putting her through an uncomfortable dinner date.

"Because I didn't know until now," was his lame reply.

"So you're saying that being with me was what convinced you to go back to some other woman?"

That was pretty much it, yup.

Except that Cam isn't "some other woman"—she's his wife. Still.

He wanted to remind Kate of that, but he didn't. He wanted to feel sorry for her, too, but in the end, he couldn't do that, either. She's too hard, too bitter.

She's not Cam.

But do I even know Cam at all?

Aren't you supposed to know someone better and better, the more time you spend with them?

In their marriage, it's been the opposite. With every year that's passed, Cam has become more remote.

The funny thing is, today, when she opened the door and smiled at him, he thought he glimpsed the old Cam. In that instant, he felt that he was doing the right thing, coming back. Giving their marriage another chance.

He thought it right up until she dropped her bombshell.

He looks up at her again, and something stirs in his gut, in his heart, despite his anger.

"Can't you say something?" she asks again.

He can. And he does, the first thing that pops into his head: "Tess said you don't drink anymore."

Obviously caught off guard, Cam looks away, as if she doesn't like the idea of Tess and Mike talking about her behind her back.

"Is this why you stopped?" he asks.

"You mean, the pregnancy?"

"Yeah."

"There were a lot of reasons."

"So you really did stop? Cold turkey? Just like that?"

She nods.

"Was it hard?"

"Not really." She sounds surprised. "I mean, I started by going to AA, but . . . that's not really for me. Everyone seems so . . . desperate. I know it sounds bad, and everyone there probably says the same thing, but . . . I'm not like them. I never thought I belonged there in the first place."

"Then how did you end up going?"

She hesitates. "This woman . . . Kathy."

"Who is she?"

"Just . . . She's someone who lives back home."

"In Montclair? A friend of yours?"

"No, just . . . I used to see her around the neighborhood a lot, and she was always friendly. We got to talking a few times. It sounds crazy, because she's really a stranger, but I always felt like I knew her, in a way."

"It does sound crazy," Mike says, trying to picture Cam letting anyone into her private world, much less a total stranger.

"Anyway, she'd mention that she used to have a drinking problem. And I knew she went to AA. She used to talk about it a lot. And one day, she just . . . asked me if I wanted to come to a meeting with her."

"Why would she do that?"

"I don't know, maybe she thought I had a problem, too."

Maybe it was obvious that you did, Mike thinks grimly.

"So you went with her?" he asks Cam, incredulous.

"No! Not then. I mean, even when I finally went to a meeting, I never went with Kathy. But when I realized I had to do something about it, I knew where to go. And I knew she'd be there. And, of course, she became my sponsor."

Of course?

Mike doesn't know how AA works, but for some reason it bothers him—the thought of Cam telling a total stranger about her problems when she wouldn't even open up to her own husband.

You're just jealous, he tells himself. *You need to get over it. Be glad she's sober*.

"So are you still going to AA, then?"

"No, because I'm over the hurdle, and—"

On the other end of the house, a door creaks.

Cam breaks off; they both look toward the sound of footsteps, along with a heavy thudding.

Tess is coming, lugging her bag along with her.

Cam reaches across the table, lays a

hand on his forearm. He realizes she's trembling, and again, something stirs inside him.

"Don't say anything to her, Mike," she says in a low voice. "About the baby. Promise me. We should tell her together . . . when we know what we're going to do."

"What do you *want* to do?"

"Have the baby. Raise it." She shrugs. "You can be a part of things or not."

"It's my child. Did you think I wouldn't want to be a part of things?"

"That's not what I meant."

He knew that. But he can't resist making this harder than it has to be.

"What did you mean?"

"You can come back, or . . . Or you can be a single dad, with a visitation schedule for the baby just like you have for Tess."

Yeah, sure. It's hard enough for Cam to let a fourteen-year-old walk out the door. How is she going to send an infant away for hours, even days at a time?

It would be so much simpler for all of them if he just moved back home.

Simpler?

Is that a good reason to go back? Because it's simpler?

Tess appears in the doorway. "Dad!"

"There's my girl!" Mike stands, hurries to hug her. Hard. "Ready to hit the road?"

"Yeah. Mom . . ." She goes over to Cam, still sitting at the table. "Are you sure you'll be okay?"

"I'll be fine!" Cam says brightly. Unconvincingly. "Have a great time in Washington. Give my regards to George."

"Which George?"

"Take your pick. DC's full of Georges, right?" Her tone is forced. "Whatever. Have fun."

"Love you, Mom."

"Love you too, Tess."

Mike, already halfway to the door with Tess's bag, doesn't say anything at all.

Chapter Ten

Ike figures he probably shouldn't be driving in his condition.

What else is new?

He doesn't have far to go, and he knows these streets as well as he knows his own face in the mirror.

Wait—bad comparison.

Glancing at his reflection in the rearview mirror, he sees an old man looking back at him.

How the hell did this happen?

Some nights, when he's flying high, sitting in with a band for a set or two, beating those drums and singing his heart out, he feels like he's twenty again.

Yeah, and some mornings after, he wakes up feeling like he's ninety and has just been hit by a garbage truck. Smelling like it, too.

The worst is when he has no recollection of what happened the night before.

Well, that's what you get when you party too hard.

Or when you're getting too old.

This was one of those mornings.

Last thing he remembers was being on the mainland, somewhere in Manahawkin, jamming with a friend.

That was sometime yesterday . . .

Or was it?

It's too damn easy to lose track of time these days. Ike never was one to bother with a watch, much less a calendar, but this is getting ridiculous lately.

Anyway, he was in Manahawkin, and the next thing he knew he was waking up in his own backseat this morning in a familiar parking lot.

So he obviously found his way to Long Beach Island. That was fine with him. He got a greasy egg sandwich for breakfast, then stopped in at a few of his favorite haunts for some hair of the dog.

Then he remembered that it's summer

now, and his daughter and her family are on the island. So he decided to surprise them. It's been awhile since he's seen everyone, and a man needs family. Especially when that's all he's really got left in the world—just his daughter, his son-in-law, his granddaughter.

And Brenda, wherever she is.

An image flits into Ike's brain and is gone.

Brenda's face.

Huh.

Did he see her somewhere again? Maybe last night?

The Brenda in his vision just now was beautiful and young.

Must just be a long-ago memory popping up to taunt him. He couldn't have seen her. Not looking like that.

She might have been a teenager when they met but she'd be a senior citizen by now. Still beautiful, but sure as hell not young.

Even Ava wouldn't be young now. She'd be middle-aged. Would Ike recognize her if he saw her?

Probably. She always looked so much like Cam.

Then again, people change. They get older, grayer, wrinkled. They have plastic surgery, dye their hair, gain and lose weight . . .

Hell, half the time, you don't even recognize yourself in the mirror.

Meaning there's a good chance Ike wouldn't know his own daughter, his own wife, if he came face-to-face with them today. That's why it's important to look beyond surface appearances.

Because you just never know.

As he pulls up in front of Cam's beach house, Ike sees her station wagon with the oval L.B.I. sticker in the rear window.

He's vaguely reluctant to park his crappy old car in the driveway behind his daughter's Volvo, but it's much easier to do down here on the island than in Cam's fancy neighborhood in Montclair. Anyway, Ike reminds himself, she won't care what the neighbors think there or here, because he raised her right.

Still, he tucks his T-shirt into his jeans and pulls a rubber band around his straggly gray hair before walking toward the front door.

* * *

"I can't believe you came with us," Debbie tells Cam as they emerge from the crisp, air-conditioned car into what feels like a hot, sopping sponge.

"I can't believe it, either." Nor can Cam believe Debbie isn't calling out to Jonathan, who has already scrambled out and is racing through the parking lot toward Ships Ahoy, the waterside entertainment complex.

"So . . . Why did you come?"

Cam hesitates. She really isn't sure.

When Debbie called earlier this afternoon, she was on the couch in front of the fan, with a cup of iced herbal tea and a stack of Marble notebooks on the table.

She couldn't bring herself to go through them just yet, but she was planning to.

She wasn't going to budge for the rest of the day. The rest of the weekend, really.

But for some reason, she heard herself tell Debbie yes when she meant to say no.

So here she is, going to a minigolf course up the highway, a painstaking trip in holiday weekend island traffic. She must be out of her mind. Which is what she says to Debbie now, in exactly those words.

"Yes, you must be out of your mind," Debbie agrees with a shrug, aiming her key remote at the car and locking it with a double staccato chirp, "but I'm glad you are, or I'd be having no fun by myself."

"Instead, we can have no fun together—is that it?" Cam asks, and Debbie grins.

"That's exactly it. Too bad Petra and Gwen didn't come along, too."

"Yeah, well, *they're* not crazy."

"For the record, Petra *is* crazy, but she said no. Her kids are with her ex." Petra has shared custody with her ex-husband, who lives across the causeway. "And Gwen's not home, or I bet I could have talked her into it."

Maybe not.

Unlike Cam, Gwen probably didn't wake up this morning with reconciliation on her mind. Gwen didn't spend the day obsessing over everything she said, everything he said, everything either of them could have said, didn't say. She didn't have notebooks filled with notes about horrific visions of missing persons—mostly traumatized children—that she was planning to reread this weekend, just in case . . .

Well, just in case.

Nope, that was me.

And I guess I'm here because I needed to escape all of that.

Anything—even minigolf—sounded better than spending another solitary moment in that cottage.

"Talk about a crowd scene," Debbie murmurs, as they walk around a car that has its turn signal on, waiting for a space.

"This place is always jammed."

"You've been here before?"

"Oh, yeah. I think I've been to every minigolf place on the island. Tess loves it."

Mike does, too.

Not Cam. Probably because she was never was any good at it. It's not easy to hit a ball through a moving paddle wheel after a couple of glasses of wine.

Who knows? Maybe now she'll be able to hit a hole in one.

But neither Tess nor Mike will be here to see it, she reminds herself glumly.

"Come on, Mom!" Up ahead Jonathan darts around a minivan that's backing out of a parking spot.

Cam fights back the urge to tell him to be careful.

He's not *her* child, not *her* responsibility.

Her child is miles away, someone else's responsibility this weekend.

Someone else?

Mike. Her dad.

You can't really blame him, she tells herself yet again, *for how he reacted.*

He was blindsided by the news. Once he's had time to let it sink in . . .

What?

He'll say he wants to come home?

That doesn't seem likely.

But there were a few minutes there, before Cam broke her news, when she could have sworn something had sparked between them again.

Maybe that was just wishful thinking, the heat, pregnancy hormones . . .

Or maybe it was real. Maybe once the dust settles . . .

"Did you go to the beach today?" Debbie asks.

"No. Did you?"

"Nope. Too hot for the beach."

Cam laughs. "I thought hot days were perfect beach days. Isn't that the whole point?"

"Not if you don't go into the water. Who wants to sit and bake all day?"

"You can always go into the water. No matter how cold it is, on a day like this, it would feel great."

"I don't go into the water here."

"Why not?"

"Sharks." Debbie shudders. "This is where the movie *Jaws* happened, you know."

"That was supposed to be New England."

"It was based on something here in Beach Haven. A great white attack. Haven't you ever heard about it?"

Who hasn't? The rogue shark is island lore; Cam's father told her about it—in gory detail—when she was a little girl. She remembers the incident well; they were in a poolroom somewhere on the island and one of Pop's friends—some biker chick with yellow hair and dark roots who hung around the band for a few summers—scolded him.

"Why would you scare a little kid like that, Ike?"

"Look at her," Pop said with a laugh and pointed at Cam. "Does she seem scared to you?"

In truth, she was. But she was careful to hide that fear—and every other. Pop was always boasting about how grown-up she was, how resilient, how independent. She worried that if she showed him the slightest insecurity, he'd leave her behind.

"Yeah," she tells Debbie, "of course I've heard about it. But it happened a long time ago."

"You think it can't happen now?" Debbie's tone is challenging . . . almost amused.

For some reason, that bothers Cam. "Of course I don't think that. It can happen anywhere. Any time."

"That's the point," Debbie says ominously.

She's talking about a shark attack, but something shifts uneasily in the back of Cam's mind.

All day, brooding over Mike, she's felt a lingering trepidation as well. She can't pinpoint the cause, or what it is she's even worried about.

It's as if the sky is clear and the meteorologists haven't forecast rain, yet Cam is certain a storm is brewing. "You feel it in your bones," as her mother-in-law might say.

Maybe it really does have something to do with the oppressive weather, and nothing more than that.

"Have you heard from Tess yet?" Debbie asks, removing her own phone from her pocket and checking it as they walk.

"She called earlier."

"What did she say?"

"That they were there, checked into the hotel."

"And . . . ?"

"And that was it."

Her conversation with Tess was stilted, and she knew Mike was right there. Not that she thought Tess would confide anything earth-shattering even if she was having a conversation out of his earshot. But it bothered her that he was there.

And that she was here.

Come on, face it: you're just jealous that Mike gets to spend the weekend with Tess and you have to spend it alone.

Or at least without Tess.

She did try to reach her father. Maybe he'll call back and come visit, or Cam can go to him, wherever he is. Someplace nearby, she's certain. Maybe even here on the island. He often plays beach bars at this time of year.

Debbie's around, too, but she's getting on Cam's nerves already.

You should have stayed home. Why are you here, on your feet, in the heat?

Feeling claustrophobic, she takes off her sunglasses. They seem to be trapping hot air against her face.

"Hey—are you wearing makeup?"

She looks up to see Debbie looking curiously at her. "You mean it hasn't all melted off?"

"I've never seen you in makeup," says

Debbie, whom Cam has never seen without it. "You look nice."

"Thanks."

Something about the way Debbie's looking at her tells Cam she's not going to drop the subject, and she's right.

"So why do you have it on?"

"Why else? I wanted to look my best for minigolf," Cam quips. "Doesn't everyone?"

"Come on, you wanted to look good for your ex-husband."

"Right," Cam says with a shrug. Why bother to deny it? Who cares if Debbie's on to her?

"I hope you got fixed up just to show the creep what he's missing, and not because you thought you might win him back. Because, trust me—that's not going to happen," Debbie says flatly. "It never does."

Annoyed, Cam shifts her gaze away, instinctively checking on Jonathan.

There he is, up ahead.

Waiting in front of concrete block wall that's painted bright blue. On it, red bubble letters spell out SHIPS AHOY MINIATURE GOLF.

* * *

Walking back toward his car, Ike scowls.

He comes all this way, and nobody's home?

You could have called first, Pop, Cam's voice says in his head.

I never call, he retorts.

Never has, never will.

You can't change the way you do things at this stage of the game.

Hell, Ike couldn't change the way he did things from the very beginning. Not even for Brenda.

But that's not why she left.

No? Why'd she leave?

Not because I needed my space, that's for damn sure.

Brenda wasn't the kind of woman who needed a husband with a nine-to-five job, coming through the door at the same time every night—or even coming through the door every night. Brenda liked her space, like he did.

They were good together that way.

Not so good together in other ways.

But I never stopped trying. I never

walked away for good. Not like you did, Bren . . . if that's what you did.

Maybe someone took her away.

Maybe she's dead.

Maybe she's not.

Frustrated, Ike looks back at Cam's cottage, wondering if he should stick around waiting for someone to come home, or leave.

The air is muggy and still; a mosquito buzzes somewhere around his ear and he swats it away.

It's too hot to hang around here waiting. For all he knows they went back to Montclair in Mike's car.

He does have a key to their place–Cam insisted on giving one to him, back when they first bought the cottage, and it's presumably still tucked into his wallet somewhere.

"Use the house anytime, Dad," she said. "You can crash there whenever you're on the island, whether we're there or not."

Maybe he should let himself in now, wait for someone to come home.

Maybe he shouldn't.

Climbing behind the wheel of his car,

Ike reaches for the beer in the cup holder. The bottle's warm and just about empty, but he swallows the backwash.

Feeling a twitch on his bare forearm, he sees that the mosquito has landed there—right on top of his tattoo.

He slaps it, hard, with his other hand.

Did he get it?

Lifting his hand, he sees that he did—and winces.

BRENDA is smeared with fresh blood.

Some kind of omen?

She believed in them.

Maybe Ike does, too.

Shaking his head, he reaches into his pocket for his wallet.

Yeah—the key is there. Good.

He'll just go into the house and wash off the blood, get cleaned up a little.

SHIPS AHOY MINIATURE GOLF.

GOLF . . .

The last word . . . the last two letters . . . jump out at Cam.

LF . . .

The paint on the sign must be fresh,

she thinks irrationally. Because it's dripping down the wall.

No—it's not paint at all. It's blood.

Cam blinks, and the blood is gone.

But she notices, for the first time, that a girl is standing there.

There, at the far right side of the sign.

It's her.

Oh my God.

It's her.

Cam breaks into a run, hurtling herself through the crowd toward the girl.

"Cam! What the hell are you doing?" Debbie calls behind her.

Cam ignores her, eyes fastened on the girl.

She's about Tess's age, cute, a carrot-top with a pair of braids that hang just past her chin. Her freckled cheeks are sunburnt. She's wearing a green cotton top that has spaghetti straps tied in little bows over her shoulders—also freckled and sunburnt. Her feet are in white sandals, her toenails polished hot pink.

Around her neck is a silver chain with some kind of small triangular black pendant hanging from it.

A shark's tooth.

In her hand is an oversized waffle cone of chocolate ice cream, studded with fudgy chunks. It's melting in the blazing sun, dripping over her hand. The girl licks it, her face flushed and shiny, her bangs damp.

The ice cream is dripping and the girl is licking, and laughing, and looking at someone beside her, but Cam doesn't see who it is.

She zeroes in on the chocolate oozing over the hands, and the chocolate, like the paint, becomes blood. Blood is dripping over the girl's hands, and now it's smeared all over her clothes, and her face, and her hair, and she's not laughing, she's crying, she's screaming in terror, she's—

Cam blinks again to shut out the gory image and the girl is laughing again, licking chocolate ice cream off her hand.

But something's going to happen to her.

She's in danger.

Cam pushes her way forward. She has to get to her. Has to warn her.

"Sorry, excuse me," someone says, and her path is momentarily blocked by a family: mother pushing baby carriage, father carrying toddler on his shoulders.

They pass, and Cam realizes that the spot where the girl was standing is empty.

No. Please, no. Don't disappear.

Looking around frantically, she sees a flash of green in the crowd. There she goes.

"Wait!"

She darts in that direction, eyes peeled, but the crowd shifts, swallows the girl. She's gone.

"Cam?"

Dazed, she looks up. There's Debbie, with Jonathan at her side.

"Are you okay? What are you doing?"

"Oh, I . . . I thought I saw someone I knew. But I lost her."

"Well, you'll never find her again in this madhouse."

I have to, Cam thinks grimly. *I have to find her. I have to warn her.*

Then, as she turns away, something catches her eye.

She steps closer, and the world screeches to a stop.

* * *

Coming out of the minimart with yet another cold bottle of soda—her umpteenth for the day—Kathy immediately scans the parking lot for Cam.

No sign of her.

Not surprising.

The island is big, and crowded. No reason to think she's going to run into Cam at every turn. But that hasn't kept her from looking for her everywhere, just in case.

So how long are you really going to hang around in Beach Haven without letting Cam at least know you're here?

That depends.

On how long it will take her to come up with a compelling reason to give Cam regarding why she happens to be here.

Since I can't tell her the real reason.

Wouldn't that *be something, though?*

Imagining Cam's probable reaction if she actually did reveal the truth, Kathy uncaps the bottle and takes a long, unsatisfying swig. Unsatisfying because it won't quench her thirst—she should be drinking water in this heat—and unsatisfying because it's just soda.

Unsatisfying.

Story of my life.

Climbing into her car with the sun beating down is like stepping into Death Valley.

Kathy turns the key, rolls down all the windows, sets the air-conditioning on HIGH, shifts into REVERSE . . .

Then hesitates, her foot still on the brake.

Which way?

Back to that horrid, sweltering little guesthouse with the busybody owner and nosy guests?

Or perhaps, a walk on the beach?

Or . . .

Is it really time to go find Cam?

Maybe just drop in for a friendly little visit?

That might freak her out.

Yeah. You think?

The last thing Kathy wants is to alienate her. Cam has already pulled back; hasn't shown up in Montclair, hasn't returned Kathy's phone calls in days.

Still . . .

I need to see her. Just to make sure . . .

Her mind made up, Kathy heads toward Cam's cottage.

"What are you getting, Dad?" Tess asks her father.

No reply.

She sighs.

He doesn't seem to hear that, either.

He just sits, looking at the menu he's holding, either intently reading every last word on it, or thinking about something else.

Tess doubts anyone could be that fixated on seafood and burgers, so it must be the latter. Especially since Dad has seemed quiet and preoccupied all day.

It wasn't a big deal in the car, even though the drive down took almost twice as long as it should have, thanks to the holiday traffic.

"Do you know how long this trip would take in the middle of the night with no traffic?" Dad had asked at one point, shaking his head. "And it would take a matter of minutes to fly between DC and the island."

"Then maybe we should have chartered a private plane or something," Tess said with a grin.

Dad didn't return it. He was lost in thought again.

Tess plugged into her iPod and listened to music the whole way, which is what she's always done on long road trips with both her parents.

She expected her father to protest, since the whole point of the weekend is for them to spend quality time together, but he didn't. He just stared out the windshield at the road, like he had something on his mind.

Once, his cell phone rang. He took it out of his pocket, looked at it, then threw it down on the seat.

"Aren't you going to answer it?" Tess asked.

"Nah. It's work. I'm on vacation."

But Tess doesn't think it was work at all. When they stopped and he got out to pump gas, she checked his phone. The call had come from someone named Kate.

Dad remained subdued while they checked into the hotel with adjoining rooms. Mom would never let Tess have her own room, much less close the door between. Dad doesn't seem to care.

He opted to sit by the pool and read a magazine while Tess took a swim. Then, deciding they were both famished, they got dressed for an early dinner, and here they are.

Usually, Dad makes an effort to talk to her when they go out to a restaurant together. But he hasn't said anything at all in at least five minutes now. It's like he's forgotten Tess is even here.

She wonders what he's thinking about, and whether it has anything to do with Kate and the phone call he ignored . . . or with Mom, maybe.

Tess figures the two of them probably had an argument right before she and Dad left this morning. There was definitely some tension when Tess walked into the kitchen.

Too bad it took her so long and they had to spend all that time alone together. But she had to make sure she hadn't left behind the one thing she couldn't afford to leave behind.

She was pretty certain she'd packed it

into her bag late last night after they got home from the Marrimans's, but then she couldn't find it. So she had to search her entire room, trying to remember where she might have hidden it when she got home from the beach yesterday.

It's a lot easier to hide stuff from Mom in her room back home, where she has tried-and-true spots no one would ever stumble across.

Not that Tess ever had much of anything to hide until now. Just her diary, and a bag of M&Ms—Mom doesn't like her eating in her room—and a forbidden DVD of one of those NC-17 slasher movies Mom wouldn't let her go see when her friends did.

Nothing like this.

In the end, after all that searching and worrying this morning, she finally found what she was looking for. She had tucked it not into her duffel bag, but into a zippered compartment of her camera case, where she knew neither of her parents would ever look.

Brilliant hiding place—even you *couldn't find it.*

"Do you know what you want, Tess?" Dad asks, cutting into her thoughts.

Yeah, I want my normal life back. I want you to come home. I want Mom to be happy. I want us all to be happy.

"How about the fried shrimp?"

Dad is talking about food. She looks up to see that at least he's apparently snapped out of his own glum mood.

"I was thinking lobster," she tells him. "Can I? With battered French fries?"

"Sure. I was thinking the same thing. With a side of potato salad and coleslaw, though. It's too hot for fries."

"Mom made homemade fries one night at the beach house, when it rained," Tess informs him. In case he was wondering.

He doesn't seem to have been wondering, because he blinks and says blandly, "That's nice."

"Yeah. She's been cooking a lot. She makes great potato salad, too, remember? Maybe she'll make it this weekend."

"I doubt she'll cook just for herself."

"Oh, she's got a bunch of friends," Tess hears herself say, and wonders why.

But suddenly, Dad looks interested. "She does? Who are they?"

"Just . . . you know, some people she's met on the island." She deliberately says *people*, instead of *women*. "She went out with them last night."

Maybe it's a good idea to let Dad think Mom might be hanging around with other men.

And, come to think of it, Mom did look great this morning, for a change, when he showed up to get Tess. She's still heavier than usual, but she always gets a nice deep tan, and she was wearing makeup and that cool hemp ankle bracelet Debbie helped her pick out.

Tess felt a pang when she saw it; that kind of jewelry reminds her of Heath.

The mere thought of it does again now, but she pushes Heath aside.

Tyler, whom she hung out with last night at Beth's, is pretty cute. Even though Beth says he's way too young for them. She's got a crush on one of the lifeguards, who has to be at least eighteen.

But Tyler seems like he might be kind of interested in Tess, and he's nice. And after what happened with Heath Pickering, Tess thinks it might be nice to be the older woman with the upper hand.

Not that anything's happened with Tyler, or is about to.

"Who are these people?" Dad is asking, frowning a little.

"People?"

"The ones your mother's going out with."

Oh. Right.

"You know . . . just people." Tess grabs her menu again, not wanting him to press her too hard. "Can I get an appetizer?"

"Sure." A pause, then Dad asks, "Did she meet them at the beach, or . . . ?"

"On second thought," Tess talks over him, "I don't think I'll get an appetizer. I'll save room for dessert. I feel like something chocolate."

Normally, Dad would say, *"That's strange. You don't look like something chocolate."*

But he just nods, and looks lost in thought again.

Tess sighs to herself.

This long weekend is truly going to be a long weekend.

Chapter Eleven

Leah Roby.

The name—and her exact age (thirteen)—helps fill in part of the puzzle Cam has been carrying around in her head since May.

Unfortunately, the puzzle is far from completed and the rest of pieces are missing.

So is Leah Roby, a sweet-faced blonde pixy.

She was last seen getting off a school bus in a Philadelphia suburb, carrying a purple backpack, and wearing a white blouse, knee socks, and a Black Watch plaid uniform. She was also wearing a silver med-alert bracelet warning of her severe nut allergy.

No mention is made in the flier of the

distinctive shark's tooth pendant—the one Leah wore in Cam's vision, and the one the redheaded girl was wearing both in her vision and just now, in real life.

"What are you doing?"

Cam turns to see Debbie and Jonathan watching her.

"Oh—this girl . . . She looks familiar."

"Who does? You mean the girl in the poster?" Debbie sounds as if she's decided Cam really is crazy, and Jonathan—without benefit of sunglasses to mask his expression—rolls his eyes.

Who cares what anyone thinks?

Cam reaches out and tugs on the flier. It comes free easily, stuck there with masking tape whose glue is probably melting, along with everything else, in this heat.

"What are you doing?"

"Taking it with me," she tells Debbie. "So I have the number. Just in case."

"You honestly saw that girl? Where?"

You wouldn't believe me in a million years.

"I don't remember . . . somewhere,"

she tells Debbie, who tilts her head dubiously. "I'm sure it'll come to me."

"Let's see her."

She holds the picture out to Debbie, who studies it without removing her shades, then shrugs. "I don't know . . . She looks like anyone else, don't you think?"

"What do you mean by that?" Cam is feeling prickly, and not just from the heat.

"I mean, it's not like this girl has warts or three eyes or whatever. A lot of kids look like her, so you're probably thinking of someone else."

"Probably." Cam's tone is short.

Why did she think it would be a good idea to make new friends? Or look up old ones, for that matter?

She doesn't need to listen to stupid comments, or answer questions, or worry that someone's going to figure out that she sometimes sees people—children—who aren't really there.

But the redheaded girl—just now—was really there.

And the little girl she saw cowering in

that cellar somewhere really exists, and is missing.

Did you ever have any doubt?

Cam folds the exposed part of the tape over, pressing it against the back of the flier, then folds the sheet in half twice and shoves it into her pocket.

She looks up to find Debbie still watching her. "What?" she asks, wishing she hadn't come.

But if she hadn't come, she wouldn't have seen the redhead or the flier.

She was meant to come.

Things happen for a reason.

"Who were you chasing after just now, that you thought you knew?" Debbie asks. "Not this same girl?"

"No, that was . . . someone else." She shifts her weight, uncomfortably aware of Debbie's hard stare from behind the sunglasses.

"Come on, Mom . . . Can we please just go play golf?" Jonathan asks impatiently.

"All right, already," Debbie snaps. "Let's get it over with."

As they make their way toward the blue building with the red bubble letters,

Cam searches the crowd, hoping for another glimpse of the girl with the silver shark's tooth necklace, and wondering what it means.

As she turns onto Dolphin Avenue, Kathy has yet to come up with a plausible reason for being here on Long Beach Island.

Vacationing?

Why wouldn't she have mentioned that before?

Polite concern as an AA sponsor?

Would anyone really go this far out of the way for that?

Visiting family?

She doesn't have family—not real family. Not anymore. Cam doesn't know that, but . . .

Business?

What kind of business would one have on a resort island over a holiday weekend?

Pure coincidence?

Come on.

Slowing the car as she spots the familiar cedar-shingled cottage ahead, Kathy decides to wing it when she gets inside. Which isn't her style. But here she is, almost helplessly drawn to Camden Hastings, for reasons she'll never be able to confess.

A man steps out of the house just as Kathy pulls up to the curb two houses away, keeping a wary distance.

Kathy watches him scuttle toward a junky car parked in the driveway, head bent furtively as though he's not supposed to be here.

He almost looks like . . .

Can it be . . . ?

Yes. That's him.

Ike.

Fancy seeing you here, after all these years.

Through narrowed eyes, she watches him get behind the wheel and drive away.

She waits a moment, then, on a whim, decides to follow.

Early evening sunbeams slant across the grassy, rectangular National Mall in the heart of Washington. As the holiday weekend kicks off, it's crowded with tourists and impressive security detail.

Tess and her father make their way across, heading toward the stately museum buildings on the north side.

But it's still early, and Dad found out from their dinner waiter that the Smithsonian National Museum of Natural History is open for another hour.

"What do you think?" he asked Tess. "Want to go?"

Stuffed after a one-and-a-half-pound lobster and Chocolate Mousse, she would have preferred to go back to the nice, air-conditioned hotel room and climb into bed with a book.

But since her father has apparently decided to put aside whatever has been bothering him, the least Tess can do is humor him.

Even in this muggy heat and relentless sun that have her feeling sticky and gross. Not that it's likely to be much cooler in the shade.

Tess thinks longingly of the beach as she feels around in her purse for the packaged wet wipe she pilfered from the lobster dinner. If she was at the shore with her mother, she'd be diving into cold waves right about now.

"Look at the way the light is hitting the Washington Monument and the Capitol building," her father comments as she mops her forehead with the wipe. "You have your camera with you, right?"

Yes, she has her camera bag tucked into the bottom of her purse. Not that she was planning to use it.

But her father doesn't need to know why she brought it along.

Too bad he won't just leave her alone for a minute so she can take care of business.

"Why don't you snap some shots?" Dad prods.

Gazing from the impressive dome on one end of the mall to the distinct towering white obelisk on the other, Tess decides it is pretty photogenic.

She gingerly reaches back into her purse and unzips the camera bag, not wanting to pull it out and take any chances of her father seeing what she has stashed there.

"Have you been using the camera?" he asks as she sets up the first shot.

"Yup," she lies.

She snaps again and again, and suddenly misses her mother, who is sure to want photographic evidence of everything.

"Smile, Dad." She aims the camera at him, and he obliges.

He looks good, in his black Maui Jim sunglasses and the navy Ralph Lauren Polo shirt Tess wound up getting him for Father's Day. Well, Mom actually picked it out. Tess didn't have the heart to go shopping after what happened at Lily's.

She'll show Mom the picture of Dad in the shirt, so she'll know he liked it. Probably a lot better than he would have liked the puka shell necklace Tess originally wanted to buy for him.

That makes her think of Heath Pickering.

Which plunks her back to reality with a sad, sick feeling in the pit of her stomach.

"It's too hot to stand here taking pictures," she says, abruptly closing the camera lens. "Can we go now?"

The nice thing about Dad—as opposed to Mom—is that he tends not to read anything into what Tess says and does. Mom would detect distress in her voice, look closely at her, and ask her what's wrong.

Dad, however, just shrugs and they're on their way.

"This is going to be great," he tells Tess as they climb the wide steps with roughly a million other tourists, by Tess's estimate. "You love dinosaurs."

"I do?" she asks crankily.

"Don't you?"

"I mean, I like them, I guess, but . . ." Tess wipes sweat off her cheeks and decides Washington is the most humid place on earth. Why are they here?

"I remember when you were obsessed with them. You wanted everyone to call you Steggy."

"Steggy?"

"As a nickname." They trail the line of sweaty people heading into the museum. "Steggy—short for *Stegosaurus*."

"I don't remember that. Are you sure it was me?"

"Who else would it have been? Ask Mom. She'll tell you."

Mom.

Not *your mother*.

Tess feels a flutter of hope, and the crankiness subsides a little.

"How old was I," she begins, to keep the promising conversation going, "when I wanted to be Steggy?"

"Oh, I don't know . . . four . . . maybe five? Seven?"

"Mom might know."

"She might." They inch closer to the door, and air-conditioning.

"So did you guys call me Steggy?"

"Sure. For awhile."

At last, they've reached the entrance—and what Tess sees inside makes her legs go limp.

"Have your bags open, please," a uniformed security guard announces from the head of the line. "All bags, briefcases, purses, and containers need to be searched."

Tess clutches her purse close to her side, feeling as if she's going to faint and wishing she would.

Anything to keep her camera bag out of the security guard's hands.

* * *

Pacing barefoot across the small living room, Cam sips from a cup of ice water and tries to calm down. The heat and the stress aren't good for the baby.

She forces herself to sit on the edge of the couch, directly in the warm breeze from the floor fan. Setting her cup on the table, heedless of the wet ring it will leave, she sees the Marble notebooks.

There was no need to put them away when she left with Debbie. It wasn't as if Tess or Mike were going to come along and find them.

Mike.

This morning's unpleasant little conflict has been all but forgotten at this point.

Cam spent the past few hours pretending to focus on minigolf, all the while keeping an eye out for the red-headed girl. She never saw her again.

But the effects of the bloody premonition didn't subside. If anything, the sense of foreboding has grown stronger by the minute.

When Debbie asked why she was so quiet in the car on the way home, Cam feigned an upset stomach. That was preferable to bringing up the missing child poster again, which Debbie and Jonathan seemed to have forgotten.

"You don't look good. Have you eaten shellfish?" Debbie asked promptly. "You should never eat shellfish in this heat."

Cam pretended that she had, and Debbie chided her.

Then she reminded Cam, again, about her barbecue tomorrow.

"You're coming, right? You have to. I won't take no for an answer."

"In that case, I have to come, I guess."

But a barbecue is the last thing on her mind now.

Restless, she stands and paces again, running through what happened at the miniature golf complex.

It's no accident that she spotted the redhead—alive and in person—moments before seeing Leah Roby's missing child flier.

Chasing the redhead led Cam right to Leah Roby's picture.

Both girls were wearing the same unusual necklace.

That means—in Cam's logic, however

skewed it might be—that the two girls are connected somehow.

Somehow?

One is missing.

The other about to go missing, if she hasn't already.

And if her instincts are correct they have even more in common.

Is the same person responsible for Leah Roby's disappearance planning to abduct the redhead?

Never before has she had two visions coincide this way.

What are you going to do about it?

If only she knew where to find the girl, the redhead, tonight. But she hasn't a clue. She could be anywhere.

Maybe she's left the island, Cam tries to convince herself, standing in front of the screen, facing out into the street.

So what if she has? That doesn't mean she's escaped an ugly fate.

The aura of danger about that vision is too strong to ignore.

Long blue shadows of dusk are falling over the island. Soon it will be dark.

A dog barks in the distance. A motorcycle guns up the boulevard. In a neighboring yard, an illegal firecracker whistles and snaps; children shout.

Nothing good's going to happen after dark tonight.

The sultry air is weighted with a palpable mantle of foreboding.

Cam turns away from the window, not sure whether to wish Tess was here, under her roof, or to be glad Tess is a safe distance from the island.

At an explosive report from outside she jumps, gasps, presses her hand to the base of her neck.

Some kid with firecrackers again. That's all it is.

Better get used to it, or it's going to be a long night.

No.

It's going to be a long night no matter what.

Because Cam is certain that whatever is going to happen will happen here, on the island, tonight.

Her only relief is that it's not going to happen to Tess.

* * *

Mike has maintained a stony silence from the time he and Tess left the museum.

Now, with the door to his hotel room closed and bolted, he turns to his daughter, knowing he has to say something.

Nothing that comes to mind seems suitable.

"Can I go into my room?" she asks, eying the closed adjoining door.

"No. Sit down."

Tess refuses to make eye contact as she sits on the edge of the bed and fusses with the straps on one of her sandals.

"Tess."

"Yeah?"

Her head is still bent. He can see that her hands are shaking.

"Look at me."

She does. Her eyes are shiny.

Damn. He finds himself longing for Cam's presence as he asks, "How could you do this?"

"I told you—"

"No, you told the security guard. He bought your story. I don't."

"It's the truth." Her tone is defiant despite the shaking and tears.

"I don't believe you."

"Why not?"

That question, and the tremble in her voice, give him pause.

Really, why *doesn't* he believe her?

Because she's fourteen. Because I'm not naive.

Kids her age lie, and sneak around, and drink and smoke and do drugs and have sex and cheat and steal . . .

Come on. Not all of them.

Surely not Tess, formerly known as Steggy, a sweet, obedient little girl living happily with two parents under one roof.

"You always told me to tell you the truth, Dad. About everything. You said honesty's the best policy. And I listened. Why don't you believe me?"

He shrugs.

You're thinking she's lying because you actually buy into the that's-what-kids-do stereotype, aren't you?

And because she's been moody and remote?

So . . . what? You're looking for evi-

dence that your moving out has sent your baby girl down a bad path? Is that it?

Maybe it did. Mike rakes a hand through his short hair. Who the hell knows?

Or maybe Tess really is telling the truth.

How is he supposed to know?

He hates that he's here alone with her in a hotel two hundred miles from Cam. He hates that what happens next is solely up to him.

"Sit down"—he pulls the chair away from the desk and gestures for her to take it—"while I call your mother."

"Why do you have to call her?"

"Because she needs to know what happened."

"Why?"

"This is serious, Tess."

"So you're going to put it all on Mom? Make her deal with it, as usual?"

Mike goes still.

Cam's words—spoken weeks ago, when Tess's friends pulled some kind of prank on her—hurl back at him.

"You just don't get it, Mike. You don't get it, because you're not here."

Well, he *does* get it. Now.

This is what it's like for Cam.

Spending day after day, night after night, a single parent.

Yeah, he sees Tess . . . but not enough to be there every time a difficult situation arises. Not enough to really *get it* the way he used to.

If he and Cam stay on the path they're on—living separate lives—this is how it's always going to be. Not just with Tess, but with the baby. Right from the start.

He'll never know his second child the way he knows Tess . . .

The way he *knew* her, anyway.

Not anymore.

He can go on like this, and let his daughter and his wife—and, yeah, his new baby—become strangers.

Or you can go home, where you belong, and work it out.

That's what Cam wants.

But things would have to change.

She'd have to let me in. She'd have to stop hiding, tear down those walls.

She's already stopped drinking. That's a huge step in the right direction.

But she didn't even tell him about the baby. For more than three months, she didn't tell him.

Can you blame her?

Yeah. I can. She should have known I'd come back if I knew. She should have believed in me. She should have trusted me.

That's the problem, right there. Cam doesn't trust him. Not entirely. She never has. Right from the start, she's always held back a little piece of herself. Gradually, it became a big piece—the whole damned thing.

He doesn't know why. He supposes it has something to do with the way she grew up—her mother leaving, sister's suicide, father's aimlessness.

Still . . .

She should have trusted me. I was always there for her. I loved her.

I love *her.*

Her, and Tess. And this unborn child.

Yeah? So what are you going to do about it?

* * *

The Long Beach Township Police Department is on Long Beach Boulevard, so close Cam could walk there if she wanted to.

She doesn't want to.

She doesn't want to be here at all.

But she forces herself to climb out of her car in the parking lot, and she forces herself to walk through the dusk toward the entrance.

It's the right thing to do.

Just stay calm. Stay focused. Breathe.

Her sandaled footsteps slap against the warm asphalt.

From the adjacent Little League field comes the sound of a bat cracking a ball, met by cheers from the onlookers.

Cam would give anything to trade places with the parents hanging out in the stands, watching their kids play ball on this hot summer night.

They're the reason she's doing this, though. The parents who turn their backs for seconds, minutes at a time. And the kids who think they're safe in this beautiful haven by the sea.

They're not.

Not tonight.

Somewhere out there, she desperately hopes, is the girl Cam saw in her vision that day in her kitchen: Leah Roby, snatched from a suburban street fifty miles away.

And somewhere out there is another girl with red braids and sunburnt cheeks, a girl whose fate is drenched in blood.

Once upon a time, Cam would have run scared, drowning the images in booze.

Not anymore.

With a trembling hand, she opens the door and walks into the police department.

A uniformed brunette is sitting behind the desk, talking to a dark, handsome man who's leaning against it. They both look up.

Cam wants to walk right back out again, but forces herself to approach the desk.

"Yes?" the woman asks. "Can I help you?"

From her purse, Cam pulls out the flier with Leah Roby's picture, unfolds it, and holds it up.

"I need to speak to someone about a missing child."

In Loveladies, there are no motels to draw transient summer guests who tromp over the dunes at all hours. Here, there's just a stretch of homes, some of them grand seaside retreats, most privately owned by people who value the relative seclusion.

This particular beach isn't deserted tonight, but it's far less populated than the beaches on the southern end. Here, away from the access paths, there's a long stretch of dark, empty sand.

Down the way, in either direction, bonfires flicker. Children wave sparklers in the night. Roman candles soar to shower shimmers in the night sky.

In the shadows beside a heap of sea-battered washed-up wood, steady hands train the night vision binoculars on the dunes. Every so often, a pair or group of strangers crosses the distant access path, their features startlingly distinct in the magnified infrared lens.

She, however, has yet to appear.

She should have been here ten minutes ago.

Did she decide to ignore the note sent with the shark's tooth necklace?

Did her parents find it and forbid her to go out alone at night?

Is she simply late?

Amid the crashing surf: a snatch of distant laughter, guitar music, snapping firecrackers, whistling bottle rockets.

Still, no sign of her.

What if she doesn't come at all?

She will. She has to. Be patient.

When she arrives, everything will have to move swiftly. She can't be given an opportunity to flee.

The moment she sees me, realizes who I am, she'll try to flee.

That's how I should have known the other girl, Leah, was an imposter. She never recognized me. She was a total stranger to the end. How could I have made that mistake?

It doesn't matter. The mistake won't be made again.

This time, I really have found her.

Again, movement on the path between

the parallel wooden fences down the way.

And then, all at once, there she is: emerging expectantly from the dunes, red hair—expertly dyed—blowing back from a face that was obviously, cleverly, surgically altered. The masses of freckles—on her face, her arms, even her legs—are impressively done. So impressively authentic-looking, in fact . . .

What if it isn't her?

What if this is another case of mistaken identity?

It is. It has to be.

And she's wearing the necklace, just as I told her.

Good girl.

The binoculars are swiftly tucked away; the syringe is produced and held at the ready. Just yards from here, up beyond the adjacent dunes, an SUV is parked on a remote stretch of road, waiting to take her away.

There's always the possibility that someone will come along at precisely the wrong moment, and see the girl being placed in the SUV.

But it won't matter, anyway. She'll be

incapacitated at that point, and I'll explain that she's my daughter and fell asleep and I'm carrying her to the car.

By the time she's reported missing, I'll be long gone.

Things are falling into place nicely.

Here she comes, looking nervous, expectant.

After all these years, she's almost within arm's reach.

After all these years, she's mine again.

It's going to turn out to be the guy who runs the bumper cars. Rebecca Pearson is sure of it.

She saw the way he looked at her the other day, when she and her sister got on the ride. Looked her up and down, gave a slow, appreciative nod.

He was cute, in a grungy, carnie kind of way. Ragged jeans, even in the heat, a backward baseball cap, and a five o'clock shadow. That was the clincher.

The guys—ha, *boys*—back home love to talk about shaving . . . as if they have anything to shave. This guy, the bumper car guy, her secret admirer, has to be at least eighteen.

Eighteen! And he went to the trouble of tracking down Rebecca, leaving her this really cool necklace, and asking her to meet him down here at the beach after dark.

Which took a lot of guts on Rebecca's part.

Not that she's a chicken. Not by any means. But she's never snuck out of the house before when everyone was asleep.

"You're not really going to do it, are you, Becca?" her sister asked.

"Sure I am. And you're not going to tell. You swear?"

Nina swore. She's a good kid, when she's not accidentally erasing every song on Rebecca's iPod, which she did last month, causing Rebecca to stop speaking to her for an entire week.

Okay. So where is this guy? Rebecca didn't think the beach would be this deserted late at night.

It might actually be romantic if it wasn't so . . . creepy.

But I'm not scared, Rebecca reminds

herself as she emerges from the dunes onto the open sand.

Not scared at all, she thinks, just as someone grabs her and she feels a sharp, stinging sensation in the side of her neck.

Chapter Twelve

"Here you go."

"Thank you." Cam accepts a plastic cup filled with water from the man who was talking to the desk clerk when she first walked into police headquarters.

He introduced himself as Detective Randall Barakat. With his good looks—exotic blue eyes, unusual with such dark skin—he's got a lady-killer aura about him.

He brought her into this small interrogation room, took down her name and address, asked if she wanted a glass of water.

She didn't, but she accepted, needing time to gather her thoughts.

Now the water is in front of her on the table and the nice detective is sitting across from her and it's time to tell him exactly why she's here.

After which, it'll be time for the nice detective to haul her off to the psych ward.

For God's sake, Cam, why didn't you just stay home and keep your mouth shut?

Because the girl with the red braids is somewhere on this island, and someone is going to do something terrible to her if you don't stop her. That's why.

"Mrs. Hastings?"

Mrs. Hastings. Yup, that's her. When the detective asked her marital status, Cam said "Married." It was easier.

But she realized, with a sick feeling in her gut, that the day is coming when she'll have to say *divorced*.

"Tell me about the child," Detective Barakat nudges gently. "You've seen her?"

Slowly, she nods.

Pen poised over paper, he asks, "And when and where was this?"

"I'm . . . not sure."

"You're not sure when? That's all right. You don't have to be exact."

"I don't mean . . . I mean . . ." She shakes her head, feeling sweat in her hair despite the air-conditioning. "I'm not just not sure when, I'm not sure where."

He frowns. "Excuse me?"

Getting nowhere, Cam is aware that the clock is ticking. She can't afford to waste time. It might be too late for Leah Roby.

"There's another girl," she says. "I don't know her name . . . or even where she lives. But she's in danger, too."

"How do you know?"

"Just take my word for it."

She sees suspicion in his blue eyes and realizes immediately she's made a serious misstep. "I'm not involved," she says quickly. "I'm trying to help."

"But you don't know her name or where she is."

"No, but I can describe her." She does, and the detective takes notes.

"And you know her how?"

"I don't, actually. I've just seen her."

"And you know she's in danger because . . . ?"

Cam is silent. How can she answer

that without possibly incriminating herself? He'll never believe her.

What are you doing? You shouldn't be here. This is wrong.

No, it isn't. It's right. I'm here because I'm trying to save a child's life, and—

"Mrs. Hastings?"

Just tell him the truth.

How can she not?

Then again, how can she?

If she makes something up, he'll probably think she's lying.

Yeah, and if you tell the truth, he'll definitely *think you're lying.*

Still . . . She's got no choice.

Taking a deep breath, she begins, "This is going to sound crazy . . ."

The detective gives a jaded, I've-heard-it-all shrug. "Try me."

For the second time today, Cam attempts to carefully choose her wording.

For the second time today, she fails.

"I'm a psychic," she blurts.

Detective Barakat nods.

Nods!

Doesn't gape, or laugh, or shy away, or pick up the phone and dial the psych ward.

No, he just nods.

He really has heard it all.

Cam feels her body seem to ooze into her chair and realizes just how tense she was. Every muscle she has must have been clenched until this very second. Now her limbs and spine are pudding.

The detective rubs his chin between his right thumb and forefinger, watching her thoughtfully for a long moment.

"So you . . . what? Had a vision of something happening to this girl?"

"Yes."

"What?"

"I don't know . . . nothing specific . . . just, blood. I see her covered in blood, and I know it means something's going to happen to her."

For the first time, she sees a glimmer of doubt in his eyes.

"My visions used to be more specific, years ago, when I used to have them," she rushes on. "They always turned out to come true. I stopped having them for a long time . . ."

You don't have to explain the years of self-medicating, trying to shut out all those awful visions. He might really decide you're on something again.

Then he says, "There's someone you should talk to."

Lying awake in her hotel room, Tess is certain her father is lying awake in the adjoining one.

The television's blue light flickers in the dark, the sound turned low.

She put it on some late-night talk show.

Not because she's interested in any of the guests. But because anything is better than finding herself in total darkness and silence.

She'd never fall asleep then.

You'll never fall asleep now.

Dad doesn't believe her. That's what hurts.

Does he honestly think, after all these years of watching her mother crawl into a bottle night after night, that Tess was planning to drink the vodka?

Yes, she took the little bottle of Smirnoff's from Beth yesterday when Beth snuck into her mother's stash, pilfered from the airline. What was she supposed to do? Tell Beth she doesn't drink?

It would have been the truth, a stern voice reminds Tess.

Yeah, and the truth might have made Beth, her only friend, decide Tess is too young and sheltered to hang out with. And then where will she be this summer?

Alone.

Which is right where she'll be in the fall, back home.

So she pushed aside her conscience, took the bottle, and thanked Beth, who said it would help Tess get through a "long, boring weekend" with Dad.

Back home after the beach, she knew she had to hide it from her mother.

Not because she was afraid of what Mom would do to her if she found it.

But because she was afraid of what Mom—faced unexpectedly with temptation—would do to herself.

Tess had to get the vodka out of the house. So she hid it in her room, then smuggled it to DC, where she planned to dispose of it in some garbage can first chance she got.

A likely story.

The museum guard didn't exactly say that, but he thought it. Tess could tell. Still, he confiscated the vodka, then let them go.

They left immediately. Neither was in the mood for dinosaurs anymore.

Tess wonders what her father would say if she asked him to take her back to Beach Haven tomorrow.

Would he be hurt if she wanted to leave? Relieved?

Maybe both.

He's done plenty of stuff that makes you feel bad, right?

That's what Beth said yesterday, and she was right.

So why should Tess care about hurting Dad's feelings by telling him she wants to cut their trip short?

He deserves it. That's what Beth would say.

"He got what he had coming to him" is how she phrased it the other day, when Tess asked her why she doesn't see her own father anymore. "He deserves to be alone and miserable for what he put us through. It's payback," she added almost gleefully.

Payback.

The problem is, Tess can't imagine taking pleasure in someone else's pain. Especially someone she loves.

When her cell phone vibrates in her back pocket, Lucinda has just taken the first sip of her second ice-cold beer and the cover band is wailing a guitar riff, halfway through "Sweet Home Alabama." They aren't Lynyrd Skynyrd, but not half-bad for a dive beach bar.

She really doesn't feel like picking up the phone. There isn't a soul she really wants to talk to . . .

Well, maybe there's one soul, but it belongs, along with his heart, to someone else.

Heart and soul? *Christ, one beer, and you've turned into a total sap.*

Plunking down her wet green bottle on the sticky bar and rolling her eyes, she pulls out her cell phone and answers.

"Lucinda?"

Well, if it isn't the *Soul* himself.

And her *Heart,* damn it, skips a beat.

Why is Randy calling her at this hour? Did he forget that he has a wife?

"What's up?" she asks over the music, wondering what she'll do if he wants to see her.

She'll say no. That's what she'll do. That's the right thing to do.

But he won't ask.

Because it all happened a long time ago and they've both moved on and if that's really true, what's she doing on Long Beach Island? Was it really a psychic vision about Leah Roby that brought her here?

"Where the skies are so blue . . ." the lead singer booms.

Randy—*where the eyes are so blue,* she thinks giddily—is asking, "Are you still here? On the island?"

Uh-oh. Here we go.

Lucinda considers lying. Maybe she should tell him she's back in Philly. Because if she sees him, she's not sure she can stay strong. And if he's calling to see her, he's not so strong himself.

But Lucinda can't lie. Not because it's morally wrong, necessarily, but because the music is blasting and this is an open-air bar and Beach Haven isn't exactly a spread-out metropolis. It's a small town. Windows are wide-open on this hot night, in cars, in houses . . .

For all Lucinda knows, Randy can hear the strains of "Sweet Home Alabama" from wherever he is.

"I'm at the Rusty Anchor," she admits.

"That's about two minutes from here. Can you come?"

Tell him no. Remind him that he has a wife, and—guess what?—you have a life.

Or—go ahead!—tell him yes.

It would be wrong—highly inappropriate, to quote Bitsy Sloan—but when was the last time you did something just for the hell of it? Just because it felt good and to hell with the consequences?

Once upon a time, Lucinda Sloan lived her entire life that way.

Not anymore.

When were you happier? Then, or now?

"Where are you?" she asks Randy tentatively, toying with her beer bottle.

"Does your conscience bother you?"

the lead singer sings appropriately, and Lucinda wonders if it's some kind of sign.

There are no accidents.

"I'm at work, and I've got someone here you need to meet. It's about that kid you're looking for," Randy says, and all inappropriate thoughts vanish from Lucinda's head.

"I'm on my way," she tells him, already heading for the door.

"I'm going to introduce you to an old colleague of mine," the detective informs Cam, sitting across the table from her again. "Her name is Lucinda Sloan. Maybe you've heard of her?"

Cam shakes her head, setting down the water cup she just drained—again. "Should I have?"

He shrugs. "She's pretty well known in some circles."

"She's a psychiatrist?"

"A psychiatrist?" Randall Barakat looks confused. "Why did you think that?"

"Just a guess," Cam murmurs. So

maybe he doesn't think she's crazy. When he said there was someone he wanted her to talk to, that was her first thought.

"Lucinda has been working to find missing people for years now."

"Oh! So she's a cop?"

"No." The detective shifts his weight, steeples his fingers, looks at Cam. "She used to be, but now she's . . . a psychic detective, I would call her."

"So your friend has premonitions, too?"

"I wouldn't call them . . . Well, a premonition is something that's going to happen in the future, right?"

Cam—apparently the newly anointed resident expert on the paranormal—nods.

"Well, as far as I know," he goes on, "Lucinda sees things that have already happened. Usually people who have been murdered."

Cam considers that with a shudder. She herself has always felt helpless about her own visions, but at least the calamities she sees haven't yet come to pass. At least there's still hope, a chance that she might be able to intervene.

But if this Lucinda only sees violent events after they've happened . . .

Then for her, and the people in her visions, it's always too late. There's no chance of saving a life. No hope.

"That has to be really hard on her," Cam murmurs, shaking her head.

"She's a tough cookie. But it is. Because the thing is . . . She's never wrong. When she sees something—no matter how awful it is—it's for real."

"So she lives in Beach Haven, then? Or on the island?"

"No, in Philly. She's here working on the Leah Roby disappearance. She just came yesterday, so you have great timing."

Cam nods.

There are no real coincidences.

Someone recently said that to her. Who? Debbie? Gwen?

Whoever it was, they were right.

"I'm sure Lucinda's responsible for hanging that flier you found," Detective Barakat tells her.

"Why is she looking for Leah here,

though? If she's from Philadelphia, and Leah lived there, too?"

Lived.

Past tense, Cam realizes.

Slip of the tongue?

There are no real coincidences.

"Lucinda had a hunch that there was some connection to the island, I guess. I'm sure you understand."

Cam nods. She does understand. She has the same hunch.

The thing is . . .

She doesn't feel like Leah Roby is *here* . . . or even that she ever was.

There's a connection, yes. But that's not it.

She wonders if Lucinda would disagree.

I'll have to find out what it is that she sees . . .

And how, exactly, she sees things in the first place . . .

And about a million other things I'm dying to ask . . .

A flutter of excitement darts through her at the thought of meeting someone else who can do what she can. That's never happened before.

Almost immediately, her mind flits to her lost sister.

As always, the thought of Ava brings with it a profound sense of longing.

Cam knows her life would have turned out differently if her sister had lived. There would have been someone to talk to from the start; someone who understands what it's like to hear voices in your head.

Ava. Poor Ava.

I'm lucky that the worst that ever happened to me was booze.

Cam could have ended up like Ava. She could be dead.

There's a knock on the door.

Detective Barakat stands and opens it.

"Hey," he says, "there you are." His tone is gentler than it has been all night. He sounds affectionate, almost, Cam decides as she takes in the willowy, gorgeous woman in the doorway.

She has wide-set brown eyes, a full mouth, a small, delicate nose. Her hair is her most striking feature of all: tousled, long auburn waves that hang halfway down her back.

She's wearing casual black cargo

pants and a simple white cap-sleeved T-shirt that hugs her narrow waist and generous breasts.

Suddenly conscious that her own white T-shirt bears a faint coffee stain and that she hasn't combed her own hair since this afternoon, Cam thinks, *I should hate her.*

Her next thought, as she watches Detective Barakat give the newcomer's hand a quick squeeze, is *My God—he's in love with her*.

It's not about his tone, or body language, or anything he implied when he mentioned her earlier.

Cam is going on pure instinct, but she's as certain as if the detective had just come right out and announced it.

She isn't certain if he's ever acted on his feelings, or whether they're mutual. But she doesn't miss the way Lucinda's eyes fasten on the detective's handsome face as he gestures her inside. Nor does she miss the gold wedding band on the detective's left hand as he closes the door behind her.

"Thanks for coming. This is Camden Hastings. I think you'll be interested in hearing what she has to say. Mrs. Hastings, this is Lucinda Sloan."

At last, Lucinda shifts her attention to Cam. Almost immediately, her eyes betray startled, disturbed recognition.

Just a fleeting look and then it's gone, replaced with a polite, if somewhat tense, smile as Lucinda murmurs a greeting.

She saw something when she looked at me, Cam realizes, and a chill of foreboding creeps down her spine. *She definitely saw something. Something that bothered her*.

A steady line of headlights are aimed east over the causeway toward Long Beach Island, but there's little traffic headed in the opposite direction.

It takes no time to get back onto the mainland, keeping the speedometer within five miles of the limit.

Not that being stopped for speeding would necessarily give anything away.

A glance at the backseat shows that she's still there, stretched out, eyes closed. A traffic cop peering into the

SUV would see a worn-out kid who had too much sun and fun today.

From here on in, it's smooth sailing . . .

Except for the slightest shred of doubt that just won't subside.

It's not that she doesn't look like her, because aside from her build, she doesn't—that's a given—and it doesn't matter. It never did. It's not about looks. Looks, you can change.

I should know.

It's more about a certain instinct.

I was looking, and when I saw her, even from a distance . . . something clicked.

Just like before?

And all those other times, in all those other places?

No, but this time, I knew it was her. I just felt it. I was so sure I was right . . .

Until the very last second, anyway. When she made eye contact just as the syringe went into her neck.

In her eyes, there was shock, horror, terror . . .

But not a glimmer of recognition.

Of course, that's probably because she was caught off guard. She was expecting someone else. Some secret admirer who had sent her a necklace and set up a romantic rendezvous on the beach.

That's why she didn't realize it was me.

But it's her. This time, it's definitely her.

It has to be.

While passing a truck it's tempting to pick up speed and stay out in the left lane; tempting to race all the way home.

But that's not a good idea. Better to pull into the right again and ease the needle back down to seventy.

A glance in the rearview mirror reveals a pair of headlights that just switched lanes, too, pulling in a little too close for comfort.

Is it following?

Nah.

The car ahead is going a mere fifty-five and has to be passed.

The car behind ventures into the left lane again as well, almost as if in pursuit.

Paranoia?

That's to be expected, after all this.

It's probably nothing.

But I'm going to make sure I shake

those headlights before I get anywhere near home—that's for damn sure.

"I've got to get you home where you belong, little girl. It's about time, don't you think?"

No answer from the backseat.

She's going to be out for awhile. Well, that was a powerful sedative, and she's still a pipsqueak.

"When we get there, I think I'll light a nice fire. Oh, I know it's warm, but we won't let it burn all night. Just long enough."

Long enough to make you mine.

"So you didn't feel that the cellar where Leah Roby was being held is on the island?" Lucinda is determined to maintain focus on the matter at hand, despite her nagging concern over the stark, vivid image that struck her earlier, when she first laid eyes on the Hastings woman.

"No. I'm not a hundred percent sure, but . . . You know how it goes."

Lucinda nods. Does she ever.

"It felt like somewhere on the mainland—not all that far away," she goes on. "You know—Jersey, Pennsylvania, Delaware, maybe New York . . ."

"That's a lot of ground to cover," Randy pipes up, and Lucinda flashes him a look. "I'm just saying . . ."

"Why don't we let Mrs. Hastings do the saying?" she suggests, not wanting to intimidate the woman, who seems nervous enough as it is. She's actually squirming a little in her seat.

"Call me Cam."

"Right. Cam, I'm assuming the digging you heard means she's buried somewhere?" Randy asks.

"I hope not, but, it seems that way." Cam rubs her eyes, looking wan.

Clearly, she isn't used to being grilled like this. Lucinda gives her a lot of credit for holding it together this long.

"Getting back to the necklace," Lucinda says, "Leah's parents never mentioned that she was wearing anything like that. According to them, her only jewelry was a medic-alert bracelet. We did find an empty jewelry gift box in her room though."

Lucinda decides not to say anything

about the sand particles in it and hopes Randy won't, either. Better to keep a few details private. Just in case.

Her instincts tell her that Cam Hastings is a trustworthy, upstanding citizen though.

"I'm thinking the necklace might have been in the box," Lucinda muses, propping her chin on her hand and looking from Cam to Randy. "And that whoever gave it to her . . ."

"Was the person who kidnapped her," Cam finishes the sentence, nodding vigorously. "That's it. That's what happened."

Randy looks at her questioningly.

"I mean, that's what I *think* happened," she amends, squirming again in her chair.

"That's what I think, too."

"Well then," Randy says with a shrug and a flash of his dimples, "me three."

He's so damn adorable, Lucinda thinks. Inappropriately.

And so damn married.

Lucinda asked him about that yesterday. She had to, just in case.

Just in case . . . what? He was wearing

that gold band on his ring finger for luck?

When he awkwardly confirmed he'd married Carla, standing there in the salty sunshine, Lucinda couldn't help wishing a big fat gull would come along and crap all over him.

For luck, of course.

"Would you stop calling me that? My name is Rebecca."

"You don't have to pretend anymore. I know who you are. Game over. Here . . ."

On the ground, her back pressed against the stone wall, the girl flinches in the flashlight's beam. "Don't touch me."

"I'm not touching you, but I'm going to have to in a minute when I do your hair. Right now I'm just giving you a bottle of water. If you don't drink water, you'll die. You don't want to die, do you?"

The girl accepts the bottle silently, with fearful contempt, yet a perceptible hint of defiance hangs in the dank air.

"Go ahead. Drink it."

"Is it poisoned?"

"Of course it's not poisoned."

"Of course it's not poisoned?" The words are shrill with disbelief. "You kidnapped me. You injected me with something and knocked me out. You shoved me into this godforsaken hole in the ground, and you burned—"

"Shut up!"

She wisely clamps her mouth shut, but her eyes still blaze with disrespect. Little smart-ass.

"Drink the water or I'll force it down your throat and, trust me, I won't care if you choke on it."

Been there, done that.

Not with water, though.

Leah Roby. What a mess.

One sad, sorry mistake from start to finish.

She was the wrong girl.

It's not as though she was targeted for murder. Like the first girl in Santa Monica, and the ones who came after, hers was an accidental death . . . No one could dispute that. She was allergic to peanuts, she ate peanuts, she died. Period.

Died and lay here, rotting, for days until something had to be done.

She wasn't a pleasant sight by then. Bloated with gas, her skin covered in blisters, fluids oozing from her eyes, her mouth, her ears . . .

It wasn't as though she could be hoisted, carried up out of the cellar in one piece. An old firewood axe, a couple of big black construction garbage bags, a wheelbarrow . . . it was a horrible, time-consuming job.

What's left of Leah Roby is buried a good distance away, but the smell lingers. Stench this bad takes a long time to dissipate.

There must have been another way.

Not that it matters now.

The girl—the right girl—lifts the bottle to her lips, her hand shaking so hard the water sloshes over the neck. It spatters onto the dirt floor.

"You're spilling."

"So?"

"So you really shouldn't waste water."

"So? Who cares?"

Something is off about her.

The attitude, the voice—*what is it?*

Maybe nothing more than imagination. Paranoia, again.

It's been such a long time.

Still . . .

She was always strong-willed, but in a more subtle way. Now, even in the face of sheer terror, she's a brassy little piss pot, seemingly heedless of what can happen to her here, of the various punishments that would fit her particular crime.

It isn't like her. She should remember. She should know this place.

She might have forgotten . . . though how likely is that?

She might simply have changed. Not just physically.

Still . . .

Frustration is beginning to slip in to snuff out the earlier euphoria at having found her at last.

Wouldn't I perceive that it's her anyway, beyond a shadow of a doubt? Wouldn't I—shouldn't I—feel . . . something?

Looking at this girl who claims, over and over, that her name is Rebecca, it's impossible not to wonder whether she, too, is a mistake.

No. Stop. Don't even think it. Just go on doing what has to be done.

"I have to brush your hair now, put it back into braids."

"What? You're not touching me, freak." She glances up, the picture of defiance.

On her forehead, the raw, fresh brand is clearly visible.

MINE.

That's what it says, only . . .

You were wrong. You know it, don't you? You don't want to admit it, but you know.

No! It's her! It has to be!

Oh, come on. She's an imposter. Again. Just admit it.

"Can I ask you something?" Cam Hastings's voice interrupts Lucinda's thoughts.

"Sure. Shoot."

"When you have a vision . . . Are you ever wrong?"

"Never," Lucinda answers promptly.

"In case you hadn't noticed, Lucinda is a very confident person," Randy says dryly, and she rolls her eyes at him.

"I mean, I might interpret something

incorrectly, but . . . what I see has happened. Or is going to happen," she adds uncomfortably.

"I thought you only see the past," Randy says. "That's what I told her."

"In case you hadn't noticed, Randy is a very confident person." Lucinda shakes her head at him and he throws his hands up, smiles, shrugs.

"Seriously," she turns back to Cam, "in this line of work, what I see has usually already happened. But sometimes, of course, I have premonitions. It's not an absolute science."

"I didn't think so." Cam sighs. "I was just hoping maybe I was wrong about something happening to this girl."

"Yeah." Lucinda lays a hand on her arm. "I know it's hard."

"Thanks." Cam clears her throat. "Most people don't understand."

"No kidding. Really?" Lucinda manages a tight grin.

She likes Cam. She's trying so hard to seem stoic, but there's a potent vulnerability about her.

I wish I hadn't seen what I saw.

I wish I understood what it means.

"I'm sorry," Cam says, "but I need to excuse myself to go to the ladies' room. I'm pregnant, and . . ." She gestures vaguely at the empty water cup, then looks embarrassed.

"Hey, congratulations," Randy says promptly.

"That's great. When are you due?" Lucinda tries not to wonder if Randy and Carla have any babies. She couldn't bring herself to ask him about that yesterday.

"Around the holidays."

"Is this your first?" Randy asks.

"No." Already at the door, Cam tosses back over her shoulder, "I have a fourteen-year-old daughter."

Those words sweep over Lucinda like a January gust.

A daughter.

A fourteen-year-old daughter.

Now the puzzling, troubling vision Lucinda had when they met makes absolute sense.

Of course Cam Hastings has a daughter.

And her daughter, Lucinda comprehends with grim, sickening certainty, is going to die.

Rebecca jerks her head, hard, trying to free herself. "Let go of me, you freak! What are you doing?"

"Shhh, just be quiet and let me do your hair."

Her stomach lurches as she feels cool fingertips graze her skin. Loose strands are pushed back from her forehead, away from skin still raw and oozing from the hot iron held there until Rebecca thought she would die from the horror and the pain.

Even now, she's certain she's going to vomit, especially feeling those fingertips stroking her wounded skin. Somehow, though, she holds back the wave of bile.

You can't lose it. You've got to stay in control.

Her life, she suspects, depends on it.

This can't really be happening. It's got to be a nightmare. It's too unlikely, too horrific, too . . .

Too surreal, she thinks, feeling bristles moving through her hair now.

The strokes are oddly gentle, the voice almost sing-song, crooning, "You need to brush a hundred strokes a night, baby. You know that."

"Are you for real? Get your hands—oww!" Rebecca howls as the brush snags, sending fiery pain to the roots.

"Be still!" A hand, no longer gentle, clamps down over her scalp. "Did you forget that if you squirm around it makes it harder for me?"

"Harder for *you?*" Fury boils in Rebecca's blood. "You're out of your mind. Seriously. You're insane and I'm not—ow!"

"Sorry, baby. But it's your own fault. You haven't been brushing it, have you? Not at all. I can tell."

"Baby? I am not your baby!" Rebecca bites out, jaw clenched.

"Don't say that! Sit still!"

Tears sting Rebecca's eyes as the brush moves through her hair again, snags again.

"Stop it! I'm not your baby, you crazy f—"

"Shut up!"

"You shut up, and get your hands off me!"

The brush pivots abruptly and Rebecca's nerves explode in agony as a thick clump of hair rips from her scalp at the roots.

A primal howl escapes Rebecca; she can only hope someone, somewhere, will hear it and come to her rescue.

"Look what you made me do! You're going to have a bald spot now, are you happy?"

Rebecca instinctively clamps her mouth shut.

Summoning every ounce of self-control she has, she manages to still her body, manages to say, softly, "I'm sorry. I shouldn't have done it."

"No. You shouldn't have. But you're the one who has to live with this unsightly bald spot, not me."

Unsightly bald spot? *What about the unsightly gaping wound in the middle of my damn forehead?* Rebecca wants to screech.

But she forces herself to stay quiet, stay still.

The brush is moving through her hair again.

"There, now, isn't that better? If you just—"

The brush yanks at a snarl and Rebecca bites her lower lip to keep from crying out.

"If you just would have listened to me in the first place, none of this—none of it—would have happened. You'd be in the house opening your Christmas presents like a good girl."

"Christmas presents?" Rebecca echoes, then catches herself.

"They're all wrapped and waiting under the tree for you. And I baked gingerbread, just like I promised you."

Tree? Gingerbread? Good Lord, this freak is even more insane than I thought.

"Thank you," Rebecca makes herself say politely. "That was kind of you."

Gag.

"Well, I'm nothing if not kind. You know that. Even when you don't deserve it. But if you're a good girl and you behave yourself from now on, maybe you'll get presents and gingerbread after all."

Yeah, right. Or maybe you'll slit my throat when I'm not looking, you freak.

"What do you say, baby? Can you be a good little girl?"

"Yes," Rebecca says meekly. "I can be a good little girl."

Then she dips her head forward abruptly and slams it back as hard as she can. Her skull meets its target with a satisfying thud and explodes in blinding, nauseating pain.

Dimly aware of her tormentor's outraged bellow, Rebecca falls to her hands and knees on the dirt floor.

"You little bitch!"

Rebecca feels herself reeling, spinning. She begins to crawl, toward the ladder, feels cold, hard hands grabbing her ankles. Her knees are yanked from under her and she's down on her stomach, being dragged backward.

"I'm sorry!" she screams, desperate. "I didn't mean it! It was an accident! I didn't mean to hurt you!"

The dragging pauses. "You didn't?"

"No, I told you, it was an accident." Rebecca's head throbs and her body is trembling so violently she can literally feel her bones rattling.

"Really? It was an accident?"

No. I wanted to kill you. If I could have, I would have.

"Yes," Rebecca manages to say through the pain. "Really."

"All right then, baby. Accidents happen. Now, let's fix your hair, because you really look hideously ugly right now, you know that? Why on earth did you dye your hair that god-awful shade of orange?"

Before she can stop herself, Rebecca jerks her leg up in a swift, hard kick. It makes contact, but she knows that she just made a terrible mistake.

"You little . . ."

Her assailant is upon her.

Rebecca fights back, clawing, biting, growling. She manages to wrench herself free and struggles to regain control, but the pain in her skull is too intense. Hot, acid vomit rushes up her throat now, choking her as she futilely struggles toward the ladder.

She feels a rush of movement behind her. She forces her eyes open, spins her head just in time to see the brand coming at her again.

This time, though, it isn't red hot.

Just hard and heavy and—

The brand comes down with a mighty force into Rebecca's forehead, obliterating the very message inflicted there just hours ago: MINE.

Chapter Thirteen

The Atlantic is a little rough, rocking the small fishing boat as the engine cuts to an idling putter.

Ten miles out at sea, the coastal lights long since vanished in the predawn haze. Nothing out here but the incessant waves sparkling in the early-morning light, the smell of sticky salt air, the screech of an arcing seagull high overhead.

"Planning on chumming?" asked a middle-aged fisherman back at the dock. He came out of nowhere to eye the sealed five-gallon buckets as they were being loaded onto the boat.

He seemed satisfied with the casual, affirmative reply. "Well, good luck out there. The fish are biting today."

With a friendly wave, he strolled toward his pickup truck parked nearby—unaware that its vanity license plate had just been memorized: New Jersey, JMurph2, with a black plate holder from a Beach Haven dealership.

JMurph2's future—his life—is now hanging in the balance.

Just like Eddie Casalino, he'd noticed too much, said too much.

Something will have to be done about his interference.

Later, though.

For now, the important thing is . . .

Chumming.

The Internet contained specific instructions for that method of baiting. The first step: hang a milk crate off the back of the boat, low enough so that its base just touches the water.

That's the easy part.

Time for the hard part: prying the cover off the first bucket while trying not to pass out from the overwhelming smell.

A clean bandana tied tightly over both mouth and nostrils doesn't come close to blocking it out.

Steady there. Don't get sick, faint, fall overboard . . .

Just focus on what you have to do, and do it fast.

The contents of the bucket hit the crate with a sickening, sloshing thud.

Saltwater laps over the slimy, bloody heap of eviscerated flesh, shattered bone, oozing entrails, washing it into the sea.

It shouldn't be long now.

Yawn. The sleepless night's effects are starting to take hold.

So is thirst.

A few bottles of water on the boat would have been a good idea.

That, and maybe some nice, loud music.

So I don't drift right off to sleep out here.

Then again, one would be hard-pressed to find a fitting soundtrack for these particular circumstances.

Speculation in that regard is an amusing diversion until something breaks the surface of the water a good distance away, then disappears.

Was that . . . ?

Oh, yes. It sure was.

The dorsal fin crests again, barreling this way.

With it, the most appropriate background music of all springs to mind: the theme from *Jaws,* of course.

That lackadaisical thought is quickly discarded. This is no laughing matter.

The contents of the second bucket are quickly poured directly into the water.

The third as well.

And then the last.

Fascinating—and a little frightening—to watch the frothy feeding frenzy that ensues.

In no time, the boat will be headed back to shore and this unpleasant little episode will draw to a close.

How could you have made such a careless mistake?

As the creatures from the ocean's cold depths dispose of Rebecca Pearson's unrecognizable remains, the most menacing predator of all watches through narrowed eyes from the boat, knowing the hunt must begin again.

Today, even.

There's no time to waste.

She's somewhere on that island, and you're going to find her.

Cam awakens, bathed in sweat, to bright sunlight and a ringing telephone.

What the . . . ?

What time . . . ?

Past twelve.

PM.

The standing fan at the foot of the bed creaks as it pans across her body, and the phone rings again.

She should answer it. Sitting up, she swings her bare feet around to the floor and rubs her eyes.

She hasn't slept this late since . . . college, probably, Cam decides as she fumbles around for her cell phone.

Noon, yet she didn't even get a full eight hours.

It was after midnight when she got back from the police station. She sat up for awhile, poring over the notebooks she'd left on the coffee table, remembering every detail about some visions, having forgotten some others even existed, even with the notes.

They all started to blend together after awhile . . .

Girl, about sixteen, dark hair, green eyes, in bathing suit . . .

Kid, college-aged, scruffy beard, Teva sandals . . .

Boy, in jeans and gray Nike T-shirt, on skateboard . . .

She found herself wondering what happened to them.

She reminded herself that she already knew.

In the latest notebook, she added Leah's name to the first page.

Then she sat reading about her and the other girl, willing more information to come to her; praying for another vision.

Nothing happened.

Maybe she was just too tired.

Finally, she put the notebooks aside and went to bed.

It wasn't until she sank back against the pillows that she realized something.

Not only had she just survived one of the most stressful nights of her life without a drop of booze, but she hadn't even craved it. Caught up in the unfolding drama, she never once considered numbing her emotions with liquor.

A milestone—that's what it was. A turning point in her ongoing battle. Kathy told her there would be many of those along the way. She warned Cam not to let her guard down, get too confident.

"The second you decide you've won the war," Kathy said ominously, "you're asking for trouble."

Cam had a terrible time falling asleep. She was still lying awake when the sun came up; still on edge; still thinking of that redheaded girl, feeling as though it's too late for her, just like all the others.

She might be wrong.

She desperately hopes she is.

But even now, in the light of day, the aura of doom persists.

The phone stops ringing just as she finds it in the pocket of the shorts she had on yesterday.

That's fine with Cam. She doesn't feel like talking to anyone anyway, and her bladder is painfully full.

Then she remembers. Tess.

If Tess was calling . . .

But she wasn't.

The caller ID reveals a local number. Fine. Whoever it was will leave a message.

Cam hurries into the bathroom, the earlier part of last night—at the police station—rushing back at her.

Detective Barakat said he'd be in touch, took her number, gave her his card.

Lucinda didn't volunteer her contact information, and Cam didn't ask.

As much as Cam would have loved to get together again—talk, compare notes—she was too shy, in the end, to extend an invitation.

No wonder you haven't made a new friend in so long.

Other than Debbie . . . whose barbecue Cam is supposed to attend in less than two hours, come to think of it.

That might have been her calling just now.

Standing over the sink, she squeezes a gob of Crest onto her toothbrush.

Or it could have been the detective.

But when she checks for messages, there aren't any.

* * *

"Couldn't reach your friend?"

Hanging up the telephone receiver in the parlor, Lucinda looks up to see Martha, the inn's owner, watching her from the doorway with a plastic laundry basket in her arms.

"Oh . . . no. No answer." She moves away from the phone, almost tripping over a stack of magazines in a fake-antique box that reads FIREWOOD.

More clutter. Lucinda—who happens to be something of a pack rat herself—has never seen so much of it in her life.

"Most people have answering machines these days. He doesn't?"

Well aware Martha is fishing with that strategic *he,* Lucinda asks, "Who doesn't have an answering machine?"

"Your friend. The person you called."

He's not a *he*—and *she* does have voice mail, which Lucinda just hung up on—but she isn't about to tell the old snoop any of that.

"Do you know what time it is?" she asks, instead. She forgot her watch upstairs when she went for a walk on the beach just now, thinking she should sort things out in her head.

Martha gestures at the mantel clock. "Quarter past twelve."

Lucinda thanks her, then heads into the foyer. She peruses the stack of daily and weekly newspapers on the table.

"Only one that's missing is the *New York Times*."

She looks up to see that Martha has followed her.

"That woman who's staying in the cottage out back took it to breakfast with her, and then it disappeared. So did she."

Kathy—the woman Lucinda met yesterday morning. The one she was so certain was hiding something.

She didn't figure out what it was, though. And Kathy beat a hasty retreat. She hasn't seen her since.

She wishes Martha would make herself scarce as well, but here she is, making small talk about the weather.

Lucinda should never have asked her to use the guesthouse telephone in the first place. But she didn't want to place the call from her cell.

She never likes to give it out when she's working on a case. Or ever, for that matter. Handing her phone number to a stranger opens the door to all kinds of potential trouble: prank calls, desperate requests from the bereaved, fortune-teller buffs wanting their palms read.

Lucinda learned the hard way that it's best for her to be reachable only through Neal. He's her liaison to the general public. And he's not here with her, so . . .

End of story.

Except this is different. Randy is involved, and Camden Hastings isn't exactly the general public, and she isn't seeking psychic feedback. She's a psychic herself.

So why didn't you give her your number last night?

Habit, she supposes.

Then why are you so determined that she doesn't get it even now?

"What have you got planned for today?" Martha asks conversationally. "Going to the beach?"

Having momentarily forgotten all about

her, Lucinda glances her way and finds her still hovering.

Ignoring the question, she poses one of her own. “What time is checkout?”

“Checkout? You mean, for tomorrow? It’s noon.”

“No, I mean for today.”

“Today? It’s too late. It’s past twelve already, remember? And you said you were staying until—”

“I need to leave today,” Lucinda says abruptly.

Martha’s straggly white brows furrow. “I’m afraid you can’t do that. There’s a three-night minimum on holiday weekends.”

This is the first Lucinda’s heard about that, but she shrugs. “Sorry,” she says, “I can’t stay.”

“But I’d have to charge you for—”

“Go ahead. Just bill it to my credit card.”

Martha scowls, then heads for the stairs with her laundry basket.

Lucinda waits a few minutes, flipping through the papers, not wanting to follow her right up.

Yeah, it’s time to go. Definitely. The

place is a dump, she's made no progress with the Roby case, and Randy went and married Carla.

Why stick around?

An image of Cam Hastings pops into her head.

Yeah, and now that Lucinda has figured out what the vision means, she has all the more reason to avoid Cam, right?

Right.

Or maybe she has all the more reason to confront her with a warning.

Which is what she was thinking when she tried calling her just now.

But when Cam didn't pick up, she talked herself right back out of it.

What's wrong with you? This isn't like you—bullshitting around, wondering what to do.

She knows what to do.

Didn't she learn the hard way, years ago, what can happen when you try to warn a person that something horrible is going to happen to a loved one?

But Cam isn't just some random person. She understands about premonitions. Has them herself.

All the more reason to approach her.

Lucinda turns away from the newspapers and heads for the stairs.

So, say you do tell her that her daughter is in danger. What's she supposed to do about it?

You don't know where, or how, or when it's going to happen.

For all you know, it already has.

And now you're making no sense whatsoever.

All Lucinda knows is that she saw a girl—whom she now understands is Cam's daughter—engaged in a futile struggle with a man in some kind of dark hood.

Just a snippet of a scene, but the outcome is going to be violent. She didn't see that part, but she could feel it.

And death. Looming, ready to pounce.

She's felt it before.

She's never been wrong.

Never once.

So what would warning Cam accomplish?

She'd be beside herself with anxiety. Any mother would be.

For a pregnant woman, at her age especially, that wouldn't be good.

In the end, it will change nothing.

If her daughter is destined to die—and she is—then she will.

So I won't tell her mother, Lucinda decides. *I can't save the world. I just do what I can, same as always.*

Her cell phone rings in her pocket as she reaches the second floor hallway.

She pauses to answer it before starting up the next flight to the hotter-than-Hades third floor. There's no sign of Martha. She's probably upstairs stripping Lucinda's bed for the next unwitting sap who comes along.

"Hello?"

"It's Randy. What are you doing?"

"I'm about to pack and head back to Philly."

A pause.

Then, "You might want to rethink that plan."

"Why?" she asks again.

"Because a girl named Rebecca Pearson disappeared from her bedroom at her family's summer house in Loveladies sometime overnight."

Lucinda sucks in a breath. "Let me

guess. Thirteen years old, red hair, freckles . . ."

"Yeah, and she was wearing a necklace."

"I'll guess again—shark's tooth on a silver chain?"

"Exactly. Her sister said she got from a secret admirer."

"I'll just bet she did." As Lucinda shakes her head, clutching the phone, she hears a faint sound.

A creaking floorboard.

Someone is lurking, concealed somewhere nearby. Listening.

"Coming with me to talk to the family?" Randy asks.

Wary, Lucinda answers with one word. "Definitely."

"Good. Get right over here, then. And I wouldn't check out yet if I were you."

"I already did."

"Check back in."

"I doubt that's possible." She casts a glance down the hall. Still no sign of Martha, or a fellow guest.

"I'll try to find you another place, then. Worse comes to worst, you can stay in our guestroom."

His and Carla's guestroom?

That would be *worse* comes to *no way in hell*.

She'd sooner come crawling back to this pit than set foot inside their happy abode and come face-to-face with the woman who put that gold ring on Randy's finger.

"I'll work something out," she assures him.

Tess stares out the car window at the green landscape lining the Garden State Parkway, wondering what her mother's going to say when she walks in the door.

She—or her father—should probably have called to say she was coming back early.

But pretty much the moment she told Dad she wanted to leave—after they both slept in until well past ten—he started packing.

Not in anger, or hurt. No, he seemed more . . . resigned.

As if he's simply given up on Tess.

Which isn't the best feeling.

He had the car loaded before breakfast and they were in it less than a half hour later, heading north.

The trip was a repeat performance of the one down to DC the day before yesterday: slow-going, holiday traffic, Dad brooding, Tess plugged into her iPod.

A few times, overcome by guilt, she almost told him to turn around and go back.

But she managed not to.

She doesn't want to go back to Washington with him.

She doesn't want to be on Long Beach Island without him, either.

The whole thing sucks.

Tess sighs, seeing the sign for Route 72, the exit leading to the island causeway.

Dad must have seen it, too. She hears the rumble of his voice above the throbbing bass in her ear and realizes he's saying something to her.

She unplugs one earphone. "What?"

"What if your mother's not home?"

"She will be."

"How do you know? You should call her and make sure."

"It's not a big deal if she's not there.

It's not like she's gone for the weekend. She'll show up eventually. You can wait with me until she does."

Tess waits a minute for him to respond, but he says nothing.

With a shrug, she plugs her earphone in again and goes back to staring out the window and hating her life.

"Pop?" Shocked, Cam stares at her father, who just materialized on her threshold in a white wife beater, cutoffs, and flip-flops, a red bandana tied over his straggly gray hair, doo-rag style.

"Happy Fourth of July." He hands her a cardboard and cellophane box.

She looks down to see supermarket donut holes, glazed, with red, white, and blue sprinkles.

"It is the Fourth of July, right?" Ike asks.

"Right."

"I really need to get a calendar one of these days. Among other things."

Cam reaches across the threshold and gives him a hug. "Come in! What are you doing here?"

"You said to come visit. I found myself on the island, so . . . here I am."

Drunk as a skunk, too. She finds herself enveloped in liquor fumes—and other unsavory scents—and her stomach churns a little.

"Where's my grandbaby?"

"Tess? She's . . . out with Mike."

Cam will have to tell him the truth. But it won't sink in unless she sobers him up first.

He could use a good scrubbing, too, she decides, wrinkling her nose as she closes the door behind him.

"It's so hot and sticky out . . . Why don't you go take a nice cool shower?" she asks. "I'll throw your clothes into the washer for you and find something else for you to wear."

God knows what.

Mike left a few things behind in a drawer last August when they closed up the house. They all did, as usual, wanting to think they might prolong summer by making another weekend trip to the island sometime in the fall.

They never have.

When it's over, it's over, Cam thinks

grimly. *Like everything else in life, apparently.*

"I reek, don't I?" her father asks, as she leads the way to the bathroom.

"A little. But I love you anyway. Where have you been hiding?"

"Who says I've been hiding?"

He sounds prickly. He can be a nasty drunk on occasion, though he's usually pretty jovial.

"It's just an expression," she says shortly. "Towels are in that cabinet. I'll go make some coffee."

"I'd rather have a beer."

"Fresh out. Sorry."

Cam leaves him in the bathroom, shaking her head.

In the living room, where the shades are still pulled down, the Marble notebooks sit on the table beside the empty water glass from last night. Talk about careless. She has to put those away . . . not that Ike is likely to go snooping around, or would be capable of reading, in his current condition, if he wanted to.

Heading for the kitchen, she decides she'll start the coffee first, then put the notebooks back in the closet.

Of all the things she didn't need today, an unexpected visit from her father was at the top of the list.

Well, it could have been worse.

It could have been Mike, popping up unexpectedly on her doorstep to pick up where they left off.

Luckily for Cam, he and Tess are two hundred miles away right about now. Pop is going to ask about them. She'll have to tell him.

She's measuring coffee grounds into a filter basket when her cell phone rings, somewhere in the bedroom.

This time, she reaches it before it goes to voice mail.

Again, it's a local number.

"Camden Hastings?"

"Yes?"

"Detective Barakat."

With a sinking feeling she knows, before he says anything else, what he's going to tell her.

And she's right.

"Rebecca Pearson," she echoes when he tells her the name of the girl who vanished in the dead of night.

"I'm on my way now to speak with her parents."

Cam, now in the kitchen, stares miserably out the kitchen window at the beach house across the way, thinking of Rebecca's mother.

"Listen, I know you're not used to this kind of thing," the detective goes on, "but if you'd like to come over there with me—"

"No," she says quickly. "No, I can't."

"I thought you might see something else . . . if you had a chance to see her room, touch her things, meet her parents. That's how it works with Lucinda."

"It doesn't work that way with me."

"How do you know? Have you ever tried?"

"No, but—"

"You've never run into one if these victims in person before, either. But you did with Rebecca Pearson."

Cam hesitates, thinking again of Rebecca's mother.

The woman must be distraught.

"All right," she says slowly. "Maybe, if she's being held someplace, I can get some kind of psychic impression of where she is. Especially if she's nearby."

"Okay. I'll come pick you up and bring you over there."

"When?"

"Now would be good."

She agrees to meet him out in front of her house, then hangs up.

"Camden?"

The voice scares the hell out of Cam, and she gasps, whirling around.

"What's wrong? Did you forget I was here?" asks her father, standing in the doorway, towel in hand.

"Oh . . . actually, I did," she admits, and sinks into a chair, trembling. She wonders how long he's been standing there eavesdropping.

"I wanted to ask if you had a disposable razor so I can shave before I get into the shower. I caught sight of myself in the mirror and thought I was looking at Santa Claus."

"There's a *razor* in the drawer on the right beneath the sink," she tells him, and forces herself to get up again, keep talking. "Listen, I've got to go out and run a few errands. Take your shower, have some coffee, take a nap . . . I'll be back a little later, and we'll catch up then. Okay?"

Ike shrugs. "Why not?"

As he makes his way back to the bathroom, Cam, exhausted, rakes a hand through her hair and looks down at her swollen midsection.

"I'm so sorry," she whispers, laying a gentle hand over her stomach.

As if in reply, something—a tiny foot or fist—flutters within.

The baby's first kick.

Hastily wiping a blur of tears, Cam heads for the door.

Not only is Cam's Volvo in the driveway, but Mike also sees his father-in-law's car parked at the curb.

"Looks like Granddad's here," he tells Tess.

In the passenger's seat, she's finally pulled the earplugs out and is shoving her bare feet into her flip-flops. "Good—we haven't seen him in, like, forever. Not since winter."

Winter—before Mike left.

He's not particularly eager to face his father-in-law. Ike can be an easygoing guy, but he does have a temper. He can't be happy about the separation, or his daughter now alone and pregnant, his granddaughter in a broken home.

That makes all of us, Mike thinks glumly.

He's had a lot of time to think things through on the drive back.

He's going to be a father again.

Another tiny miracle in his arms.

Another chance.

Maybe he and Cam really should try again to make things work. For the baby's sake. And Tess's. And—who is he kidding?—for their own.

Yeah.

He needs to talk to Cam as soon as possible. If Tess hadn't asked to go home today, he might have suggested it himself.

The street is lined with more cars than usual. "Looks like someone's having a party," Mike comments as he pulls in behind the Volvo.

"Yeah, friends of ours are." Tess's hand

is already on the door handle. "A few houses down. Mom's there, I'm sure."

Friends of theirs.

Not his.

Strange, that his wife and daughter have friends he's never met; go to parties to which he isn't invited.

This can't go on. It's strange, and it's wrong, and things are going to get back to the way they were.

Granted, the way things were wasn't so great, either, but . . .

Mike is going to make things better. He's going to work at his marriage, try hard to get it right.

What if Cam doesn't want to, though? Yeah, she's stopped drinking, but that doesn't mean she'll be the same old Cam. She might let you back into the house, but that doesn't mean she'll let you in.

Mike pushes aside the nagging memory of Cam's emotional fortress and opens his car door.

"What are you doing?" Tess asks promptly.

"Coming in to talk to your mother."

"I just told you . . . She's probably at the party."

"Maybe not. Granddad's here."

Mike nods. For all he knows Cam is down the street with her new friends and Ike is inside, passed out cold in front of an empty six-pack. The scene isn't exactly set for a romantic reunion.

Maybe he should wait.

Figure out how to get it right.

But then, he heads for Japan in about a week, and by the time he gets back, the summer will be half-over.

"You can leave, Dad," Tess says. "I'll go find Mom and tell her I'm back."

"You don't think she might wonder why you're home two days early and want to talk to me?"

"You don't think I'm capable of explaining it to her?" she shoots back.

He fixes Tess with a look, wondering how, exactly, she would spin their early departure from DC without his input. But that's beside the point.

"There are some things I need to discuss with your mom, Tess."

"Oh. Yeah. You mean the bag-search thing? Because you don't necessarily need to talk to her about that in person. And anyway," Tess goes on, "I'm telling her my side of the story either way. She'll believe me."

"Yeah, well . . . so do I."

"What?" Tess gapes.

"I said, I believe you."

"You do?"

"I've been thinking about it, and I realized you've never lied to me before."

"No." She shakes her head. "I told you. I never did."

"So I'm going to give you the benefit of the doubt. I know what it's like to try to fit in with friends at your age—although you do know that taking a bottle of vodka from that girl was wrong, don't you?"

Tess nods vigorously. "I wasn't going to drink it. I just didn't want her to think I was a baby."

"But you've learned your lesson, right? Because if I ever catch you with booze again, or with anything that—"

"Dad! You won't! Do you think I'm actually going to drink after seeing what it did to Mom?"

He's silent for a moment. "No. I really

don't. But there are other things, Tess . . . things kids will want you to do."

"And you don't trust me to be smart enough not to?"

"Sometimes it's not about being smart." Mike shakes his head. She's got so much to learn at this age. So many hard choices ahead. She's going to be a big sister, a role model for someone who's going to grow up looking up to her.

And I want to be there to teach her. Guide her. Watch over her.

One step at a time, Mike.

"The thing is," he says, "I believe you. I believe that you were worried about your mother, and you didn't want her to start drinking again, so you took that bottle with you when you left."

"She got rid of everything. I thought if she found that vodka, she might start again."

"She's stronger than you think, Tess," he says quietly.

"Yeah, maybe she is. So anyway, are you going back now?" Tess asks, obviously eager to join Cam at the party with all those people who are part of their life on the island, which he is not.

"No." Mike gets out of the car. "I'm staying here."

Tess's eyes widen. "For good?"

I wish.

"No, just . . . I want to talk to Mom. Let's go in."

"Nina." Lucinda turns to the missing girl's younger sister, a shell-shocked twelve-year-old with the same red hair and freckles. "Did your sister mention how that shark's tooth necklace got to her? Was it mailed, or . . . ?"

Nina shakes her head. "She found it in a bag hanging on her bike handlebars the other morning."

"Where was her bike?"

"Parked under the overhang by the patio. That's where we keep all our bikes. Mine, Becca's, Mom's, Dad's."

"So someone must have known which bike was your sister's?" That question comes from Randy.

"I guess." Nina looks down at her white Keds.

"Was it obvious?" Randy asks.

"He means," Lucinda says, "was Rebecca's name on it or something?"

"No. And mine and Nina's are just like hers, only different colors," Rebecca's mother, Diane, says thinly. "Rebecca's was pink."

"It's her favorite color," Nina adds, and her mother nods.

"We always tease her about it because it clashes with her hair." Diane makes a sound that starts out as a laugh, but winds up a sob.

Her husband, Bob, puts an arm around her, and the other around Nina as she, too, begins to cry.

This is brutal.

Lucinda glances at Cam to see how she's handling this.

Seated in the chair closest to the door, she looks as though she wishes she could run right through it. Lucinda tries to catch her eye, wanting to offer an encouraging smile, though she's not sure why.

There's nothing encouraging about the scene at the Pearsons's house, a modern three-level oceanfront property in

Loveladies. The forensics team is still working in Rebecca's bedroom so the rest of them are here in the living room on the top floor. The three Pearsons are on the couch, with Lucinda and Randy flanking them in comfortable chairs.

Lucinda figures they assume she and Cam are also detectives. They were too distraught to ask any questions when Randy introduced the two of them by name only.

"We know how hard this is for all of you." Randy's voice is laced with concern and compassion. "I know you've been over this a few times already, Mr. Pearson, but you were the last one to see your daughter last night. Would you mind telling me everything you remember again?"

"He's not a suspect, is he?" Rebecca's mother asks, sounding alarmed.

"The parents are always suspects, Diane," her husband responds. "But it's okay. I'll tell you anything you want to know."

Restless as Bob goes over the details again, Lucinda rises from her chair and paces across the room.

Glancing out at the blue patch of sea in the distance, she sees something flash in her mind's eye.

A dorsal fin.

It rises out of the water, just like before, that day in Leah Roby's bedroom.

But this time, there are more fins.

And churning water, bubbling red with blood.

If Lucinda was holding out any hope for Rebecca Pearson, in that instant, it evaporates.

She knows without a doubt that the girl was murdered, her remains disposed of at sea.

Shaking her head in sorrow, she turns abruptly away from the window and finds Cam staring at her.

She knows, Lucinda realizes, seeing her bleak expression. *She feels it, too.*

She shakes her head slightly at Cam and tilts it toward the family on the couch.

Cam shakes her head back. No, she won't say a word to them about it, either.

"We're going to put out an Amber Alert," Randy is telling the Pearsons, "and we're pulling in all our resources to find her as quickly as possible."

Without anything concrete to go on, it's better to let them stay in the dark for now.

Just as it's best to do the same for Cam herself.

Chapter Fourteen

"So, what's doing?" Granddad asks as the three of them—he, Tess, and Dad—sit down at the kitchen table together.

Granddad and Dad are having coffee; Tess a couple of glazed donut holes her grandfather had brought.

"Not much," Dad says. "Washington was hot. Crowded. That's why we left early."

Not really, but Tess nods, grateful to go with that explanation.

"Washington?" Her grandfather looks from Dad to Tess and back again, apparently confused.

That's not surprising. He seemed a little out of it when they came in, and Tess could smell booze on his breath. Maybe he's drunk. It wouldn't be the first time. Like daughter, like father.

"Who was in Washington?" Granddad asks Dad.

"We were. We just got back."

Granddad looks around. "Cam, too?"

"Cam is here in Beach Haven . . . You just said you saw her, remember?" Dad sounds a little anxious. "You said she went out to do some errands."

Which doesn't make sense, Tess thinks, because Mom's car is here. She must be down at Debbie's. Granddad must be confused.

"I thought that's what she said," Granddad says, frowning. "I *thought* I saw her. But now you're saying you were all in Washington . . ."

"Just me and Tess."

"Not Cam?"

"No."

"Good. I was hoping I wasn't seeing things. I could have sworn I talked to her." Granddad sips his coffee, makes a face. Then he looks up sharply. "Why didn't she go with you?"

Now Dad looks uncomfortable. "She

had, other, uh, things to do this weekend."

"Like what?"

Tess decides to get things out into the open.

"He doesn't know," she tells her father. "About you and Mom."

"Obviously not," Dad mutters, and shoots her a dark look.

To Granddad, he says only, "Why don't we all discuss this together when Cam gets back?"

"Discuss what?"

"Mom and Dad are separated, Granddad," Tess says. At her father's dismayed expression, she asks, innocently, "What?"

He shakes his head.

"I'm just being honest, Dad. You always said that was the best policy. Remember? And I always tell the truth. *Always*." The last word is pointed.

"You and Cam are separated?" Granddad sounds sad.

"Yeah, Ike. I didn't realize you didn't know. I didn't want to be the one who told you."

"What the hell happened?"

"I wish I knew."

Tess looks at her father in surprise, just as a knock sounds on the door.

"I'll get that." She seizes the opportunity to hurry out of the room.

Beth is standing on the other side of the screen door. "Hey! What are you doing here? I thought you were in Washington."

"I was. What are *you* doing here?"

"My mom sent me over to get your mom for the barbecue."

"She's not there?"

"Nope. It started awhile ago. Mom's been trying to call for like an hour but she must have her cell phone turned off. Where is she?"

"I don't know . . . errands, I guess." Tess frowns. What kind of errands would Mom run without her car?

She supposes someone could have picked her up . . . but who?

Remembering her old passing suspicion, back when they were at home and Dad first left, she wonders if her mother is out with another man.

That has to be it.

Mom was cheating.

That's why Dad left, after all.

"Come on," Beth says, and holds the door open.

"Come on where?" Tess is reeling.

"To the barbecue. Your mom can meet us there."

"I can't go."

"Why not?"

"My grandfather's here, and my dad still is, too, so . . ."

"So?"

"So I can't just abandon them."

Beth shrugs. "Bring them. Whatever. You have to come. I need you."

"Why?" Tess asks, pleased, nonetheless, to be needed by Beth.

"Because you've got to meet this lady my mother hired to stay with us when she goes back to work. Dolores."

"She's there?"

"Yeah. I hate her already."

"What did she do?"

"She's just evil. I can tell." Beth frowns, then, just as quickly, shifts gears with an excited, "Oh, listen, you have got to hear who I met on the beach today! I was gonna text you about it."

"Who?"

"Guess. You'll never believe it."

"Bruce Springsteen?"

"Bruce Springsteen?" Beth rolls her eyes.

"You said I would never believe it."

"Why wouldn't you? He hangs out down here all the time. He's from Freehold or something. But anyway—no. I mean someone good."

"Bruce is good."

"Please." Obviously Beth doesn't agree.

"I don't know," Tess says impatiently, "Who?"

"Someone from back home."

"Where do you live again?"

"Not *my* home, you goof. Yours. Someone you know."

"Who?" Tess asks again, trepidation creeping in.

"This hottie lifeguard . . ."

"Who?" Tess practically screams it this time.

"His name is Heath."

"How are you doing? You still okay?" Randall Barakat asks Cam as the three of them step over the threshold into

Rebecca Pearson's bedroom on the first floor.

"Hanging in there." She tries to smile at him but can't quite muster one.

Rebecca is never coming back here. She's dead.

The impression washed over her as they sat upstairs talking to her parents and sister, all of them clinging to the hope that Rebecca ran away, even though that's not like her. Mr. Pearson even speculated that she's being held for ransom somewhere and told Randy that he's willing to pay to get her back.

"Do me a favor," Randy said in response, "don't say that to anyone other than me, okay? There are a lot of nutcases in the world."

Yes. And one of them stole Bob and Diane Pearson's daughter in the night and killed her.

Cam can't put her finger on exactly how she knows it, but she does.

So does Lucinda.

She can tell.

Still, Lucinda walks around the bedroom, now covered in fingerprint dust and little tent markers that indicate possible evidence locations.

"There were no signs of a break-in," Randy comments in a low voice, "and we don't think anyone came and took her out of this room, no matter what her parents claim."

"She wouldn't sneak out of the house late at night. Not their little girl," Lucinda murmurs with a nod, as though she's heard it all before.

I'd say the same thing about Tess, Cam realizes. *Not my little girl.*

Only Tess isn't a little girl anymore.

Still, she would never—

The dizziness blows in out of nowhere and Cam blindly grabs the doorjamb.

Images flash in and out of her head: a bizarre slide show at warp speed.

Tess, terrified, with a tear-stained face.

Tess, panting, staring wide-eyed at something—someone—Cam can't see.

Tess, pleading.

Tess in danger.

Tess afraid.

Tess unable to breathe . . . strangling, throat constricted, lungs bursting—

"Cam? Are you all right?"

Dazed, she looks up to see both Randy and Lucinda, concerned.

"It sounds like you're hyperventilating." Lucinda touches her shoulder. "Do you want a paper bag, or . . . ?"

Hyperventilating?

It was Tess. Tess can't breathe.

"No," Cam says weakly, "I just . . . I really need to get out of here. Please."

"Under the bo-ard-walk. Bo-ard-walk," Ike sings along with the Drifters, lounging on a plastic chaise on someone's deck in the sunshine.

He doesn't know whose deck—just some neighbor of his daughter's. Who cares whose deck it is? Ike was invited, and he's here.

Someone hands him another cold beer. He drains the old bottle quickly and lifts the new in a toast. "Thanks, buddy!"

"You're welcome," whoever it is says cheerfully, and reaches into one of the ice-filled coolers again.

Great party.

He doesn't know a soul here besides

Tess—who disappeared a few minutes after she and Ike arrived—but again, who cares?

A deck barbecue on a beautiful July day on the island?

Yeah, he'll take it.

Someone's cooking burgers and hot dogs on a grill, the music is cranking over a couple of decent speakers, there's a lot of beer—good beer, imported, in longneck bottles—and Frozen Piña Coladas.

The pretty little brunette poured him one when he first got here. She laughed when he drained it in one big gulp, gave a satisfied, "Ahh," and plunked the cup down to be refilled again.

"You're Cam's dad?" she asked, obliging.

"Yup. And you are . . . ?"

Debbie, he thinks she said, though he could be wrong. He's met so many people in the last hour . . . or is it two?

"I'll have Dolores go make another pitcher."

"Dolores?" That name, Ike remembers. He knew a Dolores once, years ago. Down here at the shore. Can it possibly be her? How many Doloreses can there be?

"She's my hired woman."

He can't imagine his Dolores being a hired woman. Anyway, what are the odds he'd run into her here, on his daughter's street?

That would be a huge coincidence, that's for damn sure.

"If you need another refill," Cam's friend said, "just go into the kitchen and Dolores will set you up."

Ike didn't bother. Beer is fine with him. He's not one of those fancy types who likes girl drinks, like the ones at the Sandbucket.

Too bad Cam's not around. She should be showing up sooner or later, though, right? He left her a note—or maybe it was Tess who wrote the note. He can't remember, exactly.

It wasn't Mike, though. Mike, he's pretty sure, left to drive back to the city.

Alone.

Ike may actually have told him to get the hell out of his daughter's house. Or life.

Or maybe he just wanted to say it, but kept the words to himself.

The details are a little fuzzy now.

He's certain of one thing, though: Mike and Cam split up months ago, and no one told him till today, and he's mad as hell.

Don't they know you don't just give up and walk away?

Way to ruin a great day . . . only Ike's not going to let it.

"On a blanket with my ba-aby . . . is where I'll be," he sings, and guzzles some beer.

My baby.

"Excuse me . . . ?"

Ike looks up into the sun to see Ava standing over him.

His jaw drops.

He blinks.

Turns his head a little, the light shifts, she moves her head.

Oh. It's not Ava.

The woman looks nothing like Ava, in fact.

You were just looking for her, same as always. For her, for Brenda, for Cam . . . your girls . . .

"Are you Camden Hastings's dad?" the woman asks, all friendly.

"Sure am. Who are you?"

"I'm a friend of hers. I heard she's involved in that missing persons case?"

Ike's heart stops beating. The Drifters stop singing. The world stops turning.

"Missing?" Ike puts his hand back to prop himself straight; his fist goes through the plastic slats. "Cam is missing?"

"No, she's not missing. She's helping. On the case. Right?"

His heart beats, the Drifters sing, the world turns.

He leans back again.

Jesus.

"She's some kind of witness or something, I heard. Someone said she was working with the cops."

Cops? Witness? Cam?

Ike decides that either the woman's stoned out of her mind, or he is . . . though he doesn't remember getting high. But that's nothing new.

"I have no idea what you're talking about," he says pleasantly. "She doesn't tell her old man everything, you know."

Come to think of it, she doesn't tell him much of anything at all.

"So." Randy looks at Lucinda over the rim of his coffee cup.

"So."

"She's dead, isn't she?"

Lucinda sips her own coffee, sets it down. "Did I say that?"

"You didn't have to. I figured it out."

"You're psychic?"

"No, but you are, and I can read you, Sloan, like a book."

"Don't be so sure."

"You're telling me the Pearson girl's not dead?"

"I didn't say that. But trust me . . . I'm not an open book."

"Trust *me* . . . I know that."

They look at each other for a few seconds.

Randy is the first to shift his gaze.

He gestures with his laminated one-page menu. "Know what you want?"

"Just coffee."

"Just coffee? What happened to the famous Lucinda Sloan appetite?"

"I lost it," she says, folding her arms across her stomach, "right about the time I realized that poor girl was fed to the sharks."

Randy sets aside his menu and leans forward. "You're serious?"

"Pretty much."

"Was she alive? Before . . . during . . . ?"

"No," she says quickly, and shudders. "It was her body."

"Being eaten by sharks."

"That's what I saw."

"Was it symbolic?" he asks thoughtfully. "You know . . . because of the necklace she had on, and Leah Roby, too?"

She's been asking herself that very question.

"I don't think so."

There's a difference—a subtle one—between visions that are meant to be interpreted symbolically and scenes that depict actual happenings.

This, Lucinda is pretty certain, was the latter. It was so vivid. Gruesomely vivid.

"You think that's what Cam saw, too, when she got upset, there, in the room at the end?" Randy asks.

"I have no idea. She didn't say."

Back at the Pearson home, they sent a pale, shaken Cam off in a police cruiser with two officers who promised to see her safely home.

"Did you see the look on her face when she said she had to go? She must have seen something."

"She's not used to this," Lucinda says. "It was hard on her."

"It's got to be hard on you, too." Randy reaches out and touches her hand.

She pulls it away like she's just been branded.

"Me? I'm used to it. I'm fine."

She can feel him nod, can feel his eyes on her from across the table, but she doesn't dare look at him.

Why did she agree to join him at this coffee shop after leaving the Pearsons? They should have just gone their separate ways.

The waitress arrives. She's been hovering, plenty of time on her hands. No one wants to hang around inside a greasy spoon on a day like today.

Randy orders a turkey club, cheeseburger, fries, iced tea, chocolate shake.

Hearing his order, Lucinda rediscovers her appetite. She's drained, depressed, hungry.

But she told him she wasn't, and anyway, if she doesn't order anything, she can just finish her coffee and go . . .

Somewhere.

"Turkey club *and* cheeseburger?" Lucinda asks when the waitress walks away.

"Cheeseburger's for you."

She raises an eyebrow.

"So's the shake. You didn't, by any chance, see who fed her to the sharks?" Randy asks, back on the case.

"No. I didn't see much of anything."

"Just the sharks."

"And the water. Blood." She shudders again.

"So you're saying a body's not going to wash up at Surf City or somewhere a few weeks from now and scare people away from the beaches?"

"Randy . . . for God's sake."

"Lucinda, I'm trying to get a handle on what you're telling me. This girl vanishes less than twenty-four hours ago, and she's . . ."

"Never coming back, Randy. She's never going to wash up on a beach, either."

"Some people might say 'never say never.'"

"I'm not one of them."

"Yeah, no kidding."

Lucinda Sloan frequently says *never*. Means it, too.

Like when she told Randy to get out of her life. Never come back.

She meant it.

He listened.

"Are you going to stay in our guestroom tonight?" he asks, resting his chin on his hand and looking across the table at her.

"Don't you think that would be a little awkward?"

"For who? Carla doesn't know."

"For you. For me." That's better than saying for *us.*

There is no *us*.

Hasn't been in years.

"I wouldn't feel awkward at all," Randy

informs her, a little too casually. "So unless you would . . ."

She would.

Before she can tell him that, he goes on, obviously remembering what she told him about the unpleasant guesthouse experience, "Listen, we've got plenty of room, air-conditioning, and great coffee. What do you say?"

"I say . . . I can't."

"You *can*. You're more than welcome."

"Thanks but no thanks. I'm going to eat a cheeseburger, drink a shake, and head back home."

"All the way to Philly?"

"Where else?"

She leans back, relieved.

It's the right thing to do.

The hardest thing is always the right thing to do. Didn't she figure that out when she was just a little girl?

"So you're just going to blow out of here and leave me hanging in the middle of a case." Randy's expression is laced with regret.

Regret because of the case?

Regret because she's leaving?

What does it matter?

She's leaving.

Her mind is made up.

The waitress refills Randy's coffee.

Lucinda puts a hand over her own cup and shakes her head.

"Look, I'm sorry," she says when the waitress leaves. "I've done what I can. I've told you what you need to know."

No, she hasn't told Rebecca Pearson's family. Guilt washes over her; same old story.

How can she tell them? What would she say?

Your daughter is dead. No, I don't have any proof. How do I know? Because I'm a psychic. You'll just have to take my word for it. Give up hope.

She can't give closure to the Pearson family. Not now, anyway.

Randy is still looking at her. Still waiting.

For what?

She exhales through puffed cheeks. "What more do you want from me? Why would I stay? I'm not a cop, Randy, or a detective, or . . ."

"I know."

"So I don't have to see this thing

through for months on end, looking for clues, tracking false leads. That's not up to me."

"No, I know. I get it. I just . . ." He trails off.

Plunking a spoon into his coffee, he stirs it hard, though he takes it black and unsweetened.

You just what, Randy? she wants to press.

It would be so easy to get him to go there, to go there herself . . .

So easy to fall right back into it.

And so damn wrong.

"See? I told you. That's him, right?"

Gazing across the beach at the white wooden lifeguard stand, Tess nods.

"Yeah," she tells Beth, "that's him."

High on his perch, Heath Pickering faces the water, twirling a whistle on a string.

"What did he say about me again?" she asks, plunking herself down in the sand, thoughts whirling.

Dismay over her mother's affair is on

hold for the time being. Heath Pickering's presence on the island has eclipsed all that.

"I already told you what he said."

"Tell me again. Please?"

Beth sits beside her. "It wasn't much. When Jared introduced me to him"—Jared is another lifeguard, Beth's latest crush—"he asked where I was from, you know, and then I asked where he was from, and he said he used to live in California but now he lives in Montclair. And I did the whole—'Montclair? My friend lives there, too . . . Do you know her?'—and he was like, 'Yeah, I know her.'"

"That's it. That's all he said."

"What he said was, 'I know her, but not that well.' And that was pretty much it."

"Pretty much?"

"Tess! That was it." Beth shakes her head, her sleek black hair swinging across her bare shoulders. She's wearing a bikini top and cutoffs.

Tess is, too, but of course, she looks a lot different in hers.

She wonders what Heath thought of Beth when he met her.

"Look, it's time for his break." Beth points to the stand, where another lifeguard is ascending and Heath is waiting to come down. "So should we go talk to him?" Beth starts to get up.

"No!" Tess grabs her arm, pulls her back down.

"Why not? I thought you liked him."

Like doesn't even begin to cover it.

Just hearing his name mentioned earlier, for the first time in weeks, brought back a lot of old feelings. Not just, to Tess's surprise, the familiar humiliation and hurt, but the equally familiar longing and desire.

Seeing Heath again now—even from a distance—seals the deal.

Beth cups her hands. "Heath! Hey, Heath!"

"Oh my God!" Tess clutches her, frantic, as Heath looks in their direction. "Cut it out! What are you doing?"

Beth waves. "Being bold. My mom says that if you really want something, sometimes you've got to take a bull by the—"

"Oh my God! He's coming this way!" Tess's hand flies up to her hair.

"Relax. You look great. Just act natural."

On the verge of hyperventilating, Tess watches Heath walk over the sand toward them, bare-chested, tanned, muscular, glorious. He's wearing only swim trunks, sunglasses, and one of those surfer-style necklaces.

What should she say?

What should she do?

How should she act?

No time to figure that out; he's here.

"Hey," he says.

"Remember me? I'm Beth."

"Yeah, I remember." His mouth smiles. White teeth. Tess is going to faint.

"You remember her, too, right?"

Heath points at Tess, still smiling. "Tess, right?"

She can only nod.

He holds out his hand. "We never met. But you go to my school."

"Tess . . . Hastings." She says it with careful deliberation, lest she slip and call herself Tess Pickering out loud.

That, she knows, would be her doom.

What she thought was her doom—the

incriminating notebook falling into the wrong hands—may not have been fatal after all.

Because Heath Pickering is standing here, smiling at her. God knows what he's thinking, since she can't see his eyes, but he's here, and he's smiling, and she's going to faint or throw up or both.

"I texted you."

Tess blinks behind her own sunglasses. Is he talking to her?

He can't be. He's not looking at Beth, but he must be talking to her, because he didn't text Tess.

"You texted Tess?" Beth asks.

"No," Tess says, shaking her head, trying hard not to be insanely jealous.

Of course Heath texted Beth. Of course he's going to fall in love with her. Look at her.

Except . . . he's not.

Looking at Beth, that is.

He's still looking at Tess. Still smiling. Saying, once again, "I texted you. A long time ago. Right when school got out."

"Maybe she didn't get it," Beth says.

"No, she did. She told me to leave her the hell alone."

Oh my God.

Tess's thoughts flash back to that night—that horrible, horrible night—back in Montclair. Lying in bed, her foot aching from the wound, her arm aching from the tetanus shot, her heart aching far worse than anything else.

The text from an unavailable number.

Hi Tess. This is Heath.

It really was him?

Tess is speechless.

"Why would she do that?" Beth asks incredulously, and turns to Tess. "Why would you do that?"

Tess just shakes her head, mute.

"There was this thing that happened," Heath tells Beth, "and her friend told me about it, and I felt bad, so I got her number and texted her."

"I thought . . . it was a joke," she says now, lamely.

"I guess I can see why," Heath says.

"Well I can't." Beth is shaking her head. "What happened?"

Is Heath going to tell her?

No. Heath, Tess's hero, says simply, "Nothing happened, really. It was stupid."

"But what was it?" Beth persists.

"It doesn't matter," Heath says. "Old news."

Tess nods gratefully.

"So . . . What are you guys up to?" Heath casually grinds his big toe in the sand. "I just got off work."

What if he's not making fun of you? What if he's really a nice guy? Isn't that why you fell in love with him in the first place?

It's Beth who answers Heath's question. "We're just hanging out."

"Yeah?"

"Yeah. What are you doing?"

"Why?"

"Because my mom is having this barbecue so we're going to go back there and have something to eat. Want to come with us?" Beth asks easily.

"I have to go somewhere later, but

sure, I'll come now for awhile," Heath says, just as easily.

Just like that.

And, just like that, Tess wonders if she might be able to put her worst nightmare behind her after all.

Chapter Fifteen

For the second day in a row, Cam's car is here in the driveway, but no one is answering the door.

Kathy turns away with a frown. Is Cam inside, watching her through a crack in the blinds? Avoiding her? Suspicious?

Why would she be suspicious?

She has no reason to believe Kathy is anyone other than who she claims to be: a concerned AA sponsor.

One so dedicated she'll go to great lengths to check in on her sponsee on a holiday weekend.

Far-fetched, but believable.

All right, so Cam must not be home.

What now?

"Excuse me?" a voice calls.

She looks up to see a trio of kids at the curb. Sunglasses, towels, bare feet . . . obviously just coming from the beach. A handsome older teenaged boy, and two pretty girls—one who looks about seventeen and built, the other younger, slimmer, less certain of herself . . .

Don't say her name. She doesn't know you, remember? And you're not supposed to know her.

"Are you looking for someone?" the older-looking girl calls, and Kathy knows she was the one who spoke in the first place.

"Yes, Camden Hastings. I'm a friend of hers from back home, and I was in the neighborhood so . . . I thought I'd stop by and say hi."

"I'm her daughter, Tess," the young-looking one says. "She's down the street, I think, at a barbecue, so—"

"That's where we're headed," the other girl cuts in conveniently, "if you want to see her."

"All right. Just for a few minutes. Just to say hi."

* * *

Sitting on the highway, the car in PARK and the air-conditioning turned to HIGH, Mike fiddles with the radio and wishes he'd left Beach Haven five minutes earlier . . . or not at all.

But at least he didn't leave one minute earlier. Just visible in the roadway ahead, about a mile from where he sits, is a massive accident.

A mile.

A minute.

That's all it comes down to.

Pure chance.

Mike twists the dial past Donna Summer's "Last Dance," past an aria, static, more static, a phone-in political talk show . . .

If he hadn't taken the time to shake Ike's hand—though Ike was glowering at him, disgruntled after hearing about the separation—or to give Tess a bear hug and meet her friend Beth . . .

Static on the radio, and then, ". . . We have Route 72 closed in both directions just east of the Garden State Parkway for a multivehicle accident with multiple injuries and two fatalities. Residual effects are—"

Mike changes the station.

It could have been him in that wreck, gravely injured, being airlifted via that helicopter buzzing overhead to some nearby hospital.

Two fatalities.

It could have been him, being zipped into a body bag at the side of the road.

There but for the grace of God . . .

Mike thinks about the unwitting strangers who are about to get devastating phone calls, their lives impacted by the drama unfolding before him.

If it had been him, Cam would have gotten the call. She'd be widowed, Tess fatherless, and the baby would never know him at all. He'd have been erased from their lives in an instant.

It wasn't him.

Still, you've already erased yourself from the inner circle, their daily lives.

If they continue on this path—he and Tess not living under the same roof, Cam a single mother, the baby seeing him only on scheduled visita—

". . . Whatever happened to you and I . . ."

Mike pauses, hand on the knob.

He knows this tune.

"I Don't Want To Go Home."

It's an oldie. Southside Johnny. Cam's favorite.

All those nights come rushing back at him . . .

All those nights he'd get off the commuter train to find Cam waiting at the station, waving from behind the wheel in her pajamas, Tess strapped into the backseat, Southside Johnny on the CD player.

Whenever this song came on as they drove toward their house after a long day in the city, Mike would sing along, changing the refrain.

"I just want to go home" were his revised lyrics.

Yes, their marriage was already strained, even then. But he loved Cam, and he loved Tess, and he thought everything was going to work itself out. He thought love was enough.

When—why—did he decide that it wasn't?

Selfishness, a classic midlife crisis. He started listening to his father—a know-it-all snob who never believed an underprivileged Jersey girl was good enough for his son.

And, to be fair, Mike listened to his own inner voice, telling him Cam wasn't the woman he thought she was back when they first met.

I was right, though. She wasn't the same. She had changed, hadn't she?

Or maybe she was always that skittish, distant person and he was too blinded by love in the beginning to see it.

And what about the booze?

But that's over. She's not drinking anymore. She's sober now, remember?

Yeah. Now.

What about after she has the baby?

There are no easy answers.

All Mike knows is that the love is still there. He still feels it. Not blind, giddy honeymoon love.

Mature love. The kind that deepens over the years—in good times, and bad. Isn't that how it's supposed to be? Didn't he vow to love Cam and honor her all the days of their lives? No matter what? Good times, bad times, sickness, health, rich, poor . . . Didn't he vow to weather every storm by her side?

Yeah.

You did.

And you walked away anyway.

Jesus. Why wasn't it ever this clear until now?

Maybe he had it right, way back at the beginning when they were newlyweds, and new homeowners, and new parents.

Maybe love is enough.

Remembering all those nights he couldn't wait to go home with Cam and Tess, Mike feels his eyes starting to sting.

I still just want to go home.

He looks helplessly at the accident ahead, then over his shoulder at the line of traffic snaking as far as he can see.

You're not going anywhere anytime soon.

"Pop?" Cam calls, stepping wearily into the house. "I'm back."

No reply.

He must be sleeping it off in one of the bedrooms.

That's fine with her. She needs more

time to pull herself together after what she saw at the Pearsons's house.

Now she knows . . . the cut foot, the friends' betrayal, the broken heart . . . that wasn't it. That wasn't what was meant by her earlier premonition involving Tess.

Her daughter—her baby girl—is in danger.

We have to leave the island.

That was Cam's first coherent thought, sitting in the backseat as the police inched her toward home through endless beach traffic.

Whoever took Leah Roby and Rebecca Pearson has some connection to the island.

Then again, Rebecca lived here—but Leah didn't. For all Cam knows, she never visited the Jersey Shore. Nor was she brought here by her abductor.

She—her body—is somewhere on the mainland.

Cam is as sure of that as she is that Rebecca Pearson was murdered in the past twenty-four hours by the same person.

But the more she thinks about it, the

more certain Cam is that simply fleeing the island won't keep Tess safe.

For all she knows, that move could somehow put her in harm's way.

There was nothing in her vision that showed Tess falling victim to the same person.

But that would make sense . . . wouldn't it?

Nothing makes sense.

Shaking her head, she gets up . . . and stops short.

Why didn't she see that before?

Tess's duffel bag, on the floor by the door.

"Tess? Tess!"

Panic sweeps through her.

"Tess, are you home?" she calls, racing through the house, opening doors, checking silent, empty rooms. "Tess?"

No sign of her.

No sign of Pop, either.

"Tess!" Cam screams helplessly, standing alone in her house, clutching the sides of her skull. "Oh, God, where are you? *Tess!*"

* * *

Mike's cell phone rings as he's still sitting, claustrophobic, still listening to Southside Johnny on the radio.

He instantly recognizes the number and answers the phone, wondering where to begin. "Cam, I'm so glad you—"

She cuts him off with an incoherent rush of words.

"What? Slow down. What are you saying?"

"She's gone, Mike! Tess! She's gone!"

"What?"

"Tess! Someone kidnapped her!" she screams and Mike is catapulted into an icy sea of dread.

Tess . . . kidnapped . . .

"Oh, Mike . . ." Cam is wailing, frantic, almost incoherent. "Help me . . . What are we going to do?"

Tess . . . kidnapped . . .

Mute, he founders.

He cannot wrap his brain around the enormity of what she's telling him. It just doesn't make sense. It's impossible. He just saw Tess, just a short time ago. She was perfectly fine.

An ambulance races down the shoulder, lights flashing, siren wailing.

Just a short time ago, the people in those cars up ahead were driving along on a sunny afternoon without a care in the world.

And Tess was perfectly fine.

Nothing is impossible.

Mike finds his voice at last. "Where are you? Cam, you have to calm down."

"I . . . I . . ." She sounds as though she's hyperventilating. "Home."

"You're home?"

He has to get to her. He has to find his little girl.

Jesus.

Please help me.

"It's okay," he tells Cam, and shifts into DRIVE.

"Please, Mike. Please . . ."

"I know, I know . . . I'm coming." There's nowhere to go. He's almost on the bumper of the car in front of him. He shifts into REVERSE. As if that can possibly help. "I'll get there as soon as I can."

He shifts into DRIVE again.

Then, realizing it's futile, back into PARK, slamming his hands on the wheel in despair.

He can't move. There's no way. He's trapped.

Cam is sobbing, gasping their daughter's name in his ear.

"Okay, okay, okay, just talk to me, Cam. Breathe. Okay? Take a deep breath."

He hears her inhale sharply. Hold it. Exhale.

"Again," he says soothingly, somehow, despite the bedlam in his head. "You have to tell me what happened. Tell me everything. What happened?"

"I just got home," she says raggedly.

She just got home. She just got home.

The words sink in.

"And the house is empty, and Tess—"

"She's down the street!" Mike cuts in as a tide of blessed relief pulls him back to reality.

"What?"

"You haven't been home yet? Since I was there?"

"No. I walked in just now, and I saw her luggage, and . . ." She releases an audible shudder. "What are you telling me, Mike?"

"Tess is okay." *Thank God, thank God,*

thank God. "She's over at your neighbor's party with your father."

"How do you know?"

"Because when I left, that's where she was going. She and Ike."

"Are you sure?"

"That's what she said. Her friend was here, and she invited—"

"Her friend Beth?"

"Right, and she invited Tess over, and said to bring Ike, and when I left they were on their way."

"Are you sure?"

Cam still sounds edgy. Why? Tess is fine.

"What if she's not over at Debbie's?"

"Debbie's the one having the party? She's there."

"What if she's not?" Cam asks shrilly.

Unreasonably, really, and an unsettling possibility creeps into Mike's head.

"Okay, even if she's not there, I'm sure she's fine." He tries hard to keep his voice level, to hold his suspicion at bay. "I mean, there's no reason to think she's been kidnapped or—"

"Yes, there is. Oh, God."

"What? What reason is there?"

"Just—never mind. I just . . . I got worried. I'm fine. I guess I got carried away."

"Yeah. I guess you did." He pauses. She's not fine. She's high-strung and irrational and erratic. Why?

"You said there was a reason you thought she'd been kidnapped," he reminds her. "Tell me."

Silence on the other end of the line.

"Cam? You came home and Tess wasn't there so you decided out of the blue that she'd been kidnapped? That makes no sense."

"I had a vision, okay?" she blurts.

"You had a what?"

"A psychic vision."

Good Lord.

Clearly, she's out of it.

He opens his mouth to say something—what, he isn't sure—but he doesn't get the chance.

It's as if someone shook up a bottle and took off the cap. Words are spewing out of Cam, crazy talk that's making his head spin.

"I've been having these visions my whole life, and they're usually about missing kids, and I never wanted to tell you because I thought you'd think I was crazy and leave me and I guess the joke's on me because you left me anyway, and now I've had this awful vision about something happening to Tess, and she couldn't breathe . . . She was gasping for air . . . dying."

Spent, she simply stops talking.

Stupefied, he's not sure where to begin.

Maybe he should just drop the subject entirely. Leave it alone.

No. You should ask.

You need to know.

"Cam . . . Have you been drinking?" he hears himself ask.

There. It's out there.

So much—everything—is riding on her answer.

It takes a moment for her to reply. When she does, her voice is taut. "Mike . . . I'm pregnant. How can you even ask that?"

"I just—you sounded so out of control that I—"

"I thought our daughter had been kidnapped!"

"Because you're seeing things? Having visions?"

"So you figure I must be drunk and out of my mind?"

Yes. That's exactly what he thought. *Thinks*.

He doesn't say it, though.

He doesn't have to.

"So that's what you think of me. That I was pregnant and intoxicated. That I would risk our child's life."

"Cam—you have to understand why I—"

"I understand you. Believe me."

"No, you—"

"I don't have time for this right now. I have to go find our daughter—who wasn't even supposed to be here today. Yet for God knows what reason, you dropped her off two days early and didn't even tell me."

"I was going to, but Ike was there and when he found out about the separation he—"

"*You* told my *father*?"

"I didn't know he didn't—"

"Great. That's just great. I can't believe you would—"

"If you'd give me a chance to—"

"You know what? I don't have time for this. I've got to go find Tess."

"Cam—"

Too late.

She's hung up.

Jesus.

Resting his head against the steering wheel, Mike listens to an approaching siren's lament and, on the radio, Southside Johnny, still singing about not wanting to go home.

He turns the knob abruptly.

An announcer is saying, "In other local news . . ."

Mike leaves it there, no longer in the mood for music.

The party is in full swing, people spilling out of the house onto the deck and off the deck into the small yard below. The warm air smells of citronella and sunscreen, beer and charcoal and hot dogs. Voices talk and laugh amidst the opening keyboard chords of *"December, 1963 (Oh, What A Night)"* on the CD player.

The sun is beginning to slant into the west—nowhere near dusk yet, but the descent is under way. Soon today will be tonight, and tonight will be over, and she'll still be out there somewhere, ever evasive.

No. I have to find her. Before dark. I can't let another wasted day go by. She's here someplace. The shark's tooth I found that very first day was a sign that she's here.

"Oh, look, there she is now!"

What? Where?

Oh. False alarm.

Whoever spoke was talking to someone else, about someone else.

Of course, because no one here can read my thoughts. No one knows who I am, really, or who I'm looking for.

"Cam! Hi! Where've you been?" someone calls.

Hmm. Cam isn't looking her best today. Far from it.

Her hair is caught back in a black headband with straggly strands escaping at her temples. Her features are drawn. She looks completely thrown together in baggy jersey shorts, Keds without socks, and a white sleeveless blouse.

A too-snug blouse whose buttons gape over her protruding stomach.

Even from way over here, on the opposite end of the deck, it's obvious.

Cam is pregnant.

Well, well, well.

Pushing through the crowd on the deck, Cam is looking around worriedly, asking, "Is Tess here? Has anyone seen her? Tess? My daughter?"

Her daughter.

Tess.

It figures.

Just when Lucinda is desperate to get off this island, away from Randy, the whole damn world shuts down.

Playing one of her favorite CDs over and over—*U2's Best Of 1980–1990,* disc one—doesn't take her mind off the fact that she's stuck in traffic on the causeway. Literally trapped between two worlds, Randy's and her own.

How's that for a cosmic coincidence?

Every song has meaning for her. For them.

Maudlin, she forces herself to live in the pain.

"All I Want Is You," "I Still Haven't Found What I'm Looking For," "With Or Without You" . . .

She refuses to cry—Lucinda Sloan never cries—so she sings.

Wailing the lyrics along with Bono at the top of her lungs is cathartic. She turns up the volume almost as high as it goes, windows open, sea breeze in her hair, and she sings.

Then—as The Edge plucks out the haunting opening guitar pings of "The Unforgettable Fire"—the car fills with the sound of rhythmic heavy breathing.

Startled, Lucinda turns down the volume.

The breathing stops.

Oh. It was part of the song, she realizes. Funny. She's heard it hundreds of times and never noticed the breathing until now. Why?

And what is the panting meant to symbolize?

Is someone running hard? Making love? Dying?

It doesn't matter, really.

She just wants to know.

The breathing is supposed to imply passion, she decides, as Bono sings about eyes as black as coal. Passion and desire.

Lucinda thinks of Randy.

Wonders when she'll ever see him again.

Then, *if*.

Better not to, much as she can't bear the thought of that.

It's harder still to imagine seeing him again maybe a year or two down the road, with Carla, and maybe a couple of cute kids by then.

Her cell phone vibrates in her pocket.

She turns down the music midrefrain—

"Walk 'til you run
And don't look back
For here I am . . ."

"Hello?"

"Lucinda—You're all right?"

Randy.

Now. In the midst of a song about passion and eyes; in the midst of her wondering if he's out of her life forever.

No. She sure as hell isn't all right.

What does he want from her? Does he want her to admit she still has feelings for him? That she knows he does as well?

Married or not, there was a vibe. Something flickering between them, something that refuses to die.

What does he want to do about it?

Have an affair?

I won't do that. I won't go there.

And if Randy is willing to . . .

Then he's not the man she thought he was.

Maybe, she tells herself, that realization is what it will take to finally snuff the flame.

"Why are you calling me, Randy?"

"I knew you were heading out, and there was an accident. Tractor trailer, bunch of cars . . . I thought you might have . . ."

"No," she says, "I'm all right."

"Thank God."

She hears him exhale shakily.

So that's it. That's all. An old friend, a good cop, checking up to make sure she hadn't been annihilated on the highway.

And now that he knows . . .

"So," she says, "is that it?"

"Yeah, that's it. I just wanted to make sure you were okay."

"I'll be fine," she assures him. "I just have to go home."

"Yeah. Me, too."

A pause.

She wonders if he's going to say something else.

Maybe.

But she isn't going to let him.

"Good-bye, Randy."

Spotting Debbie handing out Popsicles, Cam makes a beeline for her with a silent prayer.

"There you are." Debbie offers Cam the box. "Where have you been?"

"Debbie, is Tess here?" Cam impatiently waves the box away, still searching the crowd for her daughter's face.

She has to be here. Mike said she was.

With Pop. Cam doesn't see either of them, but that doesn't mean—

"Who *isn't* here?" Debbie shrugs. "It's like the whole damn island heard about my barbecue. I mean, I know I told a lot of people, and I told them to invite whoever—"

"Debbie, Tess—have you seen her? Is she here?"

"I'm sure she's still around somewhere."

"Still? So she was here?" The fist that's clenching Cam's lungs loosens a little. Just enough so she can take a breath. But her lungs are still constricted, and will be until she lays eyes on Tess.

"Yeah, she was here. A little while ago she was sitting on a chair over there talking to Beth and some guy."

Cam takes a few steps in that direction, cranes her neck. A couple of strangers are sitting there now. Tess is nowhere in sight.

"Doo dit doo dit dit," the Four Seasons sing jauntily, *"doo dit doo dit dit."*

"Oh my God. Are you . . . ?" Debbie

asks, and Cam turns to see her looking at Cam's stomach.

"You're pregnant," Debbie accuses, just as Petra and Gwen materialize.

They, too, look at Cam's stomach, which in her frantic state, she neglected to camouflage. Then they look at each other and, finally, at Cam, seeking confirmation.

"I need to find Tess. Has anyone—"

"Mom?"

Cam whirls around.

"Tess. Thank God." She grabs on to her daughter, holds on tight, giddy with relief.

"Mom, you're crushing me."

"I'm sorry."

Tess grunts. "You're still crushing me."

Cam releases her . . . but not all the way.

"Popsicle, Tess?" Debbie holds one out. "It's grape. You like grape, right?"

"Sure. Thanks." Tess unwraps it.

"So, Cam."

She turns to see Debbie, Gwen, and Petra looking at her.

"When are you due?" Petra gestures

at her stomach with the orange Popsicle she's holding.

Cam immediately feels Tess's shoulders clench beneath her hands.

"Due?" Tess echoes. She looks down. Gasps. "Mom!"

"Tess—"

"You're pregnant?"

"You know I didn't even know her name," Frankie Valli sings.

Her name?

Well, it's not *Tess* . . . that's for damn sure.

Tess.

She might be calling herself that now, but it's *her,* all right.

Standing there talking to the woman pretending to be her mother. Cam—now pregnant with a child of her own. Surprise, surprise.

When Cam showed up looking for "Tess," she was frantic. Far more frantic than an ordinary mother of an ordinary teenager would be under ordinary circumstances.

Well, I know why you were so worried, Cam.

You thought darling daughter might have run away. You know she has a way of doing that, doesn't she?

Or maybe Cam was worried someone had found out all about their little secret and taken "Tess" away, brought her back where she belongs.

Guess what? Someone has found out.

But don't worry.

I won't do anything about it just yet.

It was interesting to see how Cam reacted to not knowing where "Tess" was for a few minutes. Imagine what it will be like for her when she loses her grip on "Tess" forever.

That day is coming. You'd better get ready.

Then again . . . She'll get over it. She's pregnant. She has another child coming. One who will really belong to her.

"Tess" is looking dubiously at Cam's stomach. What is she thinking?

It would make sense for a girl who's already been living as Cam's daughter to wonder how this new baby will impact her own future.

Will she be cast aside? Neglected? Sent to live elsewhere? Maybe she'll revert to her old ways and run away.

I'll have to keep a careful eye on her.

If she tries to run, I'll be right there, waiting to catch her.

When Cam's friends realize that her pregnancy is news as much to Tess as it is to them, they tactfully disperse.

Left alone with her daughter—if there's such a thing as alone at a crowded party—Cam says, "We need to go home and talk about this."

"Not yet," Tess says evasively. She obviously needs space, still trying to absorb the news. "I'm going to go hang out with my friends again."

She looks over the railing toward a group of kids in the yard. Beth is among them.

So, Cam realizes, is a tall, blond guy who's catching Tess's eye. He looks familiar—one of the lifeguards, maybe? But he's a lot older. Too old to be looking up so intently at a fourteen-year-old, Cam thinks uneasily.

"I'm having fun here," Tess goes on, still focused on the guy as she licks a drip from her Popsicle, "and anyway . . . Granddad's here somewhere, so we can't just leave."

Pop. Cam forgot all about that.

She automatically looks for him in the throng. "Where is he?"

"Around. Maybe he's in the house."

"You haven't seen him?"

"I did earlier, and he was having fun, talking to some people. When I got back Debbie said he's been the life of the party."

Terrific. The life of the party. Cam glances around again, wondering where to start focusing damage control.

Then it hits her. "When you got *back?*" She looks at Tess. "Where were you?"

"Beth and I went for a walk to the beach."

There are so many things wrong with that scenario that Cam falters, wondering who, exactly, she should blame. Tess? Pop? Debbie?

She settles on Mike. Mike, who just dumped Tess off without bothering to see if it was okay with Cam that she's home two days early. Did he not consider that she might have had other plans? Did he not know you don't just leave a fourteen-year-old unsupervised and drive away?

For all he knew, Cam was away for the weekend herself.

Then again, he talked to Pop, so he knew she was around—although under certain influences, Ike has been known to see people who aren't there.

Mike is always saying her father's brain is fried from all those years of hard partying. He knows better than anyone that Cam's father is no reliable guardian for Tess. He's always marveled that Cam herself got through childhood unscathed, and they certainly never considered using Pop as a babysitter for Tess.

She's fourteen—does she really need a babysitter?

That's what Mike will say in his own defense when Cam lays into him about this.

And you'll say . . . what?

"I had a vision that something horrible is going to happen to her, and I'm scared."

After which Mike will accuse her of being drunk again, or worse.

Thinking again of the volatile conversation she and Mike just had on the phone, sick inside when she remembers what she told him—and how he reacted—she asks Tess sharply, "Why did you come back early from the trip?"

"I don't know. We just weren't having a very good time. Dad was kind of . . ." Tess shrugs.

"Kind of what?"

"Just quiet. I guess maybe he was thinking about the baby."

"Maybe he was."

A beat, then Tess asks, "So can I go?"

"Go where?"

"Talk to my friends."

After this nightmarish twenty-four hours, Cam wants nothing more than to leave—with Tess—crawl right into bed, and sleep for hours.

Instead, she gets to go round up her wayward father, fend off curious stares and questions from friends she's known for mere weeks, and deal with a daughter who needs to come to terms with the pregnancy—and who, disturbingly, is once again casting a longing glance at Surfer Boy over there.

Surfer *Man* is more like it.

And he looks like he's getting ready to leave.

"We really need to talk about all of this, Tess."

"What?" Tess asks absently.

"The baby. I know you must have a lot of questions. I didn't want you to find out this way. I was going to—"

"I'm okay."

"Look at me."

Tess does.

"It's all going to work out. I promise."

"What about Dad? Is he . . . ?" Tess trails off.

She's asking if the baby is Mike's.

Cam nods slowly, her stomach turning just as it did when Mike accused her, on the phone a few minutes ago, of drinking.

Somewhere in the back of her mind, she knows he has a right to question her sobriety, to doubt her tale of psychic visions.

It's what you expected from him all along. That's why you never told him.

Why you never should have tried to tell him now.

Still, it hurts.

"Dad knows all about the baby. He's happy about being a father again," Cam assures Tess, choosing her words carefully, aware that a curious, eavesdropping audience may still hover in the vicinity.

This is no one's business but Cam's and Tess's. When the summer ends, everyone here—including Debbie and Gwen and Petra, friends or not—will go their separate ways.

"So you're saying that Dad's the father."

"Of course he's the father!"

"I wasn't sure. I thought maybe you—"

"Well, I didn't."

"Okay. Good."

"Come on. Let's just go."

"Mom, please. I just want to be with my friends right now. Okay? You don't have to stay if you don't want to. You can go get Granddad and go home."

"I'm not leaving you here alone!" Cam says sharply. Too sharply.

Tess rolls her eyes. "How old do you think I am? You left me alone the other night when you went out to dinner with your friends!"

"You weren't alone."

"And I wouldn't be now." Tess gestures at the crowd scene with her dripping purple ice pop.

Cam shakes her head. No way is she taking her eyes off Tess tonight. Or anytime soon.

"So can I stay?"

"Go ahead," she tells Tess wearily. "We'll both stay. But not for long."

"Thanks, Mom!"

Wow.

One moment, Tess was struggling to absorb life-altering news. The next, she's glibly going off to flirt.

Teenagers.

But Tess is okay. She's right here, safe and sound, in one piece.

That's all that matters now.

Cam refuses to acknowledge the terrifying vision that led her to believe any other outcome was remotely possible.

So it's really her.

Incredible.

You've looked right at her how many times, and didn't even recognize her? You were so focused on that other girl—the wrong girl—that you almost missed the right one, hiding in plain sight under your nose.

She's holding a grape Popsicle now. The sticky purple juice drips down her hand. She lifts her wrist to her mouth, twists it, licks it.

The artless gesture erases any lingering doubt.

She always was a mannerless slob.

What would she do if I told her, right now, that the charade is over?

That I know who she really is? That she might be fooling all of these people . . . but not me.

I know her.

I've found her.

She won't slip away again.

She can try all she wants, but she might as well be a pogie trying to evade a great white that smells blood in the water.

You don't have a chance, "Tess."

I'll even call you that to your face . . . Play the game your way this time.

Win your trust.
And just when you think you're safe . . .
I'll come in for the kill.

Tess starts away, then turns back. "Oh, yeah, Mom?"

Hmm. Maybe she's not as fickle as Cam suspected.

"Yeah?"

"I forgot to tell you—this friend of yours stopped by earlier."

"Stopped by here?"

"Well, she was at our house, but she walked over here with us hoping she might get to see you. But you weren't here."

"Who was she?"

"I've never seen her before, but she said she knows you from back home. She was an older lady."

An older lady . . .

Mom?

The possibility that Brenda Neary might have come back for her at last is momentarily staggering.

Now, when I need her so much . . .

Then reality sets in.

Cam remembers: She's not a bewildered, motherless little girl anymore. She's all grown-up with a daughter of her own and a baby on the way.

Yes, and the hard-won wisdom that allowed her to accept, over a decade ago, that her mother is never coming back.

So why think of her now?

Because it's been a hell of a day, and I'm sad and scared and vulnerable and lonely, and I want my mommy.

"Who was the woman, Tess?" She rests her thumb on her jaw and massages her brow with her fingertips, trying to hang in there. "Did she give you her name?"

"Yeah, it was Kathy. She's staying down here for a few days."

"Kathy?"

Tess nods.

Can it be Kathy from AA?

Far more unsettling things have unfolded around Cam today.

It would almost be par for the course to have her AA sponsor wander in on the drama.

In fact . . .

Cam might actually welcome Kathy

right about now. Someone who's been in her shoes, who understands what it's like to be under constant scrutiny by loved ones who aren't entirely convinced of her sobriety.

Oh, well. If Kathy is on the island, she's sure to pop up again sooner or later.

All is quiet around the little gray house on Dolphin Avenue. It seems the whole neighborhood is at the barbecue down the street.

That's why this is the perfect time to slip away and do a little browsing around the empty house.

Amazingly, not only is the front door unlocked, but it's actually standing ajar.

Cam obviously ran out of here in a hurry, and she crashed into the barbecue like a frazzled young mom who's just lost a toddler on the beach.

Well, pregnant women do tend to overreact. Hormones and all.

Still . . .

Where was Cam this afternoon when she was supposed to be at the barbecue?

According to someone at the party, who heard from a friend of a cop, Cam is involved, somehow, in the search for Rebecca Pearson.

News about last night's up-island disappearance is already hitting the local gossip mill. Rumors are flying, as rumors do in small communities. People are saying Rebecca ran away to Atlantic City, snuck out for a midnight swim and drowned, was kidnapped by a pedophile . . .

As if they know a damn thing about it.

Which is why the passing rumor about Cam being involved is meaningless.

Why would she be involved?

Why was she so frantically searching for "Tess"?

Why, indeed?

Maybe she was afraid someone has figured out her little secret: that someone knows her precious daughter isn't really her daughter.

The irony: no one suspected a thing until she showed up, discombobulated, frantically searching, and called undue attention to herself and to "Tess."

I might never have realized the truth if she hadn't done that.

Oddly, it was almost as if Cam's frantic, premature search—for a girl who has yet to go missing—sealed her destiny.

Now, however, isn't the time to stand around speculating.

It's time to move past the packed duffel bag sitting just inside the door.

The living room is in casual disarray and the blinds are drawn, as if no one bothered to open them and tidy up in here this morning.

On the coffee table beside an array of magazines: an empty glass and a stack of Marble notebooks.

A quick perusal of the covers shows that they're all painstakingly dated with a range of months and years. The pages are covered in handwriting. Notes of some sort.

There's a long gap between the notebook that reads February 1994–October 1994 and the one that begins just last month—without an end date.

The first page of that one is filled with

details written in blue ink, in careful script.

Details that, even at a preliminary glance, are disturbingly familiar.

Blond hair . . .

Purple backpack . . .

Held in stone-walled cellar . . .

What? What is all this?

What does it mean?

At the bottom of the page, printed in black ink and circled, is a name.

LEAH ROBY.

John Murphy hates living alone.

Hated it when he did it back before he married Helen and hated it even more after they divorced.

It's been years since she traded the small cedar-shingled Cape on 22nd Street in Spray Beach for a condo across the causeway in Manahawkin.

You'd think by now he'd like having the house to himself, but he doesn't.

Most of the time, he's too lonely to appreciate the perks.

Like not having to park his pickup

truck on the street so she can park her car in the tiny driveway.

Like being able to keep all his fishing gear right in the utility room instead of stored in the flimsy shed out back.

Like watching bad movies on Cinemax late at night in bed.

Which is what he was doing earlier, when he drifted off to sleep.

Now he finds himself awake in the empty house, the movie long over and an inexplicable restlessness drifting over him.

He glances at the digital clock, wondering if he should just get up and go fishing. That's what he does most mornings, but not this early.

It's never too early for fishing.

That's what John's father, John Senior, used to say when he woke up his son in the wee hours as a boy.

Dad was John's best friend in the world. He's been gone almost as long as Helen's been out of his life.

These days, John fishes alone.

It wouldn't seem right to have someone else out on the boat with him. He and Dad were a team: *JMurph1* and *JMurph2*.

With a sigh, John rolls onto his back, thinking he should get some sleep.

In the instant before he closes his eyes, he sees a figure looming over his bed.

Before he can open them again, it's all over.

PART IV: AUGUST

Chapter Sixteen

When Cam was a little girl, she and Ike went to a beach party here on the island.

It was late August, maybe September. That day, under a cloudless blue sky, sparkling in the sunshine, the sea was calm and inviting, as warm as it ever gets on the Jersey coast.

Cam remembers wading in to cool off as her father sat on the sand with his friends and a beer.

She wore a blue bathing suit and had a cheap red plastic sand pail and one of the little plastic prongs was broken off the rim so the white plastic handle was dangling from one end. She'd had the pail all summer, and her father kept threatening to throw it away, but every time he did, she would cry.

Chasing a little silvery fish, Cam tried to scoop it into the bucket but it kept flitting just out of reach.

She was careful not to go too far out, careful to keep her head above water.

She couldn't swim.

The fish kept darting past her outstretched hands with the broken pail. She edged her way toward it, perched on her tiptoes, bobbing in the gentle waves.

Edged forward, though she could feel the ocean floor sloping down before her.

She could feel the water pulling her inch by inch down the slope as she craned her neck, struggling not to go under.

She knew she was losing the battle.

She was sure she was going to drown, right here on Long Beach Island on a gorgeous late-summer day, in the midst of all these people, not one of them, not even her own father, aware that she was in trouble.

The memory has haunted Cam for a month.

Ever since the day Rebecca Pearson disappeared, and she had the premonition about Tess, and came home that night to find that one of her notebooks—the most recent one, with the notes about Leah Roby and Rebecca Pearson—seemed to be missing.

It hasn't turned up since.

A lifeguard pulled Cam out of the water that long-ago day.

"You're lucky to be alive, little girl," she remembers him saying. "Where's your mother?"

"I don't have a mother."

Even then, she comprehended the knowing, sympathetic look he gave her.

If she'd had a mother, the lifeguard was thinking, she would never have had such a close call.

She recalls standing there on the sand, drenched, still coughing saltwater out of her lungs, and watching the broken red bucket drift out to sea, wanting it back, needing it back.

Mothers watch over their children. Keep them safe.

Now, resting a hand against the aching small of her back, Cam stands on the beach, making sure Tess is still sitting on a blanket down the way with her boyfriend.

Bare upper arms touching, heads tilted close together, she and Heath are talking intensely about something, as usual.

Tess is safe.

And Cam is watching.

Who is Camden Hastings, really?

The question lingers even now, a full month after it became apparent that she's been harboring a child posing as her own, along with a bizarre collection of notebooks.

The older handwritten notes weren't of nearly as much concern as the current, dated this summer.

Why was Cam so interested in both Leah Roby and Rebecca Pearson?

Can she possibly know?

If she does, she's not letting on.

There's a ragged edge where the third page was torn from the notebook. What was written there? Where is it now?

It's all very unsettling.

Maybe Cam's got a secret identity as a cop?

A private investigator?

Some kind of bleeding heart advocate for teenaged runaways?

Hard to tell.

If Cam does know, though, she might be planning to bolt . . . and take her so-called daughter, "Tess," with her.

That's why something needs to be done soon.

Now.

Tonight.

Before she disappears again.

August in the City of Brotherly Love: hot asphalt, cold fountains, fruit-flavored water ices; open windows and open hydrants in row house neighborhoods; museum docents in Colonial garb leading packs of camera-toting tourists on cobblestone walking tours.

"I can't wait to get out of here tomorrow," Lucinda tells Neal as they head away from the U-Penn campus, down 39th Street toward the parking lot and their respective cars.

"Lucky you."

"You're going away, too, aren't you? Next week?"

Neal's bushy gray brows furrow. "To my daughter's in Scranton, so we can watch the twins while she has the baby. Some vacation."

"Who are you kidding? You love all those grandkids."

"I don't love Scranton. Sixty-one years old and I've never been west of Pennsylvania. I'd kill to go on a ten-day Alaskan cruise right about now." Neal wipes a bead of sweat from his balding head.

"It's only seven days, not ten." Lucinda had originally considered going for ten, but decided a full week of solitude at sea—if there is such a thing as solitude on a floating behemoth with three thousand other people—will probably be enough.

"Seven, ten . . . Alaska in August. You're one smart cookie, Cin."

No one but Neal ever calls her Cin.

Or a smart cookie.

Glancing affectionately at the curmudgeon who's become a father figure these past few years, she wants to tell him he's got it all wrong. She isn't taking a cruise to the far reaches of Alaska because she's smart.

She's doing it because she's running scared.

Back in Philly after seeing Randy again last month, she did her best to get back to business as usual.

Edgy, distracted, she realized the energy she normally channels into her work was draining into a useless reservoir of feelings for a married man.

Something had to be done.

Wallowing isn't her style. Fabulous vacations are.

One thing she's wanted for years—aside from Randall Barakat—is to visit Alaska. So she booked a suite on board the *Norwegian Star* and off she goes, tomorrow.

Today means taking care of business with Neal, who's summoned her to help find a missing sorority girl. Lucinda just spent three hours roaming around the Theta Delta–something house and talking to the sisters, to no avail. The only image that popped into her head was

Randy's, repeatedly—and she did her best to push him right back out again.

She hasn't spoken to him since Long Beach Island. A few times, she thought of calling—just to check in. See if there are any new developments on the Rebecca Pearson case.

She doesn't need him for that, though. Thanks to the Internet, she knows there are no developments; Rebecca hasn't been found.

She never will be. Of that, Lucinda remains certain.

Nothing for her to do but move on, put all that happened on Long Beach Island behind her.

Rebecca.

Randy.

Even Cam Hastings.

She's been in the back of Lucinda's mind for weeks. She and her daughter.

A few times, Lucinda considered calling to see how they are. Just to make sure things are all right.

But why bother?

The day is coming when things won't be all right. Sooner or later, something's going to happen to Cam's daughter. Lucinda has seen it, over and over.

What is she supposed to do about it? Sit around and wait for something to happen, so she can say *I told you so . . .* if only to herself?

She can only hope the fresh Alaskan air clears her head so she can get back to work after the trip.

"Make sure you keep me posted on this case, Neal," she tells him as they reach the parking lot and prepare to go their separate ways.

"Didn't anyone ever tell you that you should leave the real world behind when you go on vacation?"

"Why do you think I'm going all the way to Alaska?"

"Sounds to me like you might be running away from home."

"I ran away from home once already in my life."

Neal—who grew up over in Two Street, a family neighborhood between Society Hill and South Philly—has been a part of Lucinda's real world from the start. He knows all about her past; how she gladly exchanged the Sloans's gilded fantasy world for the real world; how her family never understood her, never forgave her.

"I have to get going. I've still got to pack, run some errands, pay the bills."

"Safe travels," Neal says gruffly, giving her a hug. "Give my regards to Mount Hood."

"That's in Oregon."

"I told you I've never been out West."

"Someday you should go. Take Erma."

"She'll want to bring all the grandkids along."

"So will you," Lucinda accuses, and he grins.

Patting her on the arm, he says, "Maybe you'll meet Mr. Right on the boat and give your parents some grandkids of their own someday soon."

"That's about as likely as my parents taking a bunch of grandkids on an Alaskan cruise."

"Hey, you never know."

Sometimes, Lucinda thinks, *you do.*

"Is she still there?" Gwen asks Cam from under the umbrella.

"Still there," Cam confirms, shielding her eyes from the sun as she checks on Tess and Heath again.

"Still madly in love?" Petra wants to know, sitting beside Gwen.

"Still madly in love."

Yawning, Cam eases herself waaaaay back down into her seat, wondering why sand chairs always have to be so low. If summer wasn't going to be over with by the time she enters her third trimester, she'd have to start carrying a director's chair to the beach.

"Tired?" Gwen asks, as Cam yawns again.

"Yeah. I slept from eight to eight but I swear I could take a nap right here, right now."

"Go ahead."

"Can't. I have to keep tabs on Frankie and Annette down there."

"Who?"

"Didn't you ever see *Beach Blanket Bingo?*" she asks Petra. "Frankie Avalon and Annette Funicello on the beach, falling in love . . ."

"Nope."

"Is that the one where Eric Von Zipper kidnaps the singing star? Sugar Kane?"

Kidnaps.

It doesn't take much to jar Cam out of a momentary lapse in hypervigilance.

"Eight to eight?" Gwen asks, as Cam leans forward to check Tess again. "You went to bed at *eight?*"

"I could have gone at seven. I'm exhausted lately. I haven't seen nine o'clock in a week."

"So I guess the whole *Beach Blanket Bingo* scene isn't keeping you up nights, then?"

"No, but it keeps me on my toes the rest of the time. I guess it wouldn't be so bad if it were winter. But this whole summer romance thing—all that tanned skin, hardly any clothes . . . It's not good."

"Definitely not." Petra says, shaking her head. "Thanks to Frankie and Annette down there, I've got Tyler moping around like a lovelorn Charlie Brown, poor kid."

"Wait, I don't get it." Gwen touches her cheek with her forefinger and furrows her brows in exaggerated confusion. "Is Tess supposed to be Annette, or the little red-haired girl?"

Red-haired girl.

Rebecca Pearson.

At the thought of her, a familiar sick feeling engulfs Cam.

There's been no sign of Rebecca in the month since she vanished.

At first, the apparent kidnapping was the biggest news story on the island. It was all anyone could talk about.

The police didn't release all the details Cam was privy to during the initial investigation. There was no mention of the shark's tooth necklace or secret admirer in published reports. And certainly no mention of Lucinda Sloan. Or Cam Hastings.

Yet to her surprise, a few people have asked Cam in passing if she was involved in the search. Local gossip travels faster here than it does back home.

She denied any involvement, of course. And she never mentioned it to anyone. Not even Tess.

Then, maybe two days after Rebecca Pearson disappeared, her story was overshadowed by another headline:

LOCAL MAN SLAIN IN BED

It was almost unheard of—a cold-blooded murder right in Beach Haven.

The victim: John Murphy, a long-divorced middle-aged elementary schoolteacher who lived alone on 22nd Street in adjacent Spray Beach.

No suspect or possible motive, aside from robbery. John Murphy's wallet was missing. It was later found, minus whatever cash might have been in it, in a construction Dumpster just over the causeway in Bayside.

Randall Barakat—one of the detectives assigned to the case—was quoted in the paper as speculating that the robbery might have been staged. Though why anyone would want John Murphy dead is anyone's guess.

Even John Murphy's ex-wife claimed he didn't have an enemy in the world. It wasn't as if he had gambling debts, a drug habit, a married lover. He was just a nice, quiet guy who was a Eucharistic Minister at his church and an avid birdwatcher and fisherman.

Yet someone shot him point-blank in the head as he slept.

That just goes to show that anything can happen to anyone, anywhere, anytime.

The newspapers played down both the disappearance of Rebecca Pearson and the murder of John Murphy as time went on. It was no Great White attack, but local business owners were concerned about the potential impact on the tourist trade.

The powers that be have put tremendous pressure on Detective Barakat to solve the murder and/or find the missing girl.

Certain the latter isn't even a remote possibility, Cam drags her thoughts back to her friends' banter.

"Maybe we can introduce Tyler to Casey when she comes down next week," Petra is telling Gwen. "Do you still have that picture I can show him?"

"I do, but remember, she's an older woman."

"How old is she again?"

"Fifteen. Who knows," Gwen says,

"maybe Tess will ditch the hunky lifeguard and fall in love with Tyler."

"And maybe," Petra replies flatly, "it'll be the other way around."

"Tyler's already in love with Tess."

"No, I mean maybe the hunky lifeguard will ditch her. Debbie keeps telling you to brace yourself for the big breakup, Cam."

"Maybe Debbie should be bracing herself for the day when Beth's hunky lifeguard ditches her," Cam says.

All three of them look over at the white wooden tower where Beth, supermodelish in a leopard-skin bikini, is leaning and talking to Jared, her summer flame.

"I want a hunky lifeguard," Gwen declares, grinding her soda can into the sand so it won't tip over. "Everyone else has one."

"*I* don't have a hunky lifeguard. Petra doesn't."

"I don't even have a *life,*" Petra says wryly.

"Yeah, well, who does when you're pushing forty and raising kids on your own?" Cam asks.

"Debbie does." Gwen and Petra say it in unison, and they all laugh.

The fourth member of their single mom summer quartet is back to jetting all over the globe several days a week, leaving Beth and Jonathan here in the care of the dour yet capable Dolores.

Cam always thinks of old photos of Amelia Earhart when she sees Dolores. She's older than Earhart was when she disappeared—probably in her fifties, or maybe her sixties; it's hard to tell. But she's got the same lean, mannish build, an outdoorsy, weathered-looking face, and a shock of unkempt short hair, only hers is salt and pepper.

Cam mentioned the resemblance to Tess, who passed it on to Beth, who reportedly said, "Too bad Dolores hasn't fallen off the face of the earth, too."

There's no love lost between Debbie's kids and their summer caregiver.

"She's creepy," according to Jonathan; "a royal pain in the butt," according to Beth.

"Suck it up and deal" is their mother's usual response.

"As long as my kids are alive whenever

I come back, she's doing her job." So said Debbie to Cam, Gwen, and Petra just last week.

Cam is sure she was joking in her cavalier Debbie way.

Well, pretty sure.

She herself wouldn't joke about kids being alive—or not.

The first couple of times Dolores came to the beach with the kids, Cam or one of the others invited her to join them. They had gravitated toward this same spot every sunny day, with an unspoken arrangement to meet here around eleven and hang out till three or four.

Dolores always said no—then set herself up beneath an umbrella situated just close enough to make things good and awkward.

She's there now, a few yards away, down toward the lifeguard stand.

Cam has to admit, she keeps a better eye on Debbie's kids than Debbie does. In fact, she seems to keep a joyless surveillance over the whole scene, never bringing a book or magazine, or leaning back to nap in the shade.

With old eagle-eye Dolores on the

beach, Cam should probably rest assured that nothing's going to happen to Tess if she herself looks away for a moment.

The horrific recurring vision about Tess has never been as vivid as it was that first day, at the Pearsons's house. Maybe that's because Cam was so in tune with what had just happened to Rebecca. And the house was teeming with people, charged with emotional energy.

Armed with the growing yet inexplicable conviction that Rebecca is no longer alive, Cam still wakes up every morning wondering if this will be the day they'll find her somewhere. Her remains.

Yet deep down, she's starting to sense that it's not going to happen. Ever.

She gets the feeling that every physical trace of Rebecca has been obliterated—how, she doesn't know. She can't bring herself to consider the scenarios.

Every time she has a terrifying flash of Tess afraid, Tess in danger, she has to fight the urge to do something about it. Something other than stay on top of her

24/7, insist that she travel in supervised groups, install new dead bolts in the beach house.

She had to tell Mike she wanted to change the locks—it's half his house, and anyway, he pays all the bills. When she brought it up, she braced herself for him to accuse her of being drunk and paranoid again.

Surprisingly, he didn't say a word; he just told her to get the locksmith there and have the bill sent to him. She did send it, along with a set of new keys. It was the right thing to do.

Having the new bolts on all the doors and windows helps her sleep a little better at night . . . although, when you think about it, someone could easily cut a screen and come in that way. And it's too hot to sleep with the windows closed.

Nagged by uneasiness, Cam rises from her chair to check on Tess again.

This time, both Tess and Heath happen to see her.

Tess shakes her head and looks away, and her body language says it all.

I'm so sorry, sweetie, Cam thinks, hating what she's doing to Tess, and to herself.

But she can't help it.

She knows what she saw.

She knows what's going to happen to Tess if she's not careful.

Still, there's a part of her that wonders . . .

Are you going to watch over her every second for the rest of her childhood? The rest of her life?

"Dude, your mother is intense."

Tess rolls her eyes. "No kidding."

She likes it when Heath calls her Dude. It's kind of his pet name for her. Which makes it romantic.

That's what she told Beth, who didn't see it that way. According to Beth, there's nothing romantic about being called Dude.

"How come your mother's always checking up on you when you're with me?" Heath asks. "Doesn't she trust me?"

"She doesn't trust anyone. It's not

about you. She checks up on me all the time, no matter who I'm with."

"Why?"

"Who knows? It's freaky. She was never like this before. I think maybe it's the pregnancy hormones or something."

Heath shrugs, looking uninterested.

Tess isn't particularly interested in pregnancy hormones herself. She only knows that Mom blames them for a lot of things. Being moody, eating half a mushroom pizza in one sitting, losing her keys.

That was the worst—the day with the keys, a few weeks ago. Mom had them in her beach bag as usual, but when she and Tess got back to the house and she went to unlock the door, they weren't there.

They had to backtrack all the way back down to the beach and look through the sand. Mom was sure they had fallen out of the bag. She even checked with the lifeguards, and the Lost and Found.

Nothing.

When they got back home, there were

Mom's keys—sitting on the walk by the front steps.

"I must have dropped them somehow," Mom said, looking puzzled. "I wonder why we didn't hear them hit the ground."

"I'm hot." Heath cuts into her thoughts. "Want to go in the water?"

"Sure." Tess allows him to take her hand and pull her to her feet.

Naturally, her mother makes a beeline for them as they head toward the water, still holding hands.

"Tess!"

Tess ignores her.

"Um, I think your mother's calling you."

"I think you're right." Tess flashes Heath a tight grin.

"Tess!"

With a sigh, she looks back.

"Be careful!" Mom calls. "Not too deep!"

"Whatever," Tess mutters, embarrassed.

To Heath, she says, "You don't know how lucky you are that your parents aren't around this summer."

"Oh, yeah, I do."

The Pickerings—both of whom have

high-powered corporate jobs in the city—are back home in Montclair. Heath is staying here on the island at their beach house with his older brother Brooks. Heath's parents occasionally come down on weekends. She knows which house is theirs—on North Atlantic Avenue, pretty fancy, with a hot tub and an in-ground pool. She's never been there, or met his parents, or Brooks, who graduated college last year and works nights as a bartender. He pays little attention to Heath's comings and goings.

Must be nice.

"Brrr," Tess says as the cold seawater washes around her ankles.

"Come on, it's not that bad." Heath throws himself into the surf.

"It's cold."

"Yeah? You think so?" Floating on his back, Heath eyes her, and she admires his smile and his tan and his sun-lightened hair, marveling yet again that he's actually her boyfriend.

It happened so fast. He kissed her for the first time on the Fourth of July, beneath a canopy of fireworks. It was straight out of her imaginary fantasy life; so surreal that even then, when it was happening, Tess was still thinking it might be a joke.

But here they are, a month later, and going strong.

Yeah, and they'd probably be going stronger if it wasn't for Mom breathing down Tess's neck every second of every day—and night.

Back at the very beginning, Heath wanted to talk about what had happened in Montclair. But he didn't specifically mention the notebook and Mrs. Heath Pickering. He just said someone—Chad?—told him that Tess Hastings liked him, and pointed her out to him.

"I thought you were cute," he said, "so I got your number and texted you."

And she told him to leave her the hell alone.

Yeah.

Nice work, Tess. Way to waste an entire month you could have had with Heath.

"I thought you were someone else," she told him.

"Someone else named Heath Pickering?" he asked dubiously, and she just shrugged.

He let it go at that.

Heath isn't the type to dwell on things, and Tess is trying not to, either.

The water laps above her knees and she shivers again.

"Coming in?" Heath paddles closer, stands.

"I have to get used to it first."

Heath reaches out and picks her up in one quick motion.

"What are you doing?" Tess screams.

"Getting you used to it."

"It's freezing! You're freezing!" Tess shrieks and wriggles against his bare, wet chest, laughing as he carries her deeper.

The next thing she knows, they're both in the water up to their necks.

"That was a dirty trick!" Teeth chattering, she flicks water at him.

"I was doing you a favor. You can't wade in little by little. Only way to do it is plunge in headfirst."

"Maybe that's your style, but it's not mine."

"Hey . . ." Heath reaches out and touches her cheek. "You're bleeding."

"I am?" She touches the spot.

"Just a tiny bit. It looks like you got scratched or something while we were fooling around. God, I'm sorry."

"It's okay."

"Does it hurt?"

"Not at all."

He leans closer and kisses it. "Sorry," he says again.

And suddenly the water isn't feeling nearly as cold.

"It's totally fine. But maybe now you learned your lesson about grabbing people and throwing them into the water."

"I have. Definitely." Heath is looking at something behind her.

"What's wrong?"

"Is that . . . ?"

"What?" Tess looks over her shoulder.

"Nothing. I just thought I saw . . . never mind."

"What?" she asks, his expression making her uneasy.

"A fin. But it might have just been a shadow."

In a flash, she remembers the legend of the Great White Shark off Beach Haven. And she's bleeding.

Screaming, she splashes her way frantically toward shore, half-swimming, half-running. Any second, she's sure, something is going to bump up against her legs underwater—maybe savagely tear off a limb, or eat her alive in one ferocious bite.

"Tess! Tess!"

Heath is calling her. People are turning to look.

"Tess! Stop! There's nothing out here!"

She turns back to see Heath laughing.

"I was just kidding!" he calls, swimming toward her. "Dude, it was a joke!"

A joke?

About a shark?

"That was the least funny joke I ever heard." Tess isn't sure whether to be embarrassed or annoyed.

"I'm sorry." Heath reaches her, embraces her. "Do you forgive me?"

How can she not?

He's Heath, the guy of her dreams.

Tess would forgive him for just about anything.

* * *

Taking a pack of cigarettes from the top of her packed beach bag, Petra looks at Cam. "Do you mind if I . . . ?"

Yeah, Cam minds, but it's Gwen who speaks up. "Oh, Lord, if you're going to smoke, go do it somewhere else."

"That's what I love about you, Gwen. You're so damn frank," Petra says in a tone that makes it clear she doesn't love that at all.

"I just don't want to die young from second-hand smoke."

"Yeah, I get it." Petra takes her cigarettes and ambles down the beach, lighting one as she goes.

"Is it just me, or is she really touchy lately?" Gwen asks.

"Everyone's touchy lately. It's the heat."

"No one's as touchy as Petra," Gwen grumbles as Cam stands and checks again for Tess.

Still fine, still swimming around out there with Heath, still madly in love.

"She's just stressed about her kids or whatever."

"Who isn't?"

Cam sits again with a groan. All this up and down is killing her.

"You know, Tess is fine," Gwen says. "You're making yourself crazy. Why are you so worried about her all the time?"

"She's my baby girl."

"Not for long."

Startled, Cam looks up.

Oh. Gwen is pointing at Cam's stomach, protruding in a black maternity bathing suit.

"Pretty soon that'll be your baby girl," she explains, seemingly oblivious to Cam's initially ominous interpretation.

"Or boy."

"The ultrasound tech thought it was a girl, though, right?" Gwen asks, and Cam nods.

She had the routine sonogram last week, back in Montclair.

Tess came with her, grudgingly at first, because she didn't want to miss a day with Heath.

But when the white blob appeared on the screen and the technician started pointing out her unborn sibling's tiny beating heart and jerking limbs, Tess was fascinated.

"Do you want to know the sex?" the technician asked, and Tess answered for both of them.

"Yes!"

The technician looked at Cam, who hesitated.

"What about Dad?" she asked Tess. Mike was in Japan on business. If he hadn't been, she'd have asked him to be there.

"If Dad doesn't want to know what it is, we won't tell him," Tess said.

Dilemma averted.

The technician thought it might be a girl. Tess was elated by the thought of a little sister.

"You do know that the only way to be positive about the sex is an amnio, right?" Gwen asks Cam now.

"I know. If a boy pops out, I'll be surprised, but . . . whatever. It's fine." Mike, she suspects, would love to have a son. Mike III.

"So you're not having one?"

"An amnio?"

When Cam shakes her head, Gwen does, too. "You should, at your age."

Dr. Advani said the same thing.

Cam tells Gwen what she told the obstetrician: "Too many risks involved with the test, and I don't need to know if there's something wrong with the baby before it's born. I wouldn't do anything about it anyway."

"No?"

"No. Absolutely not. Would you?"

Gwen shrugs. "Moot point. I'm done having babies."

"You never know. What if you meet someone and—"

"No, I mean I can't." Gwen looks away, down the beach, where Petra is walking along the waterline and puffing away.

"I'm sorry," Cam says uncomfortably.

"No biggie," Gwen returns. But it is.

Cam can tell.

Great. Why does she seem to keep sticking her foot in her mouth everywhere she goes lately?

Don't beat yourself up. You've been distracted.

Things were stressful enough with the pregnancy, sobriety, Rebecca, and those visions involving Tess . . . and other visions as well.

Here and there, glimpses of children in trouble. Whenever they strike, she writes down what she sees, in a fresh notebook she keeps hidden under her mattress.

Add Mike to the mix, and no wonder she's a basket case.

He's coming down tomorrow to spend the weekend.

His idea.

He'd called—not long after the curtailed DC trip with Tess and the unresolved telephone argument—to say they needed to talk. In person.

"I think that would be good," Cam said cautiously, sensing he had reached some kind of resolution. "When do you want to come?"

"I can't get away till the beginning of August since I took that extra time over the Fourth, and I'm in Tokyo until almost the end of July."

"So come in August."

"How about the first weekend?" he asked. As if she might have other plans.

"We'll be here." She hesitated. "You're staying with us, right? In the house?"

He hesitated, too. "Is that okay?"

It would be uncomfortable if he didn't. Probably even more uncomfortable if he does, but . . .

"Yeah," she told him. "Of course."

She's been wondering ever since where he's expecting to sleep.

That, she supposes, will depend on where he wants to go from here.

The couch is a pullout, and not all that comfortable. Her father occupied it for a few nights earlier this summer, until just after the Fourth of July. One morning he woke up, hugged her and Tess goodbye, and said he'd see them again soon. Then he ambled off in his Ike way, and they haven't heard from him since.

What if he shows up again this weekend?

Then Mike won't be able to use the couch.

Meaning, he'll just have to sleep in the bedroom with Cam, regardless of where he wants to go from here.

Or, she supposes, Tess could sleep

with her and Mike could have the twin bed in her room.

But that would be awkward.

Almost as awkward as sharing a bed, once again, with her husband.

So far, it basically sounds like there isn't an aspect of the looming weekend that won't be awkward.

It doesn't help that Mike—without consulting her—sent Tess a gift from Japan.

A cell phone.

Not just a cell phone, as Tess—thrilled—explained to Cam, but some kind of tiny, fancy Internet phone. Cutting-edge technology. Mike's forte, not hers.

"Isn't it the coolest thing ever?" Tess kept asking, eager to show it off to her friends. "Now Dad and I can stay in touch even better."

As far as Cam is concerned, the coolest thing ever would be if Tess could stay in touch with her dad simply by living under the same roof.

That, however, isn't likely to happen.

Not if he's upgrading their daughter's cell phone. Probably making plans to move to a bigger apartment, too, where Tess can have her own room.

Seeing Petra coming toward them again now, Cam wonders if Mike might even go for shared custody, like Petra's husband did.

Let him try.

She'd fight it.

If Mike wants a divorce, he can have a divorce. But he can't take away her child.

"Mike!" Standing in the doorway, his mother goes pale beneath her ruddy summer complexion. "What are you doing here?"

"Is Dad home?"

"Yes . . . Is something wrong? Did something happen?"

"I just want to talk to you. Both of you." He crosses the threshold into the familiar home where he was raised.

It smells of bleach and bacon. Mom has been cooking and cleaning today. Same as every day.

It's a modest home but now worth millions. His father is proud of that; proud to be able to say that he made all the right moves in his life, at all the right times.

"How's Tess?" his mother asks.

"She's good. I haven't seen her in a few weeks, though. I've been away. I'm going down to see her tomorrow."

"Give her my love." His mother pauses, tucking her hands into the pockets of her lemon-yellow summer slacks. "And Cam, too."

"Yeah. I will."

Cam. The thought of her fills him with guilt.

Again he thinks of that day, in the car.

Of her far-fetched claim to be a modern-day Nostradamus.

Of the moment of truth that struck him—well, more like hit him over the head like an anvil—right after he hung up the phone.

He knew, then and there, what he was going to do.

But he was helpless, stuck in traffic, and the moment passed.

When the road opened again, it was late. He drove back to New York. Went back to his life, back to work, to Japan . . .

But the truth dogged him every step of the way.

He follows his mother to the kitchen, past a gallery of framed photos from the annual ski trip. Cam and Tess are conspicuously missing from the most recent. Mike quickly looks away, again plagued by guilt.

"Dad's out on the deck. I just got back from the hairdresser."

Some things never change. His mother has had a standing Friday-afternoon appointment for as long as Mike can remember.

"You look beautiful, as usual, Mom."

She smiles and pats her hair. "Do you want something cold to drink?"

"Just ice water. I can get it."

"I'll get it." She opens the cupboard for a glass, fills it with ice, then hands it to him with a bottle of Poland Spring. "Are you hungry? Did you eat lunch?"

"I'm fine, Mom." He opens the slider to the deck.

His father, wearing a pink polo shirt and sitting in a carefully weathered teak chair facing the sound, looks up from a golf magazine. "Mike! What's up, son?"

His mother says, "He wants to talk to us."

"About what?" Mike sets the magazine aside. "How about some ice water, Marge? It's hotter than hell out here."

Just once, Mike thinks as he watches his mother head back into the house, he would love to see her tell his father to get up and get something for himself.

"How was Japan, Mike?"

"It was fine."

"Did you catch up on some new technology?"

He thinks of the tiny cell phone he sent his daughter. The one he promised would keep them linked no matter how far apart they are.

"Yeah," he tells his father. "I did."

"Are you still seeing that woman? Kate?"

Mike wishes he had never mentioned that in the first place. But he did, back when he started seeing her, knowing Mike Sr. would approve.

Before he can answer the question, his mother reappears with another ice-filled glass and water bottle.

Good.

"Sit down, Mom."

"You're scaring me, Mike. What is it?"

"Cam is pregnant."

"What!" his mother squeals, then clasps a hand over her mouth and looks at his father.

"Was this something you planned?" is his first question. Of course.

"What difference does it make?" Mike asks. "Life doesn't always work out the way you planned."

"Just because she got herself pregnant doesn't mean—"

"She didn't get herself pregnant, Dad. I did."

"Are you sure about that?"

He hates the question. Hates that he'd asked it himself, in so many words, directly of Cam.

"Yeah," he tells his father. "I'm positive."

His father nods thoughtfully. "What are you going to do about it?"

"So what do you think?" Heath asks Tess as they tread water, facing each other.

"About what?" she returns, though she knows very well what he means.

"Want to ditch your mom and do something fun for a change?"

"Like what?"

"I don't know . . . You can come to my house or something," he suggests.

"When?"

"Whenever." He shrugs. "We better go in. I've got to get ready to start working."

Together, they start swimming toward shore.

"How about tonight? Why don't you come to the party with me?" Heath asks. It's a bonfire, all the lifeguards are going. So is Beth.

"I told you—my mother won't let me." Tess already asked. Twice.

"Tomorrow night, then?" Heath persists. "Do you want to do something then?"

"What am I supposed to do about my mom? She'll never let me go out with you alone at night."

"Don't tell her. Just say you're going over to Beth's. She'll cover for you."

"Yeah, but Dolores won't, and I don't know when Debbie's coming back."

"I think Jared said tonight or tomorrow. You should check."

Tired of kicking, Tess swings a leg down to see if she can stand yet. Nope, still too deep.

"Why don't you just tell your mother you and Beth are going to a movie or something? She can drop you off there and everything. I'll meet you and we'll go someplace until the movie would've been over. Pick a long one."

Tess isn't sure how she feels about that plan. Not that it matters.

"I doubt my mother would even let me do that," she tells Heath. "She's been acting really weird. She'd think she had to wait up, and that would be impossible because lately she falls asleep at, like, eight o'clock. Which is the only break I get from her watching me breathe."

Seeing the look on Heath's face—and worried he's deciding a younger girl with an overprotective mother is too much trouble—she adds quickly, "My dad's coming tomorrow for the weekend. Maybe he can talk some sense into her."

"Your dad's coming? I didn't know that."

"I didn't, either, until last night."

"I thought he's in Japan."

"He was. He's back. And he's staying with us for two days."

"What's up with that?" Heath asks. "Are they getting back together or something?"

"Maybe. Who knows?" She doesn't even dare to hope.

Again, she swings her leg down to see if she can stand yet.

"All I know is that I want to be alone with you, Tess."

"I want to be alone with you, too." Tess's feet hit the bottom, but she can't help feeling like she's still in way over her head.

"Petra looks happier now that she's had her nicotine fix," Gwen comments.

"Definitely."

"I wish she could just quit."

"I'm sure she does, too." Cam knows

just how hard it is to kick an unhealthy habit.

Or addiction, when it comes to Petra and smoking.

Habit, addiction.

There's a difference, Cam has come to realize.

She no longer believes her own drinking was a bona fide addiction, or that she's an alcoholic, or needs a twelve-step program.

Yes, it helped her to realize she had been drinking too much, for too many years, and that she had to stop.

But she only started in the first place to block out the visions.

She's no longer struggling against them. No, it's the opposite now. She'd welcome a vision if it meant she'd potentially be able to help a child in danger. The more she's able to see, the better.

"There's no way in hell I'm ever going back to drinking," she told Kathy when they spoke on the phone last night. "It's over. I'm not even tempted."

"You're pregnant," Kathy reminded her. "Sometimes your body naturally has an aversion to things that aren't good for the baby. You can't let your guard down. You have to work the program, one day at a time . . ."

Blah, blah, blah.

Kathy's AA rhetoric still gets on Cam's nerves sometimes. Kathy doesn't understand why Cam started drinking in the first place; doesn't understand why—aside from the pregnancy—she was able to stop.

But at least Kathy no longer calls Cam every day, asking if she's been to a meeting. And Cam doesn't feel the need to avoid her calls when she does check in a few times a week. It's kind of nice to talk to someone who cares; someone who will be there when she gets home to Montclair in a few weeks—especially since she's really starting to get the idea that Mike will not.

Last night when they talked, she asked Kathy if she's coming down to the island again anytime soon.

"Maybe before the summer's over," Kathy said.

"I'm sorry I missed you when you were here in July."

"So am I. It would have been nice to see you."

Kathy said the trip was spur of the moment. She and some friends decided on a weekend getaway, and one of them suggested visiting another friend who was staying in a rental house on Long Beach Island.

"The next thing I knew, there I was, right in the neighborhood," Kathy told Cam, "and I knew I had to look you up."

"Too bad that was such a crazy weekend for me," Cam said. Understatement of the year.

She asked Kathy where her friend's house is, but being unfamiliar with island geography, Kathy wasn't sure.

"All I know is that it was near the beach," she said—which means, it could have been just about anywhere.

Oh, well.

"If you come down again, let me know in advance," Cam said, and Kathy promised to do that.

Cam just hopes it won't be this weekend, with Mike here.

"How was your walk?" Gwen asks Petra as she sits down in her chair again.

"Great. Your daughter's boyfriend has a mean streak, though, Cam."

Cam frowns. "What do you mean?"

"I saw him teasing Tess out there, pretending there was a shark in the water. She was petrified."

"Boys will be boys," Gwen says lightly.

"I don't know . . . I can't imagine Tyler ever doing that to someone he liked."

Gazing out at the water, where Tess and Heath are swimming toward shore and looking amiable, Cam doesn't know what to make of it.

She can't help but remember what happened to Tess back in Montclair with her so-called friends, who also happen to be friends of Heath's.

What if he's playing her now?

It's possible, Cam supposes. She doesn't know him all that well. Or particularly trust him.

But then, who do you trust, where Tess is concerned?

Yeah. You're paranoid.

Anyway, consider the source.

Right. She shouldn't go jumping to conclusions about the integrity of Heath

Pickering's intentions based on Petra's opinion.

Didn't she just say in so many words that she hopes Tess and Heath break up so that poor lovelorn Tyler can date her?

Looking out at the swimmers bobbing in the water, Cam realizes she can no longer see Tess and Heath.

Leaping to her feet, heart pounding, she scans the beach. No sign of them.

"What's wrong?" Gwen asks, and stands, along with Petra.

"Cam? What are you looking at?"

"Tess—where's Tess?" She starts for the water, panic washing over her.

"Cam! She's right there!"

Hearing Petra's shout, she stops short.

Tess is, indeed, right back where she should be, rubbing her eyes as though she's just popped up from underwater.

Oh. Thank God.

Cam presses a hand against her racing heart.

Her friends watch her with obvious concern as she walks back over to the chairs.

"Sorry," she says sheepishly. "I lost sight of her for a second."

She sees Gwen and Petra exchange a look.

They're thinking she's ridiculously overprotective.

Or maybe just crazy.

She doesn't blame them.

They don't know what she sees, what she fears . . .

What she knows.

Again, she thinks of the missing Marble notebook.

She's now almost a hundred percent certain she brought it down here to the shore with her. She could swear she remembers seeing it the night she came home from the police station, even remembers writing Leah Roby's name in it.

But it was so late, and she was tired . . .

Maybe she dreamed the whole thing.

Maybe she left that notebook behind in Montclair.

She should have looked for it when she stopped back to check on the house last week after the ultrasound.

Either the notebook was there all along, or it was here . . . and she somehow lost it. Or someone took it.

Sitting in her chair again, Cam shivers in the sun.

Chapter Seventeen

Sitting in front of her laptop, waiting for the web page to load, Cam can hear the water still running in the shower.

Tess has been in there for at least fifteen minutes. When she gets out, she'll take forever to dry her hair and get dressed—especially since she knows Cam is waiting for her to go to the supermarket.

"Go without me," she said, when Cam told her the plan on the way back from the beach. "I don't want to go shopping."

Of course, Cam told her she had no choice.

She's trying to make the most of this waiting time, straightening up the house for Mike's arrival tomorrow, doing laundry—everything is sorted and the dryer is humming along. She can't start the wash again until Tess gets out of the shower, so she decided to kill some time on the Internet.

Specifically, browsing through the missing children sites she's been frequenting for weeks now that the visions are back.

She begins scanning the case records, checking each face to see if she recognizes it from a recent premonition.

So far, no sign of the little towhead, missing his two front teeth, she saw in a vision the other day, or the beautiful African-American teen who's been haunting her for two weeks now.

Hearing the water turn off in the bathroom at last, she mutters, "It's about time."

In the laundry room off the kitchen, she tosses in a load of whites, then goes to the closed bathroom door. Knocking, she calls, "How about putting a move on, Tess? I don't want to be at the store all night."

"Then go ahead. I'll stay here."

"You're coming. Hurry up."

"Don't rush me." Tess, ornery, is bound to drag this out forever.

With a sigh, Cam returns to the computer and resumes scrolling through the web pages.

Minutes later, a familiar face catches her eye.

The girl is about Tess's age. Shoulder-length dark hair. Glasses. Brown eyes. Pretty.

Cam scans the details quickly.

Her name is Kimberly Claire Osborn. Age thirteen. About four foot eight inches tall, seventy-five pounds. Last seen wearing denim shorts, a white T-shirt, and Nikes, disappeared from Santa Monica five years ago, a probable runaway.

The accompanying photo was taken on the day she disappeared, in one of those photo booths you find in old-fashioned five-and-dime stores and arcades.

None of it rings a bell—and, thinking back over her recent visions, Cam can't put her finger on any that involved this girl.

Not recently, anyway.

Maybe it was years ago . . .

Although she's been poring over the old notebooks, and she doesn't remember seeing anything that might have been in reference to this teenaged runaway.

And she can't help but feel as though she saw the girl more recently.

Could she have spotted her in person somewhere?

She'd practically be an adult now. Eighteen. She wouldn't even look like that anymore.

Glancing back at Kimberly's face, Cam tries to imagine what it might look like today.

That's when she sees it.

Around Kimberly Osborn's neck is a shark's tooth hanging on a silver chain.

It's been a good ten minutes since Cam's Volvo drove away down Dolphin Avenue.

Now is the time. Now or never.

And never isn't an option.

The street is quiet; it's the dinner hour. The air smells of beef seared over charcoal. It brings back memories of happier days.

Grilling for one just isn't much fun.

It never should have had to be this way.

But things are going to change.

The key turns easily in the back door lock.

Cam left the washer and dryer on. Does that mean she's coming right back?

No time to waste.

The floor plan is familiar, unlike at John Murphy's house that night last month. There, it was necessary to fumble around in the dark, finding the way to the master bedroom.

He never knew what hit him. One shot to the head, and there was no longer a chance that if ever some fraction of Rebecca Pearson's DNA was to wash up somewhere someday, anyone would possibly connect it to an early-morning chumming expedition.

Sure, it was a slim chance John Murphy could ever have made the connection, but even a slim chance is unacceptable.

John Murphy, like Eddie Casalino, is out of the picture, a necessary casualty in a war that should never have had to be waged in the first place.

None of this is my fault.

It's hers.

And she'll pay for what she's made me do.

Through Cam's living room, down the hall, second door on the left.

It only takes a minute.

There.

Now the stage is set. There's no going back.

"All we still need to get is Pringles," Cam tells Tess, looking up from her shopping list to consult the sign above the next aisle. "Where do you think the snacks are?"

"Hmm?"

Cam looks at Tess, standing there with her hands on the handle of the grocery cart, a faraway expression on her face.

Cam has been lost in thought herself, still fixated on Kimberly Osborn and the shark's tooth necklace.

It's probably a coincidence.

Lots of people—lots of kids—probably have necklaces like that. Especially kids who spend time in beach towns, where they're a dime a dozen in gift shops. Kimberly lived in Santa Monica.

But when you saw her picture—before you noticed the necklace—you already thought she looked familiar.

She almost called Detective Barakat to tell him about it, but stopped herself. Officially, the necklace is insignificant to the Pearson case, other than the fact that Rebecca was wearing it the day before she disappeared.

So it's better for Cam to wait to mention it to the detective until she figures out where she might have seen Kimberly Osborn before.

If you ever have seen her before.

Maybe she's mistaken about it.

With her wearing the necklace? It can't be a mistake.

There has to be a connection.

"We need a mop in aisle four, please. Cleanup in aisle four."

The announcement breaks Cam out of her reverie.

"We have to find the snack aisle," she tells Tess again. Then she frowns and leans in closer. "What's this?"

"What? This?" Tess reaches up to touch her cheek. "Oh . . . nothing. I got scratched."

"How?"

"Who knows? It's fine."

Cam nods, not liking the expression in Tess's eyes but uncertain what it means.

Just focus on something straightforward. Like grocery shopping.

She leads the way to the next aisle—condiments, oils, and dressings. No Pringles here.

"Maybe we should do some chicken on the grill," she decides, picking up a bottle of barbecue sauce.

"Hmm?"

"I said, maybe we can have barbecued chicken while Dad's here." As if they're all one happy little family again.

"That would be good. Listen, Mom . . ."

"Yeah?" She adds the barbecue sauce to the heap in the cart.

"I want to go to the movies tomorrow night with Beth. Okay?"

Cam looks at her.

Tess suddenly becomes very interested in the nutrition chart on a jar of mayo.

She's lying, Cam realizes. *She's not going to the movies with Beth. She's going with Heath. Or maybe she's not even going to the movies at all.*

"No," Cam says decisively. "I want you with us this weekend."

"So I can't see my friends at all?"

"You can see them. With us."

"I thought you and Dad had to talk. I thought that was why he's coming."

"What does that have to do with—"

"Don't you need to talk in private? What am I supposed to do?"

Cam considers that.

Tess has a point.

If she's otherwise occupied, Cam and Mike can have some time to themselves, to talk about working things out or . . .

Or to decide not to.

But what if something happens to Tess the moment Cam lets her out of her sight?

"You can't go off anywhere with your friends this weekend."

Tess opens her mouth to protest.

"Sorry," Cam cuts her off, "but case closed."

"That's not fair. You never let me do anything."

Cam can't argue with that.

Nor can she explain to Tess that it's for her own good.

All she can do is continue to say no, and keep Tess in a virtual prison for the rest of her life.

Some way to live, she thinks grimly.

But it's sure as hell better than the alternative.

The photograph is an old one, chronologically organized in a leather-bound album filled with pictures of illustrious people, exotic places.

But tonight, Kathy isn't interested in revisiting her social circle, her travels, even her beloved four-year-old Bichon Frise, Louis, who takes up his fair share of film.

Tonight, as she sits with the album on her lap, she turns the pages quickly, knowing what she's looking for and where to find it.

There.

Tucked between the travelogue shots from Kathy's African safari five years ago and several of Louis as a puppy, is the picture she wanted to see.

Strange, and telling, that after all those years of sharing a roof with her, there's only one photograph. In it, she's wearing her black housekeeper's uniform, as always. Smiling at the camera . . . but it was a smile tempered with sadness, as always.

Years went by and Kathy never thought to ask the woman she knew as Ann Johnson anything beyond the cursory questions about her past. Of course, the information was never volunteered.

She had her secrets, as everyone does, and she meant to carry them to the grave. She probably would have, if she'd lived to a ripe old age.

But dying young, and slowly, does something to a person. Diagnosed with a terminal illness, she felt the need to unburden herself.

Kathy was the only one there to listen.

The story was tragic.

Haunting.

Incredible.

On her deathbed, when the time came, she asked Kathy to make her three promises.

She's kept two.

She's about to break the third.

Carefully, with manicured fingernails, she slips the four corners of the photo from their holders. Then she picks up a fountain pen.

Turning over the photograph, she slashes a line through the name written there years ago. Before she knew.

Ann Johnson.

Beneath the crossed-out wrong name, she writes the right one.

Brenda Neary.

Back home, Tess immediately heads for her room.

"Hang on there," her mother says. "I need help dealing with these groceries."

Tess scowls and starts unpacking a bag.

"Thanks, Tess."

Thanks? Does she have a choice? About anything?

It takes forever to unload the car and put stuff away. It's like Mom bought out the whole store, and there's not a lot of cupboard space here at the cottage.

"I've got one more load of laundry to do. Want to watch a movie and help me fold, Tess?" Mom asks, putting the last can of Dr Pepper into the fridge.

"No thanks," she says curtly, thinking of Heath at that lifeguard party without her.

"Come on, you don't have to help fold if you don't want to. I'll make some popcorn. Or we can have some of that Ben & Jerry's I just bought."

Tess softens. Just a little. Ice cream does sound good.

"I thought it was for Dad."

"Not all of it." Mom tries hard to cover a yawn. "What do you want to watch? You can pick."

Pick a long one. That's what Heath said, when he was trying to get her to sneak out, supposedly to a movie with Beth, and meet him instead.

"You won't even last through the opening credits," she tells her mother, frowning.

Her mother, yawning openly this time, can't exactly argue with that, but she says, "I'll make it as long as I can, and if we don't get through the whole thing—"

"Forget it," Tess grumbles. "What good is watching a movie if you can't see the ending?"

Tess goes into her room without a backward glance and starts to slam the door.

Thinking better of it, she closes it. Hard enough to let her mother know she doesn't want to be disturbed, but not hard enough to get herself grounded.

Although . . . What's the difference?

She might as well be grounded as it is.

As she turns on the lamp and starts toward her dresser to find some pajamas, something catches her eye on the bed.

Stepping closer, she sees that it's a little paper gift bag.

* * *

With a sigh, Cam dials Debbie, hoping she's not thirty thousand feet over the North Atlantic with her cell turned off.

She isn't.

But she is in the middle of something. Cam can tell by her distracted tone when she says, "Hey—what's up?"

"Where are you?"

A slight pause, then, "Heathrow. I can barely keep track anymore. I actually had to check and see."

"When are you coming home?"

"Hopefully late tomorrow, but there's weather in the afternoons at this time of year, so you never know. Why?"

"I was going to ask a favor, but . . . that's okay. Forget it."

"Are you sure?"

"Positive."

Debbie doesn't push the issue, nor does she linger on the phone. She's not big on favors. Doing them for other people, anyway.

Which is why you shouldn't have bothered calling in the first place, Cam tells herself, hanging up.

Even if Debbie was going to be here, she wouldn't exactly jump at the chance to chaperone two fourteen-year-old girls at the movies so that Cam and Mike can have some time to talk about their marriage.

Oh, well. For all Cam knows, Mike is going to show up here tomorrow with divorce papers.

And then what?

And then it's over, that's what. You lose.

Everybody loses. Including Mike.

But chances are, he'll be long gone before he ever figures that out.

The gift bag is bright green, with hot-pink tissue paper sticking out the top.

Mom must have left it here earlier, before they went to the supermarket.

Frowning, Tess wonders what the occasion might be. Maybe Mom is just feeling bad for being so strict all summer.

She reaches into the bag and finds a note.

YOU'RE INVITED is etched at the top of the card, which has a colorful green and pink plaid border that matches the bag.

So it's not a note, but an invitation.

Someone wrote it on a computer, using a fancy font.

PLEASE JOIN ME FOR A MIDNIGHT SWIM. SKINNY-DIPPING OPTIONAL, BUT YOU MUST WEAR THIS. NO RSVP, JUST MEET ME AT THE POOL. SIDE GATE WILL BE OPEN. HEATH

Skinny-dipping?

Tess swallows hard.

Wear this?

What does that mean? Wear what?

And more importantly, how did Heath get this into her room?

She glances over at the open window.

Could he possibly have crawled in through the screen?

She crosses over to take a look. The screen is all the way down, latched at the bottom.

But that doesn't mean Heath didn't pry it open, sneak in, sneak back out again, and close it.

She tells herself that would be a totally romantic gesture, but for some reason, the thought of him coming into her room doesn't sit well with her.

Then again . . . he's Heath.

And she's crazy about him.

And he wants her to meet him tonight at midnight for a swim.

Or skinny-dip.

Whoa.

What now?

Remembering the gift bag, Tess pokes through the tissue paper.

Tucked into the bottom, she finds a small white gift box wrapped in a white bow.

It fits into the palm of her hand and something tells Tess, as she unties the bow with a trembling hand, that it's not a bathing suit.

Yawning, Cam double-checks the dead bolt on the front door.

Locked.

Back door.

Locked as well.

Returning to the living room, she turns off the lamp, then the floor fan. It *creak-whirs* into silence.

Beyond the screens, she can hear crickets and a night breeze stirring the leaves. She steps closer to the window and peers out.

Lights from neighboring houses beam reassuringly, yet Cam feels distinctly uneasy.

She finds herself wishing this was tomorrow night, with Mike here . . .

Oh, please. What kind of bullshit is that?

That's what Debbie would say.

You don't need a man around to keep you safe.

No. She really doesn't. Cam's done a good job of that on her own, for several months now.

If tomorrow Mike tells her that their marriage is over, she'll survive. So will Tess.

No matter what, she thinks fiercely, and turns away from the window.

Her gaze falls on the laptop. She spent another hour perusing the missing child profiles, and kept going back to Kimberly Osborn's. She still can't place her. Maybe it'll come to her later.

On the coffee table is a plastic laundry basket filled with dryer-hot clothes she just finished folding. It was the last load and smaller than the others, the reds.

She can leave them to put away tomorrow . . .

Or do it now, and have a good reason to check in on Tess.

She picks up the basket and heads down the hall. Balancing the laundry on her hip with one hand she knocks on Tess's door, hoping she isn't deafened by her iPod headphones.

A grouchy voice comes from within. "What do you want?"

Cam cracks the door open. "I've got some stuff to put in your drawers."

Tess is lying on her bed, wearing a pair of summer pajamas.

No iPod, no book or magazine.

Clearly, she's moping.

"Are you okay?"

"Not really."

"Anything I can do?"

"Let me have a life."

"You have a life."

"Not one worth living."

Teenaged melodrama.

That's all it is.

Yet Tess's words make Cam more uneasy than ever.

She lifts a small pile of laundry off the top of the basket. "Here are some of your clothes," she tells Tess. "Do you want to put them away, or should I?"

"I will. Just leave them."

Cam deposits the stack of folded red garments on the dresser, then bends over and plants a kiss on her daughter's forehead. Then she gently touches the small scratch on her cheek.

"Does that hurt?" she asks.

"No."

Cam pauses. "You know, Tess, things will look a lot better in the morning. They always do."

"No, they don't. Not always."

Cam heads for the door, realizing nothing she says is going to make a difference, just glad that they've gotten through another day unscathed, other than a minor scratch on Tess's cheek.

One day at a time, as Kathy says.

That's all it takes.

* * *

Precisely at midnight, Tess arrives, breathless, at the Pickerings's oversized house on North Atlantic Avenue.

She almost didn't make it.

While lying on her bed waiting for the minutes to tick by, she dozed off to sleep.

When she awakened, it was twenty of twelve.

She stripped off her pajamas, under which she was wearing her bathing suit, and quickly pulled on the pair of shorts she'd worn earlier, and a T-shirt from the top of the pile her mother left to be put away.

After grabbing her sandals and her cell phone, she stuck her head into Mom's room to make sure she was sound asleep.

Yup. And snoring.

She never used to. Yet another side effect of those pregnancy hormones, Tess figures.

She snuck silently out of the house, then practically ran all the way here, worrying the whole way about what's going to happen.

Mom would kill me if she knew what

I'm up to . . . but she won't know. I'll be back home in bed long before morning, she reminds herself with a twinge of guilt.

But she wouldn't have to resort to sneaking around in the night if her mother would just give her a little bit of freedom.

It's not like she's asking if she can go backpacking in Europe for a month.

All she wanted was to go to the movies with Beth.

No, it wasn't.

That was a total lie. You just wanted to be alone with Heath.

Yeah, but Mom didn't know that, and she still said no.

Tess looks up at the house, which is three stories tall and set back from the street.

Why, she wonders, is it so dark? Not just inside, but outside as well. You'd think Heath would have at least left the outdoor lights on.

There's no moon tonight to help her along as she starts to pick her way along the side path, separated from the driveway by hedges.

Uh-oh. She stops short, remembering.

In her haste to get out of the house, she forgot to wear the shark's tooth necklace.

Cam awakens with a start and looks at the clock.

Midnight.

Yawning, she swings her legs over the edge of the bed and stands.

She shouldn't have drunk so much water before bed. Not that it seems to matter, lately, how much she drinks. Her bladder is feeling the full effects of the pregnancy these days.

She's in and out of the bathroom quickly, wanting only to get back to bed, back to sleep.

Passing Tess's closed door, she wonders if she's still sulking in there. Maybe she should talk to her.

Cam hesitates.

Goes back to the door and knocks softly.

No reply.

Maybe Tess is plugged into her headphones.

Or maybe she's asleep by now, having sweet dreams.

I should let her rest.

In her own room Cam climbs into bed, sinks back against the pillow, and waits for sleep to reclaim her.

Up ahead, Tess can see the dimmest outline of the gate, propped open as Heath had promised.

She can hear the pool pump somewhere beyond, humming along, intermittently drowned out by the crashing of the distant surf.

"Heath?" she calls in a hushed voice, inching her way forward.

He doesn't answer.

But he's there.

She can sense his presence, but she can't see him.

The pool water is catching light from somewhere to cast eerie, moving shadows up into the surrounding boughs.

Tess doesn't like this.

Not one bit.

Remembering the prank Heath pulled on her in the water today, pretending there was a shark, she wonders if he's going to jump out at her.

"Heath?" she says louder, not caring that it's midnight. No one besides Heath can possibly hear her. His brother must be working at this hour, and the other houses are too far away.

"Heath! Cut it out! I know you're there."

Still no reply.

Cam's heart is pounding as if she's just run a marathon, yet she hasn't moved a muscle. All that's racing is her brain as she lies here, eyes open in the dark, body tense.

Another vision.

It came out of nowhere.

Tess.

Not here, safe and sound in her bed, wearing pajamas.

She has on the brick-colored L.B.I. T-shirt Cam had left on her dresser earlier, on top of the pile of laundry.

In the background is some kind of stone wall.

Cam has seen it before . . . in her vision about Leah Roby.

A shadow looms on the wall behind Tess.

"Stay away from me," she whimpers. *"Don't come near me with that."*

With what?

And who's there? Who is it?

Tess recoils, turning her head.

On her cheek is a small scratch.

Familiar.

Fresh.

The scene dissolves even as Cam comprehends that it doesn't portend some far-off future event.

The scratch, the shirt . . .

It's going to happen soon.

She shouldn't have come.

She should turn around right now and—

Tess screams as, doing an abrupt about-face, she sees a shadowy figure looming in the path directly behind her.

It pounces.

Presses something over her nose and mouth . . .

Then everything goes black.

* * *

Cam throws open Tess's door.

The bed is empty, the coverlet rumpled.

Don't panic.

It doesn't mean—

Something glints on the table beside the bed, and Cam steps closer.

A shark's tooth on a silver chain.

Chapter Eighteen

The girl who lived until now under the guise of Tess Hastings lies in the backseat of the SUV, eyes closed.

Out cold, she hasn't stirred since Beach Haven, an hour and a good sixty miles ago.

Smothering her with an ether-soaked towel was much easier than trying to inject an anesthetic, like last time.

No muss, no fuss.

I'll have to remember that for the future.

Wait a minute.

There won't be a need for it in the future.

It's over.

It's not going to happen again.

She's back where she belongs at last.

With me. And she'll never run away again.

The headlights arc into a long, tree-lined dirt lane.

"Here we are, sweetie pie." The car bounces over ruts in the road; ruts that help keep prying locals at bay.

"Oh, look, baby, are you awake? Do you see?"

The house has come into view. Bright strings of old-fashioned colored bulbs twinkle from the porch eaves and in the front window, the Christmas tree glows warmly.

"See how pretty? I've kept it all just like it was when you left. Home, sweet home, at last."

Conan O'Brien is interviewing some skinny girl who's famous for no apparent reason whatsoever, and Lucinda has no clue whatsoever why she's watching.

Except that she can't sleep, and anything is better than tossing and turning in bed in the next room.

Anything?

"I really think Paris Hilton is, like, underestimated," Conan's guest declares.

No sooner has Lucinda aimed the remote and zapped her into oblivion than the silence is broken by the telephone.

Phone calls after midnight never bode well. As she lifts the receiver, her mind runs the gamut of probable callers, possible scenarios.

All except this:

"Lucinda. It's Randy."

The breath is sucked right out of her at the sound of his voice, and she can't find her own.

No matter, because he's doing all the talking.

"If there's any way you can possibly get out to the island, I need you here. Another kid has gone missing and it looks like we've got a serial crime on our hands. Can you come?"

Lucinda looks at her packed luggage across the room, thinks about her trip tomorrow. The one that's supposed to carry her far, far away from Randy, give her a fresh perspective.

"I'm leaving for a trip in about six hours," she tells him.

Then he says the one thing that could possibly make her own plans irrelevant.

"The kid who got snatched is Cam Hastings's daughter."

Mike. I need Mike.

He still doesn't know.

During that first frenzied telephone conversation with Detective Barakat after Cam realized Tess had disappeared from the house, he instructed her not to call Mike yet.

"Why not?" she asked, distraught.

"I'll tell you when I get there. Just sit tight."

Sit tight? When your only child has vanished in the night?

Somehow, Cam managed not to run out of the house in hysterics. Mercifully, she doesn't remember much about the wait for the police to show up. She only knows they got here quickly.

Now she and the detective are standing in the bedroom where just hours ago Tess was lying on the bed in her pajamas.

A pair of crime scene investigators talk

on radio transmitters, dust surfaces for fingerprints, take measurements and photographs.

But it's nowhere near the fever-pitch frenzy Cam would have anticipated under the circumstances.

That's because there's no hard evidence that Tess was kidnapped. Nothing other than Cam's gut feeling.

Even the shark's tooth necklace means little to the investigation at this stage.

Yes, Rebecca Pearson had one.

But that could be circumstantial, as far as the authorities are concerned.

No one but Cam—in a psychic vision—ever even saw the necklace on Leah Roby.

The police—with the exception of Randall Barakat, who hasn't left Cam's side except to call Lucinda Sloan—think Tess simply ran away.

That, or her father took her: fallout from a messy marital separation.

That's why they won't let Cam call Mike. They're trying to find him first. They tried his apartment, but he wasn't there.

Randall Barakat didn't actually tell Cam that Mike is a suspect, but he didn't have to. It's obvious.

Cam remembers Rebecca Pearson's father being questioned that day, taking it in stride, reassuring his wife, *"The parents are always suspects."*

Cam can't take that in stride.

"Mike doesn't have anything to do with this," Cam keeps saying, and she's pretty sure Randall—though he alone—believes her.

As Lucinda speeds toward the exit for the island causeway, she'd give anything to make a U-turn and go right back home. Home, or to Alaska . . .

Anywhere but here.

She knows what she's going to find when she reaches Cam Hastings. She's visited the same scene over and over again.

The house filled with cops, the child's empty bedroom, the traumatized mother . . .

Only this time, Lucinda might not be

able to maintain that famous Sloan detachment.

This time, it's personal.

This time, she knows the mother all too well.

This time—unlike ever before—she saw the event before it actually happened.

She shudders, remembering the vision—the premonition, actually—of a fierce, futile struggle between Cam's daughter and a hooded figure.

The vision has revisited her since.

She's seen how it ends.

If there was even the slightest chance Lucinda could be mistaken about that . . .

But there isn't.

You know what you saw.

You've never been wrong, never once.

So there's no hope for Cam Hastings's daughter.

All Lucinda could do, when Randy called, was tell him about her vision. Describe the scene that materialized in her head, so that he'll know where to focus the investigation.

In Manhattan.

* * *

"I know it's been years, but the house hasn't changed much since the last time you were here, see?"

The voice reaches Tess across a great echoing chasm.

She realizes she's on her feet—sort of. Someone is holding her up, more or less dragging her along in the dark, up some steps, over a threshold.

There's a click and a flood of light.

Tess struggles to blink away the glare and the stupor, tries to get her bearings.

Her heart racing, she takes a deep breath and her lungs are assaulted by dust and mildew as the scene comes into focus.

Dazed, Tess tries to make sense of it.

Unfamiliar wallpaper and light fixtures.

Heavy, old-fashioned chairs, couch, tables—all blanketed in dust.

A television that in itself is a piece of furniture, built into a wooden console with a small, curved screen.

"Look, look at the tree." The voice is almost gleeful.

Tree?

Bewildered, Tess tries to make sense of it.

"Do you see what's under the tree?"

Tess must be hallucinating or her captor is, because they're inside, and there are no—

"For God's sake, would you look! Did you forget where we put the tree?"

A hand grabs hold of Tess's head and turns it, wrenching her neck painfully.

And there, across the room, she sees a tree.

A Christmas tree strung with big, old-fashioned oval lightbulbs in bright colors and shrouded in thick garlands of silvery cobwebs.

"Look under the tree!" the voice commands again, more harsh than gleeful now.

Tess sees a heap of wrapped presents.

"They were all for you. But you left. I should have thrown them all away, but I didn't because I love you. I love you so much that . . . you know what?" A small candy-striped package with a green bow is snatched from the top of the pile. "I'm going to get you settled and then let you open just this one present. Then, after your punishment, you can have the rest."

It's all too much. The word *love* . . . the word *punishment* . . . the eerie scene . . .

Red-hot panic bubbles to life in Tess's core.

"Guess what? Your room is exactly the same, too. I kept everything just the way you left it—your desk . . . all your stuffed animals . . ."

Her room?

Where *is* she?

"It's all there for my baby girl, just waiting."

"Mom?" Tess croaks.

"Yes?" replies the voice that doesn't belong to her mother at all.

It's vaguely familiar, though.

"You know what happens to bad little girls, don't you?" the voice asks ominously.

Stunned, Tess realizes who it belongs to even as her panic erupts and sweeps it all away: the voice, the tree, the lights . . .

* * *

The detective's cell phone rings.

Cam screams. She can't help it. Screams, cries, buries her head in her hands.

Please don't let it be bad news about Tess. Please, God. Please . . .

"Barakat here."

Cam tries hard to calm herself down, to listen.

"Where was he?" Barakat asks.

Pause.

"I see. I'll be right there."

He hangs up.

Turns to Cam. "Your daughter's boyfriend was just located. She's not with him."

Cam cries out in dismay, starts sobbing all over again, though she knew that would be the case all along.

Tess didn't merely sneak out to meet Heath in the night.

Someone has her. Someone who means to harm her.

"You have to get ahold of yourself, Mrs. Hastings. This isn't good for you, and it isn't good for the baby. Here, sit down. Have some water."

She sits, but pushes the water away. "Tell me about Heath."

"The kid claims he hasn't seen Tess since this afternoon and doesn't know anything about what happened, but they're questioning him now. I'm going to go down there."

Cam nods miserably. A shuddering sob racks her body.

"Is there someone you can call?" the detective asks, laying a hand on her arm.

"Mike." He's the one person she needs. Desperately.

"Not yet. They're trying to track him down. Is there other family?"

Just her father. She could try his phone, but why bother? He never answers.

She shakes her head.

MIA father.

Long-gone mother.

Dead sister.

So much for family.

"A friend, maybe," Barakat suggests, "who can come over here and be with you?"

Debbie isn't on the island.

Kathy, either.

Petra? But she has the kids tonight. Can Cam call her at this hour?

Gwen? She'd be alone, and she's nearby.

"Look, Cam, you need someone."

Maybe she should just call Mike, no matter what anyone says.

Detective Barakat is looking impatient.

"I'll try my father," she says, sniffling. "Maybe I'll be able to reach him."

"Good. You really shouldn't be alone right now."

No, she shouldn't.

Now—or ever.

Cam wipes at her eyes with a wad of soggy Kleenex and starts dialing.

"I know how anxious you must have been to see your room, aren't you? It's been such a long time."

Just a muffled groan from the backseat.

"It's too bad you won't be able to sleep there tonight. I'm sorry, but I have to punish you. You know why, don't you? Oh, you might want to brace yourself and hang on back there."

The tires leave the dirt drive and roll over the grass.

"Rough road ahead. It isn't far, remember?"

Nor is it a road at all, but a field that stretches toward the far reaches of the property where the orchard once thrived. Twin trails flatten the overgrown meadow grasses ahead, tracks from recent trips to the old root cellar.

"You know, this used to be a farm. Back before there was ever such a thing as suburbia this far down in Jersey. Did I ever tell—?"

Somewhere, a cell phone rings.

Hers? Or mine?

Mine.

And it's coming from Cam's number.

"Hello?"

Cam falters at the impatient greeting.

"Hello? Who's there?"

Cam shouldn't have called. She knew it.

No going back now, though.

You could always hang up.

What about caller ID, though? It'll be obvious that it was me.

Then again, who really cares?

Then again—she shouldn't be alone. Detective Barakat said so.

"I'm so sorry, it's Cam . . ."

"Cam! Are you okay? What's wrong?"

"It's Tess," she manages to say, before a wave of desolate tears engulf her again.

"Look, I'll be there as soon as I can, Cam. Okay? Just hang in there."

The cell phone snaps closed.

You should probably turn it off.

That way, if Cam does try to call back, she'll think the battery died or something.

The girl moans in the backseat.

"Hmm? Oh, that was a friend of yours. But she won't be bothering us again for awhile."

The headlights illuminate the heap of brush and, nearby, the gardening shed.

"I'll just get the shovel. You can stay here while I dig."

* * *

"Sounded pretty good, Ike," Billy calls as Ike sinks onto his bar stool again, still panting from the exertion of the set.

"Sounded like shit," Ike returns. "I'm getting too old to play with these young kids."

"Nah." Billy comes over, slides him a fresh beer. "You'll never be old. You're a legend, remember?"

A legend. Yeah. That's what Ike has always liked to say. From the dawn of doo-wop right through the days with the Boss at the Stone Pony . . .

The good old days were pretty good.

Now, he's old.

And that's not good.

Age does strange things to a fellow. Even a legend. Lately, instead of looking back fondly, Ike's found himself looking ahead.

He doesn't like what he sees.

Growing old is bad enough.

Growing old alone is worse.

Not growing old at all . . .

Well, that scares the hell out of him.

He finally bit the bullet and saw a doctor yesterday. Found out there are a whole lot of drugs he should be taking at his age, with his conditions . . . and a few choice drugs he shouldn't.

The doctor was blunt. If Ike doesn't change his ways, he's going to drop dead one day soon.

So, yeah. Maybe it's time to clean up his act.

Spend less time hanging around in bars, more time hanging around his family.

Maybe he can talk some sense into Cam and Mike. Tell them not to throw it all away.

"Hey, Ike." Billy points at the bar, where Ike left his keys and cell phone when he went to join the band. "I almost forgot—your phone rang while you were up there."

In the wake of yesterday's doctor visit, Ike decided to start carrying the phone with him again. Now it's ringing . . . and only one person has the number.

"Must've been my daughter," he tells Billy.

He checks the messages.

Of course it was Cam. She called just a few minutes ago.

"Hi, Pop. I just wondered if you were

around, but . . . you're not. So . . . that's it. Good-bye."

Her voice sounded strained.

Something's wrong.

"Who are you calling, Ike?"

"My daughter."

The phone bounces into voice mail.

He's about to leave a message, then decides it would be better to just go down to Beach Haven. If Cam needs him, he wants to be there for her.

Just the way he was when she was little.

"Mrs. Hastings? You want to come take a look at this?" one of the cops asks, standing by Tess's bed.

She crosses the room.

He seems to be holding a piece of paper.

"I found this under the mattress."

"What is it?"

Holding it between latex-covered fingers, he tilts it to give her a better look.

Pink and green card stock.

An invitation.

Reading it through, Cam gasps.

Heath.

Striding into the Beach Haven Police Department, Lucinda hopes Randy is still here.

He was when she called from the causeway, and he said they had a possible suspect in custody.

Here on the island.

That can't be right.

Lucinda knows what she saw.

The struggle in her vision was taking place in Manhattan. Downtown, judging by the angle of the skyline she glimpsed for an instant.

Tess Hastings's father lives in Lower Manhattan.

He's going to murder his own child.

God help that little girl, that poor mother, pregnant with another of his children.

"I'm Lucinda Sloan, here to see Randy about the Hastings case," she tells the desk sergeant. "Is he here?"

"Yeah, I'll let him know." He picks up the phone and hands a bulletin across the desk to Lucinda. "You might want to take a look at this while you wait. It just went out."

Lucinda gives it a cursory glance. "What is this?"

"The Hastings girl."

Staring at it, Lucinda nods slowly.

Restless, Cam paces the house, unable to bear another moment of waiting for something to happen.

Presumably, they're questioning Heath right now about the note.

Kitchen to living room, living room to kitchen . . .

Cam never trusted him, from the start.

Over to the window, and back again.

True, she didn't trust anyone around Tess.

Front door, back door, front door.

Heath seemed like a normal kid—just older. Too old for Tess, who looks younger than her age as it is.

Oh, Tess.

Cam paces.

Prays.

Remembers every detail of the day before, trying to come up with some clue, something that might have led her—and Tess—to this point.

Tess, where are you?

Did Heath stash her somewhere?

She was so evasive about the scratch on her face. Because he did that to her?

All the pieces seem to fit, and yet there's something . . .

Could an ordinary high school boy really have kidnapped three—maybe more—girls?

What about Kimberly Osborn?

She was a runaway. No one thinks she's connected to this.

No one but Cam.

But how can she be, if Heath is involved?

Yes, he's from California. Tess said something about his moving to Montclair from there.

But Kimberly Osborn disappeared—ran away—five years ago.

She had a shark's tooth necklace.

Cam can't get past it.

Heath, in the water, pretending there was a shark.

Tess had a shark's tooth necklace like Rebecca and Leah.

It always comes back to that.

The pieces seem to fit, and yet . . .

It doesn't make sense.

She goes over yesterday again. The beach. Heath. The fake shark.

Petra's disapproval. She said her Tyler would never do that. She said—

Cam stops short.

That's it.

Dear God.

She knows where she's seen Kimberly Osborn before.

The pain in Tess's right leg is unbearable.

Lying on the clammy dirt floor of the old cellar, trying not to cry out in agony, she wonders if it's broken.

It might be. That was a long drop—at least eight or ten feet from the trapdoor.

So intense is the bone-shattering pain that she can think of little else.

Other than, *Why is this happening to me?*

It makes no sense.

And now she's far from home, hidden away underground, and no one is ever going to know where to find her.

The trapdoor is shut, but she didn't hear dirt thrown against it or anything dragged on top of it. If she could possibly hoist herself up there, she might be able to escape . . .

She moves slightly, then winces as pain slices through her leg.

She's not going anywhere.

She's as helpless as a caged animal, imprisoned by a lunatic masquerading behind a familiar face. A face Tess would have trusted, even Mom would have trusted.

She's crazy.

And she thinks Tess is her long-lost daughter, whose name was scribbled on the holiday tag attached to the Christmas present she made Tess open.

Inside the box were two small silver charms: a starfish and a lighthouse.

Mike's cell phone rings, startling him from a sound sleep.

He awakens and it takes a moment for

him to realize that he's not in bed in his apartment in Lower Manhattan.

Yes. Right.

As he fumbles around for the phone, he remembers where he is.

At the house in Montclair, in the king-sized bed he once shared with Cam.

He drove over from his parents', rather than returning to the apartment in the city. The thought of that seemed too depressing, and Montclair gives him a head start on the drive to the shore in the morning, and anyway . . .

He belongs here.

This is home.

Well, it will be, when Cam and Tess are back with him.

That's what he told his parents. That he's coming home, that he loves his wife, that he's going to make his marriage work.

His mother was elated, of course.

His father—not so much.

When, Mike wonders, has his father ever been happy about anything?

But he's over worrying what his father thinks, over trying to think like him, over listening to him.

Finding his phone, Mike answers it even as he catches a glimpse of the bedside clock and realizes it's the middle of the night.

"Hello?" he asks worriedly.

"Mike? It's Cam."

Her voice is low. Barely controlled.

He sits up in bed, dread wrapped around him. "Cam—"

"Please just listen . . . I know this is going to sound crazy, and I know I've said it before and that you thought I was drinking . . . I'm not drinking, Mike. It really happened. And they know who did it, but—"

"What? What happened?"

"Tess was kidnapped. By this woman I know here, and nobody knows why, or where she took her, but her own daughter has been missing for five years. Her name is Gwen."

Chapter Nineteen

The brand glows red-hot in the night, ready at last. It took a long time, much longer than she wanted. The sun will be coming up soon.

Gwen carries the brand carefully toward the trapdoor, careful not to brush the heated metal against dry leaves or grass along the way.

Once she's made her mark on Casey's forehead, she'll be safe. She won't have to worry that her daughter will run away ever again.

It's the only way to stop her.

Lord knows Gwen has tried everything else, and nothing ever worked. Bribes, scoldings, threats—not even locks.

The first time Casey ran away, she was only in grade school, still wearing her hair in braids Gwen plaited so painstakingly every morning. They were living right here in Monmouth County, on this very property. Gwen had to punish Casey for a failing grade on her first trimester report card.

She remembers it clearly. School had just let out for Christmas break and a wet, heavy snow was falling that afternoon. Her daughter was bent on building a snowman, though the grass was barely coated. Gwen bundled her daughter against the cold and sent her outside with a promise to bake a batch of gingerbread cookies later.

She kept one eye on the futile snowman project as she emptied the bulging purple backpack: lunch remains, PTO notices, a candy cane from the teacher . . . then the fateful report card. With an *F*. In math, of all things. Gwen herself had excelled in math. Excelled in everything. Now her daughter was failing?

A bitter gust nearly picked up the front door when she opened it, slamming it against the siding with a loud bang.

"Kimberly Claire, you get in here this instant!"

She never used her daughter's full name unless she was in trouble. She never had cared for the name Kimberly; only used it because Doug liked it. She thought it would help.

He left anyway—ran off in the night when the baby was a few months old.

When Gwen realized he was never coming back, she started calling her daughter by her initials: K.C. It evolved into Casey.

Casey, who, like her father, took off one night with no intention of ever coming back.

That first time, she got all the way into town before a police officer found her and brought her home shivering, crying. Her hair was undone, crimped waves matted from melting snow. It was the day before Christmas Eve, but what was Gwen to do? Casey had to be punished for both running away and getting the *F* on her report card. Punished severely.

One might think, after a solid week alone in the dark, locked in the root cellar with just bread and water—missing

Christmas, even—Casey would have learned.

But she didn't.

Nor did she appreciate that Gwen had saved her pile of wrapped gifts and a plate of painstakingly decorated gingerbread cookies, stale by then but still edible.

Did Casey eat them? Did she say thank you for the gifts? No. She was sullen, whiney, screaming bloody murder as Gwen patiently combed out the mass of snarls and rebraided her hair, back the way it belonged. The way Gwen herself always wore her own hair when she was young.

A few days later, just after New Year's, Casey tried to run away again.

This time Gwen caught her before she got anywhere, and they left Jersey. They could afford to get away for awhile. Gwen owned the house outright, having inherited it from her parents, along with a nice nest egg. She and Casey went to Florida for the winter and decided to stay on past spring in a condo community near the beach.

Things were good for awhile. But Casey

started acting up one day, and one of the nosy elderly neighbors reported Gwen as an abusive mother. Social Services showed up. Who needed that?

She took her daughter and they moved to Texas, where they rented a small house in cattle country.

Things were good there, too. Until she caught Casey, just twelve, kissing a ranch hand under the mistletoe. Christmastime again, but Gwen had no choice. Casey had to be punished. There was no root cellar, but a small closet off the kitchen had a sturdy lock. Spiders were known to nest in the rafters there. Not poisonous spiders—just big, ugly, hairy ones. The kind Casey desperately feared.

Gwen had to do it. It was for Casey's own good.

She didn't want her daughter to end up as she had . . . a pregnant teenager.

"It's for your own good . . ."

That's what Gwen's parents always said to her, too, when they had to hurt her.

Again, Gwen saved the Christmas presents. She even bought a few more for Casey, and baked fresh cookies to have waiting when the solitary confinement in the closet was over.

Again, Casey was unappreciative.

Again, she ran away.

This time, she was harder to find.

When she turned up in Dallas weeks later, she had ditched her glasses, pierced her nose, and worst of all shorn her hair and bleached it a harsh yellow blond. Gwen didn't recognize her own daughter at first; it was like looking at a stranger. Amazing, how a person's appearance could change so drastically.

Casey tried to accuse Gwen of abusing her, telling the cops and anyone around that she was being tortured.

Luckily for Gwen, the cops understood the difference between abuse and parental discipline.

"You get on home where you belong and learn to listen to your mama," the good ol' boy in charge told Casey.

Furious, Gwen dragged her home.

Seeing the cows in the field beyond their door, she got an idea. A way to make sure Casey remembered where she belonged.

Gwen borrowed one of the ranch's brands and used it on Casey's bare backside.

Casey told the ranch hand, who told the landlord, who kicked Gwen off the property.

From there, they went west to the sea for a fresh start. Santa Monica.

It was good for awhile.

Then Casey reverted back to her old, disobedient ways.

One day, the police came to the house and picked her up for shoplifting. A store owner had it on a surveillance film.

Casey had stolen a necklace, a shark's tooth on a silver chain.

Gwen was livid.

But before she could punish her, Casey ran off—and that time, disappeared for good.

Gwen has been trying to find her ever since. Casey's got to realize that she belongs with her mother. For her own good.

The first time Gwen thought she'd found Casey was on a foggy night by the Santa Monica pier where a bunch of homeless kids hung out. The girl was off to the side, keeping to herself, and seemed a little lost. She even looked like Casey from afar, with glasses and long brown hair, wavy, the way Casey's was when she took the braids out at night. It wasn't until Gwen hauled her into the car that she realized it wasn't Casey. After all, Casey's hair was short and blond now, and she probably wasn't still wearing her glasses. Maybe she wasn't even in California anymore.

Gwen hated to hurt the poor kid, a runaway from Arizona who pleaded for her life. Pleaded so hard that Gwen apologized right before she slit the girl's throat, and she meant it. Truly, she felt badly. Still, she couldn't help but think that if the girl had stayed home with her mother where she belonged, she never would have wound up a bloody Jane Doe on the side of a desert highway.

Where was Casey?

Frustrated, Gwen retraced their path; looked for her daughter in Texas, in Florida. A few times, she found girls who looked just like her lost daughter—at least from afar. One even had braids, the tufts at the bottom bound in black leather laces.

Gwen cut those braids off as an afterthought before leaving the corpse in a Dumpster, much as she'd left all the other girls who turned out not to be Casey. She carried the dead stranger's braids around for a week because they reminded her of her daughter. Then she saw a picture of the girl on one of those missing children's posters, and she hastily burned the braids. No one would ever connect her to a missing waif, but why take chances?

Years went by. No sign of Casey, and too many cases of mistaken identity—too many lost souls to dispose of. All that blood on her hands, and for what?

Gwen came back to Jersey last Thanksgiving, hoping Casey might eventually come full circle, find her way home. She aired out her parents' house and got it ready for an old-fashioned holiday. Christmas lights were still strung from the porch, the artificial tree was still decorated in the living room, its boughs draped in cobwebs that looked almost like tinsel.

Gwen baked gingerbread, bought more presents for Casey, painstakingly wrapped them, and piled them with the others beneath the tree. She told the neighbors who bothered to ask that her daughter was living with her father for awhile but was coming home for the holidays.

No one questioned her story. Custody often shifted in broken homes.

Gwen started frequenting her old haunts, looking for her daughter everywhere she went. Christmas came and went; she left the house decorated, kept the presents and even the gingerbread, waiting for Casey. Winter turned to spring, then summer on the way, and still she couldn't find her daughter.

It wasn't until she got down to the island and found that shark's tooth that she realized she was on the right trail.

Now, holding the hot brand, she bends to open the trapdoor.

Yes.

This time, she finally got it right.

"You know it's for your own good," she calls. "This time, I'm going to put it right in the middle of your forehead for the whole world to see."

From below, Casey begins screaming for help.

"Oh, shush. You're wasting your breath," Gwen tells her. "There's no one around to hear you. And no one will ever think to look for you here."

"How are you doing? Hanging in there?" Lucinda asks Cam.

Cam nods, sitting beside her in the backseat of the state trooper's car as it races up the Garden State Parkway. Hanging in there. But just barely.

She's been reeling ever since she figured out that Kimberly Claire Osborn and Gwen's daughter Casey—whose picture she proudly showed off to Petra and the others—are the same person.

Cam can't grasp the enormity of Gwen's lie, and she refuses to consider the implications.

All she can think about, as the car races toward the location where they think Gwen has Tess, is her daughter's safety.

Please, God. Please let Tess still be there.

She was definitely there just a short time ago.

At least, her phone was.

The cell phone Mike gave her—the fancy one he sent from Japan—was tracked to a house in Monmouth County.

As long as Tess has the phone with her, she'll be found.

Alive. Please, God. Let them find her alive.

At this very moment, a team is being positioned around the property.

Cam tries not to think of hostage rescues she's seen in movies—armed captors, armed rescuers, victims caught in the crossfire, victims reached too late.

Panic bubbles within her again and she turns to Lucinda. "Do you think . . . ?"

"I think they're going to find her and bring her home." Lucinda reaches out and squeezes Cam's hand.

"Are you saying that because you've seen it happen?"

She hasn't wanted to ask Lucinda about that, just in case.

Lucinda shakes her head, looks out

the window at the passing landscape. "No. I'm saying it because I think it's meant to happen. Thanks to your husband. He's an amazing husband, you know, to have done what he did."

Yes. Absolutely. Amazing.

The phone Mike sent Tess from Japan wasn't just a phone. It was a high-tech device with a built-in GPS locator.

He did it, he told her in a rushed phone conversation, to be on the safe side. Because for God only knows what reason, he decided he believed Cam after all—that she'd had a premonition about Tess.

Please, dear God. Please let her come home to us.

"This is so hard," she tells Lucinda. "I just hope . . ."

She trails off, unable to finish the sentence.

I just hope it's not too late.

"Stay away from me!" Tess shrinks away from the red-hot object in Gwen's hand. "Don't come near me with that."

"I wish I didn't have to do this, but I

don't have a choice, Casey. You've proven over and over again that you can't be trusted to stay where you belong. With me."

"I'm not Casey, and I don't belong with you. I don't even know who you are."

"What? That's rich! I'm your mother. Stop being ridiculous."

"Please." Tess shrinks against the cold stone wall, tortured by the slightest movement of her leg. "Please don't hurt me."

"I'm sorry. Really. But it won't hurt for long."

She's going to kill me, Tess realizes. *I have to stop her, or she's going to kill me.*

Bracing herself for the inevitable explosion of pain, she waits for the right moment.

Then she pounces.

Gwen is caught off guard.

Tess grabs the end of the heavy branding iron, wrenching it from her hand and swinging blindly with all her might toward her captor.

The heated end thuds into flesh and

bone, searing it, and Gwen lets out an unearthly howl.

Kathy has always been an early riser, up before the sun.

The housekeeper, Carmen, sets the timer on the coffeemaker the night before so the fresh, hot brew will be waiting when Kathy comes into the kitchen.

Ann—Brenda—used to get up and make it for Kathy herself at that hour.

She never said a word when Kathy put a shot of whiskey into it, but she always looked as though she wanted to.

She'd putter around the kitchen as Kathy drank her coffee at the table there. Sometimes they'd talk.

Never, until the last few months, about anything significant.

Not until Brenda was diagnosed with inoperable breast cancer.

They gave her six months. She lasted less than two.

In those short weeks, she told Kathy her story.

Her full name—her real one—was Brenda Ann Johnson Neary. She had been married to a musician named Ike, had two daughters, Ava and Camden.

Tormented all her life by psychic visions, Brenda suspected the gift came from her grandmother, who had been placed in an asylum and died there when Brenda was still a child. Chilled by the memory, she never told anyone about the things she saw.

To keep the visions at bay, she saw doctors. Took medication. Drank too much. It all took its toll on her marriage. Brenda loved Ike, but her world revolved around her daughters. She loved her girls more than anything.

In the end, that was why she left.

Increasingly haunted by a recurring vision about her oldest daughter, Brenda became convinced Ava wasn't going to live into adulthood. The more she tried to keep Ava close, the more Ava pulled away.

Consumed by paranoia, certain she lacked the strength to face the inevitable, Brenda walked away one day.

She never meant to leave, never meant to stay away.

Even Kathy—twice divorced, childless—couldn't relate to that. How does a mother leave her children?

"I couldn't bear the loss," Brenda told her. "Waking up every morning, looking at my beautiful daughter, wondering if that was going to be the day . . . I couldn't take it."

"Why didn't you go back, then?" Kathy asked.

"It was easier not to. How could I have faced them again?"

She didn't go far. Stayed in the general area, hovering on the periphery of her family's lives. Sometimes, she even watched them.

Once or twice, she told Kathy, she slipped in while Ike was performing onstage, watching him from the crowd.

Hiding beneath a wig and big sunglasses, she saw her oldest daughter graduate from high school.

But she couldn't bring herself to attend Ava's funeral a year later.

It happened just as she had always known it would.

And that was when she knew she could never go back.

* * *

Still writhing in pain, Gwen lunges for the branding iron, grabs at it.

Tess sees the raw red wound she inflicted on Gwen's forearm.

Good, I have to hurt her again, she thinks wildly. *I have to kill her, or she'll kill me.*

Gwen's hand closes around the brand and she pulls it. So does Tess, harder. The shaft slides through Gwen's fingers all the way to the red-hot end. She screams and lets go, doubled over her fingers. The air smells of burning flesh.

Still clutching the brand, Tess scrambles for the ladder.

She has a split second to make a decision and opts to drop the brand, tossing it as far as she can. With one leg useless she needs both hands.

Breathing hard, she begins to pull herself up, resting her good knee on every rung as she reaches for the next.

Keep going.

That's it.

There's light at the top and she can hear night sounds: crickets, distant sirens.

Her hands reach and cling to one rung, another rung.

Just like she used to do on the playground back in the city when she was little.

She remembers her parents standing below the jungle gym, cheering her on as she made her way, hand over hand. Remembers how proud she felt when they marveled at her agility, at how strong her arms were.

That was a long time ago, though, and a horizontal course.

This is vertical, and she's weak from pain, and terrified, and Mom and Dad aren't here to cheer her on . . .

No, but this time, my life is hanging in the balance.

And if I don't get myself out of here, I'll never see Mom and Dad again, Tess acknowledges grimly, and hurriedly pulls herself up another rung.

As Mike steers around a curve, his headlights fall on a police barricade down the road. He forces himself to slow the car and rolls down his window.

An officer approaches. “I’m sorry, sir. Road closed. We’ve got an investigation going on up ahead.”

“I’m the father,” he says hoarsely.

“Excuse me?”

“That’s my daughter they’re trying to find. My name is Mike Hastings.” He reaches into his pocket, finds his wallet. Thrusts his ID into the officer’s face.

He takes it. Looks at it. Looks at Mike.

“Hang on a minute, sir.” He steps away, says something into his radio.

Almost there.

Freedom waits beyond the trapdoor, almost within Tess’s grasp, so close that she can smell it, literally. Now when she breathes her lungs get a taste of fresh night air, not just the wretched, toxic stench from below.

Another rung up the ladder, and she’ll be able to hoist herself onto the ground and—

“No!” she cries out, as the ladder suddenly sways beneath her.

She looks down and sees Gwen at the bottom, holding the ladder with her good hand. Her eyes gleam with madness and rage; she clutches the ladder like a ferocious, wounded bear bent on shaking a helpless kitten from a tree.

Tess releases the rung she's holding and grabs the next as the ladder jiggles beneath her.

I can do this. I have to do this.

"Help!" she screams at the top of her lungs.

Below, Gwen laughs, a harsh, evil sound. "Scream all you want. There's no one to hear you."

"Help! Someone! Please, help!" Tess bellows, praying Gwen is wrong.

Balancing on one knee, she strains with her arms overhead, reaching as far as she can. Her hand encounters the door frame just as Gwen gives the ladder a hard jolt. Losing her balance, she feels herself falling.

I'm going to die, Tess thinks in the instant before she hits bottom and her leg splinters with pain that's worse, far worse, than the first time.

But she's still alive.

And Gwen is on her, snarling, "You little beast."

* * *

When Brenda answered Kathy's ad for a housekeeper, she said she had no family in the area.

It was a lie, Kathy later learned.

Brenda's family—her surviving daughter—was the reason she was in the area.

All those years, she lived right here, near Cam, but she couldn't bring herself to face her daughter.

"I'm weak, Kathy," Brenda said. "Weaker than you can possibly imagine."

Maybe. Maybe that was why she didn't fight the cancer when it struck.

Or maybe she was just eager to see her lost daughter again.

Kathy was with her at the hospice, holding her hand when she died. She saw Brenda seeing something that wasn't there, saw her face light up, heard her murmur, "Ava."

Days before that, she told Kathy how she had come to be in Montclair. Told her about her younger daughter living nearby with her husband and Brenda's granddaughter.

She asked Kathy to promise her three things.

One, that she would get help for her drinking problem—to which, of course, Kathy replied that she didn't have one.

"Yes, you do," Brenda said weakly from behind the oxygen tubing, "and you need help. Join AA. It'll save your life. It saved mine."

The second promise was that she'd keep an eye on Brenda's family. Just check on them now and again. And if there was ever anything Kathy thought they might need . . .

"I'll help them," Kathy said around a lump in her throat.

Brenda nodded gratefully. "But don't ever tell."

That was the third promise.

Never to tell Camden Hastings that her mother had watched her build a life while living out her own a mile away.

Kathy promised.

She thought she could keep it. Even after she impulsively introduced herself to Cam one day, struck up a conversation, smelled booze on her breath.

Getting Cam to AA was tricky. Kathy

wasn't even sure it would happen. But it did, and it worked.

Who knows how it all pulled together? Kathy prefers to think it happened with a little help from above.

Yes, someone up there is looking out for Cam. Kathy is sure of it.

Tess tries to push Gwen off but she can't get the force; not with one leg useless, shattered beneath her.

Gwen's hands are around her neck. Squeezing her throat. Cutting off her air.

Injured, imprisoned beneath the weight of her assailant, Tess can't move, can't breathe.

This time, there's no escape. It would take a miracle to get her out of here.

Suddenly blinded by a burst of white light, Tess is certain she just died. This is what she'd heard it's like, the light . . .

But there's still pain, and her lungs are still bursting, and she can't be dead because Gwen is still choking her . . .

She hears a commotion above.

"Let go of the girl!" a voice calls.

Tess feels the hands tighten around

her neck; feels the blackness seeping in; knows she's passing out, knows this is it.

Mike waits, tense.

Thinks about Tess. His little girl. His Messy Tessy.

He loves her with all his heart.

And Cam, too. Cam, who kept so much hidden, all those years.

If it wasn't for Rebecca Pearson, the girl who disappeared from Long Beach Island last month, Mike might never have believed his wife.

He heard the report about Rebecca Pearson on his car radio, then saw the Amber Alert posted on an electronic highway bulletin board.

The description of the missing girl eerily mirrored what was scribbled on the pad he'd found in the kitchen in Montclair several months ago. He recognized it even before he opened his wallet, where he'd stashed the note, to check.

Girl, 13-14, freckled, redhead, short braids, sunburn, green spaghetti-strap top, white sandals, hot-pink toenail polish . . .

Cam had written it all down months ago.

Before it ever happened.

Faced with the evidence, he took a leap of faith.

But he wasn't sure what to do about it until he got to Japan and happened upon the sophisticated new tracking technology that might just give him peace of mind for the time being.

Yet even then, never in his wildest dreams did Mike imagine something like this might happen.

The cop returns to the car, looking somber.

Before he speaks, Mike hears it: the distant sound of an approaching siren.

"You need to wait here for a few minutes, Mr. Hastings."

The siren rapidly grows closer, coming up somewhere behind.

"Why? What's going on?"

"They need to let the ambulance through, and then someone's going to come up and talk to you."

* * *

Cam's cell phone, clutched in her hand, rings.

She jumps.

The baby, too, is startled. She feels the flutter of life deep inside; a reminder that there's another child. Another life to protect. Something else to live for. No matter what.

Lifting the phone, she checks the incoming number.

"It's Mike," she tells Lucinda, who nods.

"Do you want me to answer it for you?"

"No."

The phone rings again.

Cam swallows hard.

Takes a deep breath.

"It's going to be okay," she whispers, unsure if she's talking to Lucinda, or to herself, or to the baby in her womb.

She opens the phone, presses TALK.

"Cam?" Mike's voice is a sob.

"Mike." She tries to steel herself for the inevitable. Knows nothing she can possibly do will prepare her. "Please. Please don't say it."

"Cam, it's over. They found her."

"She's not going to make it."

The voice, speaking above her, is male, and maddeningly decisive.

"Are you sure?" another voice asks, less certain.

"Positive. Not with a hole the size of stinkin' Newark blown through her chest," says the first voice.

Jesus.

But it's not as if she didn't know. She heard the violent blast of gunfire in the instant before she felt the detonation in her chest and knew she'd been hit.

Still, she didn't think she was going to die.

She isn't going to die. She can't die. She won't die.

"Hey, look. Her lips are moving."

"Yeah, but she's not saying anything."

Yes I am! Listen to me! Listen, dammit! I'm not going to die. I can't die. I'm still alive. You have to help me.

"How long does she have?"

"Are you kidding? Maybe a minute. Maybe not even. Don't waste any time on her, let's just take care of this one."

I have to see her. I have to see my baby. Mine.

The uniformed strangers, who scurried down the ladder with flashlights and radios and medical equipment, have all turned their backs.

No one sees her open her eyes one last time.

No one hears one last word escape her lips.

"Casey," she murmurs, as her gaze falls on the girl lying nearby on the dirt floor, surrounded by a cluster of people, all working over her with encouraging, soothing words.

You were mine again. Mine at last.

"Okay, honey, this is going to hurt but I have to do it, okay?"

Grimacing in pain as they do something to her leg, the girl turns her head.

Her gaze meets Gwen's.

And Gwen sees, in an awful burst of clarity just before her eyes slam themselves closed again, that she isn't Casey at all.

Gwen was mistaken. Again.

But . . . This time she was so sure.

How could she have been so wrong, so blind?

A fresh tide of resolution washes through Gwen as another surge of blood pours from the gaping wound in her chest.

Casey's still out there somewhere . . . And I'm going to find her. I'll never give up, Gwen decides, just before the shroud of darkness falls and smothers her.

In her kitchen, as the first rays of morning light come in the window, Kathy pours a steaming cup of coffee and thinks about the day ahead.

She's going to drive down to Long Beach Island with the picture of Brenda, and Brenda's scrapbook filled with yellowed newspaper clippings she'd collected over the years: Ike in the shore papers with his various bands, Cam's wedding announcement, Tess with her soccer team.

It was seeing Cam's daughter last

month in Beach Haven that changed Kathy's mind about honoring Brenda's deathbed request.

Cam and Tess deserve to know about the breast cancer. That's part of it. An important part. But it goes well beyond. They deserve to know about a lot of things.

Tess should grow up knowing that she had a grandmother who was proudly aware of her existence.

And Cam—Cam needs to know that her mother didn't simply abandon her. She needs to know why she left. That Brenda loved her, and her father, too, until the day she died.

Yes. Kathy's mind is made up.

Some promises were made to be broken.

The first thing Cam sees, when she jumps out of the backseat before the car comes to a stop at the edge of the field, is Mike.

He's standing beneath an old orchard tree.

Hearing the car door slam, he turns to look.

His face lights up at the sight of Cam, and she sobs. Starts running, picking her way over uneven ground as Mike runs toward her, calling out for her to be careful, meeting her halfway.

He grabs her hard, hugs her fiercely, cries into her hair. "She's okay. She's okay, Cam. They think her leg is broken but . . ."

"Where is she?"

"Over here. Come on, they're giving her something for the pain."

Pain.

Her daughter is in pain.

"What happened, Mike?"

He tells her quickly, his arm around her as they walk toward the ambulance parked several yards away.

The troopers got there just in time. Not to the house, but way out in back of the property. Without the GPS they would never have found Gwen, with Tess, in an old root cellar.

"They shot Gwen. She didn't make it."

Cam tries to find a place in her heart to feel something—anything.

She can't. Maybe she never will.

They round the back of the ambulance, and Cam spots her.

"Tess!"

Her daughter looks up. Her face, though etched in pain, somehow lights up. "Mommy!"

As Cam holds her close, she looks at Mike over the top of their daughter's head. "If it weren't for you . . ."

"No," he says softly. "If it weren't for you."

In his eyes, she sees the answers to all the questions that have haunted her for months.

"Can we just go home?" Tess sobs. "I just want to go home."

"We will, sweetheart," Cam assures her, stroking her hair. "Soon enough. We will."

Mike nods. "We will. All three of us."

Watching Cam and Mike hovering as Tess is loaded into the back of the ambulance on a stretcher, Lucinda shakes her head.

"What?"

She looks up to see Randy watching her.

"Nothing, I just . . ." She smiles. Gestures at the petite girl with the brown shoulder-length hair sandwiched between the two most grateful people Lucinda has ever seen. "So that's Tess Ava Hastings."

"Yup. That's Tess Ava Hastings." Randy tilts his head. "So what's up with you, Sloan? I can tell there's something."

Wordlessly, Lucinda pulls the folded piece of paper from her pocket and hands it to him.

He looks at it, then at her. "This is the Missing Persons Bulletin our department put out."

Lucinda nods.

Takes it back.

At the top is the name TESS AVA HASTINGS.

Beneath is a photograph of the rescued girl.

A girl who looks exactly like her father—and nothing at all like her mother.

The moment Lucinda saw that photograph earlier, she realized that her fatal vision hadn't been about Cam Hastings's daughter after all.

It probably wasn't a premonition, either.

It—like most of what she sees—must have already happened.

She realized that Tess Hastings's fate wasn't necessarily sealed.

In that moment, she found hope.

In this, resolution.

Lucinda yawns, stretches.

"Oh," she says softly, remembering something.

"What's wrong?" Randy asks.

"Nothing, just . . . I was supposed to be leaving on a cruise today. Alaska."

"Alaska!"

She nods. "I wanted to get away from it all."

Especially you.

"Maybe," he suggests, "you can still make it."

"No," she says, "I won't. I can't make my flight, and by the time I get out there, my ship will have sailed without me."

"That stinks."

"Yeah," Lucinda tells him, "but I'm used to it."

"What?"

"Never mind."

Again, she looks thoughtfully at the Hastings family.

At Cam, in particular.

Somewhere in her past, there's a dead girl who looks just like her; a girl who struggled with a hooded figure high above a Manhattan street before being hurtled to her death.

Who was she?

And who killed her?

Lucinda will have to ask Cam about it.

But not now.

Now is a time for happy reunions.

And, she thinks, turning back to Randy, for final farewells.

Epilogue

"It's a zoo out there," Ike observes, peering through a crack in the blinds two days later. "Is that an *Entertainment Tonight* van?"

Cam, in the midst of trying to figure out where to put yet another basket of flowers from yet another well-wisher, looks up at her father. "Why would they be here?"

"Maybe they got wind of my involvement. I told you I was a legend in my own time."

A legend in his own mind is more like it. But she just nods and smiles. "Maybe they *are* here because of you, Pop."

More likely, the *Entertainment Tonight* van out there with the rest of the news satellite trucks is a figment of his imagination.

A lot of things are.

Dementia, the doctor told Cam privately after Ike's long-overdue examination. Maybe even the early stages of Alzheimer's.

But Cam is hoping for the best.

Getting her father under good medical care was the first, and most important, step. They're going to do some tests on him when the dust settles and Cam can devote herself to a new patient.

Right now, though, the only patient she can handle is Tess.

Two nights in the hospital were hard on her daughter. Hard, too, on pregnant, exhausted Cam, who refused to leave Tess's bedside until this morning—and then only because Tess was about to be released.

Cam reluctantly agreed to come home and take a nap for the baby's sake. She actually dozed off for a few hours, more sleep than she's gotten since the whole thing happened.

Yes, those nights in the hospital confirmed it: a bedside chair that converts to a cot is uncomfortable. More like a torture device, as Mike had pointed out years ago.

Cam woke an hour ago to find her father puttering at loose ends downstairs, a house filled with flowers, bouquets, and food platters from neighbors she didn't know existed, and a throng of media standing guard at the curb.

They're having a field day with the story. Especially now that Gwen has been tied to Leah Roby and Rebecca Pearson's disappearances, as well as to several others in California, Texas, and Florida.

Leah's remains were found not far from the root cellar. Rebecca's haven't been located so far.

They won't be, according to Lucinda, who confided her feeling that Gwen had disposed of poor Rebecca at sea.

According to Debbie and Petra, who keep her posted on the Long Beach Island end of things, the Pearsons are still holding out hope.

Cam wonders how long that'll last.

Maybe forever.

Maybe it's easier that way.

Look at Pop. He still believes Mom and Ava might be alive, might be coming home, even after all these years. He said it just yesterday, between bouts of lucidity at the hospital.

Yes, and now he believes an *Entertainment Tonight* news truck is out there with the other press, having connected Tess Hastings to Ike Neary, the legendary Jersey Shore musician.

"Close the blinds, Pop. Please?" Cam sets the basket of flowers on the mantel, squeezing it in among the others. They're from Kathy, who has left several messages for Cam, expressing her concern, saying they need to get together as soon as Cam is up to it.

"Wait, look!" Ike exclaims. "I see them! They're here!"

"Who?" Cam asks, and braces herself for him to tell her he sees Mom and Ava alongside the *Entertainment Tonight* crew.

"Who do you think? They're home!"

"Mom and Ava?"

Her father looks at her as if she's lost her mind.

"No," he says gently, shaking his head.

"Not them. They're gone. But look who's here!"

Cam peeks over his shoulder through the blinds just in time to see Mike's car pull into the driveway, past the barricade of cops who are keeping the reporters at bay.

"They're home," her father says again.

So they are.

Cam hears the faint *whir* of the garage door opener. She hurries toward that side of the house, through the kitchen and mudroom, where Mike's favorite Yankees hat once again hangs from the hook by the door.

She opens it to find his car in the garage. In the instant before he cuts the engine, she hears what he's playing on the car stereo.

Southside Johnny.

Cam smiles to herself.

Mike pops the trunk, and the front car doors open simultaneously. The garage door is already lowering, shutting out the rest of the world.

Unaware that Cam is there in the threshold, Mike steps from the driver's seat and removes a pair of crutches from the trunk. He arrives at the passenger's side just as Tess swings her feet out.

"How are you doing, you okay?" he asks Tess, and Cam can't hear her reply.

She feels a pang seeing her daughter's legs. One is tanned and wearing a flip-flop, the other encased in a long plaster cast.

"Nice and easy." Mike holds out the crutches, helping Tess out of the car. "You just have to get used to being on your feet again. Come on."

"I don't think I can do the stairs, though," Tess's voice is small, like a little girl's.

"Sure you can. Come on."

Cam watches Tess awkwardly stand, watches Mike help her position the crutches beneath her armpits.

"Good. Now let's go. One step at a time."

"I don't know if I can—"

"Yes, you can. You can do it."

"It's just . . . I feel like I'm going to fall."

"Well, if you do, I'll be here to catch you. Every step of the way. Okay?" Mike asks their daughter.

Tess nods. "Okay."

Together, they start toward the door, their heads bent, attention focused on Tess's leg, the crutches.

They still don't see Cam.

She waits a few moments to say anything. Mostly because she can't push her voice past the lump in her throat.

Cam watches them with tears in her eyes until Mike looks up, meets her gaze.

He smiles. Gives a little nod.

She nods back and at last manages to get the words out. Two words she's been waiting a long, long time to say.

"Welcome home."